BORN—
AGAINST ALL ODDS

For Liz
my friend
with
best of luck!

♡ Hope Silver
(Nadya)
Berkeley
2019

A Novel by
HOPE SILVER

BORN — AGAINST ALL ODDS
First English Edition
(Translated from Original Russian by
Krystyna Steiger, Montreal, Canada.)
Copyright © 2019 by Hope Silver

FIRST ENGLISH EDITION SOFTCOVER
ISBN: 1622539753
ISBN-13: 978-1-62253-975-8

Editor: LaneDiamond
Cover Artist: Brianna Hertzog
Interior Designer: Lane Diamond

EVOLVED PUBLISHING™

www.EvolvedPub.com
Evolved Publishing LLC
Butler, Wisconsin, USA

Printed in Book Antiqua font.

DEDICATION

*For my kids, who are always with me,
and for my friends who left too soon.*

Chapter 1

"Here he comes, all on his own!"

Those were the first sounds for me in this world, followed the next second by various smells. Then my eyes opened, only a crack at first due to my exhaustion, but even so, the light was so bright—too bright, really.

Two figures in blue appeared, deftly helped me out of my refuge from the world, and lay me down on something warm—on *somebody*, actually.

She looked me over curiously, the strain of what she'd just endured evident in the little red veins crawling across her face and eyeballs, fine as threads.

"Hi," she said, and then touched me gently with her index finger, as though checking to make sure I was real.

As she pored over me, I supposed she was my mother, but....

Why does she only vaguely resemble the girl I chose to be my mother, when I was still out there flying around? Do people change? Giving birth is no picnic, but.... No, no, my mistake... it's her.

No worries. She'd rest up, get herself together, and be the most beautiful mom in the world—mine! Besides, I was supposed to love her just the way she was.

"Let's call it: 12:02 a.m.," announced one of the two in blue.

My mother turned her head toward somebody behind her, whom I couldn't see.

"What does yours say?"

"Midnight and thirty seconds," a man's voice replied. "Thirty-three, now."

Mom started arguing with the two in blue over the two minutes.

So principled!

She'd often argued with others during my time inside, too—seemed to be something of a habit with her.

She shifted her attention away from me—felt a little offensive under the circumstances—and continued her argument.

The people in blue gave in and wrote down what she wanted, then picked me up and carried me somewhere, leaving my mother behind. Other people had started doing something to her, and I worried that she might still be in pain—I couldn't stop thinking about it—and....

Oh, how awful! I forgot her name!

It seemed I'd forgotten a lot, since coming into the world.

The two in blue rubbed me down for a long time, poked and prodded my stomach, weighed me, and put a band around my wrist that read:

Vorobyeva. Boy. May 27, 12.00. 53 cm. 3650 gr.

Then they swaddled me up good and tight, and left me on my own.

Before long, somebody in black came along and put a strange object with a little round mirror on me. I didn't know what it was, so I squeezed my eyes shut—they hadn't opened very wide yet, anyway. He whispered that I looked like a little old lady.

Hey, stupid, you're the old lady!

He couldn't be my dad. I'd recognize my dad just as I had my mom—after all, I'd chosen them myself... long before today.

So, I'd been born, an irreversible event. Now I'd have to live here—no more of that nice warm liquid I just lay around in, sucking my thumb; no more sense of absolute security; no more eavesdropping on adult conversations without a chance of being caught; and....

I won't be able to fly anymore.

The melancholy hit me hard, and the tears soon followed, but I was so exhausted that I could only manage a kind of silent sob. The rule seemed to be that newborns cried only so the world would know they'd been born. Nobody realized the truth behind my tears. Nobody knew the depths of my sadness.

Chapter 2

The first time I saw my future mother, she'd looked completely different – although, I didn't look like anything then. She was a curly-haired redhead with a nice tan, in denim shorts and bright yellow tank top. She laughed a lot, while sitting in a rowboat with a young man. Sunbeams glistened off the water all around them as they talked, and she appeared truly happy.

I'd been flying by with my friends – other souls, who didn't belong to anybody yet – all of us invisible. Our assignment was to find the people who could be our future parents, and I was looking for happy people who loved each other. And when she laughed....

Then it hit me. It was *her*. It's as if I knew her, a long time before this moment.

"I think I'm done, kids," I yelled. "Carry on without me from here!"

I sat down on her shoulder, and she scratched it right away, as though she'd felt a tickle or something. People do that all the time – a tickle from us feels something like a little bug crawling across their cheek.

I looked into their laughing, brown eyes and sensed something warm and joyful between the two of them. They might have been in love, which meant I was on the right track.

"Okay, Vic," she said to her friend. "Where are these monkeys already? Looks to me like we're lost."

"Don't worry, Ginger, we'll find them!" he replied.

They were looking for some island, so I decided to stay with them and observe. They took turns rowing.

"Take a picture of me, all beautiful at the oars." Ginger laughed again and leaned back a little.

She really was beautiful, or so it seemed to me, anyway. She emitted a burst of solar energy that felt like it permeated my very being, so that I, too, felt like a sunbeam. At that very moment, I may even have been visible!

"I want you to be my mom," I whispered into her ear, and she scratched it. I had established contact!

I stayed with them all day, until they finally found the little island with the monkeys, which had been kept at the Central Park of Culture and Leisure in Saint Petersburg in the summer of 1999. They hand-fed them for a while, then rowed back, returned the boat, and lay around on the grass for a long time, drinking beer and talking.

I found out that her real name was Lera, and that Victor called her Ginger because of her hair color. The two had split up two weeks earlier, but got back together a few days ago, when he came by her parents' place with some belongings she'd left at his apartment. They'd both started new relationships during their time apart, but they reconciled before their dalliances could get serious.

"But, Ginger, you're my real wife," he said with a loving gaze, and I saw how unbelievably happy that made her. "We've been through so much together!" He stroked her curly hair. "You were the only one who visited me in the hospital every day, when I broke my back and had to lie there, totally immobile for a month, and then all the rest of it.... My God! You know, I haven't been myself since the day I saw you again. I can't concentrate at work. I've been stuck on the same assignment for days, and even my colleagues are asking me what's wrong. Yesterday, I finally figured it out. It's love, Ginger!"

Despite Victor's declaration, I didn't like him, and I wouldn't want a father like him. He was like a caveman, with his protruding ears and oddly-shaped head, and he had the face of a gnome—depending on the look in his eyes, he could be kind, or vindictive. The point wasn't the way he looked, though; there was something cold and cruel in his eyes that I just couldn't gauge, as though they had a false bottom.

I definitely had to help my future mother find somebody else. I really wanted to have a look at the person she'd been seeing, before she and the caveman got back together.

Chapter 3

July 95th.

There was no such thing, of course, but all the same, that date appeared on Lera's wood-block calendar the first time I entered her apartment. With this unusual girl as my mom, I would definitely experience a variety of unusual events.

She was so absorbed in her reading that she didn't even feel me tickling her ear, but I had other ways of announcing myself. I could also send people messages — the kind that made them shake their heads and say, "It's a sign!"

I sent her one of those while she sat on the bus one morning, contemplating her relationship with Victor as she stared out the window on her way to work.

I read her mind.

"Why did we have to pick up again, when everything was already so obvious in the spring?" she mused. *"We shouldn't have bothered. You can glue a broken cup back together again, but it will always be cracked. We're running the same gamut of emotions as before, slipping into the same rut."* She sighed and leaned her cheek against the pane of glass. *"If only somebody could give me a hint, and tell me for sure, if it's* not meant to be.*"*

That very second, the bus had driven by an enormous billboard that read, "Not Meant to Be." Though only the title of a song, how could it not be a sign? Besides, it was the truth. I knew it, and she'd known it for a long time. I noticed the look in her eyes suddenly change from pensive and sad, to amazed.

We can appear in people's dreams, too, and when Lera was reading and didn't notice me tickling her, I got upset, so I decided to make her dream about me. First, I had to decide on the form I would assume. At that point, I was just a little soul, light as a breath of fresh air, and I didn't remember my past lives, or whether I'd even had any. Now, it was my time to live among people, as an earthly incarnation, provided I could find the people who would be my parents.

I didn't have a name yet, just a number: M-04041999. The 'M' stood for 'male,' and the numbers signified the date on which I'd begun the search for my parents. According to the rules, boys pick their mothers first, and girls, their fathers. Tens of thousands of others had the same number, and got analogous assignments on 4 April 1999, but I'd already lost sight of them. Just how long my quest would take, and when I'd come into the world in the form of a baby, remained anybody's guess.

Sometimes, we had to set up our parents' first meeting and make sure they didn't lose each other, before that most important event, for the sake of which they'd met: conception. Sometimes, we had to do the opposite: sever them from those who weren't right for the role of the second parent—as in my case.

Ack... the things we do for the sake of family happiness!

I would help Lera find 'the one' with whom everything would work out well. How?

Yeah... right. How?

Lera had wanted a child for a long time, and I found out from a phone conversation she'd had with a friend that she could've had a baby at the age of eighteen. As a first-year student, in a relationship that could never have been serious, she just didn't have the stomach for it.

Being young and stupid, she and a buddy, who'd had some medical training, tried solving her pregnancy problem by means of hormonal injections, but they didn't help. Then, on the advice of a girlfriend who'd recently had a similar experience, she consulted a gynecologist and told him the whole story. The sympathetic doctor treated her like a daughter, patted her on the head, and told her to come in the next day, with a housecoat and slippers.

The last thing she remembered was saying, "I'm so afraid the anesthetic won't work..." and the smile on the anesthetist's face in response.

Before Lera had even realized, it was all over.

The soul of one who'd just been a tiny daughter... was gone. She hadn't wanted to see the process of her would've-been body's extraction, so she flew straight up to her fellow souls and had a good cry over her dashed hopes—she'd already fallen in love with the teenage giggler, who'd known she was pregnant since April Fools' Day.

At first, her 'man of the hour' even took the news for a joke, which turned out to be a particularly cruel joke, indeed. The little soul's mistake wasn't in her choice of parents; it was that she'd made her choice before they both were ready to have a child. That error in judgment carried a penalty of two years—the length of time she'd have to wait before she could try choosing her parents again.

For a while, the sight of little children made Lera want to cry. She had several dreams of a little redheaded girl with gray eyes. Later, the same feeling of loss returned whenever she held her girlfriends' children. The whole time she lived with Victor, her desire for motherhood had been overwhelming.

That same year, Lera's friend, Anya, had given birth to a baby boy. She'd told Lera that she'd had a dream about him, before he was even conceived, in which he'd instructed her to name him Romka.

The next year, Lera was at Anya's place again on April 1st and, as a joke, had suggested Anya give birth on the 17th, since it was her favorite number. Imagine her surprise when it happened precisely then!

"Anya, I hope you know who should be his godmother," Lera said afterwards, laughing.

"There's no doubt in my mind." Her friend smiled. "As soon as he's a little older, we'll have the christening."

"He'll be my second godson," Lera added. "Someone told me recently that your life changes for the better when you've become a little boy's godmother, and here I'll have done it twice!"

Anya had thrown her hands up and said, "So then everything will *definitely* change for the better!"

Lera's supplication had reached us up at the Celestial Chancellery, as she held the month-old Romka in her arms for the first time, imagining for a split second that he was hers.

That day I saw her with Victor, having been actively searching for over a month, I knew that it was time to answer her plea.

That type of request, for a child of one's own, normally goes out when the woman sees a little child she likes. Something very difficult to pinpoint occurs, an inner sense of enthusiasm, or delight transpires, which emerges as the desire to have the same kind of child. This signal is then picked up by a soul seeking earthly incarnation, at from that point an energy link between them is established and maintained. I thus found Lera intuitively, without even suspecting she was the one for me.

When she came home from seeing little Romka, Lera told Victor how she felt, and immediately, their respective yearnings parted ways. Not yet officially divorced from his first wife, Victor was seven years older than Lera, his second and 'unofficial' wife. He considered himself experienced and practical, and saw Lera as young, naive, and far too emotional. A generous, cheerful prankster, on the one hand, Victor also harbored a darker side that could reveal itself at any given moment, and lash out at whoever was around.

Lera often thought of Victor as having two 'personalities' that happened to co-exist: the kind-hearted comedian she loved, and the unrelenting pragmatist with the cruel eyes, who terrified her. If you believed in horoscopes, this sort of duality was quite common for Gemini.

The 'second' Victor saw Lera as a free-spirited flake and a rotten housewife, whom he would never marry, let alone have children with. Period. But... since the 'first,' bright and cheery Victor truly loved her, the only thing his dark side could do was accept the situation.

Chapter 4

By the middle of May, when I'd first sensed there was a girl out there, somewhere, who needed me, and vice-versa, Victor and Lera's relationship was on the brink of complete collapse. The levity and romance between them having disappeared, their life together revolved around working out the banalities of coexistence, things like whose turn it was to buy groceries, and how to chop the onions for dinner. Over dinner, they talked about their jobs, without the slightest bit of warmth.

When that life had become unbearable, Lera packed her things while Victor was out with his friends. She bumped into him on her way out the door, and he simply walked her to the elevator without a single word.

The next day, a handsome young journalist by the name of Artem Golubkov showed up at the editorial office of the newspaper where she worked in the PR department. The editor-in-chief introduced him right away, leading the embarrassed rookie from office to office and begging everyone to love and respect him.

"We'll not only love and respect him, we'll even take pity on him," said Lera, unable to resist the wisecrack on seeing Artem's embarrassment. He was her type—average build, adorably puffy gray eyes, and a sensuous mouth, like Brad Pitt's. He was also a bit of a milquetoast, another plus, as Lera loved putting people on the spot. "Which of the three would you prefer, Artem?" she asked, making him blush.

Grinning bashfully, Artem decided he'd prefer leaving her office as quickly as possible, but Lera stuck in his mind. He'd always liked redheads like her, but felt they were out of his league. Still, he wanted to try his luck at this one, so he plucked up his courage and, about ten minutes later, walked back into the office.

"Anybody feel like going to the DDT concert tonight? I've got an extra ticket," he said, addressing the room, but looking straight at Lera.

"You should go, Lera. You love Shevchuk," said a colleague who noticed.

"I do appreciate his talent, but I *love* Zemfira."

"Oh well, you can see Zemfira another time. Go with the rookie." The colleague laughed. "You did say you'd take pity on him."

"Well, okay, Artem, I'll go with you," Lera agreed, and taking her cue, she added, "but only because I'm obligated."

The concert was sold out, and for some reason, they held the bleacher fans back at first. When they finally let them in, there was a mad rush, during which Lera and Artem were pressed up against each other. They didn't mind. He even thanked the pushy crowd, mentally, because it would've taken him ages to get up that close to her on his own.

Shevchuk was in top form. The concert was a great success, and when it was over, the fans descended upon the metro 'en masse.' Lera and Artem stood nose to nose in the metro car, both of them aware of the strong physical attraction between them.

How strange, Lera thought. *Just yesterday, I felt like bawling my head off, and a day later, here I am, up close and personal with another man who seems to really like me. I mean, he's very nice and cute, but he could really use a shave.*

"What's with the silly beard?" she asked, bluntly. "You're only twenty-three! We're almost the same age, by the way, but as you can see, I don't have a beard."

"I thought it would make me look more mature. Didn't it work?"

"No, it didn't. Shave it off."

"I'll think about it."

"Good! Think about it, and shave it off."

"Can't stick a finger in *your* eye," Artem said, enthusiastically.

"So don't. Why would I want a finger in my eye, anyway?" Lera laughed.

Stuck for a quick comeback, he couldn't think of anything to do but pull her hair.

Where was I right then? Why wasn't I there with them? I mean, that was the defining moment for things to go one way or another, and nobody was there to send Lera a sign that Artem was the one who shouldn't get away. She shouldn't belittle him, as he was still 'green,' and she could mold him into whatever she wanted. He could've been the right dad for me, but Lera wasn't a sculptor by nature. In fact, she could've used a little molding herself. In truth, the stuff Artem was made of, however malleable, wouldn't have withstood Lera's firing kiln. That's why things went wrong from the very start.

After the night of the concert, Artem and Lera hung around together after work a few times, just staring at each other, in the company of other colleagues. On one such occasion, an inebriated Artem unexpectedly went after her friend, Julia, who happened to tag along that day. Already sweet on him, Lera watched in disbelief, as the pair split off from the rest of the group and stood there, by the statue of Lenin at the Finland station, necking passionately for several minutes.

Whatever Artem had hoped to achieve with that stunt was beyond Lera.

For the bearded Artem, who knew nothing about socializing with women, even at the most basic level, he'd done it as a ploy to make her jealous and further pique her interest in his persona. He even shared his favorable impression of that kiss with Lera, but the whole thing backfired. Lera merely shrugged her shoulders in deeper disbelief and multiplied him by zero. And Artem's spontaneous romantic interlude with Julia had been purely a one-off occurrence.

Back in the present, I wound up in Lera's room, watching her contemplate the two pink stripes on the pregnancy test strip. I felt her distress and heard her thoughts, and was beside myself. How could this have happened? I'd wanted Lera to see, before conceiving me, that she and Victor were incompatible. Things had suddenly gotten very complicated.

God, she thought as Victor lay sleeping. *What will Vic say when he wakes up? He'll say it was all my doing, that he doesn't want it.*

I watched how peacefully he slept, his head perfectly positioned on his pillow. To me, 'the mister' looked just as unpleasant asleep as he did awake. How could Lera not realize he was holding a rock behind his back, and that any minute now, he was going to hurl it at her? He would've done it long ago, if he didn't truly love the girl he deemed so unworthy of bearing his child. So, the rock lay in wait....

Victor had been the fellow in the rowboat with Lera, when I first saw her. I would gladly have left him on that island with the monkeys. He could've used that rock for protection.

He'd been hankering for a daughter for ages, and decided to name her Katya, after a girl he'd loved platonically in school. I knew it would happen for him, only not now, not with Lera! I was supposed to be a boy, so Victor couldn't possibly become my father.

There was something wrong here. I felt detached from the big picture, as though none of what was happening had anything to do with my life. Then I made a big mistake.

Chapter 5

On a hot, sunny day in July, something happened that I didn't understand — probably too much sun on my nonexistent head.

We souls were always attracted by intense feelings between our potential future parents, and on that day, such feelings existed between Lera and Victor. They'd gone to the movies and fallen in love again. They'd spent the whole time necking in the back row, and could barely remember the plot as they left the cinema. Then they held hands all the way home.

Victor was suddenly so different, as if he'd been replaced by somebody else. The coldness I'd noticed in his eyes had disappeared completely, as though it had never been there at all. I knew their feelings were genuine, because I was powerless to resist, as they sucked me down from above like a vacuum cleaner.

Everything changed direction this night, though, along a path that Lera wasn't destined to follow, thereby deciding her fate. And mine.

Victor looked at those stripes on the pregnancy test strip, and said, "Have a baby with anybody you like, only not with me."

As they sat at the kitchen table, I could feel Lera seize up on the inside. It was all she could do not to burst into tears.

"But we've talked about your Katya together," she said, "and I want her too."

"No, Ginger, I don't think we're meant to keep the baby. Better go see a doctor."

"I will, but only if you come too."

The doctor she happened to see at the clinic turned out to be the same kind-hearted fellow who'd performed her first procedure. He remembered Lera and, as per her request, he tried convincing Victor to keep the baby.

"She's about five weeks in," he said, taking him into the corridor after the examination. "The lining is very thin. An abortion could have a negative effect on any future pregnancies. Understand?"

Victor nodded.

The doctor winked at Lera as she left, intimating he'd managed to turn the would-be father around, and Lera wanted desperately to believe it.

Chapter 6

They'd bought their tickets to Sochi, for September 3rd, before they'd discovered it wouldn't be just the two of them going. Maybe Victor had decided to let things slide for a while, because changing his vacation plans was a hassle. I didn't feel like going with them, somehow, since I could observe them and hear their thoughts remotely anyway.

I sensed that the pregnancy had destroyed the sincerity between them. Lera was devoting all her energy to convincing Vic that everything would be fine, and that the baby wouldn't interfere with the course of his life.

Conversely, my reluctant father contemplated the most horrifying things. Once, when Lera initiated a conversation on the beach, about their future and having a little girl together, I caught him thinking how he could just drown her, right then, and probably get away with it. He was still as possessive as ever, however, even though he'd already decided the baby question by then. He threw a fit on the beach when Lera wanted to tan topless. A regular storybook vacation, that was.

The whole thing made me so unbearably sad, I wanted to cry—out loud, like a baby—but I couldn't.

Lera often listened to a recording of a humorous play in verse, about a fellow named Fyodot. At that particular moment, I wondered if it was about me, as when one of the characters says:

> At times I get a puzzling thought:
> Do I really exist, or not?
> I've got troubles, but I can't fix them,
> I've got food, but I can't eat!
> There's tobacco, but I can't sniff it,
> There's a bench, but I can't even sit.

I was invisible to everyone—except those like me, and nobody but me could see them, either. I could even make myself invisible to the other souls, if I wanted, by turning on the so-called 'invisible mode.' Seriously, where was the proof of our existence? Despite having argued the question of 'What is a soul?' forever, who had actually seen one? Nobody. Souls were like rumors, and nobody really knew for sure whether they were left behind when people died, or reborn in somebody else, or whether they even existed! It seemed I'd stopped believing in myself — that is, if I existed at all.

Every evening, tens of thousands of us would get together in little groups, and those with something to tell would share their most interesting impressions of the day with the others. The souls who'd materialized inside their future mothers that day would organize a dance party, and the others rejoiced for them. One day, the soul I knew as F-12161998 gathered a huge crowd around her with the news that her mom had finally discovered her.

"She went to her friend's place with her pregnancy test results," she said, sweet Chatty Cathy that she was. "And the friend said yes, she was definitely pregnant, and my mom smiled. She has such a beautiful smile! And my dad's so fascinating! I must absolutely look like him — such big, expressive eyes," she added, dreamily. "That's what I fell in love with first, his eyes, as soon as I saw them in the rearview mirror of his car."

"And does he already know?" asked the other future little girls.

"Not yet. Olga — that's my mom — is afraid to tell him for now. She and Vlad, my dad, haven't known each other for very long. Plus, she and her husband, Klim, aren't divorced yet. I heard him threaten to hurt her or himself if she leaves him. They're a complicated family. They have a five-year-old boy, Petya, and now there's me, too. But Olga's fantastic. I'm just crazy about her! I can hardly wait till I'm a real baby girl, with hands and feet and big blue eyes just like my dad's, and she's holding me in her arms...."

F-12161998 was flitting around, daydreaming away, just ecstatic to have finally materialized in her ideal mom.

Every one of us had a particular image in mind of our own ideal mother or father, before we set out to find them, and Lera corresponded perfectly to mine.

One of my friends had chosen a fourteen-year-old girl as his mom, and he was in such a hurry that he was born only eight months from the day he first saw her, right on her fifteenth birthday. He'd been too hasty in choosing his father, though, and things were really tough for his mom, at first. She had to drop out of school for a while, and when her grandmother first heard about his imminent arrival, she almost had a heart attack.

The minute we're born, we stop communicating with each other, and we never recognize one another in our earthly incarnations, but I watched over my friend after his birth. He had a different dad now, plus a little brother, and his mom was back at school and finally happy. He made the right choice, after all.

Maybe we'll meet again, when I'm a person, too, but we'll never remember how we used to peek into people's windows and fly in through the little air vents, in search of our future parents, when we were best friends, with numbers instead of names.

Chapter 7

The first time I saw Lera after the trip to Sochi was in the doctor's office. She lay on a cot, and a white-haired lady in a white lab coat sat alongside, going over her belly with a little instrument. My mother couldn't see the grainy image on the screen of the tiny person inside her.

It was me... in my future body!

"What an obedient little baby you have," said the white lady. "I asked it to move a little, and it did."

My mother smiled. "Can you see if it's a boy or a girl yet?"

"It's still early, about ten or eleven weeks. Should I print up the image for you?

"Absolutely! I'll show the father his obedient baby."

When the photo popped out of the printer, it fell onto the floor.

"How did that happen?" the lady wondered out loud and, bending down, she half-disappeared under the desk.

I did that, so I could have a look at the first picture of my future self, but there wasn't much to see—just a little smudge against a fuzzy gray-and-black background.

Lera got dressed, took the little print with her, and started looking me over, right there in the corridor outside the ultrasound room.

"These must be the hands," she said, going over the image with her finger, thinking about how she would show Victor the first photo of their little baby. "And these are the feet."

Victor had been growing gloomier and gloomier, lately, and it scared her.

Then there was Artem, who had no idea. He sensed something was going on with Lera, but whenever he asked her about it, she only laughed him off. They'd stopped socializing after work, and any interaction between them was limited to text messages—usually on his initiative.

One such text had caused a lot of trouble. Unable to restrain himself, one night, after a few rounds with his friends at a popular tavern, the lovesick Artem started texting Lera all kinds of stupid things, every twenty minutes, like:

I want it-I want it-I want it-I want it-I want it. I'm your wanter.

Lera couldn't help but smile at that one. After an office party the previous evening, she and Artem had started talking about sex, and various attitudes towards it. He disapproved of his mother, who changed husbands and boyfriends regularly, and was shocked to discover that his sixteen-year-old sister had a boyfriend, with whom she was actually having intimate relations! He'd chosen Lera to unburden himself to.

"Well, what do you expect? Girls start early, these days," she said, trying to calm him down.

"When did *you* start?" he asked, point blank.

"Late, by today's standards." She laughed. "At eighteen."

"There you go!" he exclaimed. "Polina's only sixteen!"

"So what?" Lera countered. "It's not like I'm the benchmark, or anything."

"For me, you are," he said, without a hint of a smile, looking her square in the eye.

Lera was uncomfortable with his candor, so she tried to make a joke of the whole thing. "Stop, before you give me a superiority complex."

"Or a singularity complex," Artem quipped.

"God forbid!" Lera burst out laughing. She loved plays on words, and people who used them.

They ended up sitting on a bench in a nearby park. Unexpectedly moved to pour his heart out, under the influence of a gin and tonic, Artem filled Lera in on his own sexual experience, consisting of an incident the year before, when a woman twice his age plied him with alcohol and then seduced him. His attempts to start a relationship with someone his own age had been unsuccessful. He also told her about his family: his dead-beat dad, whom he hadn't seen since he was a child, and the well-trodden path to his mother's door by her admirers. His sister Polina was the fruit of the mother's second marriage, which she followed up with a third and a fourth, both unofficial. Her last common-law husband turned out to be a generous man, who'd left her a handsome sum — in debts. Only recently, the family had been forced to sell their apartment just to pay them off.

Telling her all of this, Artem resembled a little boy with a beard, and I felt sorry for him. I realized why I wanted him to be my father: he really was a little boy — kind, open, capricious and stubborn. I think we would've gotten along well together.

"So where do you live now?" Lera asked.

"I'm renting a studio. You should come over. I bought a couch. I have some grapes, and we can watch a movie. I'm in a kind of grape-and-movie mood," he said, getting cheekier every minute.

"A couch-warming party?"

"Something like that. I have to break it in, right?"

"I'll drop by sometime. Later. If you have hot running water. Because pretty soon, my place won't have any for two weeks," Lera replied, jokingly. For some reason, she didn't feel like telling Artem she already had somebody with which to break in couches.

Obviously, this conversation had given him reason to think something could happen between them, because the next message she received from him on that ill-fated evening was of the following 'poetic' content:

> *I'll fly through your window*
> *As a little pigeon,*
> *And sneak into your hollow*
> *With such precision....*

Lera sputtered with suppressed laughter, and that very second, Victor grabbed the phone out of her hand and read the message.

"Who the hell thinks he can send messages like this to my girlfriend?"

"Just some kid from work," Lera said, dismissing the whole thing with a wave of her hand, giving to understand it was nothing. She figured he'd probably gotten tipsy and started texting. "Just forget about it."

"Really? I think I'll give him a call."

"Oh, Vic, don't. Don't wreck his night. Let him have his fun."

Victor was suddenly jealous. "Don't wreck *his* night? But he can wreck mine with his stupid rhymes?"

"Come on," Lera said. "He's not sending them to you."

"That's right. He's sending them to my chick!"

"And it doesn't mean anything to your chick," Lera said calmly.

"Well, it does to me!" Victor half shouted. "It means he has no respect for me!"

He looked mad as a bull about to enter the ring. Another minute and he'd be puffing steam out of his nostrils.

"Oh, God, Vic, he doesn't even know you! How can he respect somebody he knows nothing about?" Lera groaned. She really wanted to end this conversation.

"Oh, I get it! So, you haven't told him you already have a man?" His voice grew louder. "Is he your Plan B?"

"Come on, Vic, stop talking nonsense. Why would I need a Plan B, when you and I are having a baby in seven months?"

"I don't want the baby! I never did!" he shouted. "Get this through your head: I would never marry a woman who can't even make a 'home,' or keep house, or do anything at all!"

Lera went completely cold inside. She couldn't utter a single word for the lump in her throat. What could she possibly say to that, anyway? She got up off the chair and walked over to the front door while Victor stayed in the bedroom. She put on some shoes, grabbed a jacket, and walked out the door, shutting it quietly behind her.

Even forgetting there was an elevator, Lera started down the stairs from the seventh story. Every time she looked down, she saw the words *'Don't leave!'* flashing up at her, from every step.

"I can't stay," she kept saying, every time she saw them. Her eyes welled with tears, but they didn't run down her face. She heard the door open upstairs and Vic's voice call out her name.

The lump in her throat was still there.

There was a pause, and then Vic's voice again. "Lera!"

Then there was silence, and the door finally closed.

The very second she got to the stop, the bus pulled up, as though it had come just for her. Lera looked through the back window at the receding apartment building, where the baby she'd wanted for so long had been conceived. She was leaving, well aware that this was likely the end. If she hadn't left, things may have worked out differently. With her sense of humor, she could've turned the whole thing into a joke and said something like, "I know, I know, I'm a crummy housekeeper, but since you're such an expert, you could give me some pointers, right?"

She hadn't, of course. It was only that easy in theory; if people could react that calmly to things that really upset them, the divorce statistics would be very different.

She saw the same billboard: 'Not meant to be.'

That's when the floodgates opened. Lera sat on the bus weeping silently, so as not to attract attention, but when she got off at her stop and cut through the deserted park toward her parents' place, she started sobbing loudly, uninhibited. She felt sorry for herself and for her future child, but right now, she was scared, too—scared for her future. She didn't want to be a single mom. Plus, she really loved Victor, but to burden him with a child, and with herself, too, as his life partner, just didn't seem feasible. Without the child, that would be impossible, but the child existed! And if it ceased to exist? Was that something she could forgive? They couldn't possibly stay together after that.

I can't think about that right now. If I do, I'll go crazy. I'll think about that tomorrow.

At her parents' place, as she lay on the sofa, she recalled that line of Scarlett's from *Gone with the Wind*, one of her favorite books as a child. She also thought about the poor little baby inside her, who could probably hear and feel everything, and who could realize she was capable of causing him irreparable damage.

I really *did* hear and feel everything. I would've been tearing my hair out if I'd had any, because I could've prevented everything that was happening now, from the very beginning.

Victor wasn't destined to be my father, and that's why the pieces of the puzzle didn't fit. One day, he'd definitely find himself a suitable wife, who'd be waiting patiently with a hot meal when he came home from work, and who'd close her eyes to the nights he didn't come home, and give him his little 'Katya.' Just how Lera had written herself into this narrative was a mystery, some sort of ill fate. She was a temporary person in Victor's life, as he was in hers, and having separated once before, they should never have gotten back together. Yet my mother had stepped into that same river twice, of her own free will, and that was her big mistake.

If you're going to leave... leave.

I wasn't helping the situation. I was actually hurting her, and myself. If she were to get rid of the baby, she could never be my mother again, and I wouldn't be able to look for another one for at least two years. I would have to spend that time performing 'corrective labor' as a kind of penalty for having made a mistake and not being born—like helping the guardian angels with their tedious daily business, for instance. Angel assistants didn't have a minute to spare, or any time at all, to think about their future birth.

Chapter 8

Lera spent the entire next day waiting for Victor to call; they had to make a final decision. After the first trimester, they only terminated pregnancies for medical reasons, and they'd told Lera at the clinic that everything was going perfectly. In her eleventh week, the very thought of getting rid of the baby she'd wanted for so long terrified her.

She finally got the call on the evening of the third day.

"Hello."

"Hello, hi." A miracle could have happened after those words, but it didn't. In a cold, unfamiliar voice, Victor said he wanted her to have the abortion.

She'd been expecting that, but when she actually heard the words, she burst into tears like a little girl and shouted, "Why don't *you* go and have them cut something out of *you* for no medical reason?"

"You're just being emotional, Ginger," Victor replied curtly. "The decision is made. I'll drop by the day after tomorrow, in the morning, and we'll go see your favorite doctor." With that, he hung up.

The next day, Lera called in sick and sat around on the sofa, hands clasped around her knees, thinking about what to do. She was twenty-two years old, and having a baby on her own was a scary prospect. She'd be graduating soon, and had just gotten herself a new job. Her bosses wouldn't approve a maternity leave that soon. Plus, her parents were the 'creative types' — here one day, elsewhere the next, and unable to help out, financially or otherwise. She had exactly twenty-four hours to decide: tomorrow was her doctor's scheduled procedural day.

I wanted to send her a dream I'd come up with earlier, while she was relaxing on the beach in Sochi, as though I'd predicted what was happening now. In the dream, she was standing on a sunbeam, holding a little bouquet of multicolored balloons that were pulling her up into the sky. Beside her was a five-year-old boy, the kind I'd be later, and he begged her not to fly away. I didn't send her the dream, though, because I didn't want to influence her decision. I didn't want her to spend the rest of her life bound to that transient person in it all because of my mistake.

"Understand one thing," said Lera's girlfriend, Anya, over the phone. She was nine years older and wiser, and could speak from experience, now that little Romka was already six months old. "Men come and go, but kids are forever. If it's a child you need, then keep it, but if you keep it only for the sake of staying with Victor, then it's probably not worth it. I love you, and I'll support you, whatever you decide."

Lera stayed on the sofa like that until nighttime, and decided in my favor. Another girlfriend, Nadya, who'd been in Lera's situation once, called that evening to learn of her decision.

"Well, maybe you're right," Nadya said, albeit doubtfully.

"You're absolutely right," Lera's father later said, authoritatively and approvingly, despite having observed Lera's life only peripherally, and knowing very little about her. "You have to keep it. Aborting a first pregnancy can be dangerous."

"I don't know, Lera," her creative mother said afterwards, one on one. "I wouldn't advise it. I realized a long time ago that Victor wasn't the man for you."

The next morning, Victor showed up, and Lera let him into the apartment without a single word. On seeing the mother of his unwanted child still in bed, the expression on his face changed... radically.

"What the... you've decided to keep it?"

"I have," Lera replied, still sitting in the exact same position as the day before, trying to appear calm.

"All right, Ginger, keep it then. It's your choice, except you'll never see me again."

"It doesn't matter. When it's born, we'll do a DNA test, confirm your paternity, and you'll pay child support," Lera snapped, pulling the blanket right up to her chin.

"Go ahead, Ginger, talk as much as you want." Victor was beside himself with anger. "Only, bear in mind that my official salary is only eight hundred rubles, and you'll get a whole quarter of that!"

Lera looked at him in horror. At that particular moment, my 'unwanted father' looked like a monster, his distorted face particularly cruel.

I could hear my mother thinking: *What if I have a boy, and twenty years later I see that same look on his face?*

That very second, she changed her mind.

For some reason, I wasn't afraid. That's probably the way soldiers on the frontlines feel, when they realize there's no escaping death but know it will help save someone else.

Victor said he'd wait in the car and left the apartment.

Lera's mother, who obviously hadn't slept all night, jumped into the corridor after him in her heightened emotional state, and shouted, "I want my daughter to have a child, whereas you—may you be damned!"

Then the door slammed shut, and the damned one took off.

Lera dressed quickly and called Nadya, who'd recently gotten her license and needed to practice driving in her first car.

"Nadya, it's a bad morning. Everything has changed. He came over, and I've reconsidered. Can you come and pick me up at 72 Maurice Thorez, at noon? Seems a bit sleazy to have to take the bus home after the procedure, and I won't ride with him."

"I'll be there. Just stay put!"

"I will. Where can I go?"

Her mother had gone into her own room.

Lera went out into the street and got into Victor's car. They didn't exchange a single word on the way to the clinic, and the rest happened in silence too: the physical exam, the blood test, changing into her nightgown. It was all so dreamlike—unreal.

Victor covered the cost.

Doctor Zhigalov, who would perform the procedure, tried talking to him but quickly realized there was no point.

Despite the excruciating pity he felt for Lera, and his own shame, Victor was relieved. Just a little while longer, and he'd be rid of that excess baggage.

It was very painful for me—not physically, of course. Lera suffered the physical pain, but luckily, they'd invented the anesthesia. I saw everything that was happening in the operating room. I saw what could've been my body, but never would, now. The doctors conversed on various unrelated, prosaic topics; the procedure was routine—all in a day's work, like sticking stamps on envelopes was for post-office employees. How many souls like me had lost their hopes of being born right here, in this tiny room, smelling of medicine and blood?

Lera was still sleeping.

In my thoughts, I said goodbye to this wonderful, strong and weak girl, who couldn't be my mom. I'd already managed to love her so much, and I really didn't want anybody else for myself, but according to our rules, there was no going back.

When Lera finally came out of the anesthetic and got dressed, Nadya was already in the waiting room, sitting on the sofa next to a pale Victor. Lera hugged her friend silently, snuggling up to her shoulder.

Then, without even looking at Victor, she said, "I never want to see you again. Ever!"

The girls got into Nadya's car. Victor stood looking through the front window, holding a bottle of orange juice. He opened the car door and placed it at Lera's feet.

"This is for you," he said. "What about your keys?"

"I'll toss them through the air vent," she said, and shut the car door.

The thread that had united them for two-and-a-half months, thanks to me, had stretched as far as it could, and finally broke when Nadya's car drove away.

I could only stay with Lera for another twenty-four hours—max. After that, I would be debriefed. What went wrong? How could I have let it come to this? Blah blah blah.... Then they'd assign me to some slacker of a guardian angel, unable to cope with his workload, and I'd have to be his apprentice for the next two years, getting his wards out of unforeseen predicaments.

I was again reminded of Fyodot, who said:

> I acknowledge my error
> And must bear its burden.
> So find me a war,
> And I'll fight, 'til the final curtain....

Again, that was exactly me. I screwed up, and now I'd have to pay. On the bright side, I'd have time to contemplate the impermanence of creation. Two whole years....

I decided to stay with Lera an extra twenty-four hours, until they started looking for me. News of idle souls down here traveled fast, but I wanted to be sure that my former mom would be okay.

Lera spent the rest of the day lying in bed, face buried in her pillow. She didn't sleep, or cry, or think about anything at all. That evening, a girl named Masha called and cheered her up a little. Lera laughed like a crazy person. Even her father looked into her room, and couldn't believe his own ears. He thought she'd lost her mind.

The next day, Lera's mom convinced her to go out for a walk. The sun shined and the sky was blue, as only a St. Petersburg sky can be, and all the birds flew around—exactly like we souls did, except much lower, and everybody could see them. I had less than an hour left to spend with my could-have-been mother's side. I snuggled up to her thick, red hair, and was overcome by the urge to cry, because I would never see her again.

"I'm sorry things turned out this way," I whispered.

She looked up at the birds, flying in V formation, and her eyes filled with tears. Suddenly, she fell to her knees and sobbed loudly.

My would-have-been grandmother got upset. At a complete loss for words, all she could do was kneel down beside her daughter and pat Lera on the head. "There, there, sweetheart, don't cry. All things must pass, and so will this. You'll absolutely have children one day, and a husband who's a lot better than this one! Absolutely! Today's a special name day— for Vera, Nadezhda, and Lyubov—so we'll celebrate Faith, Hope, and Love. I'll bake a little cake this evening. You can invite your girlfriends over, and we'll have a little get-together. Now, calm down, please!"

Lera wanted to shut her eyes, tight, in the hope that when she opened them again, things would be as before, as though nothing had happened, and she and Victor would be together again. Despite the fact that her mind couldn't forgive what had happened, she suddenly realized her heart had already forgiven him, and that she didn't need the blue sky, or the birds, or anything—without him. But there was no turning back, because their child, the only thing worth staying together for, was gone. That's the one thing she couldn't forgive him... or herself.

I could feel myself being pulled upwards by those invisible threads, and there was nothing I could do. It was time to go back home.

"Goodbye, Mama," I said at the very last second.

"Goodbye," she suddenly pronounced, looking up at the sky.

When I got back up, the one in charge wasn't there. He'd flown off, along with some other guardian angels, to the site of a tour bus crash. It happened while the angels were having fun, playing the lotto, and there were a lot of injuries. This is where they sent souls like me, who'd screwed up—to these irresponsible 'chaperones' with wings—the logic being that two screw-ups would have a positive effect on each other, culminating in mutual redemption. Put another way, 'negative times negative equals positive.'

I sat down and waited to find out who would be my mentor, and heard a voice say, "Hi."

"Hello," I replied out loud.

An angel of rather stately proportions sat right beside me. He looked like a regular guy, about thirty, but his face was very pale. He had shoulder-length, jet-black hair that he obviously hadn't brushed for a long time, and I could see his folded wings, big as he was, behind his back.

"So, should we introduce ourselves?" he asked.

"Do we need to?" I asked back, being cautious.

"You're M-04041999, right?"

"I am."

"My name's Elias. From now on, I'm your immediate superior, and you are my assistant. I hope you'll be able to fulfill your obligations better than the hundreds who've preceded you."

I hoped he was kidding.

"As of now, the number M-04041999 will be deactivated for a period of two years, so go ahead and think of a new name for yourself. I can't seem to come up with anything today."

His wings were a little disheveled, and had a grayish hue; he'd definitely needed a good rainfall for some time. The creative type, I supposed; he probably wrote poetry, like Lera's mother. His eyes were a gray-green and looked kind, to be expected for an angel, and he had the most beautiful, thick eyelashes, a little over the top even for a male angel.

"And has the disciplinary lecture been cancelled?" I asked.

"Postponed," he replied, wriggling his lips from side to side for some reason. "I mean, you know what your mistakes were, but when the big boss remembers, he'll summon you. You can count on it. For now, you're all mine. You won't be bored. I have seven people under my wing, but I haven't decided exactly whom you'll be assigned to. Right now, I have to fly, though. There's one more thing I need to do today, and you need to come up with a name by tomorrow. See you then, same time, same place."

Then he flew off, flapping his wings loudly.

A name.

Should it be just any old name? Maybe I'd call myself Artem, in honor of that sweet young man with the beard. No, I needed something more meaningful and conciliatory, and shorter. Like 'Peace!' It sounds so inclusive, and when the opportunity arises, Elias can say, "We come in Peace!" Yes, that sounded nice. And so it was. I'd grant myself peace.

With the free time I had, I decided to visit my friends, who happened to be in the middle of their evening dances.

F-161211998 saw me and yelled, "Hi there! How are you?"

"I guess you haven't heard," I said. "It didn't work out. I've been suspended for two years."

"Oh no," she groaned, sympathetically. "I'm sorry. So he turned out to be a jerk, just like you figured?"

"Something like that."

"Oh, I really feel for you! Well, maybe in two years...."

"Absolutely," I said, trying to sound optimistic. "How about you?"

"Oh, things are just fantastic!" she chirped. "At first, I thought I'd end up in your situation, but luckily, my dad reconsidered. And Olga's getting up the nerve to finally settle things with her husband and move in with Vlad and my big brother to be. Isn't that great?"

"Sure is," I said, unenthusiastically.

"I made her dream about me yesterday. You know, just to bring it all home," F-12161998 continued, "and this morning she texted my dad: 'Dreamt of a little girl, who looked like you.'"

"What about him?"

"He wrote: 'They say if a girl looks like her father, she'll be happy.'"

"You're lucky," I said, and even though I was happy for her, I got sad.

"Oh, come on, you'll be lucky too, absolutely! The two years will go by so fast, you won't even notice! I have to fly, okay? I'm going to spend some time with my dad today."

"Sure," I said. "Have fun."

The rest of the M's and F's were busy flying around, chaotically, and having the same three-minute conversations. There was rarely any real bonding between us, not like the bond I had with that friend who'd already been born. I was never able to find another kindred soul after that. F-12161998 managed to blab about my unenviable fate to several souls at once as she flew away, and now they flew up to me, one by one, to offer their condolences.

"The same thing happened to me five years ago," one of them said. "After that, I didn't feel like doing anything at all, but the angel they assigned me to bombarded me with assignments, which distracted me from my gloomy thoughts so effectively, I haven't had any to this day. However, I'm careful with my choices now."

"And do you know anything about the girl who decided not to have you?"

"No, and I don't want to, either. I was offended by that. I heard she did have a baby afterwards, but I don't think she was upset about losing me. I happened to pick a frivolous person, but I won't make that mistake again. What about yours, was she an airhead too?"

"There's no need for name-calling. She wasn't an airhead at all."

"So what was the problem? Afraid of the responsibility?"

"Probably. I haven't figured it out yet."

"Well, forget about it. Live for the present, and just don't think about her, like she never existed."

"I can't do that."

"Force yourself. I did!"

"And I'll bet you remember her anyway, and you're still offended," I said, and he didn't like it.

"Maybe I am," he retorted, "but I try not to think about it. I've decided to look for a serious, intelligent mother, around forty, who'll have been dreaming about having me for at least ten years. I'll be her last chance to have a family. Women like her don't do stupid things. And I'll be sure to pick the same kind of father."

"That's wise. Well, I wish you success!"

"Likewise, my friend. What should I call you now?"

"Peace."

"Awesome! A name is binding, though. Make sure you do it justice."

"I'll try," I said, and we flew off in opposite directions.

I was impatient to get down to my new responsibilities now, and I tried not to think of Lera.

Chapter 9

Elias was late for our meeting, but didn't seem to care. He held a sheet listing the people who needed our help, and the problems peculiar to each. After approving the name I'd chosen for myself, he got down to business.

"Okay, Peace, look," he said. "We have three poor suckers here who keep ending up in the strangest possible circumstances. I have others, too, but they have fewer problems, whereas these three—something's always happening to them, and always suddenly, and it's not always good. They're always veering off their predetermined paths. The funniest thing is, two of them recently got to know each other.

But first things first: Vladimir. He was supposed to marry Marina and have a family, years ago, but he just moped around in his room for days on end, growing a disgusting beard and paying no attention to women. As a result, Marina's whole life was turned upside down. She was so lonely, she became a novice in a monastery, and eventually took the veil. Nobody saw that coming—she'd always been such a 'people person.' Now, instead of raising six-year-old twin girls with Vladimir, she lives in an orthodox convent near Jerusalem, helping the pilgrims!"

"So, Vladimir and Marina never even met?" I asked, genuinely disturbed by the story.

"Sure they did! In January of 1994, I helped break a heel on her boot as she was crossing the bridge over the Fontanka River. She started waving at cars, and Vladimir stopped and gave her a lift, but he didn't say a word to her the whole time! Just imagine: your destiny is sitting right there, beside you, and you're thinking about asking her to pay you for the ride because your fridge is empty! I mean, come on!"

Elias even clapped his wings together out of agitation. "So he'd been living in his room in the communal apartment like an inmate, until I arranged another meeting with a really fun girl—not so anything would happen between them, but because he needed a friend, a mentor. All the better if she were a woman. She helped him look at the world differently and become more like a human being. He shaved off that beard, started thinking about seeing someone, and even bought an expensive cellphone just recently.

"You see, I'm good friends with this girl's guardian angel, so she aided me in helping the girl put Vladimir out of his loneliness. Basically, I let go of my control over things. My first few attempts to introduce him to girls had failed, but in the end, things with this particular girl worked out—much to her own surprise, too. How could I not have found a good match for him sooner? Anyway, they got together without my involvement, and this girl, Olga, was his first 'woman,' if you know what I mean. I'm sure you're well aware of what has to happen before a woman can have a baby, right?"

Elias cocked his head awaiting my response, and I nodded.

"And now everything's great," he continued. "He's on an entirely different trajectory, of course, instead of the one that would've been best, if he'd only paid more attention to his passenger in 1994. Alas, people choose their own paths, Peace, and sometimes they're only given a few. A guardian angel's job is to help their person get back on track, and I'm very happy and relieved that Vlad has finally found love. By the way, one of yours recently fell in love with Olga, too—as her future mother," Elias said, visibly exhausted by his lengthy narrative. "And the hero of the story is Vlad—the baby's father!"

"Then everything's perfect! So, what's the problem?" I asked.

"Olga's husband, Klim, if only still in the legal sense at this point. Klim's own guardian angel gave up on him a long time ago, but for some reason, Klim still hasn't been reassigned to anyone else. Right now, he's on his own. I don't have any authority over him, but between me and you, this guy is dangerous. He treats his wife and son like personal property, and he's capable of really hurting anybody who tries taking them away from him. Our job is to isolate him from Olga and the kid as soon as possible. We've got to get that thought into Olga's head, or Vlad's, since we can't influence Klim."

"All right. Who are the other 'poor suckers'? You said there were three."

"We'll save that for next time. I've given you enough information to process for now. Besides, I'm already late for a meeting. So, here's your first assignment: fly down to Vladimir's place and see what's going on there. Here's the address," he said, slipping me a piece of paper. "And tomorrow you'll fill me in."

"Consider it done, chief!"

Chapter 10

The first thing I sensed in Vladimir's room was the presence of another soul. I couldn't see it, but it was definitely close by.

"Vlad," chimed a pleasant woman's voice. "Bring me a towel, please! I forgot."

A young man of average height got up from his computer, opened the wardrobe door, took out a light green towel, and went off to fulfill his girl's request. Vladimir had straight chestnut hair and amazingly big blue eyes, the kind icons have—huge and piercing. Apart from that, he looked pretty average, with no trace of the beard that Elias had mentioned.

A minute later, he came back into the room with Olga, who was drying her blondish, shoulder length hair with the towel. There was something remarkably soft and feminine about this miniature, gray-eyed girl.

And sure enough, there sat F-12161998 perched on Olga's wet shoulder. She gasped and almost fell off when she saw me.

"What are you doing here?" she asked wildly.

"I'm their guardian angel's helper." I laughed. "Strange coincidence, right? Your fate is in my hands."

"Just like that, eh?" she snorted. "I'm trying to bring them together myself."

"And I can see you've done a good job so far, but from now on we'll be working on it together."

While she and I talked, the lovers started doing what Elias was talking about. I wasn't a novice, but felt embarrassed just the same. Noticing my embarrassment, F-12161998 giggled.

"What's with you?" she said, making fun of my culture shock. "I mean, they're constantly doing it, whenever my mama comes over!"

"But you're already... What's the point?"

"I guess they just like doing it."

We sat on the windowsill alongside two potted plants—a little fir tree, and some sort of bush with reddish-green leaves. It felt like we were in the woods, watching an adult movie we'd snuck into.

"Drive me home?" Olga asked afterwards.

"Maybe you could just stay?" Vlad asked, ruefully.

"How do you figure that's even possible? I have to pick Petya up from kindergarten, and besides, what would I tell Klim about where I'd been?"

"Olga, you should've told him about us and the divorce a long time ago."

"I think he's figuring things out on his own. We just have to wait a little longer. He's changed, somehow, recently. I could never have left Petya alone with him before, but he even volunteered to babysit when I went to my girlfriend's yesterday."

"What a hero!" Vlad smiled sarcastically. "The kid's five years old! Bring him over here next time, and I'll look after him. You should move in with me soon, anyway. You'll be showing in a couple of months. What do you intend to tell him then?"

"Vlad, don't. I'll do it... soon. I just have to collect my thoughts. I think he suspects something, but... I'm afraid of him. I've heard rumors about what he's capable of, and I know there's something criminal about his past that he's not telling me about."

"Do you want me to talk to him?"

"Absolutely not! I'll do it myself."

"All right, Olga, only give yourself a deadline—say, two weeks. Otherwise you'll be 'collecting your thoughts' in the delivery room," he said, and stroked her wet hair.

"Don't worry, I'll get it together before then." Olga smiled sweetly and closed her eyes, hinting she wanted a kiss.

Vladimir kissed her lips tenderly.

I watched them, and was happy, and right beside me, F-12161998 smiled from ear to ear with her non-existent mouth. Then, the soul of the blue-eyed little girl, who looked like her dad, flew off after the yellow Zhiguli her parents had driven away in. Vladimir was driving Olga back to her husband, the man who wasn't the father of her unborn child. That's what she wanted, and Vlad was too soft to stand his ground for very long, while Olga was being too soft, herself, to just cut the Gordian Knot.

Since they were my mission now, I followed them.

Vlad parked the car in front of a two-story building with a fenced off yard full of children, from toddlers to five- or six-year-olds, walking around in little groups. He and Olga walked over to the gate. On seeing them, a little blond boy left his group and ran over to them, shouting happily all the way.

"Mama, Mama, you came! Hi, Vlad!"

"Hi Petya," Vlad said. "Guess what we bought you."

"Transformers?" he asked, overjoyed at the very possibility.

"Right!" Olga said, ruffling his hair. "Now, run along and say goodbye to Elena Vladimirovna, and we'll go home."

"Or if you want, we'll go to that little café, right there," Vlad added, crouching in front of the boy.

"I do I do I do!" Petya shrieked, and he skipped over to his teacher. "Elena Vladimirovna, me and my mom and Vlad are going to the café now." He bounced ecstatically. "They'll buy me a shashlik, and some ice cream!"

"You see?" said F-12161998. "They're already like a real family. Oh, I want to be born as soon as possible, so they'll finally be able to see me! You know what Petya said to our mother, when he first met Vlad?"

"What?"

"He said, 'I want to have a dad like him.'"

"He said that?"

"Word for word."

"Yeah... there's definitely a void in the family, then," I surmised.

"That's for sure. His so-called 'real' father, Klim, barely even talks to him; he's always too busy. Petya doesn't identify with him at all, really. He doesn't even call him Dad, just Klim, whereas he's already called Vlad Dad twice. Vlad was really pleased. I could feel it!"

F-12161998 was an incredibly emotional being, always on the verge of tears and laughter at the same time. It'd be a real stretch to imagine her as the soul of a future little boy. Most of us—I mean men—were calmer and more rational, whereas she was so funny, but that was part of her charm. In time, she'd probably grow into a girl with a lively personality, like Lera, who I still loved very much, and whom F-1216998 reminded me of every time she laughed.

I wondered how Lera was doing, what she was thinking about, and whether she remembered me. I even wondered if should make her dream about me, although.... What for? To cause her more pain? Maybe I could fly over to her and just let her know, somehow, that I wasn't angry and that I still loved her anyway. I'll think about it tomorrow, like Scarlett, Lera's heroine.

First, I had to figure out the matter at hand, so I could fill Elias in the next day.

After the café, Vlad drove Olga and Petya to the building where they had a small apartment on the third floor. Judging by the darkened windows, Klim wasn't home.

"Tell him, Olga," Vlad said, hugging her goodbye.

"I will. I'll muster up the courage and tell him."

"Where is he now?"

"At work."

"Can you come to my place this weekend?"

"I think so. Klim's going beaver hunting. He's already cleaned his old shotgun. He'll be gone for two days."

"Everything always depends on him," said Vlad, annoyed. "And if he weren't going away?"

"Don't torment me, Vlad." Olga, almost in tears, turned and walked toward the front door.

Petya, who'd been playing in a nearby sandbox during the conversation, followed behind, as did the two of us.

Everybody was asleep by the time Klim came home, drunk. He was a completely unremarkable forty-year-old, with beady little gray eyes, the opposite of Vladimir's big, iconic baby blues. Trying not to make any noise, Klim ate the dinner Olga had prepared for him. Then he grabbed a bottle of beer, opened it on the edge of the table, and stood at the window, looking out as he drank it.

I turned my attention to his hands as he held the bottle. They looked as if they'd been cut up by fine shards of glass. Only recently, he'd secretly read all of Olga's correspondence with Vlad, who affectionately called her 'Lala.' Unable to restrain his anger, he'd put his fist through the glass cupboard door. He'd blamed the damaged hutch on a "sudden gust of wind that must have slammed the cupboard shut."

Thus, Klim knew about everything... except his wife's pregnancy.

He finished up his beer, undressed, and lay down beside Olga. He watched for a long time as she slept, and then whispered, "If you leave me for that man, I'll kill him."

He rolled over to face the wall, and was sound asleep and snoring within a couple of minutes.

The negative energy this guy gave off absolutely terrified me. Why had his guardian angel abandoned him? How was it that nobody had helped him to love himself? Maybe the opposite was true, and he loved *only* himself. Psychology wasn't my strong point, but all the same, I supposed his behavior was a reaction to feeling superfluous. People who feel that way act out in various ways, either trying to prove themselves, falling into a deep depression, ruminating incessantly on their own death, or by avenging the whole world for their own sense of worthlessness.

How could I breathe some goodness into this embittered man? Was it even possible? I flew off to meet Elias with these very thoughts in mind.

Chapter 11

"What do you say, Peace?" Elias asked, looking much tidier than he had the day before.

"You seem different today, somehow," I said.

"Yes, I had a date, so I got myself together." With a light movement of his hand, Elias pushed a lock of clean hair off his forehead. Clearly, he was pleased with himself.

"A date?"

"Well, I consider it a date."

"Angels go on dates?" I asked in disbelief.

"Why not? We're people too, to some degree, and human weaknesses aren't exactly foreign to us. If they were, we wouldn't be able to figure people out at all." He smiled. "And don't ask me about anything else, you curious soul! All right, so how's our Sad Sack?"

"Things between him and Olga seem really great. I even met a soul I know over at Vlad's—Olga's future baby. But as concerns us, things would be even greater for them, and good for Klim, too, if we found him another guardian angel."

"How simple things are to you, kid!" Elias guffawed. "What about human emotions, like jealousy, possessiveness, and the urge for revenge? They're extremely difficult to wrestle with! It takes them a long time to subside, and time is precisely what we're short on. Your little soul-friend was in too much of a hurry, and from what I could see...."

The look on Elias's face told me his thoughts were a million miles away.

"Finding Olga's husband a guardian angel is beyond our realm of responsibilities."

"Don't worry about it," I said. "Let me think about it for a while, and I'll definitely come up with something."

"Really?" Elias looked at me in amazement. "Good for you, kid! You show great promise."

"And now, who's the third?" I asked out of curiosity.

"Who's the third?" Elias appeared somewhat confused.

"You know... the third person I'm supposed to help you with. You said you'd tell me today. What's his problem?"

"Ah yes! It's a girl named Masha, who's also pregnant. Hmmm, it's as though these cases have been handpicked for you – they're so in sync with your own situation. Well, maybe they'll distract you from any sad thoughts you're having. I mean, you're probably sad, right, kid?" He had a surprisingly tender, almost paternal look in his eyes.

"Thanks, they already have, a little."

"Well, that's great." Elias smiled.

"So, what's wrong with this Masha?" I asked.

"Masha's an unusual girl. She's in her second year at the Foreign Languages Faculty, and she's very young and emotional. She left home at sixteen, because she wasn't getting along with her mother, and moved in with her grandmother. A year later, the old lady died, leaving Masha her apartment. At the funeral, Masha met Nikolai, a young out-of-towner who'd accompanied his own grandmother, Grandma's friend, to the sad event. Things developed so rapidly between the two kids – they married only two months later, certificate and all, since Masha was underage. Well, it turns out that Nikolai should never have come to that funeral!"

Elias suddenly raised his voice, as though he were angry with himself. "I didn't foresee things happening so fast, and now Masha's on an altogether different trajectory. She wasn't fated to even live in Russia, and here, out of the blue, she has a husband. I don't think the jerk even loved her. He only wanted to stay on in Saint Petersburg, so he just latched on to a naive girl, taking advantage of Masha's inexperience and good faith. He played her. I've seen him, and I know I'm right."

Elias paused and sighed.

"And there you have it," he went on. "People sometimes think their fate is decided *here* – I mean from on high – but they often decide it themselves. All it takes is a moment's distraction for their guardian angel. I can't understand where I could've been at that particular moment. Something pressing must have come up right then with someone else. After all, she's not my only ward. Some think there's no such thing as coincidence but, alas, there is."

He sighed again. "And there you go. I got distracted, and this idiot showed up on her path! Oh, you didn't hear that. Otherwise they'll penalize me for badmouthing."

"Who was badmouthing? I didn't hear a thing." I smiled.

"Nice. You're catching on." He slapped me on the back.

I didn't actually have a back—not really—but Elias could see me in any way he wanted to, though I didn't know how, exactly.

"So," he continued. "Now she's pregnant by him, and they're separated. He met another woman, older than him and very wealthy. Now Masha's in the lurch, trying to decide whether to keep the baby. She's getting all kinds of advice from all kinds of people, and she can't make up her mind. And this Nikolai couldn't care less—he's even told her he can't be sure the child is his."

I nodded. "And I'm supposed to help her decide to keep it?"

"Precisely, my clever one! There isn't supposed to be an alternative. I'm sure you'll manage it, having been through it yourself, and knowing how these things go. Don't let anybody throw her off course! And make sure it's the right course for us... and *especially* for her."

"But what'll happen to her if she ends up on her own with a baby? That's exactly what my mom was afraid of."

"She'll be fine, but if she doesn't have the baby, she won't be. Don't worry about her. The main thing is, don't let her make an irreparable mistake. It's precisely because of her future son that Masha will come to understand the imperative life lessons that will lead her forward. Mission understood?"

"Absolutely!"

"Then get to it, Peace!" Elias commanded.

"Yes sir!" I replied, enthusiastically, sensing that Elias and I had become friends.

Chapter 12

Masha really was young, studying for an exam when I dropped by. Textbooks lay strewn about the desk, and notebooks, which, judging by the handwriting, belonged to other people. She'd probably missed a lot of assignments. Sometimes she got distracted and, deep in thought, she sucked on a lock of her reddish hair. I also noticed she'd chewed her thumbnail down to the quick—two stupid habits, so far.

In terms of the energy she emitted, I picked up on something in Masha that resembled Lera, and a flood of memories hit me from the time before my future was decided. How wonderful it had been, to believe in the good! That was all behind me now, but for some reason, the nice memories outnumbered the bad. My thoughts raced, and I couldn't focus, no matter how I tried.

Luckily, Masha didn't sit there, adrift, clasping her knees like Lera had done, when we'd still had a chance. So all was not lost, and even if the baby's father turned out to be just like Victor, I already knew what to do.

I wanted to get to know this future baby's soul, but for some reason, I couldn't see it anywhere. Masha and I were the only ones in the room, the silence broken only by the disturbing, constant buzzing of an annoying fly. Unable to stand it, she stood up abruptly, pushed back her chair, grabbed a newspaper, rolled it up, and started chasing the culprit.

"Here, you stupid fly. I can't concentrate because of you!" She followed it around the room, all in vain.

The fly finally flew over to the window, probably thinking it was its salvation, only to come up against the invisible barrier of glass. It started hitting up against it while it buzzed even more loudly.

Taking advantage of the fly's stubbornness, Masha said, "Die, you worthless being!" She brought the rolled-up newspaper down on it, hard. Success!

"If you were a bee, I would've caught you and let you out. Too bad you were only a fly, a useless insect, and you interfered with my studying."

She flicked what was left of the fly into the wastebasket with the newspaper, and returned to her studies. Before long, though, she was interrupted again by a phone call.

"Oh, it's you, hi," she said, dully. She'd spoken in a livelier voice to the dead fly. "Well, what have you decided? A divorce?"

She listened silently to the caller for about a minute, and then said, "No, Nick, dear, I won't be going with you. Why not? Because I'm pregnant, and I'd like the child to be born in wedlock—the one in which he was conceived. It seems only logical."

Another long pause; the person on the other end talked for a long time.

"Yes, I understand. It's quicker and easier to divorce if we both agree to it. I know you're in a rush to marry your rich old lady, but I don't need a divorce, and so I don't intend to file for one," she snapped. "Whereas you can do whatever you want! But any decisions concerning our child will be mine. Exclusively."

She hung up, even though Nick was still talking.

"You jerk. What a jerk!" she said a few times, then suddenly started bawling. Masha cried as bitterly as Lera had, the last time I saw her, and I felt really sorry for this trusting young girl.

Being such an openhearted person, she needed someone to talk to right away, so she picked up the phone again and called someone immediately.

"Hi," she said, "it's me."

I heard a woman's voice on the other end say, "Am I imagining things, or are you crying?"

"You're not imagining things," Masha replied, blubbering. "Nick just called to tell me he's going ahead with the divorce. I really need to talk to you. Can I come over right now? Or maybe we can meet somewhere?" After a brief pause, she said, "Okay, your place, in an hour."

In following Masha, the first thing I had to do was go down into the metro. We went underground at the Vasileostrovskaya Station, with an unbelievably huge crowd. The people on the stairs at the entrance were divided into two camps: the honest, and the sly. The honest ones leaned against each other, taking baby steps, while the sly ones just butted in. Naturally, the honest ones were also meek, and merely snorted at the injustice of it all.

What a strange place it was, with people breathing into the back of each other's heads and moving so very slowly.

Masha finally got into the lineup to the booth, where everyone bought either a pass or a token, and then proceeded to another lineup to the turnstiles. While she waited, I observed. The really imaginative people, who didn't want to wait, just jumped the turnstile. One fellow moved in so closely behind a woman, he walked through it right behind her, perfectly in step, without using his token or even being noticed by the woman, because of the crush of the crowd.

What amazing people, and I'd have to live among them, one day, get used to their strange world order. This assumed there was some 'order' in this world, though I'd yet to see it. And so, contemplating the problems of the world, as obliged by my name, I followed Masha on the 'down' escalator, and into the overcrowded car, until she managed to squeeze herself out of it.

On the way up this escalator, I could tell, by the looks on their faces, that those going down the opposite one envied us—the lucky ones who'd be out in the open again, while they had to stand, crammed together, in a stifling subway car.

I noticed that Masha stood out from the crowd, and not just because of her funny hat with the pom-pom, her bright pink-checkered jacket, and remarkably long, striped scarf. The energy she gave off made her different, so similar to the kind that first attracted me to Lera, as did the lively way she dressed. Clearly, there was some link between them.

As Masha crossed the park among the yellow and red maple leaves shimmering in the autumn sun, I wondered where the soul of her baby had gone. It had to be worried about what this young head in the funny pom-pom hat would decide, but I couldn't hear Masha's thoughts.

When we got to where her girlfriend lived, I felt like I was 'home,' for some reason. We entered the building and walked into the elevator. Everything around me felt so familiar, so....

Oh, don't tell me!

I got the shock of my life, so to speak, when Masha knocked on the door and her girlfriend opened it.

Lera!

"Hi, come in, my poor little wretch!" Lera said with a smile. "How did we both get into this mess, one right after the other?" She shut the door behind Masha. "Should I make tea? Come into the kitchen."

Totally unprepared for such a turn of events, I couldn't believe this was actually happening. I'd seen her just a few days prior, but she looked completely different. She'd cut her hair off, and even bleached it blonde, like Gwyneth Paltrow's character in 'Sliding Doors,' whose transformation had helped her survive a personal tragedy. It was Lera's favorite movie, and she'd apparently decided to follow that heroine's example to the same end.

"Lera, I barely recognize you," Masha said. "I wouldn't have decided on something so radical. I've never even dyed my hair!"

"Come on, Masha! When I walked into the salon, I could barely resist the temptation to shave my head completely bald, à la 'Scarecrow.' Remember that movie?"

"I do. I read the story, too."

"Well, I'm just like her now, you see? An 'un-genuine' woman. He would only have married me if I was the last woman on Earth, and maybe not even then. I'm incapable of 'creating' a cozy home, or even a tidy one, he said—the ultimate loser. I hate myself, Masha! That's the horror of it all, that instead of hating him, I hate myself! In fact, I have no negative feelings for him at all. I mean, how is that even possible?"

I could hear the tears in her voice.

"Yeah.... Listen, I've come all the way here for some talk therapy, but it looks like you could use some yourself."

"Come on, then. How about we cry on each other's shoulders, for free?" Lera quipped, always ready with a joke, even at the saddest times. "Who should go first? You?"

"Okay. Basically, you and I are in similar situations, only you've already taken the final step, and I haven't. I just don't know what I'm supposed to do now."

Masha looked at her friend, hoping she could make the decision for her, but Lera didn't say anything at all.

I learned that they'd met some years ago at a summer camp, where Lera had been a counsellor, and Masha, then fourteen, was vacationing. As it turned out, they were neighbors, too. Since then, Lera had been the person Masha could always turn to for sound advice, and the two girls shared their innermost feelings with one another. The now eighteen-year-old Masha thought that, at twenty-two, Lera had a better understanding of life—like a giraffe, who had a better view.

Meanwhile, I was still reeling from the shock of our unexpected reunion.

Talk about a coincidence! Is it by accident? Or a kind of test? How am I to interpret this? How am I supposed to react?

Once again, a wave of unbelievable tenderness washed over me, that desire to snuggle up to her hair. What advice could she give the girl who'd landed in the same trap? Lera seemed at a loss herself.

"Oh, Lera, what can you tell me?" Masha snuggled up to her shoulder.

"Life is like a box of chocolates," Lera replied off the cuff. "You never know what you're gonna get."

"You and your jokes! I should probably go," Masha said, getting up out of her chair.

"Oh, Masha, don't take it the wrong way! Please, don't go," Lera pleaded, realizing she'd talked out of turn. "We'll have some tea and figure out what's best together. What do *you* want?"

"I don't know anymore! I'm hopelessly confused." Masha sat down again. "I don't know if I want the baby, or if I want to just forget about it, like some bad dream."

All of a sudden, I heard a strange sound, like somebody crying, only very softly. I looked around, and there, behind the lace curtain, was the soul of Masha's son, hiding.

"Hey, why are you crying?" I asked him.

"I'm so afraid. I don't want to die," he blubbered.

"Souls don't die, silly! Look at me. Lera could've been *my* mom. It didn't work out, but I'm still alive!"

"You are?" he asked, looking at me in disbelief and still sobbing. "Then why are you here? You're not even together anymore."

"I don't know myself. I was assigned the mission of saving you, and here I am. Where have you been all this time?"

"Flying around," he replied, distractedly. "*Can* you save me? Is there still a chance that Masha will decide to keep me?"

"There's always a chance. Listen, what should I call you? What's your number?"

"M-07091999."

"My name's Peace. I'm what's called a helper, to a guardian angel named Elias."

"And where's he?"

"He's occupied with other business right now."

"So this is probably happening because he's always busy with other things, instead of paying attention to her," he said, nodding in Masha's direction.

Deep down, I agreed with him, but I didn't let on. I wasn't allowed to speak ill of my chief, and besides, Elias had been nice to me. Like all people, he had his shortcomings. Well, he had one: he just couldn't seem to focus on the matters at hand. Now, he seemed to have fallen in love, too—from bad to worse, with every passing hour.

I needed to map out a plan of action, to determine how to help Olga stop being afraid of her husband, and convince Masha to keep her baby. I was being crushed under my unprecedented load of responsibility. How would I manage it all? And now there was Lera, too. I thought of her often, as things were, and now she'd be around me almost constantly.

When it rains, it pours!

"I promise everything will be just fine with you and Masha," I said. "You'll be born when you're due. When is that, by the way?"

"In almost seven months."

"So, there you go, in seven months," I said, when suddenly a particular thought struck me: our respective situations were a little too similar.

"Listen," I said. "When you met your mom, did you like your future father?"

"Not really," M-07091999 said. "I just really liked my mom. Why do you ask?"

"Well, it looks like you and I made the same mistake. We were in too much of a hurry, and look what happened. Lera made a snap decision at the very last minute, and there was nothing I could do about it. I think that we souls can sense the men our moms are out of sync with. What they feel is probably only an illusion of love, whereas we're supposed to be born of genuine love. Then the moms wouldn't have those doubts. I mean, if they really loved the guy, the thought of parting with his child wouldn't even occur to them, whether they'd stay together afterwards, or not. See what I mean?"

"I think so," the little soul said, a little more optimistically.

The tea kettle let out a piercing whistle. Lera turned off the stove and moved to pour the tea.

"Tell me honestly, Lera, do you regret it?" Masha asked. "I need to know what to expect, afterwards."

I listened closely, desperate to find out, myself.

"How should I put it, Masha. I don't even know. I don't know what would've happened if I'd decided to keep it, and Vic had just up and left. What would I have thought? How would I have felt? Would it have been more painful for me—more than it is now? So many 'ifs.' You won't know unless you go through with it, either way."

"Probably," Masha said, having grown pensive.

"I guess you have to look at things from a practical perspective," Lera said. "Will you be able to raise a child on your own, plus earn enough money to live on, considering he or she would be with you 'round the clock? Would you work from home? You could earn a living doing translation from English and French, but you have another four years of school before you graduate. People do have babies and manage, somehow. If you believe that 'God provides the child and *for* the child,' then you have to keep it. The thing is... I'm a realist."

Masha sighed. "I don't want to just *manage somehow*. I don't want us to go hungry. I could easily do translation work to supplement my income, but with no work experience, who would take me on? And with a newborn baby, no less."

"What about your mom?"

"She's almost always working—for next to nothing. Besides, she's skeptical about becoming a grandmother."

Lera nodded. "So, immediate family is out, then?"

"Right."

"And Nick won't help out, not even financially?"

"Oh, please." Masha smirked. "Nick's filing for divorce the day after tomorrow. He's under a spell or something. Anyway," Masha said somewhat gruffly, all of a sudden. "I don't want to talk about him anymore, and I wouldn't take a single ruble from him."

"Oh, such a proud girl!" Lera shook her head but smiled.

"You got anything to drink?" Masha asked out of the blue.

"You're not really supposed to—"

"Not really?" Masha retorted. "I may not even have the baby. Pour me a shot, if you have something, would you? To calm my nerves?"

"I think my dad has some vodka. You sure you want some?"

"Yes."

Lera reached into the cupboard and took out a bottle that was less than a quarter full, and poured Masha a shot.

"Why am I drinking alone, like some wino? Come on. You have one too."

"Okay, I'm allowed to now." Lera smiled.

The girls clinked glasses, and Masha said, "Here's to us, and nuts to them, right?" She smiled a strained smile, raised her shot glass, and downed it.

"Exactly. Nuts to the both of them."

"Let's do it again, right? 'One after the other.'"

"'Otherwise, why bother!'" Lera said, finishing the popular saying.

M-07091999 and I watched in silence as our grieving mothers polished off what was left of the vodka in a few minutes, munching on apples in between shots.

"Come on, then, call your 'magic' doctor and book an appointment for me," Masha said abruptly. "I won't be able to manage it. Besides, I've drunk vodka, so I can't have the baby now."

"Masha, you dummy! I asked you about that!"

"Yes, Lera, I did it on purpose, so there's no turning back. Now, go on and make the call. When is he on duty next?"

Little M-07091999 curled up into a little ball right before my eyes. He seemed even more transparent than before. Thanks to our having met, I found out that we souls really could cry. My efforts to cheer him up were useless, as he cried and cried inconsolably, and quite loudly. I tried as hard as I could to make Masha hear him.

"Lera," she suddenly said. "I'm hearing things... like the sound of a baby crying." Now drunk, she started crying too.

"Now, now," Lera said, caressing Masha's hair in the way her own grandmother had done to soothe her when she'd skinned a knee. "You know, I dreamed of a baby a few times. He'd be lying there, all cheerful and smiling.... I wonder about how many more days it would've been, now, until he was born. I've decided to scratch 'Katya. April 2000' on the hood of Vic's car this spring."

"The best thing for both of us is just to forget about it all, as soon as possible," Masha asserted, before getting down to the details of her appointment at the clinic. "Do I have to be there early in the morning? And will you go with me?"

"Of course I will! I wouldn't leave you in the lurch at a moment like this, even though my own memories of the place aren't exactly pleasant. Nobody should have to end up there twice, if at all."

The tear-stained M-07091999 now lay curled up in Masha's lap, looking up at her.

I had one day left to save him.

Masha tried to study for the exam again, but still couldn't focus. She took a shower, turned out the lights, and crawled into bed, but she couldn't sleep, either. She just lay there, eyes closed, thinking about the transitory nature of human existence, about how everything can change on a dime, and about how, sometimes, one has no control over circumstances. Here she thought she knew her husband and could trust him implicitly, but she'd had the rug pulled out from under her so suddenly, that she just couldn't regain her balance.

On the one hand, she felt a certain sense of relief now that she'd made up her mind. On the other hand, the thought of getting rid of the baby sickened her. She looked at the pros and cons of keeping it, and the cons definitely outweighed the pros, which, more than anything, were metaphysical in nature. She'd have to compartmentalize her emotions and push them far, far away.

Out of sheer exhaustion, her thoughts grew confused, and eventually, she fell asleep.

I was in her room along with M-07091999 who, tired of lamenting his fate, dozed off as well.

His mom had a dream.

She stood barefoot in the middle of an enormous field of sunflowers, many of them taller than her, and they resembled parasols. The sun was just rising as she walked between the fuzzy stalks, separating them with her hands, feeling as though this flowery forest would go on forever. She pulled one of the big sunflowers, round as a plate, down to her face and inhaled deeply. It smelled sweetly of freshness and dormant seeds. She was about to tear it off its stalk, when suddenly the voice of a child stopped her.

"Don't do that! It'll hurt me!"

She looked down at her hand and saw a tiny five-year-old, about the size of a sunflower seed, sitting on her index finger. Startled and frightened, she threw it onto the ground. Then, realizing she'd done something terrible, she started crawling around on all fours, looking for the little seed. Suddenly, she thought she could hear a child sobbing. She kept groping around on the ground, getting dirt all over her hands, but finding nothing.

Then she ran through the sunflower field for a long time, separating the stalks as she went, hearing the little voice saying, "It'll hurt me!" over and over. Bending another stalk, Masha looked closely at each of the seeds, but they were all just ordinary. She sat down on the ground in utter despair, and suddenly felt she was being raised upwards by some indeterminate force. To her surprise, she realized she was sitting on a huge sunflower that was growing terrifyingly quickly, soaring straight up to the clouds. For some reason, she wasn't frightened at all, as though what was happening were perfectly normal. The sunflower passed through the clouds like a plane in flight. Now someone in a somber-looking 'suit' stood before her, and he looked at her somberly, too, like God.

"Why did you throw the baby away, Masha?" he asked coldly.

"I wasn't throwing it aw – "

"Then why did he come to me, crying, because his mother threw him down? Onto the ground, no less – literally!"

"It wasn't on purpose," Masha insisted, completely flustered. "I thought he was a sunflower seed. I even wanted to eat it."

"Eat your own child?"

"But I didn't know... I mean, it was only a seed!"

"There are many things you humans don't understand, my child, so you plead ignorance for your actions. I love that saying, 'Man proposes, but God disposes,'" he said with a smile. "Well, that's not always so, because people just end up doing what they want, right? So where exactly does God's will come into play? I'll bet you wouldn't even believe me if I told you your child would become a talented artist, and that there's no need for you to be afraid of raising him alone. That's not your path. Go now, and try not to lose your seed again. It's the bearer of a new life, and a new beginning for you, too."

Before Masha could respond, the sunflower moved quickly downwards, and....

She awoke with a start, feeling an overwhelming sensation of freefalling. She remembered the entire dream, from beginning to end, which she rarely ever did.

From the expression on her face, I realized the dream I'd sent was a good idea. She would have the rest of the day to spend on her own and contemplate it.

In the hopes that my plan had succeeded, I flew back to Olga's place.

Chapter 13

As it happened, Olga and Petya weren't home, but there sat Klim at the table, gloomy in a wrinkled gray t-shirt and black jeans. His messy hair looked like it hadn't been washed for a long time, and his face seemed kind of wrinkled, too. He was looking at photos, staring at length particularly at those in which he was with Olga.

"So, you're deceiving me," he suddenly said out loud.

He held one of their wedding photos, glaring at it, as though he were trying to bore holes in the image. He abruptly crumpled it in his fist, and then, as if frightened by this action, he started smoothing it out again. The damage was irreparable, though, so he tore it to pieces and threw it into the garbage, getting rid of the evidence. It seemed he didn't intend to have it out with his wife, once and for all, in the immediate future.

He quickly dressed and walked out the door.

I followed him as he headed for the taxi company where he worked as a cabby. I wanted to know more about this man, so I could get a better sense of him. He emitted a certain darkness, and clearly posed a threat to Olga and her future child, and I didn't know how to protect them yet! This assignment was turning out to be a little too complicated for me. I suspected Elias had dumped on me what he was afraid of failing in himself, that it had nothing at all to do with his alleged lack of time. However, you can't pick your assignments, and I needed to pass this test without fail, in order to be allowed to continue my search for a mother. It was imperative I do everything right, since I really wanted to be born!

I decided to try to get my hands on Klim's dossier. I needed to know about his past, in order to understand what kind of threat he posed. Elias would have to help me with that. After all, if something happened to his charges, *he* wouldn't exactly be getting a pat on the back, either.

Our chancellery kept records on everybody, and only the guardian angels could access them because, in fact, they compiled them. They stored all the information in drawers, and Elias and I managed to get into this repository by drawing up a special permit together under a plausible pretext, allowing us access to information on those not directly under his care. It took us a while to find the right drawer, as nobody had looked at Klim's file for so long. It was buried deep in the archives.

"But what exactly happened to Klim's guardian angel?" I asked.

Elias shrugged. "That's classified. He either just dropped him, or he was transferred somewhere else, or maybe he was suspended for non-compliance. I really don't know. What's strange is that they didn't assign anyone else. I mean, a person without a guardian angel? It's a disaster. Clearly, the system is flawed."

Elias finally found the papers we needed, and we got down to reading them.

"Kliment Shelin. Born 18 July 1968 at 04:25 a.m. in Chelyabinsk," stated the first.

"So," Elias said. "Which period are we interested in? Each covers three years, starting with age 0 to 3." He flipped through the pages, looking for the first block of information. "Okay, so... at age two, he lost his father, who died in a car wreck. His mother worked a lot and spent her free time boozing, so the boy was raised mostly by his grandmother, from a very young age. At ten, he was already fairly independent and.... Oh! Here's a note about some conflict at age 13, with his mother. He asked her to 'stop drinking and bringing home whoever was with her at the moment.' In response, she told him to... well, do something of a sexual nature... to himself. Prone to aggression, in response to the humiliation, he —"

Elias suddenly cut himself off.

"What? What did he do?" I asked, anxiously.

"It's not good." He paused and looked at me. "He murdered his mother. His grandmother, who accidentally witnessed the whole thing, died of a heart attack. As a mentally unstable minor, he was ordered to spend 15 years in a psychiatric hospital, after which he was released under his doctor's supervision."

"How awful!"

"He spent the next few years living in the old house on his own, seeing his psychiatrist regularly, until the age of 35, at which point he decided to make a fresh start in Petersburg, where his cousin lived." Elias had finished paraphrasing the information pertaining to Klim's troubled past.

"I remember how he first met Olga," he continued. "She was waving at cars. He happened to be driving by in his cab, and so he picked her up. In return for the free ride home, he asked for her phone number. At the time, he seemed like an okay guy to me. Granted, I didn't know about his past, plus he behaved so differently then."

"So he's got a 'false bottom'?" I asked.

"Possibly. Apparently, Olga doesn't know about any of this either. It all happened in his hometown, and he's decided to keep it secret. He told her he was an orphan, that he grew up in an orphanage, and she took his word for it. Who would've thought to check him out? Olga reminded him of his mother—when she was sober. Olga was kind, accommodating, and had won him over immediately by being an excellent homemaker and, when their son was born, a remarkable mother. By the time Petya was 2 or 3, she was already taking him to concerts, sporting events, all kinds of activities. True, Klim didn't agree with that, not seeing what good it would do. He particularly hated music, because one of his mother's drinking buddies always played the guitar when he got loaded. A year ago, he categorically forbade Olga to buy a piano, but she went ahead and bought one anyway. Now he's forbidden everyone to so much as touch a single key in his presence. He's a dictator around there, not to mention the emotional blackmail. It even says right here—" Elias tapped the page with his index finger. "—that two years ago, she wanted to move back in with her parents because of his drinking. He threatened to hang himself if she left, so she stayed. Apparently, he's psychologically dependent on his wife."

"We're like detectives, right, Elias?" I asked.

"Right, Peace." He patted me right where people usually have hair on their heads.

You see, we can imagine each other however we like. As he explained later, Elias saw me as a redheaded, shaggy-haired, freckled adolescent, in green pants with a hole in the knee, except I didn't know it. Meanwhile, I couldn't figure out why he smiled every time he looked at me.

"So, what's the plan?" I asked.

"It's not something we can decide just like that. We must consider everything carefully, and maybe even consult with our colleagues. In the meantime, you just watch over them, and if you notice anything suspicious, let me know immediately. Got it?"

"I already have been."

Elias looked at me interrogatively, then shifted his gaze to the hole in my 'pants.'

"He tore up one of their wedding photos, and said he'd kill her..."

Elias remained perfectly silent for two whole minutes. I waited for him to reply, but obviously, he was too distracted by some other thought, because he suddenly spread his wings and flew off to destinations unknown—at least to me. He wasn't quite himself. Or... maybe that's how he really was—self-absorbed to the point of ignoring everything going on around him. To think, somebody like him actually managed to become a guardian angel! He needed his own guardian.

I started to fly after him, just to see where he was headed, but I lost sight of him quickly. Not knowing what to do next, I sat there, like a bird on a branch, and fell deep into thought about the frailty of everything—vanity is vanity, but losing oneself in thought is useful sometimes. I became so engrossed in my tasks and feelings, that I could've used a clean sheet of paper and a pen, so I could make a list or, better yet, a chart. Alas, I had to keep it all in my head.

What was happening that was so terrible? Essentially... nothing. Well, besides my personal tragedy, but that had already happened, so dwelling on it with such profound and persistent sadness was non-constructive. Better to realize one's own mistakes and learn from them. Now, that would be the right thing to do. What lesson had I learned? To choose both parents at the same time. I'd picked only my mother, and that turned out badly. Also, there needed to be not even the tiniest crack in their relationship, because when there isn't one, it was not a given that one would appear, whereas if there already was a crack in place, it could get bigger at any given moment.

There was a lyric from a song Lera listened to a lot, which went, "I remember all of your little cracks, and sing all of 'our' songs... Why?" That was one of many by her favorite singer, Zemfira. I memorized a lot of them, when Lera and I were together.

> You are white and bright,
> I'm dark and warm.
> You cry, and nobody sees.
> While I fog up the windows, so stupid.

You love so freely,
I'm hopelessly involved.
We tell each other secrets,
We understand it all, only it's not enough.

I remember how she'd cried while listening to these lyrics, when the thread connecting us was going to snap the next day, leaving us just enough time to say goodbye.

"Why, Mom? Why did it happen so?" I cried.

But nobody saw.

I decided to revisit Lera again, just to see how she was doing.

She was a masochist, listening over and over to the songs that would cause her even more pain, but... it's not just pain that makes you hurt.

Or just your conscience that makes you afraid.
Oddly, I lacked the will, again.
I fill the ashtray, you write the story.

"Too bad I don't smoke," she said to no one. "Maybe it would help. There's something so beautiful about crushing butt after butt, with the look of failure in the quest for meaning in your life written all over your face. Shit, I'm sorry for Masha, too. She's still so young."

This prompted me to fly back to Masha.

Chapter 14

After her conversation with Lera, Masha had tried with all her might to convince herself she'd made her decision, and there was no turning back. Still, that dream about the sunflower field and her visit with the Creator had left her unsettled all morning. She was scheduled to have the procedure, which would decide M-07091999's fate, the next day. The day after that, she would have to take a difficult exam, for which she was supposed to be studying now. Yet with so much else on her mind, she had no room left for knowledge. So rather than cramming, she sat there, diligently scribbling cheat sheets. On top of all the mental anguish, she had the nausea to deal with—every thirty minutes or so, she had to run to the toilet and throw up, or at least retch.

"Oh well, tomorrow's another day," she said to herself after another toilet run. "It'll all be over tomorrow. After that, I'll get a divorce, continue my studies, graduate, and move as far away from this toxic country as I can. And may it burn to the ground, along with my ex-husband."

She refocused on her cheat sheets.

M-07091999, who'd already stopped believing he and Masha had a future together as mother and son, stopped crying, too. He just looked at her, objectively, hot having the energy to give her any kind of sign. What could he possibly do, anyway? Make the neighbors' radio suddenly start blaring Danko's chorus, "...your kid is wise beyond his years?" Not likely.

The little soul had surrendered to apathy, and I could do nothing about it, except tell him to hope for a miracle, because miracles sometimes happen. In response, he only smiled a sad smile that said, "It didn't work for you."

Toward late evening, the phone rang. We only heard the replies, but the questions and the caller's identity were obvious.

"No, I haven't changed my mind," Masha said. "Yes, I've thought it through carefully... Okay, don't say anything else... It'll hurt a little and then it'll stop... I mean, what is a soul, anyway? Has anybody ever seen one, even once? It's probably a myth... Okay, we'll talk tomorrow... Yes, yes, half-past eight, at the Muzhestva metro."

Without even realizing it, Lera was trying to help me.

"At the 'Courage' metro," Masha repeated, in English this time, after hanging up. "I could definitely use some of that right now."

That evening unfolded like any other for Masha, except for having to stuff a robe, a nightie, slippers and clean socks into her backpack, along with her school books. She got ready for bed, as she always did, and went to sleep.

She dreamt of her growing belly, with a tiny palm pressing up against it from the inside. She saw the outline of every little finger.

The dream was M-07091999's last-ditch effort to tug at his mom's heartstrings, with no particular hope of succeeding.

Sometimes, we sent the same dream even before conception, just to let them know we were there.

Elias had disappeared, and I couldn't find him anywhere. We didn't have an appointment or any plan of action. Since he hadn't even tried to contact me, I assumed I would be on my own for the rest of my assignment.

First thing in the morning, I had to reanimate M-07091999, literally, so he'd at least be able to fly—he wasn't a fighter, poor thing. I put all my energy into coming up with a sign to send to the sweet, young Masha, in an attempt to change her mind as quickly as possible. Unfortunately, I was unable to influence her little 'unbeliever,' even though he was the only one who could help me.

After exchanging hellos, Masha and Lera waited for the trolleybus in silence, which lasted until they were halfway to the clinic. I could see that this was harder for Lera than Masha. I felt really sorry for her, as it was like being sent to Golgotha again, just two weeks later.

"I feel like I'm your mom," she said to Masha in front of the doctor's office, trying to smile.

"And I feel like a void, soon to be even emptier," Masha replied.

They entered the office together.

"Hello, Sergei Aleksandrovich," Lera said in greeting, still trying to smile.

"Oy! Hello-hello," he said, having recognized her immediately. "How are you feeling? Is there something bothering you?"

"More like some*body*. I've brought you my friend, who's in the same mess as I was."

"What's with you girls?" He shook his head. "So, what's your friend's name?" He then told the nurse to open a new file, and turned to Masha. "Go ahead and have a seat, and let me have a look at you. Lera, please wait in the hallway."

I stayed with Lera.

Masha came out minutes later, holding a few requisitions in her hand.

The doctor looked out his door at Lera, instructing her to take Masha to the lab for some blood work. He'd already performed the smear.

"You have to pay the cashier, then bring me the receipt," he said. "You know the drill, so you can walk her through it."

Lera nodded. "I do, and I will."

"By the way, how's your boyfriend?" he suddenly asked. "No pangs of conscience?"

"I wouldn't know," Lera replied. "He's not my boyfriend anymore."

"Good for you." The doctor nodded his approval. "You'll find somebody else, someone who'll understand you. Only don't make another mistake. You don't need another procedure. Next time, you're absolutely having a baby!"

"I promise." Lera smiled, albeit sadly. "Absolutely." Just for a second or two, an image of herself as a mother, at long last, flashed through her mind, and cheered her up. "By the way," she suddenly blurted out. "Do you deliver babies too? I wouldn't want anybody else to deliver mine!"

"I don't, but I can recommend a really good doctor when the time comes," he replied, as though it were a done deal.

"You can count on it!" Lera said, with a genuine smile this time.

"All right, now run along. I start in half an hour, and I have six patients today." He turned to Masha. "Want to go first?"

She nodded hesitantly in response.

"Then go do the blood test and come straight back."

Masha looked white as a sheet.

As the two girls waited their turn at the door to the lab, Masha squeezed Lera's wrist. "I'm scared," she half-whimpered.

"I can just imagine. It's your first time. Try to get hold of yourself. It'll all be over soon, and when you leave here, you can start a new life."

Masha shook slightly. "I can't seem to calm down."

"Everything will be fine," Lera assured her, well aware of the platitudes coming out of her mouth that were, nevertheless, unavoidable in situations like these. "I mean, nobody really knows, but I'm certain everything *will* be fine!" She put her hand over Masha's, whose fingers were cold as ice.

"You know, I had a dream last night," Masha started to say, but Lera cut her off when the light over the door flashed. It was Masha's turn.

"Tell me after the test," Lera said. "Now go."

Masha disappeared behind the door.

"It's over! I'm dead!" I suddenly heard in my ear. M-07091999 was screaming again.

"Calm down," I said. "I have one idea left. Can't you see she's having doubts?"

"But she's going through with it, anyway."

"The fat lady hasn't sung yet!" I half-shouted to bring him back to his senses.

I didn't know whether he understood what I'd said, but he seemed to understand that the fat lady was very important, and until she started singing, things could be fixed.

"Save me!" he begged through his tears.

"Then stop crying... now!" I was older and wiser, having already gone down this road. "Tears are not constructive."

"Make a fist," the nurse told Masha just then, tying a rubber tourniquet just above her elbow.

While she looked for a vein, Masha averted her eyes and noticed a picture on the wall of sunflowers in a vase. She kept her eyes glued to it the whole time they were drawing her blood. When they finished, she left the room, squeezing her elbow.

"Now to the cashier?" she asked Lera.

"Yeah, it's right here."

"I need to sit down for a minute," Masha pleaded, tugging Lera's sleeve.

"Okay, but we don't have much time if you want to go first."

"Do I want to go first?" She looked up at Lera, who'd remained standing as though she knew the answer.

"I don't know. It's up to you. I always preferred being the first to take the oral exams, so I wouldn't have to sit there and worry."

"Oh...." Masha moaned, half out of it.

Lera sat down beside her. "Tell me about your dream."

"Oh, yeah... I was in a field of huge sunflowers. I tore one off its stalk, and there was a baby on it, about the size of a seed. He sat on my finger, but I got scared and threw him off, and then I couldn't find him. Then I dreamt of God."

"Of *God*?" Lera's eyebrows shot up.

"Yes. He looked like our faculty head, all business-like, wearing a suit. He told me to think things over again, as if I were making a mistake."

"Did he convince you?"

"I don't know. He also said it was going to be a boy, and that he would become a famous artist."

"What a dream! If I'd dreamt something like that when I was pregnant...." Lera paused and seemed to look inward. "I did dream of a little girl, but after the fact, which made me feel even worse."

I was surprised, because I didn't know about that particular dream. I hadn't generated it. And why a girl? It was obviously a realm of her subconscious that I hadn't gotten to—the realm of wishes. She wanted a little 'Katya.' How surprised she would've been to hear that 'Katya' was going to be a boy.

"You know what?" Masha said. "I'm going to call him."

"Your husband?"

"*Sort-of* husband."

"What for?"

"He should know where I am. He's probably filing for divorce as we speak."

"All right then, call, but what good will it do?"

"Wait for me here." Masha walked a few meters away and dialed the number.

Lera sighed. While she was alone, I decided to stay with her for a minute. Despite what had happened between us, being with her still felt good. Plus, I was so tired of listening to other people's conversations. Things were out of my hands now. I'd done my part. It was no coincidence that the sunflowers in Masha's dream had been identical to the ones she saw in the picture at the lab. It seemed like they'd served their purpose, as clearly, something was going on with her already.

She spoke loudly, and I could hear bits of her phone conversation. Her emotions even caused her to shout, "You've already signed? Don't you care at all about our child? Do you not understand where I am right now, and what that means?"

Clearly, she was no longer under the influence of reason.

She called him back a couple more times, and was still talking when the doctor approached Lera to ask if Masha was ready.

"Looks like she won't be going first," Lera said.

"Right, so... maybe second?"

"Probably," Lera replied, not convinced. "We'll be there soon."

The doctor nodded and left.

Oddly enough, I harbored no ill will toward him, even though his hand had ultimately decided my fate. If my plan didn't work, it would also decide the fate of M-07091999, who was nowhere to be seen; he probably wanted to be alone.

Masha came back, her face covered in red blotches. "Is there somewhere we can get a coffee?" she asked. "I don't feel very well. I really need to have a coffee and just sit quietly for a little bit. Not here, though."

"Come on," Lera said. "There's a coffee machine in the lobby."

Masha took a cup of chicken soup, instead.

Lera joined her friend and, after a sip, finally broke the silence. "Well? I'm almost afraid to ask. What did he say?"

"He happened to be waiting in line to file for divorce," Masha said, seething. "And he referred to what I'm going through here as, and I quote, 'your personal problem.' Screw that jerk!"

"So why are you shaking then?"

"I don't know. I don't think I can do this, Lera." Masha's eyes brimmed with tears. "I can't kill this baby. It's my child, for crying out loud!"

"Yes, it is, but there can be another, can't there? I mean, when you find a guy who's not an insensitive swine! I'm sure I'll have a baby one day, even though I was here too only a week ago."

"Of course, there will be another, but what about this one? I mean, it's alive! I heard they're already formed at eight weeks. It probably has a soul by now."

"I do, I do!" M-07091999 suddenly shouted out from behind her. He'd made himself so tiny, out of fear, that I barely even noticed him.

"Oh, Masha, think. This is your life we're talking about!" Lera said, almost desperately. Then, after a prolonged moment of shared silence, she brought things down a notch, and seemed less emotional. "Have you decided one way or another?"

"No-o-o!" Masha wailed. "I haven't decided *anything*! I don't know what to do!" The floodgates opened at that point.

"Me neither," Lera moaned, taking Masha's hand in hers and sitting quietly for a moment. "But either way, we have to go and tell them something. They're waiting for you."

"Okay, we'll go." Masha stood up, took the empty chicken soup cups off the table, and threw them in the garbage. "But first I'm calling him, one last time."

"Oh my God, what for?" Lera cried, but she could do nothing about it.

Masha made the call.

Lera sighed and, suddenly, without knowing how, I could hear her thoughts again.

> *What if I'd decided not to go through with it? I could've gone in, asked the doctor, sweet man that he is, to pretend he'd operated, have them wheel me out of there thirty minutes later, and Vic would've been none the wiser. I would've had the baby, and he would've been all mine. What was I so afraid of? Why did I change my mind? I wanted to keep it. I was so stupid! And I'm just as stupid now, still imagining the life I could've had, but... don't! Let Masha do what she wants. She's stronger than me.*

At that moment, Masha screamed, "You're a real scumbag, just so you know! For your information, I'm not doing anything about the baby! And if I do, it'll be your fault, and you'll always have that on your conscience, if you even have one!" She hung up in his ear.

In fact, Masha called her husband back again, more than once. In the meantime, the rest of the women who'd registered that day had undergone the procedure and been wheeled into the recovery room.

At that point, the doctor stuck his head out the door to say he was about to let the anesthesiologist leave for the day. "Are we going through with the procedure, my dear?"

Masha didn't respond.

Lera shrugged her shoulders, and then turned to Masha. "No?"

Masha just shook her head.

"No, as in 'we're not,' or no, as in 'we are'?"

"No, we're not," the mother to be mumbled, like a pouty little girl. "I'm having the baby. There, it's final!"

The doctor nodded and left.

M-07091999 was bursting with happiness, as a result of which Masha's tear-stained face lit up, so much so that Lera noticed the glow too. Outside the clinic, she even told Masha her face seemed "different somehow."

Masha looked happy, relieved, even inspired, repeating "No matter what!" on the way to the bus stop. When she noticed a vase of artificial sunflowers in the window of a flower shop they passed, she stopped, grabbed Lera by the arm, and pulled her into the doorway.

"Oh, I want some of those for home," she said. "Should we go in and buy some?"

Lera smiled. "Sure. Do they look like the ones in your dream?" She immediately waved it away. "Doesn't matter. At least they'll never wilt!"

Desperate for some comic relief after their emotional morning at the clinic, both girls burst out laughing.

When they got to Masha's neighborhood, Lera suggested they stop into a little boutique selling children's toys and clothing.

"What for?" Masha asked.

"I want to buy your baby a gift, just to make sure you don't change your mind again. You have to follow through now, 'no matter what.'" Lera smiled after repeating Masha's mantra. She squeezed her friend's hand. "Most importantly, screw all the Nikolais of the world! You're a rock, and I respect you."

"Some rock," Masha said. "I have no idea how I'm going to get by. There's school, then more school, exams, the thesis defense... and a baby on the way. I need to start making some money soon."

"One day at a time," Lera said. "And if you need to sit down or anything now, tell me. I don't have a lot of experience, but hopefully I'll be able to help somehow."

She ended up buying a baby sling and a teething toy, which was also a rattle, shaped like a teddy bear.

"Carrying the baby around is easier in the sling: just tie it around yourself, stick the two-in-one teething toy in his mouth, and you're set!" She handed the parcel to Masha, and added, "A gift from the future godmother, although... forget it. I don't deserve to be godmother to the child I advised you not to have."

"Stop! You were probably right. I'm the stupid one."

"You're not stupid at all. You did the right thing. The dream you had will come true, and your kid will grow up to be another Van Gogh. We'll be mortified to think that, just this morning, we almost deprived the world of his timeless canvases!"

"Lera, you're a lucky charm." Masha hugged her.

"I know." Lera giggled, with a smile that made her eyes twinkle my favorite way.

They could've been sisters: the same height, both with blonde hair, though Lera wore hers short, whereas Masha wore a ponytail. They were even dressed the same cheerful way: Masha in her tam, Lera in dark red skinny pants, a light orange jacket and multicolored scarf.

I looked at her and tried my best to memorize her image—not a redhead anymore, but still bright and warm as the sun. She was amazing, and I'd forgiven her ages ago.

Our 'accidentally on purpose' meeting, thanks to Masha, had lasted longer than my actual association with her had. Now, sadly, it was really over.

The girls went up to Masha's place, and we didn't follow them this time.

"Thank you, Peace," said the future Van Gogh II. He came up to me as if to shake my hand—if we'd had them. "If it weren't for you...."

"Don't mention it," I said. "Just doing my job, but I have to say, I'm pretty proud of the whole sunflower theme. It was good, right?"

"Sure was. After I'm born and grow up to be a famous artist, I'm gonna paint a field of sunflowers and dedicate it to you!"

"How will I find out about it?"

"You'll be a person too, by then, and when you recognize the image from that dream, just know it's one of mine," he replied sweetly.

"Great." I felt happier. "It's a deal, Mr. Van Gogh II!"

M-07091999 flew off to share his good news with the others. He'd be a fun little kid, the creative type. Too bad he'd thrown in the towel so soon, but with the right mentorship, he'd definitely make something of himself.

The other future little boys and girls surrounded him as he eagerly told them his sad story, which, miraculously, ended happily! He made it a point to mention my name a few times.

I didn't feel like joining them. What was there to say? We had nothing in common anymore. It was like a class reunion for people: they went out of curiosity, then wondered what the point of it was. It was a waste of time, and I had more important matters to address.

First on my list now were Olga and Vladimir, that blue-eyed fellow with the big, open heart, whom I liked as soon as I saw him. For a minute, there, I even felt like I knew him.

Chapter 15

I had to help him regain his self-confidence, and if Olga finally decided in his favor, it was possible. It said in his dossier that only just recently, just before he'd met her, Vladimir had contemplated suicide, out of loneliness. His situation instantly reminded me of a phone call between Lera and a friend of hers, who'd told her he was so lonely and down, he was ready to jump out the window. I remember how angry she got with him for that, even threatening not to come to his funeral if he did anything of the sort. She was kidding, but only half. I never saw him, but I remember Lera calling him 'Vov.' It sounded too funny to be his name, so maybe it was a nickname.

Vladimir was driving along in his old, yellow 'Zhiguli,' humming a tune. He seemed to be in a pretty good mood. An air freshener hung from the rearview mirror, an orange, cardboard pine tree that smelled more like coffee than pine.

I saw his clean-shaven face reflected in the mirror, which should have reflected me, too, but I didn't see myself. When I do see myself, my exterior doesn't really lend itself to description, because essentially there's nothing to describe. Now, if Elias were here, he could describe what *he* saw when he looked at me. Elias had gone somewhere else, though, leaving me in charge of Vladimir and Olga on my own—minus the 'plan' he'd promised to come up with.

I'd work out my own strategy. I could suggest that Vlad have a little talk with Klim, man to man. It seemed like a good idea, in principle, but assumed both men could behave reasonably, Given the facts, that seemed doubtful and risky; Klim could very well kill again.

Vladimir's phone rang.

"Hi, Sunshine," he said. "How's it going? We have to get together somehow. We've never gone this long without seeing each other! I'm so wrapped up in my work."

He listened to the answer for half a minute. "I know. Sorry I wasn't there with you. Please don't be mad!" Whoever was on the phone had evidently scolded him for not paying enough attention to her—had to be a woman, because men usually didn't call each other Sunshine. "Every time I get into my car and smell your orange pine tree," he continued, "I think about how I should call you and drop by, but something always gets in the way."

I couldn't understand who could possibly be on the other end. I couldn't hear the voice, and the suspense was killing me. Was it his sister, or perhaps another lover?

"Maybe we can all get together, go to a café," Vlad continued, "you, me, and Olga. By the way, did you talk to her for long? She can't make up her mind to leave her husband. Maybe you could talk to her about it?"

It had to be one of Olga's girlfriends, but then, why would she call him, and why would he call her 'Sunshine' and beg her pardon for not having seen her for so long?

"Listen," he suddenly said. "I just got pulled over. I'll call you later, okay?" He hung up.

"License and registration, please," said a man in uniform at the driver's window. He looked strangely familiar to me.

"Here you go," said Vlad. He got out of the car and handed him a card and some papers.

"Your permit's expired," stated the man, a traffic inspector.

"What do you mean, expired? That's impossible!"

"See for yourself."

Vlad took back his card, and his eyes widened in disbelief. "Wait a minute. This is some kind of mistake! This is the wrong date. I renewed my permit three months ago."

"You don't believe your own eyes?"

"I guess not. I mean, this can't be right! It's some kind of voodoo!"

"Things aren't always as they seem," the traffic inspector said. He was very odd, speaking in riddles like that.

"So, what am I supposed to do now?" Vlad asked.

"That's an excellent question. What do we do now?"

"I've only got about a hundred rubles on me," Vlad said, preparing to pay the customary bribe.

"Please, save your money. You need it more than I do."

Vlad's eyes grew wider still. Obviously, he'd never come across an honest inspector before.

"Sorry, but I'm a little shocked," he said. "There's definitely something supernatural about this."

"Fine, let's say there is. What's wrong with that? You and your girl might've died in this car on this very spot tomorrow, if I hadn't discovered your permit had expired."

Vlad stood dumbfounded, at a loss for words.

"Is there anyone else in the car with you?" the inspector asked for some reason, and then looked inside the vehicle.

His face definitely reminded me of somebody, and I was pretty sure he even winked at me, as though he could see me.

"All right, my dear Vladimir Alekseyevich," he said. "You can have your permit back, and I won't even write you up. All the same, bear in mind that you must not get into this car tomorrow, no matter what. And double-check that expiration date later, in case it changes again. You're okay to keep driving right now, and nobody else will pull you over, but tomorrow isn't your day. My job is to warn you of that."

"Yes, of course. Thank you, but I have to ask: is this a paid service?"

The man in uniform laughed.

I know that laugh!

"The first time is free," he said, and started to shuffle away along the pavement.

"One more thing: is your unit able to foresee the future? I mean, could you maybe tell me what to do with the rest of my life?" Vlad appeared mildly embarrassed, but figured it was worth a try.

"Absolutely! Call your girlfriend, tell her to pack her things, then pick them up and take them away with you. If you drag your heels, something irreversible could happen. Only remember: do not do it tomorrow! And as a rule of thumb, be especially vigilant on the eighth of every month. Those are high-risk days, 'life-wise.' Now, tell me who's in the car with you?"

That caused the dumbfounded Vlad to turn in my direction, at which point the uniformed guardian angel spread his wings and soared upwards.

Bravo, Elias! What a teller of tales!

I was ecstatic that he hadn't neglected his responsibility after all, and I applauded him.

When Vlad turned around again and realized the 'inspector' had disappeared into thin air, he appeared visibly shaken, and even started to hyperventilate. He'd clearly never experienced the disappearance of an official, or anybody else, for that matter.

I accompanied him all the way home, to make sure he would be okay.

I looked for Olga, but she got stuck at work that day and couldn't pick little Petya up at the kindergarten, so his godmother did. The boy skipped along with the young woman now. They talked and laughed on their way to the indoor amusement center and his favorite game arcade.

I happened to get a glimpse of Godmather's figure and....

Humankind has yet to come up with an epithet to describe how I felt at that moment. Petya's godmother was Lera! It was unbelievable. Coincidences like these just didn't happen. First, Lera had been connected to Masha, and now this! And to think that Lera's friend, Vov, whom I'd only heard over the phone, was actually Vladimir, the person I'd just been in the car with, and that it was Lera who'd called him just before Elias pulled him over.

It really was a small world! Or was the universe giving me a second chance?

As it turned out, Lera was an interesting 'backup' mom, often allowing Petya things his mom denied him. Mother and Godmother, Olga and Lera, would argue about it sometimes, but Godmother always won.

"A kid needs to have fun once in a while," she'd say. "He can't just eat, sleep, and walk around at the kindergarten every day, and then do the same thing at home, too. The little guy needs more stimulation, like game arcades! You should see him hammering the cockroaches as they crawl out of a kind of cage they live in," she'd say, trying to convince Olga. "Bam! Bam! It develops his reflexes, and it's great for relieving pent-up aggression! He's better off smashing cockroaches than the other kids in his group. At least you won't have to deal with any parents. Am I right?"

"Ah," Olga would say, dismissing her with a wave of her hand. "You can always rationalize your behavior, as if your opinion is the only right one. What about all the violent computer games?"

"Okay, so he plays a couple of them, but he plays air hockey much more often. Now that's what I call a game of passion. Even I like it!"

Thus, their visits to the amusement center had become a tradition. Lera had bought tickets for special kids' shows a few times, for just the two of them, but sometimes Olga would come along. Petya loved his godmother very much, and it was mutual.

"Sorry, kiddo," Lera said this particular time. "We can't play the machines today 'cause I'm broke. Come on, I'll buy you an ice cream and your favorite cookies, and we'll go fool around in the park and wait for your mom. She won't be too long."

"Okay," Petya said, trying not to show how disappointed he was, but his godmother could tell by the look on his face.

"Hey, don't be sad, kiddo. Next time, I promise we'll go to all the attractions at the Kirov Culture and Leisure Park. And if we go on your birthday, everything's free there!"

"Awesome! I wanna go!" Petya shrieked, so excited that he even jumped up and down.

When they got to the park, they sat down on a bench and started eating cookies.

"So, Petya, how do you feel about having a baby sister or brother?"

"Good. I'm going to help change the diapers!" he said, rather seriously.

"You're a real champ!" Lera slapped him gently on the shoulder. "You'll need a doll and a box of Pampers to practice with first, so when the time comes, you'll be ready."

Petya looked at his godmother and giggled. "You're joking now!"

"No I'm not!" she said. "I'll buy everything for you the next time I get paid. Your mom will show you how it's done, and you'll start training. Look, here she comes now."

I watched as Olga walked along the path toward them in a pair of low heels, a short gray coat and colored scarf, with the breeze ruffling her hair. She looked beautiful, and so weightless, you'd have thought the next gust of wind would wisp her away.

Petya screamed "Mom!" then ran over to meet her and give her a big hug.

"Hi," Olga said, approaching her friend. "Thanks for helping out."

"Yes, well, it's been my sacred obligation for some time now!" replied Lera. "You're lucky we're almost neighbors, though." She chuckled. "Let's sit for a while. Petya can fool around on the playground. Petya, what do you say your mom and I sit around and gossip a little?"

Petya looked inquiringly at his mother.

"Go ahead, sweetie," Olga said. "We can see you from here."

He finished his ice cream along the way, as he ran over to the other kids.

"I called Vlad today," Lera said. "He was driving, so we couldn't really talk, but he's upset about your situation. As his friend and your son's godmother, and because I'm the one who introduced you, I'm concerned too."

"What do you want me to say?" Olga sighed. "The truth is I'm scared, and not only of Klim's wrath. It's going to be hard for Vlad, too. He's lived alone for so long, and suddenly he'll have a family. I haven't forgotten how spooked he was, when I told him I was pregnant."

"Well, what's the alternative? You'll be showing soon. How will you explain that to your husband? Maybe plead ignorance, and then say, 'Oh my, honey, we're having a baby!'"

"Are you kidding?"

"What, then? Tell me honestly, are you still sleeping with him? I'm worried about Vlad. Obviously, you're my friend, and a remarkable person, but I've known him ten times longer than I've known you, and twenty times longer than you've known him! I know how sensitive he is. He may have been spooked at first, but I can bet my right arm he's a decent guy, and he wouldn't leave you. Besides, if, God forbid, he chickened out at the last minute, he'd have me to deal with." Lera furrowed her brow and jokingly shook her fist.

"Klim and I only happen to share the same bed. There's been nothing between us since I met Vlad, and for two months even before that." Olga sighed yet again. "As for everything else... well, you know better than anyone how men are."

"Other men, maybe, but not Vlad. He's a rare specimen. His eyes alone are precious! And eyes are the windows of the soul. He reminds me of those icons of Jesus. On his last birthday, I even texted him about that: *Good morning, 33-year-old, with Christ's eyes!* And he texted back: *Are you suggesting I'll have to suffer as much as he did?*

Lera laughed. "I told him to wash his mouth out with soap."

Olga nodded and threw up her hands. "There you go. His pessimism makes me a little wary. He's not much of a fighter. The slightest confrontation, and he backs down. Klim is the opposite. Don't get me wrong, I'm not taking sides. I love Vlad very much, and only Vlad. It's just that I'm afraid for him. Klim swore that if I left him for Vlad, he'd kill him. He thought I was asleep when he said it."

"He said that?"

"Yes, but please don't tell Vlad. I'm begging you!"

"Why would you think he shouldn't know about *that*?"

"There's no point in upsetting him. I'll figure this out myself. Klim wasn't serious. Even before any of this, he was always threatening to harm himself."

"He should do it, then, instead of the constant emotional blackmail. It'd be better for everybody, including himself! People who threaten to commit suicide rarely do. The serious ones arrive at that decision in silence."

"How can you say such horrible things, Lera? How am I supposed to live with that thought, now?"

"Well, it's the truth."

Olga may well have agreed with her, deep down, but she was the nurturing type—kind, concerned, tentative—and the embodiment of many men's desires. She couldn't even imagine vocalizing what Lera had said; her parents hadn't raised her that way.

I wasn't able to read Lera's thoughts anymore, not since the thread between us had been severed, but I sensed her feelings, somehow, including her concern for Vlad as a friend. She was trying to take on the responsibility of something she couldn't change. In addition, she was torn between her loyalty to Vlad, her most reliable old friend, and a most remarkable but much newer female friend. Lera simply didn't know how to proceed.

"What if I could distract your husband from those gloomy thoughts of his?" she suddenly said.

"What do you mean?" Olga asked.

"Well, what if you invited me over for supper, or arranged for us to be introduced, somehow, and I flirted with him? I'm pretty good at it, and if I could attract his attention, he might stop ruminating about the horrible things he could do you and Vlad."

"Hmmm... that's an interesting idea. I'll think about it."

"Do. To tell you the truth, I don't like the way your husband behaves, or even the way he looks. I saw him once, when he picked Petya up at the kindergarten. The poor kid didn't even want to go with him! Klim called you and gave Petya the phone, so you could convince him to go home with his own dad! Let's just say he's not my type—*at all* — but I'll do it, if it'll mean a happy ending for you." She wagged her finger in the air. "No sex, though! I'll just drive him crazy with my charm, and then leave him all hot and bothered."

Olga both liked the idea and hated it. It was tough not to feel possessive — whatever kind of husband he was, he was *her* husband — but the circumstances demanded action. Such feelings aside, Lera's idea wasn't so bad. Petya spent so little time with Klim, he called him by name instead of Dad.

"Oh," Lera continued, now on a roll. "And I have nothing good to say about your husband's position on Petya's christening, either. Where does he get off proclaiming there wouldn't be one, just because *he* was categorically opposed to the idea? And instead of standing up to him, or even trying to convince him otherwise, you went and baptized him secretly. I mean, my God, how many secrets does poor Petya have to keep from his father? This has to end as soon as possible! I'm amazed that a five-year-old already knows what he can and can't say. The kid's a genius! I'm twenty-two and still haven't learned when to bite my tongue, and probably never will. I guess you either have it or you don't."

Olga listened to Lera, quietly, until her tirade was over, and then finally agreed. "Yeah, I know."

"So then, why are you always so indecisive?" Lera slapped the wooden bench for added emphasis. "Why are you not like me? If I were in your situation, I would've packed my bags and gone to Vlad's place ages ago!"

"Oh, really?" Olga retorted, however mildly. "And do you remember Vlad's reaction when he found out I was pregnant? Remember the torment I went through for two weeks, worrying about whether or not he needed this in his life?" Olga was being apprehensive again.

"Look, there are so few men who are happy to hear that kind of news right off the bat. You can count them on one hand! They make movies about them, but I've never actually met one." Lera laughed a little, but her voice remained firm, as though she were an expert on the topic. "Vlad pulled himself together, though, after I put the fear of God in him and turned him around."

"Exactly! I don't want to have to turn anybody around with threats."

"Olga, you have no other choice. I'm repeating myself, but.... You're not going to tell Klim the baby's his, and leave Vlad, are you?"

"No, I'm going to tell him the truth. It's just that I'm scared."

"Forget being scared. Forget the very word," said Lera, making circles with her palm in front of Olga's face, as though she were erasing it from her memory. "Let's do this: you'll tell him everything after he and I meet, when the only thing on his mind will be me!" She laughed again. "Although, I probably would've packed my things, taken the kid, and left a note that said something like: 'My knight in shining armor showed up out of the blue, and I just couldn't refuse. Sorry. Olga.'"

This time, they both laughed.

Suddenly, F-12161998's melodic voice rose beside me. "Hi, Peace!"

"Hi, sweetie, how's it flying?" I asked.

"The flying's beautiful, as always!" She laughed. "But if you're referring to my problems, you've already heard it all. I'm not moping around, though. I have a feeling my future's going to be bright, with a professional like you on the case." She giggled. "By the way, did you give my big brother's godmother the idea to help my mom figure things out with her husband?"

"I can't take credit for that one. Is this your first time seeing Lera?"

"Probably the third or fourth already. I like her a lot. She's so much fun, and so sure of herself—the opposite of my mom in that way—but things aren't going so great for her, either. The man she loved ditched her, and she lost her baby."

"I know."

"How?"

"I would've been that baby, and she lost me of her own free will."

"Are you serious?" F-12161998 couldn't believe her ears. "How come you've met up with her again? That's against the rules! Talk about a small world...."

"Only for the people who hang around together. Actually, the odds of meeting her again weren't that high, so it must've been absolutely necessary, especially since this is the second time."

"The second time?" F-12161998 exclaimed in disbelief. Evidently, the inexperienced little soul had suffered a tremendous emotional shock.

"Yeah, I bumped into her on my previous assignment, too."

"Doesn't it make you sad to see her?"

"Well, not seeing her makes me sadder."

"I understand. I can't imagine myself in your position. I'd probably die of grief, if I could, but you're an optimist. Good for you! Of course, Lera's easy to fall in love with. She has something in her that's... orange. She's like a little sun."

"Thanks for the kind words. Maybe she really will be able to help Olga, who seems so defenseless! Meanwhile, Elias, my boss and guardian angel to both your parents, stepped up to the plate today. He really scared your dad in the process, so maybe you should look in on him. I'm a little worried about him."

"I will, Peace. I miss him, myself. I used to spend all my time with him, but as soon as I found my future mother, I felt more like being with her. I didn't even see my friends for a few days! Do you know if anybody has news?"

"No, I haven't felt like talking to anybody lately, and I have a lot to do. Fly to them yourself, and then go see your dad. I'll stay with your mom today, and I promise, nothing will happen to her."

F-12161998 flew happily over to Olga and kissed her on the cheek.

Just as Lera had, when I first met her, Olga rubbed it.

F-12161998 took flight at full speed and disappeared into the clouds. I watched after her and thought about how happy she was. Regardless of anything, she had a future. In about five months, she'd be drinking her mother's breast milk, while her dad looked on, lovingly. For some reason, that particular image was etched into my mind as the family ideal.

Chapter 16

I had one more assignment to complete, and then I'd be allowed to browse around for my new parents, though I couldn't actually take any measures for two years. In the meantime, I was fine with my new name and important occupation. I felt needed. What could feel better than that? I'd have to contemplate Lera's idea, though—to seduce Klim— very carefully, to make sure she wouldn't be putting herself at risk. I worried about her so much! The amazing thing was that she seemed to be helping me, always by my side.

Who invented that stupid rule about not being able to pick the same mother twice? I'd be willing to risk it —

"Your thoughts are seditious, my friend," a voice suddenly intruded. "Nobody's going to pat you on the back for them, and if the top brass gets wind of them, they'll call you on the carpet." Elias wasn't close by, but he could send his thoughts remotely. This was the first time he'd taken advantage of this particular option. "I'm expecting you at our usual place in half an hour. We need to talk, so wrap things up."

Even though I promised F-12161998 to spend the evening by her mom, I couldn't ignore my boss. So, hoping our conversation would be short, as always, and throwing a final glance at the two friends talking on the bench, I left to answer the call of duty.

Elias sat with his huge white wings outspread—quite an amazing sight.

"I got caught in the rain," he explained, seeing how amazed I was. "I'm trying to dry off."

"I'd like to express my enthusiastic appreciation over the man in the uniform," I said.

"Oh, yeah... it was a spontaneous idea." He seemed pleased with my approval. "How else could I convince someone so indecisive to act more decisively? Plus, I found out he could've had a serious accident at the exact same place tomorrow. That's the last thing we need right now. Vladimir should be with the mother of his future child instead of lying in a hospital with his bones all broken—and that was the best-case scenario! Especially since they could've both been in the car, and Olga would've been injured too. There's something fundamentally wrong with those two, as though they're heading down a path not intended for either of them, but that it's too late to get off now. They need to take care of things immediately, in order to prevent a calamity in the future."

"Tell me what to do, and I'm on it!"

"Inform me of their situation as soon as possible, so we can take the appropriate action. Is there any news today, for instance?"

"Olga's talking with her friend right now, about how to diffuse her husband's jealousy. My mom suggested they distract him somehow."

"What do you mean 'your mom'?"

Uh-oh. I'd stuck my foot in my mouth.

"Well... yes," I mumbled, but decided immediately that my best defense would be a pre-emptive strike. I quickly added, "And by the way, Elias, how did I happen to bump into her on both of the assignments you gave me? Was it on purpose?"

Elias looked stunned. "Hang on, hang on... I must be missing something here. What do you mean 'bumped into'?"

"Lera, the one who could've been my mother, turned out to be a mutual friend of Masha, Vladimir and Olga. Now she's about to help Olga out of her predicament with Klim. Why was I assigned these particular cases, if she and I aren't allowed to see each other again?"

Now Elias was the speechless one, but the strain flitting all over his face suggested he was grappling with a very intense thought, contemplating the possibilities.

"Well?" I asked, as the innocent party in all of this.

"Peace, you're blowing my mind right now," he finally said. "I admit that I wasn't aware, and I can't even imagine how this could've happened. I interrupted your thoughts and summoned you here, thinking you were planning something in violation of the rules, but I had no idea.... It's like some sort of providence that's beyond even *our* control. So, the Lera who was recommended by my colleague, the female guardian angel, as a friend for Vladimir, is also your would-be mother? And also Masha's friend?" Elias asked, still in utter disbelief. "Well, this kind of thing simply can't be tolerated. I'll have to take you off this case. Besides which, it must be too complicated for you, right, kid?" His kind, gray eyes looked at me, searchingly.

I could not let this happen. To never see Lera again? To desert her, just when she'd decided on such a dangerous liaison? No way! I had to be right by her side, at all costs.

"No, no, no... not under any circumstances!" I blurted out. "If we were destined to meet again, then so be it. I won't drop her at such a critical moment."

"Silly little soul, she didn't feel sorry for you," Elias said, looking at me sympathetically.

"Drop it," I said stubbornly. "She had no choice. She was with the wrong guy for her. She was upset—"

"Fine, but we have to hide the fact, so don't tell anybody about it, not under any circumstances, okay? You haven't already mentioned it, I hope."

I wanted just to disappear as I remembered my last conversation with F-12161998, and with M-07091999 before that, and decided to keep my mouth shut.

"You're a remarkable boss," I said instead, answering Elias's question. "Thanks for understanding."

"And you're not a bad assistant." He smiled thoughtfully. "I completely forgot to praise your excellent work in fulfilling your assignment concerning Masha. The sunflower field dream was simply fantastic! How did your young little head come up with something like that?"

"I've always loved sunflowers." I laughed. "And I let my imagination do the rest."

"Excellent, simply excellent!" Elias flapped his wings to get the last drops of rain water off. "All I have to do now is get her back onto her predestined path, and I think I've already come up with how to do it. It won't be easy for a while, though, because of the decision she's made."

"By the way," I added, "the picture in the lab, where Masha had the blood test, played an important role. It was a traditional still life—fruit and regular flowers—but that very minute, Masha was looking for something to boost her confidence, so I made her see Van Gogh's *Sunflowers*."

"Hat's off to you, my little erudite, even though I don't have one!"

"You'd look good in one," I said, risking insubordination.

"Okay, I have things to do," Elias replied, suddenly serious. "So it's agreed: you'll observe all of them and inform me of everything. After that, we'll figure out together what to do next. Your Lera's decision to deal with Klim herself is commendable. Let her try, anyway. Something may just come of her little scheme."

"I'm afraid for her."

"It's up to Lera's guardian angel to protect her. If I see her, I'll warn her to be on the lookout. And if something happens, you and I won't let her come to harm. Well, I'm off." He flapped his wings a few times and, convinced they'd dried out sufficiently, raised himself about three meters above me. "Everything's happening just how we want it to, so be careful what you wish for!"

Then he flew away.

Chapter 17

I found Olga and Lera at the same place, getting ready to leave.

"Petya, let's go!" Olga shouted in the direction of the playground as she got up off the bench.

The boy said goodbye to the other kids and ran after his two mothers.

"So, it's agreed?" Lera asked Olga.

Olga nodded. "Let's try it. I'll tell Klim you're coming over on Saturday to borrow a book. Come at about two o'clock. We'll all have lunch, and then go for a walk in the park. You'll have just enough time to get to know each other a little. In the meantime, you come up with a plan of action—you know, *strategic enticement*." She giggled.

"Oh no," Lera said. "I can never plan things. 'Our credo is unexpectedness,'" she said, quoting Ostap Bender. "I can't guarantee results, but I'll give it all I've got."

The girlfriends got to Olga's place by way of the alley, hung with the neighbors' laundry. Lera had never been to their apartment.

The girls had originally met at the editorial office where Lera worked. Olga had won a photo contest sponsored by the newspaper, and Lera invited the winners to a nightclub to claim their prizes at the corporate party. They started talking over a glass of wine, and came to be such good friends, that sometime later, Olga asked Lera be her son's godmother.

Petya noticed a beetle on the one of the sheets hanging out to dry, and grabbed it by the feelers. "Mom, Mom, look!"

"My God, a coffin-cutter! Put it back, right now!" a frightened Olga shouted.

"Does it really cut coffins?" Petya asked.

"Get rid of it, so we don't have to find out for ourselves!"

Olga was so adamant, Petya carefully put it back on the sheet and, forgetting all about the bad omen, turned his attention to Lera.

"By the way, Godmother," he said. "How come you're not a fairy? They're always 'fairy godmothers' in fairy tales."

"Oh, sorry to disappoint you, Petya," she cooed. "Maybe I can become one later. All I have to do is sign up for fairy classes, get my diploma, and *poof!*"

"Now, that would be c-o-o-l!" he drawled.

"Okay, now run along." Lera pushed him gently on his way, and after a quick goodbye, headed off for her own apartment.

I spent the entire evening with Petya and his mom, and learned how boring their family life could be — so different from Lera's. During the time I'd spent with Lera, I discovered you could live in a completely different way: there was always somebody calling her, asking her to go out somewhere, for advice or help, and vice-versa. Catching her at home was virtually impossible. After work, she would head to the theater, to see a movie or an art exhibition, to somebody's place for dinner, or somewhere else. She'd even leave the office on a moment's notice for a meeting, to organize the next office event, like a welcoming party for the newest department head at the paper. I could barely keep up with her. Sometimes, I'd be so tired from all the chasing around, I'd fly back up to my own kind just to rest up a little.

Meanwhile, Olga and Petya spent their evenings in the kitchen in complete silence, or speaking only to each other. Petya often sat, as he did tonight, coloring in his favorite Karlsson book, asking his mother the odd question as she fried up potatoes with mushrooms for supper.

"Dinner's ready, Petya," Olga said. "Go wash your hands and sit down at the table."

"One second. I'm almost done. When is Klim coming?"

"In about half an hour. Do you want sour cream?"

"Yes, please, two spoonfuls. Mom, let's tell him everything today and go live with Vlad!"

"Soon, Petya, we'll tell him soon. Just wait a little longer."

"Okay, Mom, but only a little! I don't like Klim. He hardly talks to me at all! Real dads don't act that way."

"Petya, however he acts, he's your dad and you have to respect him."

"I don't think so," Petya said, sitting down in front of his plate and snatching a mouthful of potatoes. "Vlad is a hundred times better."

Olga maintained the meaningful silence, and Petya didn't say another word, either. He was growing up to be an uncommonly intelligent and well-raised child.

Because of the situation at home, the energy in their kitchen, already strained, lay so heavy and oppressive at that particular moment that I nearly suffocated. I couldn't fly away, out of a sense of responsibility, but being there was tough. I used all my might to get them to open the trap window.

"Mom, open the trap window, please. It's really stuffy in here," Petya suddenly said.

I immediately flew toward the fresh air and sat on the little window. That was my new post now.

The door opened and Klim walked in, carrying a black package. He changed into his slippers, walked into the kitchen, said "hi" to everybody, and put two bottles of beer on the table.

"Have a drink with me?" he asked Olga.

"No thanks, I don't feel like it."

"You haven't felt like having a beer with me for a long time now. I seem to remember you liking it."

"Well, I don't anymore."

"Oh, so you don't like it anymore. I get it. Well, it happens. Do you still like me?"

"Klim, a friend of mine is dropping by on Saturday," Olga said, changing the subject. "Do you mind?"

"What friend?"

"Her name is Lera. She works at the newspaper that sponsored the photo contest I won, remember?"

"I don't, but sure, let her come. What for, though?"

"I promised to lend her a book, and just to talk."

"Talk about what?"

"Are you feeling okay, Klim?" she asked, looking at him, her irritation thinly veiled. "People do talk to each other sometimes about whatever they feel like, and not just over the phone, if you can imagine that."

"Well, then by all means. So, you mean people...." Klim opened a bottle of beer without finishing his thought. "Tell you what: I'm going to eat, and I suggest the two of you go into the other room, since I can see this conversation isn't going anywhere good."

Without a word, Olga took Petya's coloring book off the kitchen table, then took the boy by the hand and led him into the tight, cluttered little corridor, which hadn't been lit since the little bulb had broken a few days earlier.

I watched Klim and tried to feel him out. What kind of person was he? Now that I'd been clued in to his past, I understood that people really did have to be very careful around him. If Olga had known everything about him, she definitely wouldn't have married him.

Before Klim, since her student days, she'd dated someone else for five years, but he'd decided to marry someone else. To ease the pain of rejection, she'd gone on the rebound and hooked up with Klim. He was older, more experienced, and had courted her nicely. Even so, Olga couldn't love him the way she'd loved her first boyfriend; she could only appreciate and respect him. Now, those feelings had transformed into an almost primal fear.

Meanwhile, Klim had fallen for her, and he became extremely possessive. He wasn't the kind of guy who parted with his property easily, and he claimed sole ownership over his wife and child. He needed love and attention, but behaved in a manner undeserving of either. After all, in order to get something, you have to give it first, and he had nothing to give. He was a void.

This man, so empty inside, sat in the kitchen phlegmatically chewing his fried potatoes with mushrooms, and like everybody else when they chewed, his jaws moved up and down. Suddenly, I imagined a huge machine on big metal wheels, upcycling everything that came its way into its cheeks.

My fantasy frightened me. *What's up with me?*

After all, this was a person, not a monster. He had feelings, too, and they had to be respected. We didn't know all the circumstances that had led to his past actions, although there was no excuse for what he'd done. Maybe he had a button that could switch on his *human* self.

If only I knew where it was....

Klim sat in the kitchen until about 6:00 p.m., thinking about something, eating sunflower seeds. He didn't need anyone to converse with: this guy was either completely self-sufficient or very unhappy, or both. When all the sunflower seeds were gone, he went into the bedroom and lay down beside Olga without a single word. About ten minutes later, he started snoring.

Chapter 18

If everything in the world happened the way we wanted it to, in the first half of the following year, two baby boys and a girl would've been born: me, Masha's son, and Olga's daughter. Our three moms would've been pushing our strollers through the park, calmly and proudly, discussing things like the best baby food and which child had cut through how many new teeth.

Although, if truth be told, it was difficult for me to imagine Lera's participation in those conversations. It seemed to me that even when she did have a baby, she'd just put it in her baby carrier and go about her business. I wished I could be the one in that baby carrier.

I couldn't get Elias's words out of my head, that I shouldn't have told anybody about my meeting Lera again. I was afraid the little blabbermouth, F-12161998, had already blabbed my secret to everybody. What was the penalty for a soul, who pursued the mother who'd rejected him? It probably wasn't good. From the looks of things, though, the brass had forgotten about me. Good thing, too. Who wanted to be criticized for something, when they'd already worn the sackcloth and sprinkled ashes upon their non-existent heads?

Up until now, I'd only seen Lera on my assignments, and she'd already become like a drug for me. If I didn't see her for half a day, I felt some kind of irresistible force start pulling me toward her. Why should I have to deny myself? Since it was Saturday and everyone was asleep, surely nothing would happen to anybody for the next few hours, so I flew off to see her, giving in to my inner calling again.

Lera wasn't at home. The bed hadn't been made, but that was of no significance. "Why bother making it?" she'd retorted once when Victor complained. "We come home so late in the evening, we pretty much go straight to bed anyway, so why bother with the superfluous body movements?"

Where could she be? I'd almost lost my connection to her, and it took a lot of effort to find her. I felt like a squeezed-out lemon, but I didn't regret my efforts for a minute, because I wouldn't have wanted to miss what I saw when I finally found her: she was hugging Artem in the corridor of a nightclub. The music wasn't as loud there, and their conversation moved me.

"However funny it's going to sound in this day and age, I'll tell you right now: if you want what's between us to go to the next level... marry me!" Lera blurted out. "I've decided I don't need a casual relationship. If things between us are going to continue, then let's solidify them with that stamp in our passports. It would really ease my mind. If the idea stresses you out, then I'm done," she concluded with a dismissive wave of her hand.

"So then, why not? Let's apply for a marriage license tomorrow," he replied without any hesitation – the man I'd wanted as my father not so long ago.

"Are you serious?" Lera asked, visibly surprised, even a little frightened by such a sudden, affirmative response.

"Absolutely!" He nodded and leaned in closer to her face. "So can I kiss you now?"

"No, wait...." Lera was still reeling from the sudden, serious turn of events. "First, we need to consider everything. Plus, you still haven't shaved off that beard." She laughed.

"Let's go to your place and consider everything, and I'll shave off the beard. I promise!"

"Remember," she added. "No sex, right?"

"Naturally! Actually, it's unnatural, of course, but seeing as we've agreed..."

"Okay, let's go. I'm counting on your integrity!" She meaningfully raised her forefinger.

Along the way to Lera's parents' place, they found a little store open and bought a bottle of red wine.

Following them, I entered the St. Petersburg underground for the second time, only this time at the Ligovsky Prospect station. Everything looked completely different from the time I was with Masha, with only about twenty people on the whole platform at this time of night.

My non-parents boarded an empty car and, just like after their first date at the DDT concert, they stood right up against each other, this time despite the absence of a crushing crowd.

An extremely drunk gentleman sat in the opposite corner of the car, trying really hard to stay awake and not miss his stop. His head bobbed back and forth as though supported by an elastic band, and his eyes opened and closed just like a marionette's.

I decided that if the opportunity ever arose, I wouldn't drink alcohol. I didn't ever want to look that stupid.

I didn't really listen in on what Lera and Artem were saying, because the wheels of the car were too noisy, and the car itself kept bouncing from side to side, as if it were as drunk as that passenger. I saw that Lera laughed, fooled around with his hair, and once even ran the back of her hand tenderly along his beard, as though bidding it farewell.

The train stopped at the next station, and from my position on the hanging strap, right beside Artem's hand, I now listened in.

"Only don't ruin my life," he said. "Please."

The smile on Lera's face suddenly disappeared, and they rode the rest of the way in silence. Even after they'd come out of the metro, they didn't exchange a single word most of the way home.

"You know," Lera finally said, "I suddenly got so scared for some reason, when you said that, because I'm capable of doing that—even against my will." She stopped for a second and looked into his eyes. "So, maybe we should just call it quits? We'll just go our separate ways, right here and now, as though we'd never even talked about it."

Artem looked terribly upset.

"Well?" Lera said impatiently, waiting for an answer.

"No. We've already decided. We're going to your place. It was simply something to say."

"It's not simple, though," she replied, nevertheless taking him by the hand.

The young couple walked to Lera's building, where I'd been so many times that I could've found it blindfolded, even if my internal navigator was on the blink.

What I managed to see wasn't the least bit like the 'process' that F-12161998 and I had observed at Vladimir's place between him and Olga. Lera and Artem spent about half an hour gabbing about various silly things and drinking the wine. Then, on realizing they wouldn't make it to the Civil Registry Office, because it was Sunday, and after reminding Artem there would be nothing physical between them yet, Lera tried to make her bed look nicer by fluffing up her pillow.

"I want to sleep so bad," she said, as though justifying the action. "You don't mind, do you?"

"I could sleep, too. Can I lie down... beside you?" Artem asked, amazed at the very notion of it.

"Seeing as you're my mother's future son-in-law," the future bride said between giggles, "yes, you may. Boy oh boy, will she be happy! All she's been talking about lately is my getting married, as if I'm already an old maid—and unless I get married soon, a total write-off.

"So how come you're in such a hurry?"

"I want something to celebrate, and a white dress, and for people to stop asking me, 'When-oh-when are you going to get married?' The neighbors love that, especially the pensioners. They can drive you up a wall with their stupid questions! This way, we can live together in legal matrimony, and if we don't like it, we can divorce, and I'll be able to tell all the nosy ones that I've been there, and that it wasn't so great after all."

"Ah-ha, so you've got it all worked out! But what if we don't divorce?"

"You're allowing for *that* possibility?" Lera asked, turning to her bridegroom. This time *she* was the one to show amazement at the very notion.

"Why not? A man should only have one wife for his whole life, like a mother, or a sister."

"Artem, what kind of nonsense is that? It's so un-contemporary! Don't ever say that to me again. You're scaring me. And by the way, you can have more than one sister."

"Fine," he said, looking at her with puppy dog eyes.

"Now, get undressed. You can't sleep in your clothes. Only... don't take off your shorts, not under any circumstances! There has to be some mystery left before the wedding." She giggled again.

Artem took off his t-shirt, and Lera, her sweater. He glanced sheepishly at her semi-see-through bra, and poured what was left of the wine into their glasses. Then, kneeling before one another, the future newlyweds carefully clinked glasses.

"To our worrisome decision!" Lera said.

"And may God grant it not be our last," Artem added.

They maintained that pose, hugging, for about twenty minutes. Finally, Artem decided to touch her lips with his, and she giggled again about his beard tickling. The sense of attraction between them was so strong that it sucked me in, as though into a whirlpool.

That minute, I realized: this was it, the moment I'd been waiting for! That's when I should've acted to unite forever these two foolish people who were loving each other without even realizing the intensity of their feelings for one another. But even if I'd had a second chance, nothing would've come of it today, anyway, as Lera remained true to her word, and things did not progress beyond the kiss.

You rock, Mom!

Chapter 19

I left to see Vladimir, who'd been frightened by his meeting with the strange inspector, and by the mysterious alterations to his license. I was glad that Lera was moving forward, and she was right. Why sit around grieving, when life is here and now? Lots of people make mistakes that lead to personal tragedies, but the main thing is not to let them grow out of proportion, not to treat the situation more seriously than it warrants.

All this led me to decide to stop being nostalgic about the past, and to live in the present.

I reasoned thus: did I love Lera? Yes. Were things good for her now? Apparently so. She was with someone whom I felt should be with her. She was getting back on track, and for some reason, fate had thrown us together again. Therefore, things were as they should be. I'd simply be near her, and whatever was going to happen... would.

Vlad was already up and preparing breakfast, looking thoughtfully at the two round, yellow eyes in the frying pan that looked right back at him. I smiled at the lack of human imagination, recalling how Lera always did the same thing in the morning, only she whipped her eggs with a fork first, and sometimes added chopped tomato. With all the delicacies in the world, people generally ate a breakfast of unhatched chicks. It was beyond me.

F-12161998 was nowhere in sight. Evidently, she'd already left her dad, unless she was so busy blabbing with her girlfriends that she'd forgotten to visit him in the first place.

The seven-room communal apartment where Vladimir lived sat in the center of the city, on the third story of an old building on Liteiniy Avenue. It was a noisy and smelly place, as the sound of people swearing, the smell of engine oil, and the noxious exhaust fumes from the street wafted in through the kitchen window day and night. On the outside, the windowpane was gray with dirt, and because of the five-story building directly across the street, the sun only came through for a few minutes in the afternoon.

Thus, the mornings in Vlad's apartment generally arrived as gray and gloomy as the building itself, his one source of happiness the Fontanka River. It took him exactly three minutes to walk there, and then he'd gaze out at the water for a long time, leaning against the granite railing along the riverbank. The water would calm him, and help him organize his thoughts, especially after the unavoidable run-ins with his alcoholic neighbors—he being an abstainer.

On this particular morning, he already seemed less carefree than he'd been the day before, in the car.

"Good morning," said a little old lady in a multicolored robe, who'd come into the kitchen with a kettle in hand. Small, shriveled as a twig, but with a face expressing kindness and intelligence, she looked like the kind of lady who sold old children's books on the street.

"Why so glum today, Vlad?" she asked.

"Hello, Nina Vasilyevna," Vlad said, and nodded in reply. "I'm just thinking, is all."

"About your darling Olga, I'll bet," she continued, probing. "Such a sweet girl—nice eyes—and her little boy is so polite. They should move in here with us. I could watch the boy if the two of you had to go somewhere. By the way, it might be difficult for them to live with neighbors. They probably live in an apartment, right?"

Vlad didn't feel like revealing any details, even though she was a remarkable old lady, the sweetest and kindest of all the neighbors. She was eighty-seven, a survivor of the Leningrad blockade, still possessing a healthy mind and an excellent memory. As a young nurse during the war, she'd looked after the wounded on the front lines. As a result, her sense of empathy was automatic, whether you needed it or not.

"All right, all right, I'll stop interrogating you," she said, catching on to Vlad's reticence and turning on her gas burner. "You know best about how to handle things, and if you don't know, then go to a church. There's one right around the corner, the Church of Saint Simeon and Anna the Prophetess. Stop in there, talk to the priest, and light a candle for Nicholas the Wonderworker. Ask him, and he'll help."

"Going to church wasn't part of my upbringing, Nina Vasilyevna. I wouldn't feel comfortable there."

"Then you need to go to confession. Shall we go together?"

"No thanks, I'm not ready for that yet. Maybe later."

"Later, then. What's important is not being too late," she unexpectedly concluded, then put her kettle onto the burner and returned to her room.

Vlad went up to the window and looked down at the passersby, all of them rushing somewhere on this Saturday morning. He didn't need to go anywhere today. He'd be working as a security guard in a couple of days at the same paper where Lera worked, and the rest of the time he worked to order, installing and repairing domestic appliances. He would've been happy to spend his day off with Olga and Petya, but he couldn't get yesterday's incident with the traffic inspector out of his head. Impossible as it was, his license was still technically expired, and he couldn't drive on an expired license.

He still hadn't figured out how to tell Olga why he wasn't driving, and he didn't feel like telling her about his bizarre experience, lest she figure him for a whacko. She'd gotten pregnant the first time they were intimate, although having met only four months ago, they were still, even now, getting to know each other.

Still, he couldn't stop thinking about the warning he'd gotten, seemingly from above, about moving Olga into his place as soon as possible. How could he make it happen if she continued to fight him on it, asking repeatedly for more time? He couldn't force her, and he decided not to worry her even more with this bit of news.

He suddenly remembered he was supposed to call Lera, but 8:00 a.m. was too early, as Lera didn't like calls before noon on Saturdays. If she picked up, she'd only grumble about how nobody would let her sleep.

Vlad was ten years older than Lera, but even so, she was his one true friend. He could confide in her about almost anything, knowing she would never betray his implicit trust in her. Despite her relative youth, she was often more experienced, and wiser in many situations, because he'd spent far too much of his life sitting on the fence instead of actually living it. She'd even found him his part-time plumbing job, when he was sitting around broke. And at Lera's birthday party, he'd met Olga. It seemed Lera had more or less taken the reins of his destiny.

Meanwhile, he'd been so caught up in his own world that he wasn't even there for her when she needed him most, during her breakup with Victor. Vlad was ashamed of himself. He'd wait until Lera woke up, then call and definitely get together with her that afternoon. He'd tell her what was going on, knowing she'd understand.

Lera's mother answered the phone.

"Hello, Marina Ivanovna," Vlad said. "Could you get Lera for me, please?"

"Is that Kostya?" she asked.

"No, it's Vlad."

Her casual way of asking who was calling her daughter, without actually asking outright, amused him. She always confused the names of Lera's various suitors, sometimes even making them up. Mortified, Lera would shout, "Mom, why do you do that? Whoever is there will think I'm sitting around waiting for a call from some 'Kostya,' when it could be some 'Sasha!'" Lera had lived with her grandmother in another city until she was ten. When her parents finally tired of their endless searching for their creative selves and took her back, they had to get to know each other practically from scratch, and they were still figuring things out.

"Oh, Vlad, dear, you haven't been here for ages! Come on over. I'll bake a cake," Lera's mom said.

"I was going to, today. I just wanted to check with Lera."

"Vlad, dear, she's still sleeping. She was out last night, and I don't even know what time she got in." She settled into a whisper now. "And judging from the pair of men's shoes in the corridor, she's got company."

"Well, I guess you'll find out who they belong to when she gets up." He smiled to himself at Marina Ivanovna's excitement. "And if he's a decent guy, just make sure he doesn't get away. I mean, grab him... literally," he added, facetiously.

"That's so true, Vlad. These days, you're lucky to find a decent person in a month of Sundays, and some of them are only pretending to be decent." She paused for a moment. "You saw how things worked out with Vic, and he seemed like a decent guy at first, too. Too bad you and Lera are just friends. I like you so much! Come on over, and we'll chat. I brought a bottle of consecrated liqueur from Karelian Saint Valaam Island."

"Thanks, Marina Ivanovna. I don't drink, but I can drop by in a couple of hours for some cake. And Lera will be up by then."

"Absolutely! I'll be waiting!" She sounded genuinely happy.

After he hung up, he thought about how all the flour in Lera's parents' apartment disappeared at the speed of light. Marina Ivanovna would come home from work to an empty fridge, and have dinner on the table in fifteen minutes. Her cakes didn't take long, either. They were as 'creative' as herself, a poet who'd published her collections in short runs so she could give them away to her friends. Baking cakes was different, though. She always said it required the ability to "see into their souls," while Lera, less considerate of their inner qualities than their appearance, would say, "These aren't cakes, Mom, they're train wrecks!"

Vlad needed to talk to somebody right away, and Marina Ivanovna's active spirituality made her the perfect candidate. And to his unsophisticated palette, her baking wasn't so bad either. He'd visit with her, and then when Lera finally got up, he could check out whomever it was she'd brought home with her, too, now that her mother had aroused his curiosity.

Listening in on his inner monologues, I thought how funny it was that I could've spent these past few hours at Lera's place and met Vlad there. What an amazing interweaving of fates Elias had assigned me to observe! To think this was Vov, as Lera had called him over the phone that day, my would've-been godfather.

I decided to go back to my default position and have a look at Lera, sleeping. I'd always loved watching her as she slept, and now I wanted to see how she and Artem slept together. In my view, the way people positioned themselves in relation to others, while they slept, reflected their true feelings. If they cuddled together while sleeping, they shouldn't have too many problems in waking life.

What I saw only reaffirmed my conviction that the two of them weren't together by accident. Lera's head lay on his shoulder, her hand on his chest, while his hand lay nestled under the small of her back.

Artem was already awake, gliding his free hand over her blonde hair and looking tenderly into her face. His unexpected bride-to-be also stirred — sleeping through the din of pots and pans, as her mother prepared to receive her surprise visitors, was no easy feat.

"My mom's baking again," she said groggily, explaining the ruckus in the kitchen. "So it's time to meet and greet. Have you changed your mind about the marriage registry? Did we dream the whole thing?"

"No, and no." He smiled and kissed her on the forehead. "What's your mom's name?"

"Same as her favorite poet, Tsvetaeva. Remember her name and patronymic?"

"I do. *'Rowans were burning with red berries on. Leaves were still falling when I was born,'*" he said, reciting the first lines of a Tsvetaeva poem. "Let me rehearse. 'Greetings, Marina Ivanovna! I'm your future son-in-law, Artem, and I implore you to love and respect me.'"

"Very good!" Lera looked enthusiastically at her future husband. I could tell by her gaze that she liked him even more now. "Go heavy on the erudition. Mom likes that. She's well read."

"I wasn't born yesterday, you know," he replied. "Is there a toothbrush I can use? I wouldn't feel right talking about Tsvetaeva with scummy teeth."

"There's an old one of mine lying around somewhere. I've been saving it for a special occasion, and this is it!" Lera grabbed Artem gently by the thick hair on his chest. "Well, I hope you're ready to meet your future mother-in-law."

"I'm always ready!" he blurted out, young pioneer-style, already almost in sync with Lera's way of interacting. It looked as though he had great potential.

"Good morning," said the joyful Marina Ivanovna, greeting them in the kitchen. She wiped her hands on her frock and extended the right one, spattered to the elbow with flour and dough, to Artem. "I'm Lera's mom."

"And I'm Artem," he said, squeezing her hand. "Allow me to guess your name." He squinted up at the ceiling for a couple of seconds. "Marina Ivanovna?"

"Why, yes, it is," she uttered, dumbfounded. "How did you guess?" She seemed genuinely amazed.

"It's no big deal, Mom. Artem is psychic," Lera said, stringing out the put-on. "He can even help you find that passport you lost."

"Really? Oh! I really do have to find it. I can't travel without it, and I'm going to Ukraine soon, to a Tsvetaeva conference. There's no way I'm missing that!"

"Mom, I'm kidding. Your sense of humor must still be asleep." Lera sighed. "He's not psychic, he's a journalist, so you'll have find the passport yourself. We work together, and we've decided to get married. There. So I beg you to love and respect him. He's my future first husband."

Marina Ivanovna sat down on a stool with a dazed smile, hopelessly confused. "Well," she started, never having learned how to distinguish her daughter's gags from the truth. "If this isn't another practical joke, it's an event to be commemorated. The cake will be ready soon, and I have some sanctified liquor from my last trip to Valaam. Vlad is coming over, too. He called when you were asleep."

"Excellent! I'm sorry Dad's away, though. We could've commemorated the day as a family," Lera said. "Okay, Mom, we're washing our hands and sitting down at the table."

Just then, the intercom buzzed and Lera answered. "Who is it?"

"The plumber." Ever since getting the new job, Vlad had always used the same reply to her.

"Come on in, plumber." She laughed and buzzed him in.

Everyone had become terribly cheerful. Recent times had been so plagued with problems, this particular day felt especially happy and bright by comparison.

Vlad was surprised to see Artem, whom he knew from the office, and who was always the last to leave. The security guard shook the young journalist's hand and congratulated him on his decision to marry the most positive girl in the world.

Everyone laughed and complimented Marina Ivanovna's latest culinary masterpiece, which she'd decorated with an inscription, made of cranberries. It read 'Artem + Lera,' in keeping with her tradition of inscribing each of her creative cakes. Half an hour later, only the 'ra' remained.

"I'd like to propose a toast," Lera's mom said, raising yet another shot glass of liquor. "To Artem: may he be the man Lera's been looking for, for so long—her friend, her rock." Then, turning to Lera with an inquiring look, she said, "Maybe I could recite a poem?"

Lera started laughing. It had taken years for her mother to start asking permission, instead of bursting into spontaneous verse that seemed endless.

"Go ahead, Mom. I don't think anybody would object," she said, glancing around the table at the others, all of whom nodded in agreement. "And now for a five-minute poetry break!" Lera announced.

Eyes filled with deep emotion, Marina Ivanovna looked at Lera. "I wrote this for, and about, you, when you were little:

> *"My little girl sees with eyes so bright,*
> *I want for her to grow up happy:*
> *Sincere, wise, gracious, kind, modest and simple,*
> *For her to meet a handsome bachelor.*

What was missing or unfulfilled in my own life
Is destined to return, as the miracle of hope,
To this seven-year-old creation.
Such is my prophecy – may it be fulfilled."

Artem applauded and Vlad joined in, although he'd heard the poem before.

"Thank you, Mom," Lera said. "A heartfelt and fitting poem. Here he is, the handsome bachelor." She hugged Artem around the shoulders. "As they say, another reason not to *not* have a drink!"

Everyone clinked their shot glasses of liquor, and Vlad's cup of tea, amiably. Despite the seriousness of the occasion, no serious conversations arose during the get-together. When Artem got ready to go home, Lera and Vlad walked him to the metro.

"Well, 'bye for now, Bridegroom," Lera said, and kissed him on the lips. "So, I expect a call tomorrow evening to confirm your intentions. We've given my mom hope, so it would be a real pity to let her down."

"Why let her down, then?" The bridegroom smiled. "Decide on which civil registry office we're going to by tomorrow. Or would you rather go to the actual wedding registry?"

"Oh, Vov," Lera said, turning to her friend, unable to conceal her emotions. "See what's happening here? My time to choose between good and even better has finally come! Life is truly beautiful and amazing."

"That's right," Vlad agreed.

Once Artem had disappeared down the escalator, Lera and Vlad went for a walk in the park. It was Indian summer and warm out, and she was lightheaded from the liquor.

"Vov, how great is this?" She led Vlad along the path by the hand. "Am I really going to have a real wedding and everything? I can hardly believe it!"

"You know, marriage is serious business. I mean, how do you feel about that part?"

"What would happen if I were to take such a serious thing *un-seriously*?" she asked, looking into his bottomless blue eyes.

"Probably nothing too serious, like multiplication by zero."

"Geez, what a downer you are." She moaned and wrinkled her nose. "Here I'm finally feeling good again, and you... I mean, what's the harm in my getting married? Artem is treating this as lightly as I am.

Besides, it'll make everybody happy. I'm so tired of moping around! It's not my thing. I need a radical change, and this is it."

"Blah, blah, blah..." said Vlad, mocking her in fun. "No guts, no glory. And you've sure got guts."

"Do I ever!" Lera burst out laughing. "Listen, let's go back to my place and watch a movie. You in a hurry to go somewhere?"

"Nope, and I don't have my car today, either, in case you're wondering. I came all the way here by metro, just to talk to you."

"About Olga? We saw each other yesterday. Things are complicated over there."

"That's precisely my point, and I had such a strange experience yesterday, if I told anybody about it, they'd think I was hallucinating — on drugs."

"What did you hallucinate?" Lera asked, keenly interested.

"Downtown, on Kolokolnaya street, a traffic inspector pulled me over right when you and I were on the phone. He said the craziest things, and then it turned out my license was expired."

"Didn't you just renew it?"

"That's precisely my point! I renewed it three months ago. It was like some supernatural occurrence. He told me not to drive today, not under any circumstances, and to move my girlfriend over to my place as soon as possible. Then he disappeared into thin air!"

Lera even whistled in amazement. "Well," she said, "I know you're not on drugs, so technically, I should believe you. But... if I didn't know that.... Listen, Vov, what if...." She paused to think. "What if it was your guardian angel?"

Vlad's big eyes grew even bigger.

"No, seriously," she went on. "I've heard of similar instances, of guardian angels coming to warn people of danger. I mean, more often than not, they come to people in a dream, but for an angel to appear in uniform — of the State Traffic Inspectorate, of all things — well, that has to be a first." She pointed up to the sky. "New technology, I guess, same as here!"

"You turn everything into a joke."

"I'm totally serious! And you'd better take what he said seriously, too! If it's come to the point where a traffic inspector actually pulls you over at an intersection, instead of taking the time to appear in your dreams, it must be urgent, and you have to act — now! If I were you, I'd move Olga's things right out of there, while her husband's at work."

She paused. "Since she can't seem to decide on that, I'm going to try my hand at making it easier for her. I'm going to their place for supper tomorrow, to woo her husband."

"That's news to me!"

"There you go." Lera wagged her head from side to side coquettishly. "Now thank me."

Vlad smiled. "I'll thank you when you've wooed him. I'm at the point where I'd like to 'woo' him too, with my bare hands," he added, though his voice was huskier now.

"Why bother? He's actually the injured party here. You and Olga will have a family, whereas he's going to end up alone. He's a jerk, but I feel kind of sorry for him, because deep down in every jerk, somewhere, there's a person. The question is, how deep down do you have to go before you find him?"

"Well, if you and your frankness manage to bring him out of his shell, maybe you'll get a glimpse of him."

"Actually, I'm not so sure my plan will work, because there are some gloomy types who just don't like me. I'm afraid he might be one of them. So, just in case, don't bet all your money on me."

"Nobody's betting anything. This isn't the hippodrome," Vlad joked, "and you're not even a horse."

"Exactly. I'm not a horse. Listen, how about you and I go skydiving?" Lera suddenly changed the subject entirely. "We'll start our lives over again, from scratch. We'll imagine the parachute won't open, and then—*Poof!*—it opens. It'll be like the start of a second life. That must be great, being born all over again. Don't you think?"

I listened to her as she drew conclusions about something she knew absolutely nothing about. Being born all over again wasn't just a matter of changing your hair color, your hairdo, and going skydiving. You needed to relive your death internally, and it was no big deal to stop existing physically.

I felt the need to talk with Elias, but he remained incommunicado despite the myriad inner signals I sent him.

What is he so busy with? That angel is full of secrets.

Chapter 20

Vlad spent the rest of the day at Lera's. When Marina Ivanovna left to attend an evening of bard songs, the two friends were finally alone to talk freely, one on one. Looking at the situation from every angle, they decided to try and convince Olga to give herself a deadline: say, two weeks. If things didn't resolve themselves by then, they'd assess the situation and act accordingly—either announce their intentions officially or, less perilously, just go quietly, leaving behind the note about 'the knight in shining armor.'

"God forbid we end up in a situation like that," Lera concluded. "When you look at things from the sidelines, at what a marriage can turn into, getting married gets kind of scary. To think spouses can go through such irreversible transformations as a family! I hope that doesn't happen between me and Artem. The minute there are any mind games, we'll divorce. We'll draw up a pre-nup."

"About what? How many times a week you can have sex?" Vlad laughed. "A pre-nup is for material things, for who gets what. Neither of you owns anything, so what's there to divide?"

"Well, yeah, so it won't be any good to us," Lera agreed. "And we'll figure out the sex thing on our own. It'll be unregulated."

"Has there been anything between you yet?"

"We've only kissed. I'm not supposed to yet."

"How come? Oh, yeah.... Have you told him about it?"

"What for? It's personal. Plus, he's too impressionable. Just recently, he asked me for some advice at the office: should he or should he not lend his friend some money for his girlfriend to have an abortion. Their situation's a mess. They're both twenty years old, no work or money, plus they're in school. He was upset, because if he gave them the money, he'd be responsible for murdering a living soul."

"So what did you tell him to do?"

"I said he had to help them, that if he didn't, they'd find the money elsewhere if they'd already made up their minds, and that he and his friend would both lose out. He could've helped him, and he didn't. And then he didn't have to take responsibility for somebody else's decision."

"Did he listen to you?"

"Yes. So, you think he'd understand? Maybe I'll tell him later. Or maybe he doesn't need to know—ever. I've already told him too much personal stuff, anyway. I mean, not every man is wise enough to take a woman for what she is, with her entire past, and not reproach her at least once. Especially not a beginner like Artem. You got lucky!" Lera suddenly added, loudly and unexpectedly, slapping Vlad on the knee.

"In what?" he asked.

"What do you mean, 'in what'? In having such a remarkable friend of the opposite sex, who can explain things when you need her to, from the female side of the barricade, who can steer you away from making a mistake, and just, you know... be grateful, man!" She pushed lightly against his chest with the palm of her hand.

"I am, man!" He laughed. "Here, let me hold your hand, my remarkable friend!"

"Take it," she said, giving him her right hand. "And if I were the Karlsson who lives on your roof, on the Liteiniy, I'd hook a bell up to your room, so you could ring it three times whenever you felt like saying, 'How remarkable, that there's such a beautiful, reasonably well-padded girl at the very prime of her abilities in the world, as you, Lera! You're a true friend and almost a sister.' Petya and I read that passage recently."

"I can just text it, instead of having a bell," Vlad said.

"Come on! That's just what I need, right now, to improve my self-esteem."

The two friends had fun and fooled around, not feeling like talking about serious topics. I watched them and was happy that Lera had a friend like Vlad, and vice versa. Their mutual feelings were utterly guileless. They were totally honest with each other and could speak candidly about anything, unhampered by the fear of being misunderstood. What could be more beautiful than having someone who's there for you, unconditionally and at a moment's notice?

"Oh, Vov, I've missed you so much!" Lera said, all laughed out. "I love you." She sighed, kissed him on the cheek, and lay her head on his chest.

"I love you, too," he replied.

Cuddling up to him, Lera suddenly felt like a little girl and, unexpectedly, her meticulously suppressed feelings of sadness burst forth, and her laughter turned to tears.

"Vov, the truth is, I feel so awful. When will it stop hurting?"

"It will, with time. Don't cry. Just think about how this too, will pass."

Yeah, I guess so, but I'll never forget about it. And what if I can never have kids again?" she asked, terrified.

"You will! When you're ready, you will. Things always work out for you, when you really want them to."

"Not all things."

"Look, they say if you manage to escape your destiny, then it wasn't your destiny. Here you're getting married soon, and things will work themselves out." Vlad stroked Lera's hair.

It cheered her up, like her grandmother used to do when Lera was little.

"Although," Vlad added, "I don't really get this Artem. There's something 'unmanly' about him. He's a strange guy, kind of flimsy."

"Yeah? I haven't figured him out yet either. I mean, I like him. He's cute, has a good sense of humor, and he's pretty cool, sociable, smart.... I'll give him a try. I have nothing to lose, right? I've already lost everything."

"Stop! Don't get yourself all worked up again. Let's have some tea, and then I have to go. We'll watch a movie another time, okay? And I'll let you know about the skydiving thing. I've wanted to do that for a long time, but I wouldn't do it alone. I'll sign up for just about anything, though, if I can do it with you."

"Thanks, friend! Let's get together more often!"

"I'm up for that, but you know my job. I have to be in a hundred places a day."

"I found Olga for you, and now I'm complaining about not getting enough attention from you. Shameless, right? Okay, get going. I can see you're in a rush. I'll call you next week and tell you when the wedding is."

"Good. Olga and I will start shopping around for your gift—something 'his and hers.'"

"Oh do, by all means!" Lera giggled, and they hugged each other goodbye.

When Vlad left, I decided to spend a little more time with Lera, since she was all alone. As soon as she closed the door behind him, she sat down at her computer and logged on to her favorite online forum, where complete strangers expressed their opinions, under the guise of advice, on various personal issues.

Whenever she read a comment she disagreed with, she'd pick a fight with its contributor. Lera always wanted to 'set the record straight,' in a way that would give her the last word. This time it was about whether a person could change radically for the better with age, be it on their own initiative, as influenced by someone else, or due to circumstance. Lera insisted it was all an illusion, and that if people did change over time, it was generally for the worse. Thanks to some examples she gave as 'Orange,' a heated argument developed that was practically impossible to resolve. Finally, 'Orange' Lera opted to change the topic.

I read all of Lera's comments carefully. We can do everything while we're still immaterial souls, but when we're born, we forget everything and have to learn it all over again. Lera's post was entitled 'Confessions from the Void.'

> *A week ago, of my own free will, my future child stopped 'being.' The back-story to all of this is lengthy, but in a nutshell, my relationship with the father came to a dead end and he insisted there be no child. There's such a terrible void inside of me now, I feel like an empty vase: just fill me up with water and stick in some flowers, except I'm afraid they'd only wilt.*
>
> *I really wanted this baby, even before he was conceived. When I got pregnant, I registered at a women's clinic, started to gain weight, and everything was fine. I've lost 5 kilos since, and the outfit I bought last month just hangs on me, like on a scarecrow. But that's not the main thing. It's that I was certain I'd be a mother in 7 months, and now I just can't deal with the fact that it's not going to happen. It's extremely painful. And what hurts even more is knowing that the person directly related to the child's creation is glad it won't be born. He feels better: no baby, no problem. Whereas I despise myself for having forgiven him almost immediately, and for having to struggle, consciously, not to call him ever again.*
>
> *Sometimes I think (or maybe it only seems that way) my baby's soul is right here, looking at me, and that it doesn't understand why I did what I did. I don't even know why, myself. It was all decided by a single negative thought I had about the father, in a flash. Before that, I'd decided to keep it!*
>
> *They say time heals all wounds. It's been two weeks now, but I'm not feeling any better. Remember the song about the girl who*

laughs her way through life? Her tried and true method of dealing with things, as if they don't exist.... They must have written it about me. I've even decided to get married, to start over again, from scratch. Am I doing the right thing? Or is this my next mistake?

Now you can all pummel me with virtual tomatoes, the way you do. I'm sure I won't hurt any more than I do right now.

This time she signed off as 'Lost Soul.'

If I could have, I would have replied, '*Mom, don't punish yourself! I love you the way you are, in spite of everything. Your Peace.*' But the 'new' technology was simply beyond the scope of our computer-illiterate heavenly division.

Afterwards, Lera did some work-related things, checking the data in some tables. Then she watched her favorite movie, 'Sliding Doors,' and went to bed without bothering to wait up for her parents. Coming home well after midnight, if at all, was normal in their family, so nobody worried about anybody.

I lay down beside her head, and also fell asleep. What a great day it had turned out to be! How nice it was to read about myself in Lera's post! It meant she was thinking about me, too, and that maybe she really did feel my presence.

Chapter 21

The next morning, both of us were awakened by the sound of a new text message.

> Artem: *Good morning, my future little wife, any plans for the day?*

He must have felt like saying hi.

> Lera: *Hi, going to my godson's for supper. Will call when I get home.*

She put herself together very carefully, preparing for the delicate task of wooing somebody else's husband, right in front of his wife, even though she had said wife's permission. The 'femme fatale' took a long time choosing just the right outfit, something she would never bother with normally. This time, she meticulously made up her eyes, and even manicured and painted her nails—she rarely did that, either.

"It's really more a question of charisma, than any of this, but what can you do. People are judged by their nails!" she said to herself and, making a face in the mirror, added, "Invisible and free!" quoting Bulgakov's Margarita. Then, even kidding with her own reflection, she added, "Well, maybe not."

Also invisible and free, I hoped Lera would connect with Klim, and that Elias and I would be involved in any further events, 'as the play progressed.'

As she approached the entrance to Olga's building, only one bus stop away, the 'vamp' examined her face in her compact one last time. Judging by its satisfied expression in the mirror, she was pleased. She buzzed the apartment confidently and immediately heard Olga's voice.

"Lera?"

"Yes, it's me."

"Third floor."

"Okay."

Olga had already set the table for lunch in the tiny kitchen. She'd prepared batter-fried fish, boiled potatoes and coleslaw. They lived modestly, doing without any delicacies. Klim and Petya already sat at the table on their stools.

"Hi, Petya," Lera said, patting her godson on the back of the head. They weren't allowed to advertise that she was his godmother, because the man of the house still didn't know about the sacred event.

"Lera, this is Klim," Olga said, introducing her husband.

"Very nice to meet you, Klim. I just love your name! Is it short for Kliment, or Klimenty?" Lera asked, beginning her 'strategic enticement.'

"Kliment."

"I've never met anybody named Kliment—not in person, that is. And what's your patronymic?"

"You don't have to use my patronymic. I'm not that old yet."

"That's not at all what I meant." Lera smiled. "I only wanted to see how your name and patronymic harmonized."

"He's Kliment Igoryevich," Olga chimed in, "and he wanted to name his son Serafim, and then leave the child to deal with it. So, I talked him out of it and proposed the name Peter."

"Why? They're good, solid names," Lera objected, still in her role. "And they stand out from the masses. As it is, there's an Alexander or an Andrey everywhere you turn."

"Exactly," said Klim, looking at Lera with interest. "You sit back and relax. Olga, serve our guest some potatoes."

"I wouldn't mind some fish, too!" Lera laughed and pulled her stool up to the table.

"And what do you do for a living, Lera?" he asked, once everyone was seated.

"I work in the PR department of the same paper where your wife won the photo contest. I presented her prize personally, and I liked her so much, we unexpectedly became friends."

"Why haven't you ever come for supper before?"

"Well, nobody's ever invited me," Lera said with a smile, looking quizzically at Olga.

"My dear," Olga said to Klim, "I've been trying not to invite anybody over for a long time now. You don't really like having guests."

"Honey, that depends on the guest! A nice girl like Lera should've been invited long ago!" Klim asserted, as Olga stared at him in disbelief. This kind of reaction on his part was extraordinary.

Lera smiled. "Be careful, Klim, otherwise I'll start believing I'm nice. I'll come and move in here forever, so I can hear it every day, to boost my self-esteem." She flirted openly.

"So, you have a self-esteem problem?" Klim asked without even a hint of a smile.

"It goes up and down, depending on my life circumstances."

"Take an example from me. Everything about me is very stable," he said, without any humor whatsoever, as he raised a forkful of fish to his mouth.

"Then I'll need to join a workshop. Can I sign up for yours?"

Olga shifted her eyes from Lera to Klim, observing the dynamic between them as Lera tried to achieve her goal.

Petya ate in silence. He never butted into adult conversations in his father's presence, because he remembered getting the belt for that — twice.

"It'll be very expensive, and individual sessions will cost you double," Klim replied, again, seriously.

Lera found this difficult. When, after the first ten minutes of socializing, her interlocutor hadn't smiled even once, she started losing interest in him. Boring people with serious miens stressed her out, and Klim turned out to be one of them.

"Mom, could I go to the bedroom?" Petya asked, tugging gently on Olga's sleeve.

"Don't you want to have tea with us?"

"No thank you."

"Well, run along then."

"How about we have some tea and go for a walk in the park? Why should the kid be cooped up in here, when the weather's so beautiful today?" Lera suggested. "Klim, will you join us?"

"I don't really feel like it, but I'll consider the proposal over tea."

"Well, I think it's a great idea," Olga said. "I'll go get Petya dressed, and you two stop being so formal with each other. You sound like a teacher and a student." She left the kitchen.

Lera sat looking at Klim, not knowing what to talk about. She could find common ground with anybody, usually, but she sensed some sort of barrier in him, and she just couldn't find the right key to unlock that door.

"Well, should we get a little friendlier then?" she asked, breaking the silence.

"But we haven't even drunk to brotherhood yet," Klim replied skeptically, shrugging his shoulders.

"So what's stopping us? Too bad I didn't bring a bottle of wine with me, but we have tea!"

He cheered up unexpectedly. "It's unusual, but let's try it."

They stood up and, crossing arms with cups in hand, took a gulp each. Klim put his cup down on the table, hugged Lera tight, and gave her a most genuine, penetrating kiss on the lips.

It was so unexpected, that despite her combative mood, she was at a complete loss. "Oh-ho!" she blurted out, trying to compose herself as quickly as possible. "Well, after a kiss like that, we're definitely on friendly terms."

"Tell Olga later," he said, licking his lips, "about what a good kisser I am. She's probably forgotten."

"What, are things that bad?"

"Let's not get into that." He stood up from the table. "Let's go for that walk. We'll buy some beer and warm our bones in the sun, while we still can." On his way out of the kitchen, he ran the palm of his hand over the rear pocket of her jeans, and gave what was under it a light squeeze.

Lera, who always reacted to this kind of thing with embarrassment, just smiled at the jerk. *Your idea*, she thought to herself, *so deal with it.*

The park stretched in full autumn splendor. Petya ran along ahead and furrowed through the rustling, golden maple leaves with his feet. Those still left on the trees were imbued with the St. Petersburg autumn sun, so that the entire park seemed alight with an amazing, warm glow.

Lera walked along, inhaling the fragrance of the fallen leaves, wondering whether there was any point in telling Olga about what had happened in the kitchen in her absence.

Klim had gone to the store for some beer, and though Olga had said she didn't want any, he bought three bottles anyway, saying that if she didn't change her mind, he'd drink it himself. The idea of buying his son a juice never even crossed his mind.

"The weather is beautiful, isn't it?" Lera asked, trying to diffuse the tension.

"Yes, it's been just miraculous lately," Olga replied, nodding at Lera inquisitively, looking surreptitiously in Klim's direction.

Lera only shrugged her shoulders in response.

"So, Olga," Klim interjected unexpectedly, without having seen their silent exchange. "What do you say I take another wife, like they do in the East? We'll divide the sex, draw up a timetable. You'll be the elder, favorite wife!" He looked steadily at Olga, but she wasn't smiling. "Or are you against it? Maybe you've been planning on getting a second husband? You just say the word, and we'll consider everything together."

Lera butted in. "But male harems aren't in style yet, and they could put you behind bars for polygamy."

"Oh," he said. "That doesn't scare me. Even if they wanted to put me behind bars, they wouldn't."

"How can you be so certain?"

"I'm insured against it," he joked, mysteriously. "What about you, Lera, would you agree to marry me? What's so bad about me? I make money—not a lot, of course—and my virility's intact."

"So, if I'm following you here, we're talking about filling a vacancy for a second wife, right?" Lera specified.

"That's exactly right."

Seeing Olga's face suddenly pale, she decided to turn the whole thing into a joke. "Well, if you get permission from your first wife, I can send in my résumé and recommendations from my previous husbands." She laughed and poked Olga in the side. "Earth to Olga! It'll be more fun as a threesome. I'll help you with Petya, and I've been told my cooking's not so bad."

"No, no, I'm fine," Olga finally said. "I'm just trying to figure out where we could fit another bed into our tiny apartment. And we can't move in to Lera's place. I mean, she lives with her parents."

"Well, ladies," said the tipsy Klim, putting his arms around both of them. "You two figure out the living conditions, and I'll handle the financial considerations."

"Is there enough money for a new apartment?" Olga suddenly quipped.

Evidently, her question hit Klim where it hurt, because he immediately grew gloomy and sat down on the nearest bench. "You really know how to take the wind of my sails, dear. Just 'Bam!' and it's gone."

It seemed he'd gotten completely drunk on just one bottle of beer. "You know what, girls? You go on ahead, and I'll just sit here. For some reason, I feel like being alone for awhile."

"Come on, let's go," Olga said, shoving the bewildered Lera forward. "It's better not to say anything when he's like this."

"What a basket case," Lera said, once they were out of earshot. "Listen, I'm even more afraid for you now. Olga, can't you see he's going crazy, because you two haven't had sex for such a long time. He might even suspect something. Why did he suddenly bring up that second husband thing?"

"I don't know."

"God, I'm afraid to leave you two alone. Do you think maybe you should move in with your parents first? Later, when he calms down a little, you can move in with Vlad. In the meantime, he could rent an apartment. I can't even imagine you living in his fourteen-square-meter room, with two kids. And there's nowhere for you to take the baby on the Liteiniy. It's such a dismal place."

"I've already thought of that, but the thing is, my mom doesn't know anything about this. She's so square, always going on about keeping the family together."

"Oh, come on, you know you can tell your mom everything. After all, she's *your* mother, not your husband's. She should understand. You're such a fraidy cat, honestly!"

"I'll tell her, and my dad, too. I have tomorrow off, so I'll go see them in Siverskaya first thing in the morning. I'll catch the train at Baltiytskiy Station. I could just go with Vlad, by car, but I'd rather prepare them first. How's he doing, by the way? He called yesterday, and said he'd spent the day at your place."

"He's all right, and I'm getting married, by the way," said Lera, changing the subject. "And not to your Klim, either. I'm going to be the 'first-and-only' wife of a reasonably educated and unreasonably nice journalist!" she boasted. "We're going to apply for the license tomorrow morning."

"That's some news! And you kept it to yourself!"

"How could I not when I only thought of it last night!"

"What do you mean, 'thought of it'?"

"I said, 'marry me if you want, and don't marry me if you don't.' And he went and agreed to marry me. So, he must want to!" She burst out laughing.

"Oh, Lera, you're crazy! Is the guy good-looking, at least?

"Seems pretty good."

"Will you invite me to the wedding?" Olga's mood improved noticeably after the news.

"Do you think I wouldn't?"

Petya ran up to them, sweaty from running around the park until now, and gave each of his 'mothers' a bouquet of maple leaves.

"This is for you, Mom," he said, handing Olga the bigger of the two. "And this is for my godmother, and this—"He slid a single leaf into Olga's coat pocket. "—is for my sister. Happy Women's Day!" He laughed.

The girls started laughing too.

"You're a clever one!" Lera said, patting her godson on the head. "You've given us March 8th in October! What a little man you have growing here, Olga. Appreciate it! With a kid like him, you don't have to be afraid of anything!"

Petya smiled and ran back off to play.

"You see?" said Olga. "He never even asked where his dad went, as though he didn't exist for him."

"I do see." Lera decided to keep quiet about the kiss in the kitchen, after all, so as not to scare Olga even more. He'd obviously only done it out of jealousy and spite.

Chapter 22

Klim sat there on the bench, alone, giving off so much negative energy, I realized immediately that I couldn't deal with this on my own. Humans called that kind of thing "reaching one's boiling point." A lot of emotion seethed in this closed person. He'd sat in the same pose for over an hour, after his 'wives' had already gone to their respective homes. Having polished off the third bottle of beer, Klim got himself another and went back to the same bench.

It seemed he wasn't in any hurry to get home, and I still had time to discuss everything with my boss. That evening, though, one of us, and preferably both, had to stay with Olga—to help in case the deceived husband finally blew a gasket.

"Hi, Peace, you flying off?" said a little voice, which I recognized as F-12161998. "I've spent an entire twenty-four hours with the girls. It was so much fun! We celebrated one of our girlfriend's birthday, and there was so much dancing! If I had legs, they'd probably be aching right now."

"I figured you didn't end up visiting your dad after all. Okay, I have things to do right now, so you can tell me later who was born and to whom."

"See you later. I'll be waiting for you!"

I reached out to Elias, and he agreed to meet me in half an hour at our usual spot.

He was late, again, and he was all disheveled. His wings were dusty and he looked around absent mindedly.

"Is everything okay, Boss?"

"I wouldn't say so."

"Did something happen?"

"Oh, Peace, you're too little for me to share these things with you. Let's just say that love is a complicated affair, and it makes you as sad as it does happy."

"Can angels really fall in love?"

"What makes us so different from people? Immortality and the fact that we have wings? Of course, we can fall in love! And I fell in love, too."

"What about her?"

"Her?"

"Well, yes, your beloved...."

"Peace, my dear Peace," Elias said, and sighed heavily. "If only it were a 'her.'" He paused as if perhaps considering if he should say more. "Some things are too complicated. Let's just say, my choice will never be approved. We have to keep our love a secret, because it might provide a reason for us to be suspended from being angels. I trust you, my friend, to keep this between us." He shrugged and said, "So, what did you want to talk to me about? Let's get down to business."

"I wanted to ask you to stay with me today at Klim and Olga's place. I'm having terrible presentiments."

"What? Did my message to Vladimir produce no effect?" he asked, gloomily.

"Only in that, the next day, he took the trolleybus when he went out. Also, he didn't see Olga this weekend."

"Idiot!" Elias blurted out wholeheartedly, but then cut himself off. "Again, you didn't hear that, right?"

"Hear what?" I smiled.

"Are you inclined to trust your premonitions?" he asked. "Have they ever been wrong?"

"Let's just say that if I'd paid attention to them earlier, I wouldn't be here right now."

"Right. Well, let's go then. I've got other pressing matters, but I suddenly feel the call of duty," he said with a wink.

This was our first flight together. I felt as excited and enthused as a puppy when the angel spread his enormous wings, flapped them, and a little cloud of fine down feathers formed around them. Then we flew for a long time. The flight with Elias was nothing like the flights I took on my own. I did it a lot quicker alone, whereas this was a real process! With every flap of his wings, I felt a wave of warm air envelop me, and little particles of down drifted all around us, like snow, or like when it's molting season. I didn't know the same thing happened with angels.

I decided it was probably a result of unhappy love, and was terribly curious as to the object so worthy of his attention, and why things were coming together in a way that made my boss unhappy. More to the point: why *weren't* things coming together? Alas, for a soul to pry into an angel's affairs seemed indecent, somehow, so I decided not to.

Elias and I acted like real spies, in our own private spy game.

In the kitchen of Olga and Klim's apartment, the light was on, one pane of the window leaned open, and we decided to observe from the outer windowsill of the second. Having looked in and seen that somebody moved about the kitchen, Elias listened in and gave me a sign to do the same.

With the sound of pouring water and the clattering of dishes, a dish suddenly broke. We moved in closer to the window as Olga swept up the shards of a broken plate. She seemed nervous, because she kept chewing her lip, a habit I'd noticed previously. A big butcher knife lay on the table, alongside a raw chicken, by now oblivious to its fate.

I couldn't say Olga was in the kitchen alone, as F-12161998, happy with life, sat on her shoulder, horsing around and taking a lock of hair from behind her mother's ear. Olga couldn't understand why it kept falling into her eyes, no matter how many times she put it behind her ear. Finally, she washed her hands, left the kitchen, and returned with a bobby pin in her hair.

F-12161998 looked insulted.

"It doesn't seem like anything's going on," Elias said, turning to me. "And is that sweet little thing on her shoulder your girlfriend?"

"She's not my girlfriend. We just talk sometimes," I replied, suddenly embarrassed.

"Sure, sure," Elias said. He flashed a cunning smile, and seemed a little more cheerful.

I looked down now and felt uneasy, as Klim approached the front door, drunk, with a bottle in his hand. A black cloud, generated by his pent-up negative sentiment, hung low over his head, threatening to burst into a downpour any second.

"Here comes our hero," Elias said, having seen him at the same time as me. "Shall we prepare for 'Operation Catch Him by Surprise'?" He started to laugh, but only for a second, then wiped the smile off his face and sighed. "Okay, that's enough. I have to be serious now. After all, I'm a guardian angel! That's a huge responsibility, you know. If anything happens on my watch, they can suspend me for negligence."

"Really? They can suspend you?"

"Just like that!"

"And what does a suspended guardian angel do with his time?"

"He becomes a simple mortal, same as that idiot with the cloud over his head," Elias said, clapping his hand over his mouth. "I just can't control my language. Sorry."

"Don't worry about it, Boss. I don't repeat bad language, or even remember it."

"Good." He looked at me with fatherly tenderness again.

That second, Klim came into the kitchen.

"Hi, Lala!" he said to Olga, loudly. "What's for dinner tonight? Chicken?"

Olga grew cold and stiff as a wax sculpture. The knife she was going to use to cut up the chicken froze in midair. Vlad was the only one who called her Lala.

Klim only ever called her Olga, or simply "wife." He never used any tender nicknames.

He knows. He knows everything! she thought.

Her heart started pounding so loudly, she was sure Klim could hear it, too.

In a single second, it seemed as though all her physical processes had stopped, except for one pulsating thought: *What's going to happen now?*

How good it was that she'd put Petya's Chip and Dale's "Hurry to the Rescue" on for him in the other room, and that for the next twenty minutes he wouldn't be coming into the kitchen. The door was closed, too, so he wouldn't hear the fight.

Terrible thoughts continued to run through her head. *Should I pretend I didn't understand what he meant? Tomorrow, while he's at work, I'll pack our things and leave.*

Though really scared, she summoned up the courage to turn and face her husband.

Klim looked at her with a drunken, scornful gaze that didn't bode well at all.

"Chicken," she answered, trying to control herself. "Oven-roasted, just how you like it."

"A good wife always tries to please her husband, if she doesn't want him to take on another one," said the drunken Klim, noisily pushing away two stools and sitting down on a third. "Right, Lala?" he repeated, even louder than before, as though challenging her to a duel.

Tears formed in Olga's eyes, as did a lump in her throat. She put the knife down on the table and sat on one of the stools.

"Why did you call me that?" she asked, quietly, raising her eyes to his.

"No reason. Don't you like it?" His speech slurred.

"No, I don't," she said, more quietly still.

"Really?" he blurted out, and slammed his fist down on the table. "I think you do."

"Do you know everything?" she asked, almost crying. "How? Who told you?"

Elias and I sat behind the window, ready, like Chip and Dale, to come to the rescue at any minute. True, we didn't have a plan, but I believed in my boss. After all, it could be no accident that in Ancient Greek, his name meant 'my God.' This rather strange angel had become just that kind of indisputable figure of authority for me.

We could see F-12161998 snuggle up to her mother's neck and hide under her hair. She was scared, too.

"Who told me?" Klim repeated her question with a smile, and then fell silent for about a minute. The tension mounted, until he finally revealed the truth. "Nobody, I figured it out myself. You know, that's all you can think about, somehow, when your wife hasn't let you have any sex for six months. You think it's easy for a guy?"

Lowering her eyes, Olga stared silently at the uncut chicken, and at that moment, she seemed like a negligent student being lectured by the school principal.

"It's not easy," he answered his own question. "And it's even harder to find out that it's not just because she has a headache, but because our Lala," he said, clenching his teeth, "is busy doing it with somebody else!" He was just about shouting by the end of the sentence.

"Klim, I'm begging you, don't—"

"Don't what?" he asked, purposely raising his eyebrows theatrically. "You mean... *I'm* the one being sleazy?"

"You're drunk. Let's talk about this after you've sobered up a little. We'll figure out how to go on living now. We should've done it long ago. It's just that I don't want to talk you right now, while you're *unsteady.*"

"But I don't want to wait until I'm *steady!* I'm tired of being steady, and I want to discuss everything now, while I'm drunk. I'm tired of waiting. Understand? I'm tired of waiting!" He stood up abruptly and reached for her.

Olga jumped back.

"Where are you going?" He grabbed Olga's house dress with his right hand, and with his left hand he swept the chicken, the cutting board, and the knife off the table with one movement. It all went crashing loudly to the floor. "I want my wife, too, and I'm legally entitled to it." He tore Olga's dress off her shoulders and, trying to set her on the table, put his hand on her naked breasts.

"Don't, Klim! I'm begging you, don't!" Olga cried now.

We needed to act right away, so in a split second, Elias shot into the room where Petya sat enjoying his cartoon.

"Petya," he said, "run into the kitchen right away. Your mom's in trouble!"

On seeing the angel, the kid opened his mouth in amazement, but without saying a word, he jumped off the chair, opened the door and ran out of the room. The words "your mom's in trouble" had impacted him immediately.

"Mom, Mom, are you sick?" he yelled, running into the kitchen and seeing his dad, bent over his mom who, for some reason lay on the kitchen table naked.

"Petya!" she yelled, and pulled her dress together. "Petya, dear, come in here. Want some milk? Or a cookie?" Olga's voice shook, knowing the boy's appearance on the scene had saved her.

On seeing his son, Klim instantly cut short his actions and left the kitchen in silence, giving Petya a hard smack on the head on his way out.

Petya started crying silently.

"Don't cry, my sweetheart," Olga said. "Everything's all right. Your dad's just drunk. He doesn't know what he's doing."

"I don't want a dad like him!" the boy blurted out in an injured tone. "Let's go over to Vlad's. He's kind and nice!"

"Okay, we'll go. I'll call him right now and he'll pick us up." She wiped her tear-stained face with the sleeve of her robe, and started dialing Vlad's number on her mobile.

"But, Mom, where did the guy with the huge wings like a bird's, only longer, come from?" Petya asked.

"What guy with wings, sweetheart? What are you talking about?" asked his mom absent-mindedly, not having calmed down yet.

"He probably flew in through the window, but I didn't see it. And then he told me you were in trouble and that I had to run into the kitchen."

"Petya, dear, I don't understand what you're saying," she said. "Guys with wings are only in the movies."

The little boy shrugged his shoulders and waved his hand dismissively. "Grownups never believe kids. Just like Svante's mom and dad didn't believe he had a friend named Karlsson, even though he did!"

"Do you have a flying friend, too?" Olga smiled kindly, looking at the boy's injured and insulted face. "Tell me about him. I'll believe you."

"That's what I'm trying to do," Petya pleaded.

Just then, her beloved's voice came at the other end of the line, and she broke off her conversation with Petya.

"Vlad, Sweetheart, I don't think it's safe for us to stay here tonight. Can you get a cot for Petya? How soon can you come and pick us up? Okay, we'll be waiting for you at the gate of the park in half an hour. No, don't drive up front. Klim's hanging around there. No, nothing happened. Things just finally came to a head."

Petya didn't return to the topic of the angel.

Olga threw the things she couldn't do without into a couple of bags, and grabbed their toothbrushes. Then, thinking she should probably leave a note, she picked up a pen and a piece of paper and, remembering Lera's advice, considered writing that her knight in shining armor had arrived, and she couldn't turn him down. This wasn't the time for jokes, though, so she wrote the first thing that came into her head, threw on her coat, and dressed Petya in his jacket and hat.

Then, holding hands, she and her son went outside.

"I'm free," she said out loud. "I'm finally free."

Her future daughter's soul sat proudly on her neck, wiggling from side to side like a little kid on his father's shoulders. When F-12161998 saw me on the windowsill, she smiled and waved.

That second, I saw her as a two-year-old, with her dad's big blue eyes and her mom's blonde hair — such an enchanting little girl! I waved back at her, but had no idea how she was seeing me.

Meanwhile, Elias walked on the other side of the window of the now empty apartment, cleaning up. Like a real, conscientious guardian angel, he swept the crumbs off the table, which Petya had left after his snack. He picked the chicken up off the floor, put it in the fridge, and put the knife and the cutting board in the sink.

I flew in through the little air vent while he read aloud the note Olga had left on the table. "We haven't been a family since way before I met someone else. We can't be together anymore. Forgive me. Don't look for us." Elias shook his head and added his own words. "You've never been a family. He always thought only of himself."

We flew out at that moment, and soared over the 'knight in the yellow Zhiguli' from Liteiniy. He drove along deserted avenues of the city to pick up his family. He'd tucked driver's license, no longer expired, into the right chest pocket of his jacket.

We then changed direction, and flew back along a different route— through downtown St. Petersburg—and ended up over St. Isaac's Cathedral. Bronze, five-ton angels lined the enormous, shining cupola.

Elias stood beside the sculptures, obviously deciding to compare himself to one of them. "Is there a resemblance?"

"I think there might be," I replied, uncertainly.

"There *might* be?" Elias snorted. "They were modeled after me!" He literally puffed up with pride.

"Really? Wow!"

"I'm kidding, you naive little soul." He laughed, pleased to have sucked me in. "Not after me—after my father! He just happened to be flying over St. Petersburg, and he injured his wing. That very second, the architect Montferrand was walking by, saw him, and said, 'Let me immortalize you.' Where could my father go? He couldn't fly any farther. So, while he was healing his wing, he posed for a certain German sculptor."

"Oh, wow!"

"Boy, are you ever gullible! I just made all that up!" Elias burst out laughing. "Angels don't have parents. We don't come into the world the way humans do."

"Then how?"

"It's too soon for you to know that." He pinched my freckled nose—freckled in *his* eyes, anyway.

"Elias, so what will our new assignment be?" I asked, deciding to change the awkward topic as soon as possible.

"My dear Peace," he said, suddenly turning solemn. "In view of your outstanding work, I've decided not to give you any new assignments for the time being. Consider yourself on a well-deserved leave. As soon as I need you, I'll let you know. However, I beg you to pay regular visits to Masha, Olga, and Vladimir, and if you feel that some intervention is required, it's imperative you let me know, like you did today."

"And I can do whatever I like?" I specified carefully.

"Can you give me a hint?" He smiled paternally.

"I'd like to spend more time with Lera, the girl that could've been my mom."

"You're a masochist, Peace." His smile had vanished.

"So, can I?" I asked again, not knowing the meaning of the new word he used.

"How can I forbid it? If that's what makes you happy, so be it."

I flew around my boss three times and kissed him on the cheek. "Thanks!"

"Fly away, dear, and good luck!" he shouted after me, as I took off to answer the call of my feelings. "And good luck to me, too," he mumbled to himself, perhaps thinking I didn't hear it.

Chapter 23

Lera read the responses to her virtual confession on the online forum, of which there were many, all of them different. Somebody said that the sufferings of the Lost Soul seemed phony, as though she didn't want that baby at all, and why compare herself now to a vase.

I got comfortable on the back of Lera's head and familiarized myself with some of the opinions.

> *My dear, where was your head when you went to bed with the guy you were in the dead-end relationship with? You should've gotten a priest's benediction first, and gotten married, whereas you lived in sin and killed an innocent soul. Go to a church, repent, and God will forgive you, but your sin will stay with you, regardless. You'll have to live with it for the rest of your life! What were you so afraid of? So many mothers raise kids on their own! They haven't committed the sin of killing the soul of a child, sent by God.*

I could see how difficult it was for Lera to read that comment. She'd already regretted putting her feelings out there for all to see and judge. It had been signed 'Mother N.,' apparently a rather pious person.

The next comment was of a completely different nature, from a longtime participant in the forum, who went by 'Bora-Bora.'

> *Don't punish yourself for what you did. There's no reason to do that. You're better off thinking about carrying on with your life, avoiding the same mistake. Find yourself a Real Man who, even if your relationship reaches a dead end, wouldn't send a woman to get an abortion in the first place, and second, wouldn't abandon his child later. That's what happened to me. My boyfriend and I split up, but he registered the child as his, gives us financial support, and comes to visit the boy. He's*

already got another family, and even though I still haven't met the right man, I'm grateful to him for not having insisted I have an abortion. If it had been up to me alone, I may not have decided to go through with the pregnancy. Now I just can't imagine not having my son.

'Augusta' offered some comforting words.

My husband didn't want a second child and I stupidly had an abortion. And, just like you, I couldn't understand afterwards why I'd done it. I suffered, and hated my husband, but the pain went away when I had another baby. Now I have a daughter whom I love very much. I think if I hadn't had the abortion, I wouldn't have had this child. Or maybe the soul of that first child lives on in this one.

'Martha' attacked one of the other commenters.

Dear Mother N.! Devoutly pious people like you really enjoy nailing everybody else to the cross (pardon the pun). Judging someone else's actions is easy, and you should walk a mile in their shoes first instead of spouting platitudes like 'God provides the child and for the child.' Orphanages are packed with abandoned kids! And there are so many children being found in garbage dumps! Isn't it better to go to a doctor in time than to despise the fetus in your uterus and sentence it to a similar fate, having secured yourself, as you choose to say, from sin? 'Lost Soul' is devastated enough without people like you, kicking her when she's down. Do you think your talk of killing an innocent soul make things easier for her? No. So why cause her more grief? I'm sure she'll never do it again anyway.

A long catfight ensued between 'Mother N.' and 'Martha.' Mother N. kept repeating the same things, whereas Martha tried to maintain the voice of reason.

Lera decided not to get involved in their polemic and not to write any more in order not to fuel the fire, and simply read some of the other responses to her post.

'Sunkissed' wrote as if from the voice of reason, or perhaps even training.

> *There are almost no questions in your story, so I can only conclude that you simply needed to get things off your chest. And don't count on 'nothing' ever being more painful than this. There will be more hard times. Forums are for people to express what they can't bring themselves to say out loud. 'Unburdening the soul' this way is normal, but you may need to get more off your chest and have a good cry. If you're not a believer, turn to your girlfriends, or a psychologist. If you believe, go to church. Life will go on. Have a baby. You must get through this stage, seeing as the damage is done. Don't get married right now, but you do have to move forward. You've taken yourself in hand, and you can smile at people. That's great, but you must let yourself cry and grieve a little, too. All in all, I wish you strength.*

'Nastasya' really hit home with her message.

> *Your pain will diminish over time, but what will always be with you, invisibly, is your unborn's soul. In my view, the period of mourning after such a loss isn't the best time for marriage. Until you own your situation and let it go, you won't be able to have a normal relationship with a man, because you'll subconsciously drag into it your personal feelings of guilt, and your trauma. Accepting what happened and getting it out of your system usually takes about a year. Then you'll be able to figure things out: what you want, where to go, which road to take, and with whom. I hope you survive this complicated but important, period without destroying yourself. After all, what lies ahead of you is becoming a wife and mother, and the baby you're waiting for would do well to have a mother who's not destroyed. Otherwise, you could get stuck on the unborn child for much too long.*

Nastasya's message surprised me. It was as though people knew about us somehow. The last sentence was a little insulting. Why not get stuck on that baby? After all, I was stuck on that mom. After I thought about it, though, I chastised myself for being egotistic. I didn't want Lera to feel the least bit bad.

The message from 'Sleepless' was harsh.

It's the fashion, now, to stand on every corner, screaming about bloody murders and how you're supposed to suffer after an abortion. Read less bullshit, I'm telling you. It's all only medical manipulation. Twenty years ago, practically all women went through it, and two or three days later, they were out there building Socialism, laying railroad tracks, and raising the kids they already had. All the moralists who step out here, having avoided abortions, denied life to a dozen kids by means of pills, IUD's, and other forms of birth control. I figure, everybody's the boss of their own psyche. If you want to suffer, go ahead, and if not, you have to forget about it and carry on in happiness, of which there's a real shortage here.

A wise response from 'Pipette' came next.

'Lost Soul,' my advice might seem funny to you. Take any vase, wash it out thoroughly, put some earth in it, and plant a seed, like a sunflower seed, for instance, and water it every day. When a little shoot appears, try to imagine it's your life, filling with meaning. I've materialized the image you described, so that you'll understand that if the vase is empty, but not broken, it's not over yet! Don't get me wrong. A seed is not necessarily a new life. It could be new love, or a new interest. Occupy yourself with something interesting, and stop ruminating about the past. Just take what you've gone through as an obligatory experience. Live in the present and build your future. It's not worth destroying yourself over someone who was just a passerby in your life.

Judging by their tags, the authors of the last two responses might have been men. The first came from 'Oracle.'

Maybe the soul of your baby really is right beside you. So, no wonder you can feel its presence. If I were you, I'd take advantage of the situation and beg for its forgiveness.

The last comment, short and to the point, was perhaps the most 'constructive.' It came from somebody called 'Potapy.'

It's all bull. The important thing is that your outfit fits!

Lera couldn't help but smile when she read that. Oh yes... where, besides the internet, could you see, as though behind glass, so many different people? All it took was to read a couple of sentences, and you could already paint a picture of their author. Lera tried to imagine each person behind their pseudonym. All these people, one way or another, were anything but indifferent to her problem, and tried to help with their advice — even 'Mother N.'

Lera didn't do it often, but she had gone to church a few times for confession. She even had her own confessor, Father Igor, who looked exactly like Santa Claus, except in a cassock.

When she'd visited him recently, the elderly priest with human insight had listened to everything the Servant of God, Lera, told him during confession, without spouting any of the hackneyed truths that Mother N. had showered her with in the forum.

Having familiarized ourselves with the opinions of strangers, Lera and I got ready for bed. Well, she did, while I flitted around her like a lovesick young boy, incapable of tearing my eyes away from the object of my worship. I couldn't read her thoughts, but from the expression on her face, it was obvious she was contemplating what she'd read.

While Lera brushed her teeth, her phone rang. It was Artem, who wanted to know when, exactly, they were going to apply for the marriage license. She suggested they go to the registry office near the Tavrichesky Garden.

"In my opinion," she said, "it's nice and cozy. A girlfriend of mine got married there this year. It's a small, non-binding kind of place," she joked. "And it's a palace! But...." She paused for a moment. "You know what? Let's wait a couple of weeks."

It seemed that some of the online advice had caused her to contemplate quite a bit.

"Aren't you sure about our decision?" Artem said, audibly distressed. "We can think about it after we apply for the license, too, you know. And then, in case of anything, we just don't show up."

"Well, no, if we're going to register, then we're going to go."

"All right, whatever you say. So, in two weeks?" The bridegroom seemed prepared to wait.

"Without fail!"

Lera had decided not to *hurry* to get married, to take a little 'timeout' instead, in order to figure out her feelings.

Before going to sleep, she stood in front of the mirror for a few minutes. The room was fairly dark, illuminated only by an orange wall lamp. The light gave one the impression of being in a fairytale cave, with a fire in it. I sat on Lera's neck and, if I hadn't been invisible, she would've seen my reflection.

"Hey!" she suddenly said, staring into the world behind the looking glass. "If you're really here, then please forgive me! I'm such a cowardly idiot."

I was so overwhelmed with happiness that I stuck to her face like Play-Dough. "Come on, Mom, stop. Just be happy. I'm right here."

Lera sighed deeply, got into bed, and turned out the light.

Chapter 24

Olga cleaned up Vlad's room while he was out. She and Petya had taken the day off because the boy's kindergarten was too far away from their new place. He helped with the dusting, and watered Vlad's two plants.

He and his mom pulled a stack of dusty old magazines from under the couch, put them in big garbage bags, and set out to throw them in the garbage. The trashcans were in the inner courtyard, and it took a while to reach them in this old building, with its winding system of courtyards. To people unaccustomed to living downtown, it evoked a feeling of terror, since it looked like the Leningrad Blockade. There was a kind of uncanny sense of devastation about the place, the only thing suggesting the passage of time since the war being the graffiti all over the tattered walls.

When Olga and Petya got back to the apartment, their neighbor, Nina Vasilyevna, greeted them at the door, having just returned from her grocery shopping. "Hello, Olga!" She seemed happy to have bumped into them. "Oh, and Petya's come along! Are you here for good?"

"Hello, Nina Vasilyevna! Yes, this time it's for good. We finally decided to move in. All we have to do now is get our things out of the old apartment."

"Well, that's excellent! I'm very happy you're going to be living here now, because the place is full of people, but there's nobody to talk to. Come by for a cup of tea. I have some books Petya would like, somewhere, that belonged to my daughter. I'll look for them today."

"Okay, Nina Vasilyevna, we'll definitely drop by. Thanks for thinking of us! And you come by our place, too."

They all went into the apartment and off to their respective rooms, which sat opposite each other across the narrow corridor.

A young student couple rented the room by the front door. They were quiet and modest. After finishing their studies at the art institute, they constantly painted something, and only rarely came out, to put the kettle on or boil some dumplings.

Another tiny room down the corridor was occupied by a woman about fifty years old, along with her twenty-five-year-old daughter. They'd already been on the list, and had been "temporarily" living out of their suitcases for the past quarter of a century, waiting to get their own apartment from the government. It was about time the girl started a family of her own, and here she was, still sleeping on top of a wardrobe, which she used a stepladder. During the day, after her mother left for work, she'd bring over a young man, and they had such noisy sex that Nina Vasilyevna, unable to tolerate it, would knock on their wall. Over the course of many years, the girl's mother had refused to contribute financially to the general affairs of the apartment, insisting that, as only temporary residents, they'd be moving out any day now.

Next door to the 'dreamer' lived an alcoholic couple, Vasya and Galya. Nobody could leave a pot of food on the stove, or those two would take it to their room and eat everything.

Two adjoining rooms had been locked up for some time. They belonged to a man who was in prison, serving ten years for murdering a former female neighbor. She had tormented the rest of the tenants to no end with her horrible personality, and it had cost her.

The apartment hadn't changed much since then, but luckily, there hadn't been any loud fights for a long time. On the night before the neighbor's release from prison, a particularly argumentative couple finally moved into their own apartment, and give their room to some quiet young people. When they left, everybody breathed a sigh of relief.

The kitchen, corridor, toilet, and bathroom had needed renovating for a long time, but none of the above-mentioned tenants showed the initiative in getting things done. Having started a second family, Vlad's father had bought him his room in the apartment over ten years ago, to get his then twenty-three-year-old, good-for-nothing son out of his hair. Vlad's mother had died of a stroke, when he was fifteen.

Olga never dreamt she'd end up in this situation with two children, but there was no other way. The apartment she'd shared with Klim belonged to his cousin, who worked out of the country, and once she and Klim were divorced, she wouldn't be able to count on anything. Vlad was her only means of support now. Knowing how he'd been drifting through life, she was worried about their future together, afraid of drowning in poverty once that baby was born. She worked as a nurse in a hospital three days a week, back to back, in addition to finishing her studies at the Pediatric Academy.

As she worked to de-clutter the place, she came across some pictures of Vlad as a child. She sat down on the couch and started looking through them.

"Hi, Peace!" said F-12161998, having appeared so unexpectedly that she made me jump. "See what I'm going to look like? Just like him, since I'm supposed to look like my dad. Look, look!"

She literally grabbed one of the photos right out of her mother's hand, as I had during Lera's first ultrasound, and it fell onto the floor. Vlad was about four-years-old in the picture, a round-faced little kid with a toy tucked under his arm, with blond hair and eyes that took up half his face. His eyes were so unnaturally large that he looked like an oversized doll.

Olga bent down to pick up the picture, then called out. "Petya, come and have a look at Vlad, when he was about your age."

Petya was walking around with a spare automobile part he'd found in the room.

"Maybe your baby sister will take after him," Olga said.

"She'll be a beautiful little sister," he announced, knowingly, after looking at the photo.

"Yeah...." Olga sighed, dreamily.

Her cellphone rang in of the pocket of her coat hanging on the rack by the door. She took it out and looked at the call display, at which point an expression of sheer terror gripped her face. I could see she didn't want to take the call, but after a few rings, she answered nonetheless.

"Hello. Yes, hi. Don't shout at me," she said, trying to speak calmly. "No, we're not coming back. Did you read the note I left?" She paused after every sentence. "No, Klim, stop trying to manipulate me. I've heard you say too many times that if I ever left you, you'd either hang yourself, or shoot yourself. Now that I've left, and have been gone for over twelve hours, what do I hear? That you're alive! A person who wants to harm himself doesn't talk about it constantly, he just does it!" With those unexpectedly cruel words, she hung up.

She'd repeated what Lera had told her a week ago, though Olga had been horrified at the time. She looked down at her shaking hands.

I'd never heard her talk that way, and was filled with admiration. She'd clearly transformed herself.

"Mama, calm down, please. Calm down," Petya said as he patted her hair. "I love you."

"I love you, too." She kissed him on the forehead.

The phone started ringing again, but Olga didn't answer it. As it rang and rang, she grabbed her head with her hands, and sat in that pose, immobile, staring into space.

What the heck? Turn off the ringer already! I thought, sending it out to her.

Olga stretched out her arm, pressed a few buttons, and the incoming call fell silent, though the name 'Klim' kept flashing on the screen.

Having seen Olga's determination, I wasn't as worried about her. All she and Vladimir had to do now was get her things out of the apartment, and not let Klim ever find out where they lived—at least until he calmed down.

She said, "Petya, we're going to have to find you a kindergarten nearby. Let's go for a walk, and if we see one, we'll go in and check it out, okay?"

Petya nodded obediently and started getting dressed.

I accompanied mother and son to an amazing little yard, decorated with mosaics, and watched them head toward a two-story building with a fenced-in playground, full of children.

Olga walked through the gate and approached one of the attendants.

Now that Vlad's and Olga's tense situation had been decided, I headed out to Vasilevskiy Island to see Masha, and make sure she was okay, too.

Chapter 25

As I flew, I thought about how amazingly beautiful St. Petersburg was. In the six months that had elapsed since I'd set out to find my parents, I'd managed to study the city. What I loved most was its downtown core, with its network of rivers, their distinguishing architectural features, as reflected in the buildings, churches and cathedrals: Kazan, St. Isaac's, and St. Nicholas Naval.

I flew through the Summer Garden and the Field of Mars toward the Palace Square, to cut across the Neva in the direction of Vasilevskiy Island, when I noticed another bronze angel. I landed on his shoulder to get a better look at him. He stood on a tall pillar, alone and desolate. How could I not have noticed him before? From the expression on his face, it seemed he wanted to protect the entire city, but doubted his ability to do so. I wondered who had posed for the sculptor, then remembered the joke Elias had played on me, and I laughed, again, at my gullibility. Still, the sculptors were amazingly accurate in portraying angels.

Our world remained inaccessible to people, and very few ever saw their guardian angels—and only when they appeared to avert disaster. If only people believed in them! Many completely ignored the signs their guardian angels sent them. People could have avoided so many unpleasant, even tragic, events, if only they'd paid attention.

With these thoughts in mind, I arrived at the fourteenth line of Vasilevskiy Island, where Masha lived, and sat down in the open vent window of her apartment.

She was putting her textbooks and notebooks into her backpack, getting ready for school. Perhaps she'd overslept and missed a few lectures, as very few started after lunchtime, but she seemed perfectly calm. I could tell she wasn't going to change her mind about the decision she'd made.

M-07091999 saw me, flew over, and embraced me.

I didn't like that kind of affection. "Okay, that's enough now." I carefully extricated myself from the grateful little soul. "I'm on vacation and just monitoring events, and flew over to make sure you two are all right. So, tell me how you're doing, and I'll fly on."

"Everything's fine." M-07091999 hung in the air about a meter away from me. "I think Masha's calm. She doesn't talk to my dad anymore, but I think it's for the best. She decided not to tell him she's keeping the baby. He doesn't seem to care anyway."

"Don't worry, be happy!" I said, repeating the lyrics of a song I'd heard. "The main thing is that you're going to be born, against all odds. Even though your mom is sometimes led by her emotions, she's strong, and the important thing is that reason always wins in the end. Although, she probably doesn't realize it, right?"

"Right," the future second Van Gogh agreed, with a smile. "She thinks that, in my case, she followed her heart."

"Oh, those sunflowers!" I exclaimed, recognizing them from the store window. I flew over and sat right in the center of one of them, and beckoned M-07091999 to come and sit on the one beside mine. Given our weightlessness, the sunflowers didn't even quiver.

"They've been here ever since that day," he said, still grinning. "They boost my mom's self-confidence. I look at them all the time and try to imagine the painting you 'hung' on the wall of the lab on the day that decided my fate."

"Why imagine it? Just look on the internet for Van Gogh's 'Sunflowers.'"

"I don't even know what 'the internet' is."

"Your mom doesn't use a computer?"

"She does, and pretty often, but mostly just for typing. I've never even looked over her shoulder."

"You're so uninquisitive! I read everything Lera writes, and what people write back."

"You mean, the Lera that was with my mom at the doctor's? What are you even doing at her place? You're not allowed to be near her at all." M-07091999 waited with great interest for my explanation.

I realized I'd said too much, again, and grew flustered. "Well, it was only once. I was flying by and decided to visit, and there she was, sitting at the computer," I said, spinning the most implausible yarn, to dig myself out that hole, but only doing the opposite.

Luckily, the sight of Masha in the doorway putting on her running shoes distracted M-07091999.

"Okay, Peace, I'm out of here. Good luck, and thanks again! And don't worry about the Lera thing. I won't tell anybody! I could never blow the whistle on the one who saved my life!"

"Thanks."

I watched Masha and the soul of the future talented artist, who'd latched onto her blue-and-yellow checked backpack like a baby koala to its mother's back. When the door closed behind them, I flew out the window vent.

"11.11.1999... how cool!" Lera marveled. "It must be a sign." She wrote the date beside her last name, which she decided to keep as a souvenir.

"Taking your husband's surname is an anachronism," she announced, categorically, "but if you feel like taking mine, I don't object."

"No thanks," Artem said. "I'm used to Golubkov, and can't imagine myself as Vorobey."

"How funny!" Lera only now realized they both had surnames after birds: Artem was a pigeon, and she a sparrow. "Wouldn't it be fun if we used both? I'd be Golubkova-Vorobyeva! What a name. I'm craving breadcrumbs just thinking about it!" She laughed. "Which is a good point, by the way: sparrows are better at getting breadcrumbs than pigeons, and especially lovebirds. They're no good at it at all."

"When you put it that way, we clumsy pigeons definitely lose out to you nimble little sparrows." Artem shook his head.

Lera noted that over the past two weeks of nightly outings to the movies, or to visit friends, he seemed to have gotten used to her good-natured mockery, and even picked up a few things from her.

The young couple stood holding the piece of paper bearing the date of their solemn marriage: 24 December 1999.

"Catholic Christmas Eve," Lera noted. "By the way, are we going to celebrate the wedding, or will it be just the two of us, in jeans and sweaters, with wedding bands made of twist ties?"

"We'll probably celebrate, if we come up with the money," Artem said tentatively. "Are we even allowed to go to the Palace in casual clothes?"

"You can go to the Palace however you like. It's all nonsense!"

"Then let's order T-shirts saying exactly that, and wear carnival masks," Artem proposed. "If we're going to fool around, then let's do it right!"

"It'll be difficult for the staff to compare our faces to our passport pictures," Lera said, bringing a little empathy into the joke. "Although, that's their problem. Anyway, there's still time. We'll figure it out. Let's go to work now, before they call out the dogs. And not a word about this at the office! We'll go in separately, and tell everybody *after* we're married, so it will be a surprise."

They walked out onto Furshtatskaya and along the avenue. I could see Lera looking at Artem with great interest, as though studying him, examining his every facial feature.

She's getting acquainted. I chuckled.

Lera thought about how strange it was that this person walking next to her, though completely foreign to her, would soon be her husband.

Why am I taking this step? Why is he doing it? The stupid things we do in our lives. It's horrifying, especially because we know they're stupid, but we do them anyway.

"Tema," she said, tenderly, calling him that for the first time, as though he were a little boy. "Are you sure we're doing the right thing? Are we really going to come here on December 24th?"

"Where else is there to go? We're coming! Only first, I wanted to talk you into a *beta-test*."

"Into what?"

"It's when you have to make sure everything's working properly. For instance, new software goes through beta-testing. I suggest we do the same. I mean, what if we get married, and it turns out we're completely incompatible?"

"Are you talking about sex?"

"Well, yes, I am," he said, mildly embarrassed.

"But I thought we decided that would come later."

"That's an irrational decision."

Lera grew pensive—Artem's words were the voice of reason, and she couldn't argue with that.

"I'll think about it, okay? Once I've made up my mind, we'll pick a date, and you'll wait for me to come over after you've filled the bathtub with champagne and rose petals. Everything must work out beautifully. If, God forbid, there's a problem, at least we'll have something to remember. See what a great idea I've come up with?" she exclaimed, articulating the last sentence as though she were on the stage, expecting applause.

Artem laughed, though tensely. Obviously, he was afraid of the same thing, and maybe he'd even suggested the test for himself.

The future married couple walked into the metro. As a heavenly being, I didn't like that mode of transport very much, and decided to stay above ground.

Chapter 26

The days leading up to Lera and Artem's wedding whizzed by.

Elias still hadn't given me any new assignments, having chosen to handle things on his own, evidently. I'd only seen him a few times during the past month and a half, and he was always in a different mood: either euphoric, joking around a lot, telling me about all kinds of humorous situations based on his extensive work experience; or despondent, and practically uninterested in my reports about Masha, Olga, and Vlad. He could be consumed by his melancholy, to the point where he seemed completely absent, even though his strong, angelic body sat right there beside me, nodding its head. Something was going on with him, but I couldn't ask him about it directly. Luckily, nothing troublesome had happened to any of his charges during that interval.

Olga managed to get her things while Klim was away from home. She and Vlad loaded some of them into the trunk, some into the back seat, and drove it all back to their room. Despite having to live in a communal apartment, Olga was genuinely happy. She'd changed her phone number and filed for divorce, and they'd managed to do a little renovating in their room, making it cozy and clean. Even the little fir tree growing on the windowsill looked puffier.

Olga had also started convincing the neighbors to chip in for some renovations to the common areas: the kitchen, bathroom toilet, and corridor. A new, not indifferent person moved into the apartment, and even the alky Uncle Kolya stopped coming into the kitchen wearing only his underpants, feeling awkward before this sweet, intelligent young woman with the rounding tummy.

The soul of Olga and Vladimir's future daughter stayed always with her mom, usually sitting on her neck like a tiny monkey. The future parents already knew for sure they were having a girl, from the ultrasound. They were waiting for Olga's divorce to go through, so they could get married, and the civil court proceedings were scheduled for the end of December. Klim hadn't shown up for the preliminary hearing.

Masha also made regular visits to the doctor at the women's clinic and followed all the recommendations. She ate constantly and had gained a lot of weight; unaware of the real reason behind it, her classmates always teased her about her voracious appetite. She didn't want to tell "those hens," as she called them, *anything*, although she wouldn't be able to hide the fact much longer.

Her divorce from Kolya was finalized exactly one month after her visit to Dr. Zhigalov, and she swore she would never call her ex-husband again. It made me feel good to hear her talking to her baby every now and then, telling him all kinds of stories from her own childhood. Lera had told her she needed to communicate with the baby, and from that day on, Masha started doing so regularly, and even bought a book of fairytales so she could read them out loud.

M-07091999, always at her side, was in absolute bliss.

What cast a shadow over the situation was that Masha couldn't find a job, and she barely managed to get by with the odd translation work. Catastrophically short on funds, she sometimes had to ask her neighbors to lend her bus fare. Plus, she still suffered from violent morning sickness: while reading fairytales to her stomach, she'd suddenly have to run to the toilet and heave. She felt so bad that she'd started counting the days until it would all be over. The baby was due in the middle of May, and Masha kept telling herself it was "only another six months."

Elias would listen to my reports, considering them insignificant. "As long as there isn't a war," he concluded, with his intrinsic optimism, at the end of one of our rare meetings, after which, as was his custom, he slapped me amicably on the shoulder that only he could see.

"And how are you doing?" he suddenly asked. "Still hanging around at Lera's place?"

"Yeah." I frowned. "By the way, she's getting married tomorrow. Olga, Vlad, and Masha are invited. They'll all be chumming it up."

"A wedding is a good thing." Elias nodded his approval. "Maybe I should fly over for a piece of wedding cake, too. Just imagine it: everybody's dancing, and here I walk in, all in white! Do you know that joke?"

Elias knew a lot of jokes, and sometimes told them to me, mixing in funny stories from his personal life.

"Is it a joke about angels?" I asked.

"No, it's about a circus. I heard it from one of my charges, who's in jail with three more years to serve. I visited him recently."

"What did he do?"

"Nothing criminal. They set him up, and I wasn't there to help him, because of which I was given my 'final warning.' So now, if something serious happens, it's immediate dismissal."

"And then what?"

"And then it's come what may, my young friend. Dismissed angels are sent down to Earth, after their memory has been wiped out. You know those people they sometimes find, who don't remember anything about themselves, so they solicit the public's help in identifying them? Do you ever wonder where they come from? Well, a lot of them are former guardian angels. I even know one who's in the hospital right now. He can't say a single thing about himself. I want to help him, but I can't go and say, 'Hey, you're one of us!' Would he believe me? And what if he did? They wouldn't take him back, anyway. It really scares me to think about it, but that could be my fate, too." He sighed with chin in hand.

"But everything's fine right now! What could they dismiss you for?"

"Well, if one of my wards suddenly died, and I was supposed to save him, but didn't. Not long ago there was another bus crash, and they sent five angels down to Earth immediately! Some people were fated to die in that crash, while others were supposed to be saved, but their guardian angels were busy playing lotto again."

"Do you like playing lotto too, Elias?"

"No, Peace, I don't like socializing with the others very much. You can consider me an 'angel-phobe,'" he said, pushing away the lock of hair that constantly hung in his eyes.

"We're the same, that way," I revealed. "I don't enjoy socializing with my own kind, either. I prefer being alone. I had one friend, but he was born, and since then I've been on my own." I paused to think about it. "Haven't you ever had a friend?"

"I did, and still do, but everything's so complicated for us, Peace. It's not something I can explain briefly. What if, the minute you're born, they'll make me your guardian angel?" He said it as though he believed it. "And when you grow up, you and I will talk about everything. I'll fly in through your window somehow. You'll be an adult and you'll be scared, at first, and later, when I try to remind you about our acquaintanceship, you'll have an incredibly hard time believing it's true. You'll forget everything, when you're born, Peace. Absolutely everything!"

I got sad and just about started to cry, even though I already knew about all that. "Absolutely, positively everything?" I asked, just to be sure.

"Utterly!" He passes his hand across his chest, as though he were wiping a slate clean. "You'll remember a little for the first few days, then less and less every day."

"What kind of work is this, anyway?" I said. "They dismiss angels, erase their memory, send them down to Earth, and it's the same with newborns. It's tyrannical!" I was so outraged that I would've stamped my foot if I'd had one.

"It's not surprising," Elias responded, much more calmly than I. "Humans aren't supposed to know anything about what goes on up here. Imagine the kind of chaos there'd be in the world if they knew all our secrets! So, it's all good, it's all good...."

He trailed off, and I could see that his thoughts were already elsewhere.

"So, am I free for awhile?" I asked.

"Sure! Go ahead and fly to the four corners of the Earth, although I can see you're only interested in one. Where's the wedding going to be? If I happen to be in the neighborhood, I'll look in on things."

I told Elias the location of the Wedding Palace and the reception hall, where the friends and family would gather to give the newlyweds a proper sendoff.

He waved goodbye with his wings, but remained seated instead of hurrying off somewhere. It was all very unusual.

Chapter 27

Artem and Lera decided to spend the night before the wedding separately, in keeping with tradition. All this time, they'd been living together at Artem's rented apartment. The beta-test had been so successful, the bride-to-be quickly forgot about 'saving herself' until after the wedding. They'd come home from work together, gone to the movies, gotten to know each other's friends—as they say, there was no shadow of gloom. The step they'd taken might have been premature, but it was the right one.

On the morning of her wedding day, Lera started looking a lot more like a grown-up 'Valery.' One of her former classmates, who'd become a makeup artist and hairstylist, came over to Lera's parents' apartment and turned her into a wondrous beauty, with pearls in her hair, and the eyes of a vamp. All the same, she was still Lera, my Lera—the laughing girl in the rowboat on that sunny day in July, with curly red hair. The unusual makeup and festive hairstyle didn't change her essence.

"I could use a cognac right about now, to help me believe this is all for real!" she said, turning this way and that in front of the big mirror, getting high on her own reflection. "Is this really me? Some kind of a stranger beauty."

A car pulled up to the doorway for them, with two large wedding rings attached to the roof.

Outside, she frowned. "Oh my God, how tacky! And we begged them: just please... no rings!" Lera said to the driver, who shrugged his shoulders. "I know, I know, you can't just tear them off." She sighed. "Okay, so we'll keep the rings. Mom, Dad, get in!"

The guests all waited at the Wedding Palace, among them Masha, and not too far away from her, Olga, and beside her, Vlad, holding an enormous bouquet in his arms. Petya hid behind Olga's sheepskin coat, feeling shy amid so many unfamiliar people.

Artem had also arrived beforehand and, when the bride pulled up, he opened the door to the wedding car with a solemn expression on his face. Here, just as in the joke Elias didn't end up telling me, she stepped out of the car all in white! The groom took her by the hand, and the two of them walked inside.

Lera giggled the whole time, clearly amused by everything, as if observing the proceedings rather than participating in them.

Having gotten into the Palace, from which a couple had just emerged, I was struck by the mixture of totally different energies still lingering, both light and dark, the latter evidently given off by those who envied the happiness of others instead of sharing in it.

The parents of the newlyweds sat in the first row: Lera's mother and father, and Artem's mom alongside a tall gentleman with a mustache, who sat gazing at her lovingly. Behind them, the rest of the sharp-looking guests sat or stood, with flowers or without. The music started, and in walked the bride and groom, smiling and stately, along the carpet leading from the door. How young and beautiful they were!

I looked at them, trying to imagine what I would've been like, if they ended up being my parents—probably just as charismatic as Lera, and handsome as Artem. Although it wasn't so important for a boy, if beauty would bring World Peace, then why shouldn't Peace be beautiful? I was pleased with my spontaneous play on words, and out of happiness, I sat down on the bride's bouquet. It was actually a little bunch of branches—of green fir, babies' breath, and a few tiny roses— on a little handle.

When the time came for them to exchange rings, Lera, not knowing where to put the bouquet, tucked it under her arm.

"I pronounce you husband and wife. Congratulate each other!" proclaimed the female registrar, pompously, using a pointer to indicate where the couple and their witnesses needed to sign. Lera's witness was Masha, and Artem's a gaunt, bearded fellow with dark hair, whom I didn't know. As promised, the groom himself had parted with his beard, which made him look almost unrecognizably young.

"Congratulations!" Lera turned to Artem and planted a kiss on his clean-shaven cheek, then started giggling. On seeing the female registrar's questioning look, she realized she should've probably added something.

The newlyweds kissed each other modestly on the lips, and turned to face their guests in anticipation of their congratulatory bouquets and embraces. Lera's mom wiped away tears, and as was later revealed, at that very moment, she was 'giving birth' to a poem.

It was a fun wedding. Lera's tea rose-colored dress, which she'd rented, declaring that she didn't understand the logic behind having to buy something you were only going to wear once, had already torn—twice. First, a bow fell off the sleeve, and then when the groom carried his bride up the stairs to the reception hall in his arms, he managed to step on the long hem, and a piece of the bodice came off. If not for the pin they'd found on the bow, which they used to pin together the tear in the bodice, the guests would've been able to behold the bride in her slip. Because of the incident with the dress, the young couple almost had an argument; Lera had lost her sense of humor, though not for long.

By the end of the evening, I realized, sadly, that Elias wouldn't be flying over. What a pity he didn't see how all three of our mutual charges, or "hapless creatures," as he called them, got to know each other.

"Masha, this is Olga and Vlad, my best friends," Lera said, pulling her shy friend over by the hand. She was holding a glass of champagne in the other hand. "What the two of you have in common is that neither of you can drink." She took a gulp. "And for the same reason. Olga, you're not the only mother-to-be at this fabulous wedding party. Masha here is having a baby too! So, you must absolutely become friends, so you can regularly exchange experiences and give each other helpful advice!"

Lera then, having concluded, skipped away to the dance floor, but came running right back. "Maybe having two pregnant women at my wedding is a good sign, right?" She then skipped away again without waiting for their confirmation.

Lera was euphoric about everything going on around her, and she danced enough for the both of them. Before long, Artem joined her, then all the parents, and even me.

I was happy to see her in such a good mood, and that she's stopped grieving.

"Another drink and our bride will start stripping," Olga joked. "Do you know whether you're having a boy or a girl, Masha?"

"It's still early, but they might be able to tell in a month. Do you know yet?" Masha asked.

"Yes, a girl," Olga replied, patting herself on the stomach. "I'm due at the end of March."

"So, I'm after you, then," Masha joked, with a corresponding hand gesture. "Mine's coming about six weeks later. In the meantime, he or she is tormenting Mommy with terrible nausea. I'm sitting here, surrounded by all this delicious food, but I'm afraid to eat. And I really want to!"

Thanks to their mutual topic of interest, the two girls quickly found a common language and conversed to the end of the evening.

Vlad listened to them for the first ten minutes, then gave up his seat at the deliberations of expectant mothers and sat closer to Marina Ivanovna, who'd gathered around her a small group of guests, to whom she recited poetry, composed for the occasion of her daughter's wedding.

Right alongside, Lera and Artem conversed with his mom, Nadezhda Petrovna, who gave her daughter-in-law a detailed account of how her son was born.

It made me smile, because that was Lera's mom's favorite topic of conversation as well. Maybe all mothers loved recalling that important moment in their lives.

"You know, Lera, I very nearly died giving birth to Artem," Nadezhda Petrovna said, shaking her head as she waited for Lera's reaction.

I could tell by Lera's expression that she had absolutely no idea what to say in response. She looked at Artem, then at his mother, who shook her head again, evidently for the sake of credibility.

Unable to come up with anything, she looked to Artem for help. "What does one say in situations like these?"

"Sorry?" he said, and all three of them burst out laughing.

I liked the atmosphere at this wedding, and I wasn't the only one.

M-07091999 and F-12161998 also got to know each other, just like their moms. Having become friends, they flew happily around the ceiling, like two little white clouds.

During their traditional 'wedding tour' of the city by limousine, they visited the Kissing Bridge—Lera's idea, to see if it really corresponded to the famous song claiming that couples who kissed on this bridge would never divorce. She wasn't committed to the idea of marriage till death did one part. She regarded it as merely a new fragment of life, equally pleasant and light for both of them. She saw Artem as a friend to whom she could say anything she wanted.

Because of his inherent journalistic curiosity, Artem asked a lot of questions, and she, with her extraordinary openness, told him about everybody she'd been with before him, but she left out the recent tragic events of her life. Before the wedding, Artem had fed Lera's illusion that everything they'd started was just as unserious for him as it was for her.

When they were alone in their room, however, packed with flowers and wedding gifts, and after carrying out their first marital obligation, still not quite free of the effects of all the champagne, combined with vodka, he suddenly opened up to his wife in the middle of the night.

"I don't know what's happening to me," he said, "but I'm very, very afraid of losing you! You are so experienced with men, and I have so little with women. I don't measure up, and I'm so afraid you'll soon lose interest in me." Then he talked more, and more.

I flew right up close to Lera, and could feel her seize up, literally, not knowing how to react to such a sudden outburst of emotion. She had no idea that Artem was so plagued by complexes about their unequal experience with the opposite sex. The best she could do was pat him on the head and whisper, "Sh-sh-sh!" That was the way Lera's beloved grandmother had soothed her, when she was a little girl.

Her answer put Artem right. He fell asleep almost immediately and, gently as a girl, he even started to snore.

Chapter 28

St. Petersburg was actively preparing to celebrate the long-awaited new Millennium. The city had put out the traditional 'New Year' fir trees in November, in anticipation of the event, and had decorated them with huge bulbs and stars. Kiosks sold tinsel, multicolored lights, and sparklers. People rushed around the shops, buying gifts and stocking up on alcohol for the ten days-long holiday season.

"It seems you and I forgot to think through our honeymoon," Lera said to Artem the morning after their wedding. "What are we going to do for the next two weeks? Hang around here?"

"Yeah, we'll hang around here, go visit friends."

"Or maybe we could go somewhere, like Egypt, for instance. Or to Paris!" She seemed pleased with her own idea.

"So that's what you're thinking, eh?" Artem smiled and messed up her short blonde hair. "Egypt or Paris?"

"I don't even know." Lera sighed. "I feel like going everywhere. If only somebody would print up some money for us."

"Well, you know some famous artists. Ask one of them, and we'll go."

"I'm calling right now," she joked back, and pretended to dial a number. "Seriously, though, maybe we could take one of those package trips. They have really good deals sometimes."

"Before the New Year?" Artem shook his head. "I really doubt it."

"Well, what if somebody cancels, for instance, and *bam*—we show up and get their package, because the flight leaves the next morning?"

"Have we got any money left?"

"We'll figure out how much we got yesterday and what we have left. If we don't have enough, we'll do it on credit, and pay it back! And we'll be left with the memories of ringing in the New Year in Paris!"

"So, after this celebration of life you organized, is there anything left?" Artem asked, doubtfully.

"What do you mean 'I' organized?" Lera retorted, mildly offended. "You mean you weren't involved in organizing it?"

"Of course I was, but all the same, it was *your* wedding, and I was only there as your shadow. I have to admit though, when you called me an idiot because I tore your dress, I thought we should divorce right away."

He sounded deeply hurt, and pouting like a little baby, causing me to feel sorry for him again. I imagined myself as his son, and in my mind, I could see us walking around the park, him holding me, a two-year-old boy, by the hand, and suddenly we both trip over a little hillock and fall down, painfully and hard. And *he's* crying, not me. I start soothing him, a full-grown guy, like Lera did: 'Sh-sh-sh!'

I started to laugh, but suddenly the fun turned into perplexity, and then sadness. It suddenly occurred to me that this signaled the beginning of problems between them. But why? Surely this time, finally, things would work out for Lera, especially when Artem had revealed his true feelings after the wedding. What had changed in these few hours?

"Getting a divorce on our wedding day?" Lera asked in a tone of voice that suggested she regretted not having come up with such a remarkable idea herself. "Oh boy! Then why didn't you suggest it?" Having learned from her bitter experience with Victor, she decided to turn the conversation into a joke.

"I wanted to, but you were having such a good time, dancing the night away, I decided not to spoil your fun," Artem replied, without a hint of a smile.

"How compassionate. Thanks for worrying about my feelings." She kissed him on the lips.

The kiss went unanswered. "Okay, that's enough, Tema, let's be friends. Forgive me, please! I was rude, but you remember that joke where the mother asks her little son: 'What did Papa say, when he was falling down the stairs?' and the kid goes: 'Can I use bad words?' so the mother says: "Of course not!" and so the kid says: 'Then he didn't say anything!' I didn't do it on purpose—it just came out, mechanically. Of course I don't consider you an—" Lera cut herself off and hit herself on the lips. "You wanna hit them a little, too?" she proposed, taking his hand and raising it to her lips.

"I'm afraid it won't help," he muttered.

"What if it did?" she said, looking at him lovingly. "Okay, so... should we try for Paris?"

"First we have to count the money," Artem said, and I could tell from his face that he was fighting his sense of injury with all his might, having realized there wasn't going to be any psychoanalytical conversing with Lera. "Bring in the public purse!" he commanded loudly.

"I'm going, I'm going, sir," Lera replied in a squeaky voice, imitating an old chancellery clerk. "Right away, good sir, right away!"

They both burst out laughing and she, so happy her husband was over it, sat in his lap.

I wouldn't describe their subsequent actions, in view of my inherent chasteness. At times like this, I usually either turned away or went to the kitchen, where I waited for the signal of two voices: first the short feminine squeal, and then the masculine extended moan. Then, and I knew this for a fact, I could go back in thirty seconds.

When I went back, the tension that had occurred during the conversation about going to Paris had drained off, but a hairline crack between husband and wife had appeared, all the same.

The young couple did manage to greet the New Year in Paris, after all. They got one of the great last minute deals Lera had mentioned as a possibility. Obviously, she'd wanted it so badly, her call was heard, and answered, by her guardian angel.

Lera's guardian angel was female. I knew it because, at the very beginning of our acquaintanceship, Elias had let slip that they knew each other. At the time, though, I still didn't know whom he was talking about. All women dreamt about Paris, and Lera's angel had helped her, not only out of female solidarity, but also because she realized the couple needed to change their situation and be alone together. Surely, she had to have noticed the hairline crack between them, unless she was as scatter-brained as Elias.

I didn't fly off to Paris. My presence there could have raised a lot of eyebrows in the top brass, and I couldn't have justified myself by saying I'd decided to find some parents in another country. It would be a long time before they would allow me to start my search again. So I turned on my imagination and visualized Lera and Artem, greeting the New Year in a cozy Parisian café, drinking champagne and eating little pastries while looking at the twinkling Eiffel Tower. For some reason, in my fantasy it had to be snowing—clean, pure white, French snow. It kept falling and falling....

Chapter 29

In Olga and Vladimir's family, the New Year's celebrations were tarnished by the fact that Klim hadn't shown up at the scheduled divorce hearing. They'd all genuinely hoped that Olga would be granted the court's ruling in January, and that they could get married before their daughter was born. The future parents had already considered their options, in terms of selling Vlad's room, and regarding the supplemental payment they'd need to buy at least a small studio apartment. In view of the upcoming holidays, however, they'd put everything off for a month, and Olga decided not to call Klim.

They rang in the New Year with Petya in their renovated room in the communal apartment—as the saying goes, 'tight, but all right.' For the first time in all the years he'd lived there, Vlad bought a New Year's tree. He'd received the one growing on his windowsill as an employee at the editorial office last year. Somebody told him then that trees grew badly for bad people, but his grew like a weed.

"You really are one in a million, unlike me," Lera had joked, on one occasion, seeing how much Vlad's little tree had grown. "Even the fir tree feels it! Whereas mine wilted so quickly. As a rule, I'm not good with plants. I forget to water them, and by the time I think of it, it's too late."

The two art students briefly popped into Olga and Vlad's cozy room, lit up with colored lights, and gave them a gift—a pencil sketch of a naked, pregnant woman, drawn from life, and in a special frame. A wasted Vasya visited and was overjoyed by their unopened bottle of champagne. Nina Vasilyevna spent the New Year's Eve away from home, having gone to visit her granddaughter and great-grandkids. The so-called 'temporary' owner-occupants, mother and daughter, hid away in their room, watched TV, and shrieked with laughter.

Thus the communal apartment members celebrated New Year's Eve 2000.

As for Masha, she went to Novgorod to her aunt, who lived alone and was always thrilled when her niece visited. She and her sister,

Masha's mother, had engaged in a longstanding quarrel. In their youth, the sisters were in love with the same guy, and they hadn't spoken to each other since. The man in question became Masha's father, who lived with them for three years before leaving, without a trace, for another woman. The only memory Masha had was of his back as he walked away, and of herself running after him in the rain, shouting, "Papa! Papa!"

The experience had left her with the feeling that, sooner or later, every man in her life would turn his back on her and leave. Maybe that was why things didn't work out between her and Kolya.

If I could have given her and the rest of humanity some advice, it would be not to attract unpleasant events to yourself, and not always to think something bad would happen to you. After all, the subconscious crossed over to certainty.

I spent New Year's Eve completely alone. I wasn't drawn to the other souls, just didn't feel like listening to their stories about their future parents, and watching their happy dances in honor of those who'd already chosen their prospective moms. My only kindred spirit in my world now was Elias. I summoned him mentally, hoping to engender a friendly conversation, but it seemed he couldn't hear me, so I decided to set out in search of him.

It was January 6, the Orthodox Christmas Eve, the most ordinary day—a day like all the rest. We didn't have any big holidays and, seeing the many occasions to celebrate that humans had thought up, I started thinking about what a boring existence we led! People had such a variety of goals, whereas we had only one: to be born and become a person, so that we could eventually have just as many goals. This excluded the angels, of course—they helped people and had an interesting job. You could even say I'd been lucky enough to get familiar with the things they did, if only because of my own misfortune.

I didn't end up finding Elias, who'd virtually disappeared into thin air. It suddenly struck me that I missed not only Lera and Artem, but my own angel, who'd unexpectedly become much more to me than just my boss. Even three days before the guys were coming back from Paris, I flitted around everywhere like some wandering soul, with no idea how to occupy myself. I felt like a computer-game character whose lives were all used up.

Lera came back, though, and as I remained under her influence, everything around me came back to life... and new anxieties began.

Chapter 30

"Lera, I can't take it anymore," said Masha, who was in almost the same mood now as when I'd first seen her at Lera's. "I feel so bad! Nothing's working out. I'm sorry I listened to you last fall, and now it's too late. So, you know what I've decided?"

"What?" Lera asked, clearly worried.

"I've decided to give the baby up when it's born. I'll either find it some adoptive parents now, or just leave it at the maternity clinic. The one thing I know for sure is that I can't manage with a baby on my own." Masha wore the most lost and desolate expression, but she spoke calmly, as though she'd genuinely thought it through and considered all her options.

As soon as Lera recovered from the shock of what she'd just heard, she said. "Are you out of your mind? No, Masha, do you even realize what you're saying? What do you mean 'leave it at the maternity clinic'?"

"And how exactly do you visualize our future?" Masha retorted. "Walking around the train stations, spare-changing people? I'm already living on credit! My life is of no interest at all to my mother. All she can do is give me the same idiotic advice she gave herself when she was young, and you can see how that worked out for everybody. She's alone and relevant to no one—even my brother ignores her, and he was always her favorite!"

"Masha, please, let's just calm down and—"

"I *am* calm." Again, Masha seemed to be speaking in earnest, appearing almost serene. "Whatever happens... happens. It's all the same to me."

Lera sat down on the sofa beside Masha, took her by the hands, and looked her in the eye. "Hello! Earth to Masha! That's a crazy idea. Don't do that. It's your baby, for God's sake! How will you be able to live with yourself if you desert your child?"

"I'll be fine, knowing he's better off than he would be with me." Masha seemed to be trying to convince herself. "At least I'm giving birth to him, so I won't have the sin on me of killing a soul."

"Listen to yourself. You sound like all those religious women from my online forum. How is it better to give birth and then give away your child, knowing he's calling another woman Mom? Or even worse, that he's not calling *anybody* Mom? In my opinion, it's better not to have the baby at all—that's the smallest sin. I say no, no, and no. Otherwise, the kid—who's a part of *you*—is being warehoused by the state, while *you*—a grown woman with two hands, two feet, and a great brain, who is fully fluent in two languages—has stuck her head in the sand like a cowardly ostrich."

"Don't torment my soul, or try appealing to my conscience. They're both asleep," Masha retorted, blandly, as though she were asleep herself. "I've made up my mind."

"Masha, I'm in shock. You're my friend. I love you the way you are, but know this: I'm in shock." Lera shook her head. "And what about your future artist? Who's going to take him to art school?"

"They'll find somebody. I'll leave them a note about it," Masha said, even able to joke about it. "I talked to my aunt in Novgorod, when I was there, and she reacted the same way. She even offered to take the baby herself."

"Well? Isn't that an option? If only at first, for a while!" Lera exclaimed, grasping at that straw.

"Come on, Lera, she can't even walk! She's been confined to a wheelchair ever since she had a stroke fifteen years ago, and needs looking after herself. A social worker looks in on her sometimes." Masha sighed. "I really upset her, of course. I shouldn't have told her I was pregnant in the first place. I could've hidden it, since I'm not even really showing yet, or I could've not gone to visit until after the birth."

The situation had turned genuinely bad, and I was supposed to tell Elias about it. Deep down, I was glad to have a serious reason to summon him to a meeting with me. He liked to just sit around and talk, of course, but I still needed a reason after all. Friendship aside, I was still his subordinate. I sent out a 'serious matter' signal, left the girls on their own, and hurried to our meeting place.

"Something like this was bound to happen." Elias remained calm in response to my emotional story about Masha's intentions. "I told you from the beginning that she'd be going through a lot of moods."

"Yes, but this doesn't seem like just a mood! She's made up her mind!"

"And she'll change it a hundred times." The angel smiled and waved a hand in dismissal. "Can't you see what an impulsive girl she is?"

I didn't expect Elias to react this way, but he seemed to be in a lyrical mood again, looking all tidy, as though he'd just come out of a purifying rainfall. Given his good spirits, I decided to press him.

"Elias, where are you when my signals don't reach you?"

He gave me a look that clearly stated I'd overstepped my boundaries.

"I only thought... maybe there's some particular place angels go to... where there's no reception... like a quiet zone," I rambled, trying to justify myself.

"There is such a place, my dear friend. It's called the metro!" He laughed so hard, he had to hold onto his stomach. "Oy, I can't take it. You crack me up."

Completely embarrassed by his reaction, I waited to hear what he would say next.

When he tired of laughing, my boss coughed and cleared his throat, as he might before a question on an oral exam. He grew solemn, without even a trace of a smile this time. "Seriously though, Peace, there are some things that children really don't need to know."

"But how can I notify you in an emergency, if our line of communication disappears and my call goes unheard?"

"There shouldn't be anything terrible happening in the near future. I've checked. Over the course of the next six months, everybody should have safely delivered their babies, and where Masha's concerned, don't worry about it. I have a plan. It's just not the right time to implement it yet. I'll put her back on the life path that's best for her, but right now, she must undergo some trials. They'll end. The most important thing is that the baby be born. He really will be an artistically gifted boy, so what you foretold her in that dream is right on the mark. It's a pity she has to suffer such emotions throughout her pregnancy, but that's payback for having chosen the wrong guy as the father of her child."

"But she's not the one who chose him. The baby's soul did, M-07091999."

"But her participation was crucial, right?" Elias countered. "Your M-07091999 chose his mother, but when it came to the father, he took what was available. I mean 'who,'" he added, clearly pleased with his own humor. "You did the same thing, right?"

"No!" I insisted. "I thought the whole thing through and even picked a different father. But then I had a moment of weakness, where I couldn't control myself and made a mistake."

Elias nodded. "Maybe so, but if your Lera hadn't chosen the guy who didn't end up being the one to share her path, what happened to you *wouldn't* have. Right?"

I sighed; I had to agree with him there. "Right."

"And there you go. So, relax. It'll all work out."

"Any new assignments for me, Boss?"

"Not for now, Peace, except for one: you have to protect Vladimir. There's some kind of danger hanging over him on the eighth day of every month, starting at the beginning of the New Year. I wasn't able to pinpoint exactly what it was, so it seems that whatever it is may or may not happen. Just in case, be vigilant, and I'll try not to lose control of the situation, too."

"Got it. So, am I free again?"

"You're always free, my little soul!" He playfully tousled my hair and tickled my nose, both of which he saw the way he wanted. "Appreciate this time in your life, and don't sweat the small stuff."

He stood up, spread his wings, flapped them a few times as though making sure they worked as they should, and flew away.

I watched his flight until he turned into a tiny speck, and when the speck disappeared, I grew anxious for him, as though something would happen. I really hoped my presentiments were wrong.

Chapter 31

The eight of the month was the fated date, according to Elias, but nothing bad had happened to Vladimir on January 8th—just the minor occurrence on Kolokolnaya Street, where he'd met the strange traffic inspector. The traffic accident that was supposed to have happened back then did happen, only later. As he made a left turn, his Zhiguli collided with an oncoming car, and they scraped each other a little. Luckily, there were no injuries, only a little scare for both drivers, who settled the issues of insurance and the costs of repairs on the spot, before continuing safely on their respective ways.

February 8th was the date of Olga and Klim's rescheduled divorce hearing. Klim had already ignored the first two—evidently, he disapproved of the idea. Vlad drove Olga over to the Magistrate's Court at 10 a.m. and waited in the car.

I didn't know what to do: stay with him, or go in with her. I decided Vladimir would be safe, as long as he stayed in the car and didn't drive off anywhere, so I flew over to the courtroom.

This time Klim showed up. He waited in the hallway by the judge's chamber, passport in hand. On seeing his wife, he stayed put and perfectly still, not even waving to her.

Olga sat down opposite him, wearing a loose grey coat and a big scarf. Thanks to her clothing, her belly, which had grown quite large, wasn't discernable.

The practically-former spouses sat across from each other in silence.

Klim trained his eyes on Olga, but I couldn't tell what he was thinking from his expressionless gaze. I sensed that his emotions had reached their boiling point but, unlike the last time I'd seen him, he wasn't letting it show. He spent ten minutes that way: staring at his wife, and staring at the big button on her coat.

The secretary stepped into the corridor and announced, "Shelina, Olga. 'Petition for the Dissolution of Marriage.' Come in. Is the respondent present?"

"He is," Klim grumbled.

They entered the chambers.

"Judge Khudyakova will lead the proceedings in the matter of the marriage of Shelina, Olga Alexandrovna, and Shelin, Kliment Igoryevich, concerning the dissolution of said marriage."

The judge read aloud Olga's petition, stating the particulars: the date she'd entered wedlock; the standard phrases regarding character incompatibility and impossibility of cohabitation; the fact of dissolved joint tenancy; and the petitioner's intention not to pursue financial claims against the respondent; and that the child's security and place of residence had been determined.

"Respondent, why have you not appeared at the previous hearings?" the judge asked.

Klim remained silent.

"Respondent, when the court addresses you, you must rise and reply."

A black cloud had formed over Klim's head again, and I sensed he hated the whole world.

Klim stood and said, "I've been ill." His voice sounded hoarse, as though he needed to clear his throat.

"Is there a medical certificate?"

"No, I didn't consult a doctor."

"Do you agree to your spouse's petition?"

"No," he said, after which he finally cleared his throat.

"So, you *don't* agree to the petition?" she repeated for some reason, emphasizing 'don't.'

"I *don't*," he said.

"Do you want a designated period in which to reconcile with your spouse?"

"Yes, I do."

"Petitioner," said the judge, addressing Olga, who'd grown as pale as the wall in the chambers. "Do you want a designated period in which to reconcile with your spouse?"

Olga stood up. "No, Your Honor."

"Why?"

"We haven't lived together for three months. I'm with someone else, and we're expecting a child soon." When she'd stood up, her belly became immediately noticeable.

When he first saw it, Klim's gaze had turned cold and cruel, but not a single muscle on his face so much as twitched. I was half-a-meter away from him, and the wave of his negative energy threw me against the window. He despised that baby with every ounce of his being, and he'd made the decision not to agree to the divorce as a matter of principle.

"But your spouse opposes the dissolution of the marriage and, per the law, I have no choice but to grant you a period in which to reconcile, if one side demands it."

"Your Honor, I beg of you..." Olga started, her eyes filling with tears.

"As a woman, I understand." The judge's voice carried a note of sympathy. "But as a judge, I'm obligated to designate a period of one month." She started leafing through her agenda. "We'll schedule our next meeting for the ninth of March, right after Women's Day. I hope the two of you will reach some agreement by then." Turning to Olga, she asked, "When is your due date? Will you be able to appear?"

"The end of March," Olga replied.

"So, you should all be able to make it, then." She turned her attention to Klim. "Respondent, take this time to consider this matter very carefully. There will be no more extensions. Even if for some reason you fail to appear, the divorce will be granted."

The un-divorced couple stood up, silently, and left the judge's chambers. They went through the turnstile and out onto the street. Olga wanted to leave immediately, but Klim grabbed her by the arm.

F-12161998 tried with all her might to tear his hand away from her mother, as though she really believed she could do it.

"So, you had a good time while we were still living together?" he said, nodding at her stomach.

"Klim, I'm begging you, give me a divorce! We'll split amicably, and you can see Petya whenever you like!" Olga spoke in a supplicating tone.

Klim snickered. "Let the guy you're living with now raise him. And about the divorce...." He paused for a second. "Well, there's still a whole month ahead of us." On those words, he yanked his hand away from Olga's arm.

He happened to notice Vladimir's yellow Zhiguli parked in front of the building. "That's him?" He pointed to Vlad.

"Yes, and believe me, he's a *very* good person!" Olga retorted, emphatically, not having considered the reaction her words could provoke.

"Oh, so... I was bad. I get it. Well then, run along, lovebirds. Drive off into the sunset." He snickered again, and looked over at Vlad's car, his eyes narrowed and threatening. "You changed your phone number?"

"I did, and when we can talk like normal people, I'll give you my new one." Olga walked over to the car and got in.

Vlad turned over the ignition and started to make a U-turn, when suddenly a big snowball hit the driver's window—hard—and splattered, stuck to the glass.

Klim had thrown it, and he stood there, watching them drive away.

I stayed with Olga and Vlad until late evening, listening to their conversations. Klim had dashed their hopes of getting married before the birth, and their mood was not the happiest, to say the least.

Still, nothing more unpleasant than the snowball happened to Vlad that February 8th.

Chapter 32

The shortest month of the year went by uneventfully, with things pretty much business as usual, except that Lera had the occasional bouts of melancholy, for reasons she couldn't explain to Artem. I spent a lot of time by her side, and sometimes I wondered if my invisible presence was making her so uneasy.

"Anya, the closer it gets to the date the baby would've been born, the worse I feel," she said over the phone to her girlfriend, whose baby would be another of Lera's godchildren. "Like that elk in the joke, who went to the watering hole with a hangover. Remember? There's a hunter shooting at him over and over, hitting him every time, but the elk doesn't fall over and thinks, amazed, 'I'm drinking and drinking, but I'm feeling worse and worse.'"

I heard laughter on the end of the line, and part of a phrase that ended with what seemed to be "not to think about it."

"Oh yeah? And how do I do that?" Lera continued. "I can't tell Artem about everything. He said he had a negative attitude toward women who've had an abortion. I've found a lot of new things about him: his best friend is a priest, and he even tried out for the church choir. All in all, he's turned out to be quite a tight-laced fellow, and here I am with my pseudo-easygoing attitude to life. I don't think it's going to work out between us, Anya, and I would like it to work. I've already said the wrong things a couple of times, looked at him the wrong way, and he remembers everything. I say something and just forget about it, whereas he'll bring it up a week later, and I don't know what to say so that I don't put my foot in my mouth again. I can't be myself, and constantly have to control myself. He's turned out to be so jealous and suspicious, too, more than I could ever have imagined! That's what happens when you're in a rush to marry someone you don't even know. Somebody called me, recently, and Artem was just going out on a job. He comes back four hours later, and you know what he asks me right off the bat? Who called me when he was leaving? I almost fell over. I couldn't even remember if anybody had called me at all! But that's what he had worried about all that time. Can you imagine?

I couldn't hear her friend's answers, but they were quite lengthy too.

Lera would sit listening and, every so often, she'd mouth a silent 'wow.' "It's a pity, because he and I are alike in so many ways," she finally said. "Neither of us likes sitting around at home. We have a lot of common interests, and we're constantly together — at work and at home. He has a remarkable sense of humor, and you know how important that is to me. See, if he hadn't started necking with Julia last summer, and if I hadn't gotten back together again with Vic that time, we might've had a normal relationship. Not like right now, when I'm down in the dumps and can't pull myself out. I mean, they warned on the forum, but I didn't listen, and now I keep thinking about the baby, counting the weeks until it would've been born. I bug him a lot about maybe having a baby, but he says, 'Where would we put it? We don't have our own place.'"

She sighed and continued. "By the way, both he and I almost weren't born. Imagine! We have similar histories: both of our mothers, finding themselves pregnant, went to get abortions, and neither of them went through with it. Mine said the doctor scared her, saying that her uterine walls were thin and any further erosion could prevent her from having children later. Just like my Dr. Zhigalov, the first time Vic and I went to the clinic. Artem's mother told us she changed her mind spontaneously — in the operating room — and just got up and left! I witnessed the same thing myself recently. I took a girl to my doctor by the hand, literally, but she changed her mind and left too. She's expecting a boy this May. Do you remember my witness at the wedding? Well, it was her. But can you imagine? We almost weren't born, but here we are!"

Now it was Anya's turn, apparently, to recount a similar instance, regarding a friend whom Lera didn't know, and Lera's turn to listen.

"Yes, yes, exactly," Lera said, having heard her out. "To this day, I don't understand why I didn't change my mind back then, and just walk away, or why I even went there in the first place. Vic might've come around. I mean, he did love me, deeply. Why on Earth did I insist he marry me? My mother kept hounding me, but we couldn't just live the way we were. You see, I kept asking him at least to divorce his wife, and I realize now that he only refused so as not to marry me. He wasn't living with his wife, but he only saw me as a temporary alternative. Then later, when I told him I was pregnant, he said, 'But I told you from the beginning, I'm married.' I remember saying then, that yes, he warned me about that, but that he forgot to tell me he was a bastard. Listen, did I tell you I called his wife after the abortion? I felt genuinely sorry for her. She's over thirty, and she's sitting around, waiting for her jerk of a husband to have his fun, regain his senses, and come back to her. I told her about what happened and said that he doesn't deserve her waiting for him. You know what she said in response? That she always knew things wouldn't work out between him and me from the minute she saw the cassette. How did she know? She's obviously a psychic," Lera concluded rather venomously.

On the other end of the line, Anya's response to this was the shortest yet; apparently, she didn't know what cassette Lera was referring to.

"The one where Vic and I are kissing," Lera replied. "When we first started seeing each other, he took a video of me in the Summer Garden and at home, and then left the camera running on the table and he got down to things. That was our very first kiss! It was quite modest. There I was, totally bashful, covering my face with my hair because it was completely red. Vic was still living with his wife then, although he'd told me there hadn't been anything between them for a long time. I realize now that all married men have the same story. Anyway, his wife saw the video and started grilling him about it, so he went ahead and admitted he was in love with the girl in the video — me. Then they drove over to their parents', told them they were divorcing, and he brought his things over to my place. But as you can see, he never did divorce his wife."

This time Anya's response was lengthy; Lera patiently awaited her turn to reply.

"There you go," she said. "Sometimes I wonder. If you believe people have a destiny, then why did we even have to meet? The relationship was disastrous from the beginning, somehow. The first time we noticed each other was at a pool tournament between our companies. We exchanged glances, and then — bam! — they're calling out our names as opponents in a game. Somebody's hand pulled them out of a hat randomly. Why? So that a year later I'd suffer such hellish heartache? For what? As far as I know, I've never been bad to anybody. Where was my guardian angel? Why didn't he protect me against that?

It's like the stone in that fairytale: you go to the left and lose your horse, to the right, your head, and straight, something else again. No matter where you go, you lose something. Turns out, it's better not to leave the house at all."

The girlfriends' conversation went on for about two hours. Lera's phone beeped quietly, more and more frequently, meaning the battery was low and it would die soon, but apart from the words, "Oh, I think my battery's dying," she made no attempt to charge it. Thus, they finally had to end the conversation. The girls managed to consider the present, recall the past, philosophize a little, have a laugh, complain about everything past, present, and potential. They talked about baby Romka's future christening, which, in Anya's words, would be coming up any day. Lera's moods swung from sad to euphoric.

I thought if you sat both of these Chatty-Cathy's in the same prison cell for twenty-five years, after they were freed, they'd probably keep talking outside the prison gates for another couple of hours, like the two women in the joke Elias had told me just recently, though I didn't remember the context.

It was impossible to know how long this telephone marathon would have lasted, had the key not turned in the door, and had Artem not shown up in the doorway.

"Okay, Anya, my juice has run out, and it seems my husband's just ran in." Lera laughed, and the conversation that had started on a sad note ended on a positive one.

At that very second, Lera's phone let out a final warning beep and disconnected. She put it back in its base to prepare for the next gabfest, went out into the corridor where Artem was changing out of his shoes and into the house slippers, and snuggled up to his back.

"Hello, hello," he said, then stood upright and kissed his wife on the neck. "Who were you talking to? It's kind of strange that you hung up the phone as soon as I came in."

"Anya," Lera said. "The phone died of our endless gossiping."

"Between you two chatterboxes, it's no wonder." Artem took off his jacket and went into the bathroom to wash his hands. "So what're you serving up today? Leftover borscht again?"

"You have something against it?"

"Of course not... I just don't really like soup."

"For crying out loud! Now you tell me! Here I am, cooking different kinds of soup, and he doesn't even like it! I can make other things, too, you know? How about 'chicken on a jar?' I was going to make it tomorrow, for Women's Day, but why wait? Let's have March 8th on the 7th!"

"Sure thing," Artem agreed, somewhat dully. "Except you don't get your gift till tomorrow. I haven't had a chance to buy it yet. So, what exactly is it, this 'chicken on a jar?'"

"You take the chicken, score it with a knife, stuff all the slits with garlic, smear it all over with salt and mayonnaise, and slip it over a small jar full of water. It's my mom's recipe. She even attaches a head, made of a beet or an apple, to the chicken and sticks a knife vertically under the wing, and *voila!* It's ready to serve!" Lera laughed. "Mom calls it something poetic, like 'Chicken in Flight.' She's been making flying chickens for as long as I can remember, for special occasions, or just for fun."

"But what's the knife for?" Artem asked.

"You mean you haven't guessed?" Lera suddenly shrieked with such uncontrollable laughter that she slid down the wall she was standing against and ended up crouching. "So you have something to cut the chicken with!"

Artem was laughing now, too, only much more quietly. "Well, since it's such a funny dish, let's make it today. Is there garlic and mayonnaise, or do we need to run out and buy it?"

"I think we've got some. The only thing we need is the jar."

"There must be one in here somewhere. I'll look for it right now." Even after having lived in the rented apartment for six months on his own, and over five months with Lera, Artem still didn't know where things were.

The two of them went into the tiny kitchen, equipped with an old-fashioned gas cooker, found a suitable jar, and started scoring the chicken together, Artem from one side and Lera from the other.

I watched them with the hopeful thought that things could still work out between them. The hairline fracture could still mend itself if they both wanted it to. I would've been happy to help them find their thread to each other, but I no longer had that right. I wasn't even supposed to be there at all.

I suddenly remembered that tomorrow was the eighth of the month again, and that I had to be at Vladimir's side without fail, so I left Artem and Lera to celebrate their early International Women's Day on their own.

Chapter 33

On the morning of the holiday, Vlad ran over to the nearest flower shop and bought seven long-stemmed white roses, then lay the bouquet on the bed beside the sleeping Olga, mother of his future baby girl.

Olga woke up and, upon seeing the flowers, smiled a completely angelic smile.

I'd never met a female angel, but imagined she'd look just like that. White roses suited F-12161998's future mom. First thing in the morning, free of makeup and carrying a new life, she was remarkably beautiful, and it didn't matter that she didn't have wings.

For some reason, while thinking of wings, I thought I heard Klim's voice beside me, saying, "Where are your wings that I loved?" They were the lyrics to the song he quoted during that stroll at the park with Olga in fall. I suddenly grew uneasy and tried to chase away the unbidden image of that hapless man, who had arisen from somewhere, and who'd become his own worst enemy. Why didn't he have a guardian angel? How was that possible?

"My angel," Vlad said, bending down to kiss Olga. "*Walk with me – you first, and I'll follow.*"

"A felicitation verse?" she asked, only half awake, but smiling in response to the kiss.

"Nah, Nina Vasilyevna taught me that. She said it was what you had to say when leaving the house, so nothing bad would happen. For some reason, it's been going around my head today."

After breakfast, they all started getting ready to go somewhere. F-12161998, who wasn't rushing off to go anywhere, sat on one of the rosebuds, pretending to be taking in the fragrance. I learned from the morning's conversations that their plan was to visit Olga's parents and spend the holiday with them. Vlad had already met his future in-laws during the New Year celebrations, so this would be the second visit in their joint family history.

"We'll have to buy some flowers for my mom, too," Olga said. "Should we maybe give her these, to save money?"

"No, Lala, we'll buy some other flowers for your mom." Vlad smiled. "These are for you."

"Whatever you say, my love." Olga kissed him on the cheek. "Should we get going?"

"Wait a sec, I'll just call Lera and congratulate her." He dialed the number. "Lera, hi! Happy Women's Day!" he said when she answered, as Olga stood there indicating 'hi from me.' "And the same from Olga," he added, "even though she's a woman, too. Well, all the best to you, and may all your dreams come true! We love you a lot, and your godson sends you kisses too." He handed the phone to Petya.

"Happy holiday, Godmother! I hope you become a real-life fairy!" Petya smiled ear to ear.

I could hear Lera's laughter at the other end, and my uneasiness immediately let go of me.

"Hopefully," Vlad said, "we'll be back from the parents early enough to drop by your place with a cake, for a cup of tea. I'll call you later this afternoon."

They went out into the courtyard, got into the car and drove off. They bought a beautiful bouquet of big white chrysanthemums along the way, for Olga's mom, who lived in the suburbs.

I sat comfortably in the back seat beside Petya, who had his own child seat and seatbelt. Right there beside us sat the blue-eyed little girl, F-12161998, swinging her feet in a pair of pink sandals. It was the first time I'd seen her as such, and I had no idea why she appeared to me that way today.

During the drive, Petya asked a lot of entertaining questions that made everybody laugh, including me and the soul of his little sister.

"Mom, Dad," he said. "Did you know that if you brush a cat for a long time, it changes from a cat to an electro-cat?"

Olga and Vlad burst out laughing at Petya's unconscious play on words.

"As a matter of fact, we did know," said Vlad. "We learned about it at school. The lesson was called 'Static Electro-Cats.'"

"Mom, am I clever?" Petya suddenly asked.

"Sometimes," Olga replied without turning her head.

"But I want to be totally clever!" he pouted.

"Why?"

"So I can be a superhero! Like Jackie Chan. And not long ago, my fifth wish came true!"

"What were the other four?" Vlad asked, eyes glued to the road.

"I can't tell you. It's not allowed!"

Everybody burst out laughing again, except Petya, who scowled at first, but then he started laughing too. What a remarkable family this was turning out to be.

The next day, the judge would finally deliver her decision on the divorce. The little girl swinging her feet beside me was almost due, and things would be great for them. I really wanted to believe that.

Vlad parked his yellow Zhiguli in the courtyard of the two-story building, almost the same color. They walked up to the second story, but nobody came to the door when they rang the bell.

Olga called her mom on the cellphone. "Hi, Mom, where are you guys?" She paused for a second, then replied, "Okay, we'll walk over and meet you." Turning to Vlad and Petya, she said, "They're at the store buying a cake. It's not far. Let's go meet them, okay?"

They went downstairs and back outside. Despite the holiday, the street sat completely deserted except for some people walking in the distance. The family had only walked a few meters when the three of them suddenly heard somebody shout, "Stop!"—at which point they turned around.

Klim walked behind them, holding a hunting rifle. It must have been the same one he used to hunt beavers. "On your knees!" he shouted in a frightening tone of voice. He was drunk.

"Klim, don't!" Olga said. She took a step forward, shielding Vlad.

Petya, who always liked to run ahead of them a little, had frozen, hands over his mouth in horror.

I tried to think what to do, but there was no time. "Elias! Elias! SOS!" I emitted with all my strength, to summon their guardian angel, but the thing I was most afraid of... happened: Elias didn't hear me. I almost cried because of my own helplessness. What could I do? Neither my dreams, nor my signs, would be able to save anybody. It was too late.

I could see by Olga's expression that she didn't believe Klim capable of shooting them. Having shielded Vlad with her own body, she now shook her head no, as though she wanted to say, 'You're only scaring us. You won't do it.'

She was wrong.

When the shot rang out, I felt as though caught in a nightmare from which I couldn't wake up. Everything moved in slow motion: Vlad lifted Olga, who'd suddenly started to sit, slowly, on the ground; the bouquet of white chrysanthemums they'd bought for Olga's mom fell out of his hands....

F-12161998 flew around beside her mother, not realizing what was happening. She looked at the blood on Olga's breast, which only a few weeks from now would've been full of milk for the little girl F-12161998 dreamt of becoming. "Mom, Mommy," she whispered. "What's wrong with you?"

Petya, screamed, "Help! He killed my mom!" He ran to the store where his grandparents had gone.

Another shot rang out, this time hitting Olga's shoulder. Everything happened within seconds, but in my perception, it took forever.

Vladimir's face expressed both fear and white rage. He realized the murderer wouldn't stop, and he jerkily tried to conceive of what he, unarmed, could do in this situation.

The nightmare continued for me, screaming in horror and unable to wake up.

Vlad carefully laid the profusely bleeding love of his life on the ground, took a few steps toward Klim, and tried to take away his weapon. During their struggle, the gun barrel turned downward, and Vlad was shot in the knee. He fell to the ground, holding his leg, his face contorted with pain.

"She tried to save you." the killer pronounced, standing over his victim, "but it didn't work out. You won't be going after what's not yours now. You took my wife, and my son."

He shot Vlad again, this time in the gut. Klim hatefully watched his rival, who lay there losing consciousness, and it was clear how happy Vlad's suffering made him.

I flew between both of the wounded. A large puddle of blood had formed under Olga, which had stained some of the chrysanthemums red. She lay unconscious.

F-12161998, who sat on Olga's chest, sobbed and raised her eyes to mine. "Peace, do something! I'm begging you!"

Klim took aim at Vlad's head.

"Elia-a-a-as!" I screamed, silently, and grabbed the rifle in a last-ditch and ludicrous attempt to stop the killer.

Oh, who am I against a rifle? Just a weightless, invisible little cloud, a puff of energy.

Yet the gun barrel suddenly jerked upwards against Klim's neck at the carotid artery.

But how?

That very second, another hand appeared by the trigger, and helped the killer's finger press down on it.

Klim's lower jaw shattered with the impact of the bullet, and blood poured from his neck, but he could still move. He took a few tottering steps to the place where Olga lay, fell to his knees, lay beside her, put an arm around her, and.... Then he moved no more.

I just couldn't understand how this could've happened, until suddenly a voice beside me said, "It's over. Now they're definitely going to banish me."

Elias stood beside me, looking at the three bodies lying on the bloodstained ground. To the people standing on the street, what happened to Klim had looked like an act of suicide. A little later, they would tell the story that way: the murderer shot the woman first, then the man, and then himself.

"Maybe we can still save them!" I shouted in a panic. "I mean, there's the baby, too!"

F-12161998 now hung from Elias's hand. "Help! Hurry up and help!" She sobbed as loudly as a real little girl. "It's your duty! You must, must, must save my mom! I want to be born!"

"Don't cry, you'll be born," Elias said in an effort to calm her down. "Please forgive me, little one. And you, too, Peace, forgive me." He raised himself about five meters off the ground, circled the area and, once certain that help was on its way, flew off.

I watched his ever-more distant form as though seeing him for the last time.

Sirens blared closer then, and a police jeep pulled up. A few minutes later, an ambulance arrived. As they lifted Olga onto the stretcher, an aging but still beautiful woman ran up to her, shouting, "Olga, my daughter, my dear daughter."

An old man stood next to her, holding his grandson tightly by the hand and quietly crying, the way men do. Their daughter lay unconscious because of all the blood she'd lost.

They rushed the wounded to the Central District Hospital, and I flew after them.

Klim didn't need medical attention anymore.

Chapter 34

The hospital left me with a painful impression: the long corridors lined with numerous doors, people in white smocks everywhere you looked. It reminded me of our infirmary, where you could find all the souls who, as determined by the management, needed involuntary hospitalization. They might have banished the misfit angels, but they directed the lost souls to the kind of hospital from which one could only be discharged after a certain period of time — the heavenly analogue of the hospital for the mentally ill. Even the name was similar: 'hospital for confused souls.'

I listened to the doctors talking. Olga had been shot in the shoulder and right lung. Her water had broken prematurely, and her contractions were weak. She'd need a Caesarian birth. The doctors hoped to save both mother and child, and summoned specialists from obstetrics to the operating room.

Vladimir had also lost a lot of blood, and they prepared him for emergency surgery. One of the surgeons said to a nurse, as he put on his sterile gloves, "The guy's stomach wound is almost as big as Pushkin's was. Too bad medicine was so undeveloped back then. They probably could've saved the poet, today."

"I feel sorry for the woman," the nurse replied. "Why do this to her, being pregnant?"

I didn't stick around for Olga's surgery. It would be enough that F-12161998, whom I would see for the last time today, would be by her mother's side the whole time.

Olga's parents waited in the corridor, hoping for a miracle, their faces puffy and stained with tears. They'd left Petya with their neighbors, after telling him the doctors would save his mom, without fail.

The surgery lasted almost four hours, and when the surgeon appeared in the corridor, Olga's mother stood up, fearful of hearing the most terrifying news of all.

"Your daughter has suffered tremendous blood loss, due to the wound and the Caesarian birth, and she needs an immediate transfusion, but her blood type is rare—AB negative. We're doing everything we can. The baby, your granddaughter, is fine."

Olga's mom put her head on her husband's shoulder and quietly started to cry.

He patted her on the back and said, "Don't cry. Don't cry. Everything will work out."

The newborn's cry came from the operating room. I peeked in and saw the tiny red body on the table as the obstetrician performed all the necessary procedures, rubbing the baby's skin and smearing it with something. They'd clipped a metal object that looked like a pair of scissors to the end of the belly button. Finally, they swaddled her and left her alone.

I looked into her blue eyes—just like the ones her little soul had dreamed of having. The little thing looked right at me, and for a second, she seemed to recognize me.

F-12161998 wasn't around anymore. She'd been born.

"Shelina. Girl. March 8, 18:25. Weight 3150 gr., length 52 cm. Write it on the tag, please," the obstetrician said, dictating to the nurse.

Just then, I heard Vlad's phone ring. A moment later, I heard Olga's phone ring. Then a female orderly in the department rifled through the patients' clothing and turned both phones off.

Lera tried to call Vlad. According to her calculations, he should've been back in the city by now. She'd prepared the holiday dinner so they could celebrate March 8th together, and Olga's divorce from Klim, at the same time.

"I can't understand why he's not picking up," she said to Artem. "He's never done this before."

"Anything's possible," he said. "Maybe he left his phone in the car."

"This is all very strange, somehow. I mean, Olga's not answering either. Did she leave her phone in the car, too?" She tried both numbers again. "And now they're both turned off. That is very strange," she said, beside herself. "What if something happened on their way back? Anything could happen on the highway. Those shuttle buses are always crashing. It's in the news all the time."

"Or maybe they changed their minds," Artem suggested, "and decided to spend the evening on their own, so they turned off their phones. That happens all the time, too."

"No, that's not like them at all. I'll keep trying, and maybe I'll get through."

"Stop bothering them!" Artem suddenly raised his voice, annoyed. He sat at the computer, focused on dashing off his next article for the paper.

His reprimand hurt Lera and, compounded by her concern for her friends, she wanted to cry. She sat down at her computer and logged onto her favorite forum. These days, she only went there when she had something to cry about.

She started a new thread using her own handle of 'Orange': *The Happy Marriage as Oxymoron*.

Meanwhile, they'd tried transfusing Olga with donor blood, but she never did regain consciousness. That night, having dozed off on the windowsill, I saw an adult female soul who quickly passed through the door of the intensive care unit and disappeared.

Vladimir remained in serious condition, and was confused after the anesthetic. He kept calling for Olga. A day after the operation, they informed him of the birth of his daughter, and of the fact that they hadn't been able to save her mother. Vlad silently buried his face in his pillow, while his shoulders shook convulsively.

They buried Olga six days later at the South Cemetery, on the outskirts of St. Petersburg.

First, they'd driven the coffin to the church outside the cemetery gates. I overheard a conversation between two women who were going inside.

"I don't think he would've killed her," said the first, "if she hadn't shielded him with her body. She took someone else's fate upon herself."

The second replied with a sigh, "I feel so sorry for the children."

The sound of singing wafted from the church, and I decided to stay outside. I saw the same soul I'd seen at the hospital. She went in at the same time as everybody else. After that, I never saw her again.

The burial was so painful: I'd never seen so many human tears at the same time. It hurt to look at Olga's parents, and Lera's eyes had so swollen from crying that I barely recognized her. She held Artem's hand, squeezing it hard from time to time.

They'd decided not to bring Petya to the funeral, in order not to traumatize him further.

Vladimir remained in the hospital, unable to walk.

I didn't know where they'd buried Klim, and I didn't care.

Only then did I realize, after the umpteenth time, just how irresponsible those in charge of assigning guardian angels really were, and just how terribly their negligence could affect people. They should never have left this lost person, angry at the whole world, on his own — not under any circumstances!

More than anything, what worried me now was the question of what would happen to Elias.

Chapter 35

Angel with the Golden Hair,
You prolonged the hardship of my youth.
I don't want to grow old, but what else is there – death?
There is no death,
But only our effortless ingress into another world.

Lera's mom, Marina Ivanovna, sat at Vlad's bedside with a hospital gown thrown over her shoulders. She'd written these lines for him, from one of her own poems, onto a postcard bearing a bird's eye view of Jerusalem.

"Vlad, dear, take this. I was in Jerusalem recently on a pilgrimage. They took us to an orthodox monastery and I got to know a female monk there who, just like you, was also the same age as Christ and from St. Petersburg. She first went there as a pilgrim, and God saved her from loneliness, and now she's completely happy. Such an amazing girl! Her name's Marina, like me." She tried her best to distract him, but didn't seem to be succeeding. "Vlad, my dear, don't cry. I can't bear to see you cry. Everything will be okay. I don't think Olga would want you to suffer this way. You have a baby daughter! Have you decided what to name her?"

"Olga decided long ago," he said. "She'll be named Lyubochka."

"Ah, Lyubov. What a beautiful word for 'love,' and such a meaningful name!" Marina stroked Vlad's hand. "She'll always remind you of the love between you and Olga. Lyubov Vladimirovna," she cooed, listening to the sound of it and nodding her head approvingly. "Yes, very harmonious."

"I mean, I couldn't even go to the funeral," Vlad said, his eyes brimming with tears again. "And instead of saving her, she saved me. He wanted to kill *me*, not her! She shielded me with her body, for crying out loud!"

Lera's mother was extraordinarily tenderhearted, and she burst out crying, along with her daughter's friend.

I was struck by how compassionate humans were. That type of thing didn't exist in our world. I hoped I would be like that when I became a human, and that if something happened to my friend, I too would hold his hand and give him my energy, in order to help.

"It's okay, it's okay," Marina said, patting the back of Vlad's hand. "Everything will work out. Time heals all wounds, and your concern for your daughter won't let you be sad."

"Right now, I can't even imagine how I'm going to deal with things. I've never even held a little baby in my arms before."

Just then, a nurse wearing a short white smock came into the room. She was a young woman of about thirty who somehow resembled Olga, not very tall with kind grey eyes and shoulder-length reddish hair.

"Vladimir, how are you today?" she said, before dropping to a whisper. "Would you like to have a look at your daughter? I can bring her in, only don't tell anybody or I could lose my job."

Marina didn't wait for Vlad to answer. "Of course, of course. Bring her in! Vlad, dear," she said turning to him. "Haven't you seen your little girl yet?"

"No, I haven't."

"What an incredible moment for me to have come, then!" The poetic woman appeared elated. "We'll see little Lyubochka for the first time, together!"

About five minutes later, the pleasant nurse returned, holding a little bundle in a blue swaddling cloth, and walked up to Vlad's bed.

"Would you like to hold her?" she asked.

"Oh, I'd love to!" Marina replied, arms extended. She took the newborn from the nurse and carried her over to Vlad's bedside, cooing, "Oh, what a miraculous little girl! She's sleeping, the little thing. Oh, she woke up!"

The baby opened her eyes and looked into her father's eyes, wet with tears, exactly like hers. Suddenly, I heard her thoughts: *"Oh, that's my papa! Exactly the way he was the first time I saw him, except a little tired. Hi, Dad!"* I even thought I saw her smile.

"Marina Ivanovna," Vlad said, "did she just smile at me? Can babies actually smile at that age?"

"Vlad, dear, right now it's just a physiological reflex." Lera nodded as if from her own maternal experience. "She doesn't know who's before her yet. She'll start recognizing you in two or three months."

What she'd said was funny to me. I felt affection toward this kind, spontaneous woman who was able to write such a lucid poem about an angel and death, and I was amazed at how faithfully she conveyed everything. Most likely, people who wrote poetry were able to feel more keenly than others.

Some people are gifted at baking beautiful cakes, while some are gifted at writing soulful poems.

I threw a parting glance at the idyllic scene, in which Vladimir looked lovingly at his daughter, and decided they didn't need me there anymore. Even when I saw Lera walk up the stairs to the hospital as I flew away, I didn't turn back.

I was very worried about my boss.

Chapter 36

I flew around from place to place and threw a barrage of questions at every guardian angel I encountered, but they all said they didn't know anything about Elias, as though he simply didn't exist. I managed to overhear a conversation about two angels who'd been sent down to Earth at once, but when they noticed me, the angels quickly changed the subject. I got the impression they were forbidden to talk about that type of thing out loud.

It occurred to me that I should find Lera's guardian angel, but I was afraid I would lose control of myself and start asking her questions—not only about Elias—and I feared finding out something about the woman who might have become my mother that I wouldn't want to hear. It was easier to live with my daydreams.

I checked out the place where new souls like me got together, and saw F-12161998's girlfriends, who were discussing what had happened.

"It's good that she was born, alive and healthy, at least!" one said to another.

"And luckily her dad lived, too."

"It's the most horrifying thing I've ever heard of in my whole life," said another, who would surely have nodded her head in the air, if souls could nod their heads.

They all hailed me, but I indicated I was in a real hurry. I wasn't into female gossip.

I kept summoning Elias by name, over and over....

A week had gone by since the last time I'd seen my guardian angel. He hadn't come to Olga's funeral. Could it be he was ashamed for not having managed to save her?

Tired of my endless, unsuccessful searching for him, I dropped by our customary meeting place. I sat there for about two hours, thinking, imagining. My contemplation of this 'could have been' scenario—which had not been—made me utterly despondent, and I firmly decided I wouldn't budge until meeting with Elias. After all, he'd have to show up there sooner or later.

I spent another half day like that, dozing, and then finally heard that familiar voice through my half-sleep.

"You waiting for me, my faithful friend?"

"Elias!" I almost hopped up and down with happiness.

"Hi Peace." He looked extraordinarily calm. "I've come to say goodbye, and to admit that you've become like a son to me during our time together. What I mean is, if angels had children, I'd want to have a son like you — trustworthy, loving, and responsible. For a long time, I've also wanted to tell you that you're so funny in these green checked pants with the hole in the knee!" Elias smiled, and slapped me on the spot where he saw the hole in my pants. "And your hair's really great, too — so thick, with all those funny little waves, and bright red. Seems you told me that's the kind of hair your Lera had when you first saw her, right?"

"I didn't know you saw me that way," I said, both happy and sad. I waited to hear what he'd say next.

"They've suspended me, Peace," he finally announced. "I'm wearing these wings for the last time today." He spread one of the wings and glided his hand over it, caressing the feathers as though he were saying goodbye to each.

"Where are your wings, that I loved?" I uttered quietly.

"Is that from a song?"

"Yes. Then it goes, 'I see fresh scars on the back, smooth as velvet. I feel like crying from the pain, or losing myself in sleep. Where are your wings, that I loved so?'"

"Powerful words. When I'm on Earth, I'll probably hear the song, except it won't resonate with me. I only have a few hours left of remembering who I am, and while I still do, I wanted to leave you with some completely inappropriate parting words."

I looked at him in anticipation.

"There are no rules, Peace!" His voice rose slightly. "Rules are nothing compared to what your soul desires. You know best what's best for you. Do you love your Lera?"

I hadn't expected this question. "So much!"

"If you love her, be with her! Think about it... somebody decided you're not allowed to try again." He laughed. "So what? Everybody sitting up there — " He pointed upwards with his finger. " — is a dumbbell, just like us. They just make themselves out to be learned men with serious faces. Whereas happiness has nothing to do with finding peace and stability, or observing the rules imposed by them. Happiness is knowing that you are your own master! You be the master of your own life, understand?" He smiled sadly and lightly tickled my nose.

"Understood," I replied, terribly saddened by having to part with him. "Elias, where are you going right now? Do you at least know what city you'll be living in?"

"Why bother having to travel? I'll latch onto some bronze angel in St. Petersburg. They're a dime a dozen there. It's just wait for my time to come, and then, go wherever fate takes me. How should I know what they do with people who've lost their memory? They might even put me on television," he said, proudly, "or hang my picture all over the city, asking if anybody's seen me before."

"It's sad, knowing that I could see you somewhere and you won't even recognize me," I said.

"My dear, never mind that. I won't even see you!" He burst out laughing. "And when I'm able to see, you won't recognize me, either!"

"Oh yeah, I completely forgot. It's all so complicated." I sighed.

"Yeah, but it's interesting! Every one of us begins a new life, and that's great!" He burst with optimism, even in the face of all this. "You will definitely be born, and you'll be a very talented and unusual little boy. You may even become a famous inventor. Everything depends exclusively on you. March ahead, and fear nothing! I mean, fly ahead." He laughed again and slapped me on the shoulder.

I sensed that he was actually happy with the prospect of becoming a human.

We sat there in silence for a few more seconds, as people do before one of them embarks on a long journey.

Then, Elias stood up and spread his wings. "Okay, then, I guess that's all. Oh, I almost forgot!" He handed me a little piece of paper. "Here's a phone number you have to give to Masha, but in a way she'll remember it without fail, and dial it when she needs to."

"And when exactly will she need to?" I asked, as he watched me shove the paper into the pocket of my green pants.

"I'll explain." He sat down again and closed his wings. "In the next six months, Masha's life is going to be anything but rosy. There won't be any problems with the baby—he'll be perfectly normal and sufficiently chubby when he's born—but our girl won't be able to handle all the difficulties, and after a few months, she'll put him in state care. No, no, she won't renounce him, and she'll visit," he said, calming me down after seeing my rounded eyes. "But her morale and situation won't improve by doing this, even though she'll find a job and start making a little money. Ultimately, there will come a time in her life when she feels completely desperate and alone. She'll start walking the streets and decide to send a text message with the question, 'Please tell me how I'm supposed to carry on,' to a randomly dialed number. But that number can't be random! This is my final important assignment for you to fulfill. Have you understood me, Peace?"

"Yes, but whose number is it?" I asked, dying of curiosity. "And what will they tell her?"

"It's the number of a good person, my curious little friend. He's Swedish, and his name is Martin. A week ago, he came to St. Petersburg for work on a year's contract, and this is the number he chose. Martin is the person with whom Masha can put her life back on the preordained path. Together, they'll take the little boy out of the children's home and go away to Sweden, when Martin's contract is up. When Masha's son is eleven year's old, he'll meet an artist in Stockholm who'll help him develop his talent for painting. So, Peace, dream up another dream for her, or write the number on the billboard across from her window, whichever your heart desires. I trust you implicitly, as you're really good at that, and I know you won't screw it up."

"I won't screw it up. You can count on me," I assured him.

"And don't drop Vladimir, either," Elias added. "Who knows when *those* guys—" He pointed up again. "—will be ready to assign him a new guardian angel."

"I promise!"

"Good luck, my dear Peace. I believe things will work out well for you, absolutely. Never give up!"

As he prepared to fly off, Elias turned his back to me, and I saw his massive wings, so precious to me, for the last time. I wanted desperately to throw my arms around his neck and tell him he was near and dear to my heart, and that I'd miss him, but I controlled myself. Some things don't need to be said to be understood.

Chapter 37

I sat on the table alongside Lera's mobile, when it suddenly started making a buzzing sound that was so eerie it scared me. Lera grabbed the phone, looked at the display, touched the screen and said, "Hi, Anya!"

"Hi, Lera," came the reply. "I know you're not in the mood to celebrate right now, but we've finally decided to christen Romka."

This time I could hear every word.

"My Aunt Lyuda's here from Moscow, but only for a couple of days. She's a real believer, and who knows when she'll be back. Can you make it Saturday morning?"

"Of course. Even if I were busy, I'd change my plans. A christening is sacred! And right now, it wouldn't hurt if my life changed for the better, which is what they say happens when you become godmother to a little boy."

"Oh, yeah, of course. I remember you saying something about that." Anya laughed. "Excellent, then. So, we'll meet at the exit from the Moskovskaya metro station at noon, and drive over to the Chesmenskaya church together. It's a very beautiful and unusual church, by the way."

"I've never been there, but that sounds like a plan! Don't worry about the cross. I'll buy one. I remember from the last time that it's the sacred obligation of the godmother."

"Great," said Anya, contentedly. "See you then!"

That Saturday, I decided to go into a church for the first time. I couldn't miss the act they called the "christening." I was terribly curious to know what they did to the kids. Plus, Romka was the same child who made me realize Lera existed in the world, and that she would've liked to have a son like me. I really wanted to see this little boy, at least once.

The nine-month-old future godson, in his bright yellow fuzzy little jacket with a hood, looked like a fluffy chick. In the church, I examined him more closely, without his outerwear. He was a sweet little kid with fat little cheeks and blue-grey eyes, exactly like his mother, Anya. He also had blond hair and thick lashes, just like Elias's. Romka didn't stay still for a second. They passed him from person to person, and he wriggled around in everyone's arms like a snake. He fell quiet only in Anya's arms, and even then, just for a couple of minutes.

Romka's father, a tall, thin blond, named Lesha, stood off to the side with his friend. They were making fun of the proceedings. They'd invited the friend, whose surname was Semeykin, to be the godfather. On hearing such a soulful surname, derived from the Russian word for 'family,' Lera jokingly lamented that if it were Artem's, their marriage would last a lifetime because, she asserted, a Semeykin wouldn't have it any other way.

To my relief, they sang no songs in the church that day. The affair took place after the morning service, and the priest, who was christening, 'the Servant of God, Roman,' only read out the prayers. Lera stood beside him, holding the heavy and very agile boy throughout the whole ceremony. The godfather with the patriarchal surname only observed the proceedings.

I felt a little sorry for Lera, and imagined that I could've been in Romka's place. Then, instead of just holding such an impressive little tot during the ceremony, she would've been able to do it every day: from the kitchen to the living room, from there to the bathroom, and so on. I empathized with all mothers of small but heavy children, and envied this particular one a little, because Lera had become his 'mother,' even if only a godmother.

They sprinkled the little Servant of God with water from a chalice they called a font, shaved a lock of hair off his head, rubbed his little hands and feet with consecrated oil, and asked the godparents to walk around the font three times with the child. At the very end, having given Lera the cross to kiss, the priest admonished her for having worn lipstick, and he uttered some sort of valediction in a harsh tone, which I couldn't make out.

After the valediction, Lera's mood was ruined. She left the church with a puzzled, even irritated, look on her face and said to everybody waiting for her, "I didn't like that priest. Nor did he like me, it seems. He said I didn't have 'the light of love' within me, which is why the baby squirmed the whole time. How wise he is? Sheesh! Well, Romka also squirmed with Lesha. I guess his light of love was extinguished, too."

I wanted to calm her down, somehow, and explain to the priest that he was wrong, but it wasn't as if I could have.

Anya advised her new 'co-mother' to forget about it, although Romka's father did try to defend him a little, at first. The company went back to the house for the celebratory buffet of hot snacks. Artem was expected to make it a little later, once he was through running around on his journalistic business.

After everybody was seated at the table, and they'd put Romka in his crib, I decided to stay with him. Hearing the muffled conversations and laughter from the other room, I lay down beside him to experience what it was like being a baby. Just for a little while, I wanted to feel like the happy one who looked at the ceiling and kicked his little feet. I lay there, imagining Lera coming over to me, picking me up, smiling at me, and then sitting in the armchair and breastfeeding me, saying, "My, what a sweet baby you turned out to be!" Artem stood alongside, looking at me, also smiling because of his role in achieving such a successful result, and because he loved me.

Romka quickly fell asleep. The little cross Lera had given him glimmered on his tender baby skin. With his thick, fluffy eyelashes, he reminded me of a little angel, and I thought Elias must've been just like that when he appeared in the world, although I'd never seen an angel-baby.

I just couldn't stop thinking about the 'inappropriate advice' Elias had given me. Previously, my fears had trumped my desires, but meeting that angel had turned my consciousness around. I didn't want to subjugate myself anymore. What's more, I categorically didn't want to be some other guardian angel's subordinate, even if he were the most remarkable of all the angels.

I decided to stay with Lera, no matter what, and when the time came, I would try again to be her son.

I didn't want to meet up with the other souls, and decided I wouldn't go back.

"Can you hear me?" I shouted, silently. "I... am... not... going... back!"

As ill luck would have it, they heard me.

Invisible threads grabbed me and pulled me up, exactly as they had on the day that Lera and I had bidden each other farewell. I tried to resist, but it was impossible to fight against their power. They didn't even let me see Lera for one last time.

The next thing I heard was the sound of the doorbell, Artem's voice, and Lera's laughter.

Chapter 38

I hadn't been to Earth for two years. Even after they subtracted my six months of service in the capacity of a guardian angel's assistant, I had to spend another twenty-four months in the clinic for confused souls. If necessary, they would *prolong* my stay, or if I had done well, they might have shortened it.

Once I got there and realized it was for a long time, I frequently recalled Elias's words: *"Your thoughts, my friend, are rebellious, and nobody's going to pat you on the back for them, and if the brass finds out, they'll call you on the carpet."* I was too careless with my "Can you hear me?" Why, oh why, did I throw down the gauntlet like that? If I hadn't, they may all have just forgotten about me, but I did it.

Time dragged on endlessly. I wandered along the long corridors, constantly bumping into other souls, and I had absolutely no desire to talk to anybody. It was a hospital only in name, because it felt more like a prison. My entire treatment consisted of the head doctor summoning me every six months, and attempting to evaluate my level of submissiveness. Obviously, he didn't like something in me, based on what he discerned from his stupid color tests, or from my responses, because he kept extending the duration of my stay.

I despised those walls, and the invisible threads that had dragged me there. I even started to hate myself for having ended up there because of my own stupidity. I felt terrible, not knowing about Lera, or Artem. In fact, I didn't know anything about anybody.

That's how *exactly* two years went by. At my final examination, I behaved with the utmost calm, said what they wanted to hear, and assured them I had no intention of breaking any generally accepted rules or norms, not even in thought! Yes, *I was going to fly off and look for my new parents now. No, there would be no attempt to return to the past, I promised. Why would I? Back then, I was wrong. That angel had messed me up.*

I spoke so convincingly, they believed me, even though I was nothing but a petty, deceitful little soul. They'd left me no alternative to my pious deception. I had to save myself now, because I just couldn't stay there any longer, and I desperately wanted to see Lera.

Still, I had to find new parents quickly. They'd given me strict timeframes, and I was supposed to decide on a mother, at the very least, without delay. Then I could wait as long as I wanted, to be conceived.

They reinstated my old number, so I was M-04041999 again. Now I had to pick out a mom who wasn't in any hurry to get pregnant, preferably one of Lera's girlfriends, so that I could be around her. I'd conceived of a plan during my 'rehabilitation.'

Chapter 39

Spring had returned to St. Petersburg, but even at the end of March, the streets were full of huge puddles from the melting ice. I circled over some houses, taking in the street air, inebriated by the mere thought that I was finally free! The city dwellers walked carefully through the streets, in many places using planks that served as bridges over the puddles.

On one of these little bridges, a woman carried the sweetest little two-year-old girl, in a bright pink hat and matching little jacket. Something familiar in the little girl's eyes made me stop mid-flight, my first in such a long time. A man with a limp walked up to them, kissed the little girl on the cheek, picked her up and started spinning her around. The girl shrieked with laughter and asked her dad not to stop.

I recognized Vladimir immediately. He'd lost a lot of weight, but his eyes remained reminiscent of an icon, as always. How everything had changed since I'd been gone! F-12161998 had transformed into a wondrous creature named Lyubochka, with her dad's huge eyes, and blonde curls sticking out from under her hat.

I didn't stop to figure out who the woman beside them was. Having seen her and Vlad kiss each other on the lips when they met, I realized she wasn't just the nanny. I'd find that out later, after meeting up with Lera. After all, they were probably still friends. Having seen Vladimir, I felt somehow closer to Lera. My entire being raged, as if on fire, just knowing I'd be seeing her soon.

I flew to her full speed ahead, trying to hide my one and only fear: that she was already pregnant.

They were renovating the apartment Lera and Artem had been renting, and some man in work clothes, spattered with paint, stood on a stepladder whitewashing the ceiling. I peered into his face, but it wasn't

Artem. Suddenly the intercom rang and the man climbed down to answer it.

"Who is it?" he asked, picking up the receiver.

"It's me, dear. Open up. My keys are at the bottom of the bag of groceries. They're too hard to get," a feminine voice replied.

I didn't recognize that voice, and when the door opened, I realized why. It wasn't Lera.

I flew around the whole city trying to find her. Sometimes, I'd come across a girl who reminded me of her image—with which I was so hopelessly in love—and I'd fly after her, only to realize my mistake. I searched for her for a very long time. Over the past two years, I'd completely lost the channel of energy that had led me to Lera in the nightclub, when she and Artem decided to get married. Now, my task seemed impossible. I cursed myself for not having followed Vladimir—I could've found out through him where she now lived. I'd naively hoped that everyone had stayed in their own places. I knew better than anybody how things could change on a dime.

I flew to Liteiniy Avenue and looked through the window of Vladimir's room. Everything was different there, too. An unfamiliar old lady sat at the table, sewing something. I then flew to Lera's parents' place, but they weren't at home. Losing hope, I bolted over to Vasilevskiy Island, where Masha used to live, but found not so much as a trace of a little child living there.

Mentally, I was glad of it, hoping that things with Masha had turned out as Elias had predicted, because I'd managed to fulfill my final assignment for him before I ended up in the clinic. True, I didn't bother with sending her dreams or signs. I just left the fateful phone number in her kitchen on an orange sticker I'd gotten from Lera's place. Masha was constantly putting stickers with all kinds of information on them on her fridge, but hers were only blue or yellow.

Completely despondent, I flew over a few more streets and landed on one of the old St. Petersburg rooftops. I looked at the building across the street, at a fellow who was smoking on a tiny balcony, and at the sunlight glinting playfully on the windowpanes.

Out of boredom, I decided to count the windows, starting with the top story. I counted from right to left and, upon getting to the fifth window, was surprised to discover that the frame was orange. The rest of the window frames were painted an unremarkable dark color, whereas this one stood out from them dramatically. I was suddenly, irresistibly drawn to this window. I flew towards its bright warm color, recalling Lera's gift of the orange car freshener in Vladimir's vehicle, and the handle she used on the internet forum — Orange — and felt a glimmer of hope.

The window vent happened to be open, so I didn't even have to go through the glass to get inside! Beyond the window sat a narrow little room in which everything looked quite humorous: a radiator, painted in gray and orange stripes, as was the heating pipe that went up through the ceiling, making it look like the tail of some tropical beast. The wallpaper was covered with chaotically glued-on orange geometric figures. The pillow, bed sheet, and quilt hadn't been removed from the chesterfield, and I was more and more certain every minute that I was on the right track. Under the ceiling, a narrow strip of paper ran from wall to wall, on which someone had stenciled: "Stop passing off your dreams as reality."

This puzzled me. Was I mistaken?

I started looking around at the bookshelves, hoping to fine some photos. What a collection of things lay scattered about besides books: dried grass, a clay rabbit, two empty marble salt-cellars; multicolored, unusually-shaped little bottles, and cologne, which I'd never seen at Lera's. Stones sat here and there, too, clearly brought back from the seaside. I did come across a typical kindergarten photo of a chubby little girl, about four, with a bow in her hair, holding a toy. The girl's face remotely resembled Lera's, but lots of kids had chubby cheeks and brown eyes, so it was a bit soon to celebrate.

Nobody expected me anywhere, so, exhausted from my endless searching, I decided to take advantage of the unmade chesterfield-bed and lie down on the pillow. I fell asleep quickly.

Chapter 40

I was awakened by someone turning on the light in the room, and by a man's voice.

"You know, I've been thinking about it for a long time," he said. "And I've decided we need to get married. Will you marry me?"

"Are you kidding?" a woman replied.

"Why would I be kidding?" the man replied, somewhat insulted.

"Because today's April 1st!"

"You can see right through me!" He laughed. "God, how unbearably boring it is to talk to people with a sense of humor!"

"Well, what did you expect?" asked the woman, mischievously. "I wasn't born yesterday, you know."

Still groggy, the first thing I did was look out the window. It was dark and the streetlights were on. Then, suddenly, a butt in black jeans was lowering itself onto me! I squirmed out from under it in the nick of time, bumped into the woman, and almost screamed out of happiness. It was Lera!

She was a redhead again, with a radically short haircut. She'd lost weight, but it suited her. I looked at her and looked at her—just couldn't get enough. My feelings hadn't changed: my heart belonged to her, and her alone. I stared at her every gesture, every turn of her head, as though trying to incorporate everything about her into myself, to compensate for having been without her for so long.

Artem had almost sat on me. He'd changed, too, but in contrast to Lera, he'd gained weight and looked a lot more solid now. I recognized his old self in his soft, gray eyes with the little squint. I was so happy to see he was still with Lera, and that my plan to be born in his likeness, minus his new, trimmed beard, would finally come to fruition.

"Let's cook up some dumplings, eat, and go to sleep. I'm so tired I can barely think," Lera said. "Catching the last show at the movies is exhausting!" She wiped her brow dramatically.

"Who's cooking?" Artem asked.

"Me. I don't want you scaring the neighbors out of the kitchen again, like the time Sveta couldn't take your flattery and ran away. Remember?"

"Why have neighbors if you can't scare them?"

"I know, but I'm the one who has to live with them!" She smiled, grabbed a bag of meat dumplings out of the fridge on her way out the door, and left the room. She returned a minute later and grabbed a towel, left the room again, and came back a few minutes later wrapped in the towel, squeaky clean.

Artem said, "I've never met a single woman who showered faster than you, or came back from the restroom as fast. Are you a man, by any chance?" He pretended to be serious.

"Maybe. Shall we see?"

"What about the dumplings?"

"If I turn out to be a woman, and we lose track of time, Sveta will turn off the burner. She's up late."

"Now, that's what I call a good neighbor." He pulled Lera closer and threw her towel onto the chesterfield. "Well, now I can rest assured."

I'd never seen Lera naked before. I'd never even imagined her this way, and the female breast had only ever been a vessel, a baby's source of nourishment, but I suddenly realized it could also be a work of art.

"Man, that's beautiful," Artem said, giving voice to my thoughts, except in a less romantic way.

"Duh! Even the old homeopath I saw about my congested nasal passages made me strip down to the waist, and suggested I display myself at the Hermitage! Do you ever realize how immensely lucky you've been to be able to snuggle up to the sublime?" Lera asked, eyes laughing.

"Ye-e-e-s! And the main thing is... I get to do it for free!" Artem put his mouth to Lera's breast.

"Smart ass," she said, knocking him gently on the back of his head.

How great it is that they're still together!

As before, they were doing what I was always too bashful to watch. The sounds coming from the room, while I waited in the kitchen and watched Sveta stir their dumplings, grew louder and louder, and the finale, much clearer and longer. The strange thing was, I didn't sense the same feelings between them as before, and I sensed no swirl of energy, the kind that could have pulled me in.

I returned to the room to eavesdrop.

"Lera, was it ever this good for you with the others?" Artem suddenly asked, one arm around her bare shoulders while the other continued to caress her breasts.

"There you go again."

"And with that Oleg, the psychologist, were the two of you in sync, sexually?"

"Artem!" she said, raising her voice.

"I'd still like to know."

"And I still don't want to talk about that. I want to eat some dumplings." She tried to change the topic. "You weren't exactly a monk, either, but you don't see me intruding on your thoughts, right?"

"You know I'm not letting you off the hook that easily," he insisted.

"Look, Artem, what do you want from me?" Lera said, cruelly, in a tone I'd never heard her use before. "You're the one who left, right? I didn't throw you out. In fact, I suggested you come back more than once. The divorce was your initiative, too, but a deal's a deal. We agreed from the get-go that a divorce would be granted on first demand. Well, forgive me for only agreeing on the third. Now that we're both free, what makes you assume you're entitled to intrude on my private life? Nobody's forcing you. Be here, if you want, and if not, then don't."

"I don't want to, but for some reason, I am," he grumbled. "But I can just as easily leave!" he added defiantly.

"I know you can. I've watched you do it a couple of times, maybe more. I'm sick of counting," she calmly replied.

"So, am I leaving?" he asked, clearly hoping she'd ask him to stay.

"If you want to," Lera said, maybe a little too easily.

I could see how painful this business was for her, and her pain instantly descended upon me. I was ready to throw myself at the door, to stop Artem, but I realized it would be senseless. While I'd been away, the hairline crack between them had become enormous.

Without another word, Artem pulled on his underwear, jeans, socks, and t-shirt, and headed for the door, where he'd left his shoes and jacket.

"Wait a minute," Lera said. "You need the keys to open the door." She threw on a robe and walked over to see her ex-husband out.

Just then, the neighbor turned off the burner under the pot of dumplings. "Lera, they've fallen apart. I forgot about them. Sorry," she called out, with a guilty smile.

"Oh, thanks, Sveta, that's okay. It happens." Lera then addressed Artem as she opened the door. "You didn't get to have any dumplings."

"More for you, then. I'll have to manage without, somehow." He huffed and stomped to the elevator like a scolded puppy. "I'll eat somewhere else."

"We married for fun, but got divorced for real, right?" Lera called out.

He didn't answer her. The elevator swallowed him up and took him down.

Lera crouched down and began to cry quietly.

"Hey, what's wrong?" Sveta asked, leaning over her.

"I'm an idiot, that's what! I just keep stepping into the same river, over and over." Lera waved her hand hopelessly, took the little pot of dumplings off the stove, and took it towards her room.

"Don't get so upset. It's all grist to the mill!" the happy Sveta joked, trying to cheer her up. Her room sat on the other side of Lera's wall, and so I followed her, thinking maybe *she* could be my mother. Could anybody be closer to Lera than her next-door neighbor?

"I see, and it'll all come out as flour," Lera said, finishing the idiom. She pushed the door open with her shoulder and disappeared into her room.

Chapter 41

What had happened over the past two years? Why did they separate? Artem really had changed; he seemed to have an eternal axe to grind. And who the heck was Oleg? I'd missed so much and wanted to know everything!

The idea of making Lera's neighbor my official mother fell through immediately. That night, I could hear a child crying on the other side of the wall. Sveta turned out to be the single mom of a month-old baby girl, and we weren't allowed to pick a mother who was either pregnant or had a baby less than six months old.

I couldn't wait that long.

As it turned out, Lera had only moved in here only recently, the day Sveta came back from the maternity home. I found out when she put the baby down for the night and dropped by Lera's for some tea. The girls sat on the chesterfield, their cups on a little stand—Lera didn't have a table yet.

"You're a champ, Sveta, that's for sure. I'll never forget the way you said, 'This is happiness!'"

"When did I say that?" Sveta asked in amazement, after a sip of tea.

"You don't remember? When I was moving in, you happened to be in the hall, and I peeked in through your door and saw your baby girl on the sofa. The room was tiny, the baby was tiny, and you were so happy, just glowing. I remember asking if you'd had the baby on your own, and you said, "This is happiness!"

"Ah," Sveta remembered and laughed. "Well, it really is happiness!"

"I don't know," Lera drawled. "I wouldn't have done that. I mean, I didn't."

"You had an abortion?"

Lera nodded.

"And I wouldn't do that, no matter what," Sveta replied, as though passing judgment.

"And you didn't." Lera offered a sad smile. "I wasn't planning to, but I'm a coward. True, I told myself then that I'd never do it again, no matter what. I swore it when I realized how painful it is—not physically, of course. Now I'm afraid I won't be able to have kids at all. I've started having 'women's' problems. I'm irregular."

"So go to a doctor! Get some blood tests and an ultrasound."

"Yeah, I should. I can't find the time, though. Work always gets in the way."

"Your health is more valuable."

"Golden words!" Lera started to laugh, until she saw the serious look on Sveta's face. "Smile, right now!" she commanded, "because I'm beginning to feel like a monster. I already regret having told you."

"No, you're not a monster, you just made a mistake. You'll be smarter next time," Sveta said. She was clearly a serious girl, and very 'correct.' "I feel sorry for the baby, though."

"Doesn't Sonia's father help you at all?" Lera asked, trying to get off that excruciating topic.

"Nah, neither of them help me," came Sveta's reply.

"What do you mean 'neither of them'?" Lera's eyes grew wide and round. "Are there two of them?"

"Well, at first I thought there was one, and then I remembered it could've happened the day before. So, it looks like there are two. I don't know which."

"Well, Momma, you really take the cake!"

"Yes, well, I like cake!" Sveta said, laughing.

"I'd take my hat off to you, if I had one," Lera said, taken completely off guard. "And you look like such a modest little thing."

"Looks are deceiving." Sveta snickered. "See how cunning I am?"

"I sure do. Just you and a baby, all on your own, in a ten-square-meter room. You really outsmarted everybody!"

"Well, set me up with somebody, and I won't have to be on my own!"

"I already did that once for a friend, and I haven't done it since."

"Did he end up being a jerk?"

"No, he's a remarkable man—my best friend—and she's dead because of it, murdered by her jealous husband. He shot them both, but Vlad survived. Olga was just about to have a baby. They managed to save the child. She's two now."

"How awful. And the husband's in prison?"

"In the grave. He shot himself at the scene of the crime."

"Just like in the movies. I didn't know things like that actually happened. No, it's better being single." Sveta appeared to be in shock.

"Sometimes I think so too, and I'm still raring to go."

"How come Oleg stopped coming to see you? Did you split up?"

"Yeah. I ran into my ex-husband, and we hooked up again." Lera nodded toward the door.

I was all ears.

"This was the third time since the divorce. We find a reason to see each other. But once isn't enough, and so we happily see each other for two or three weeks, and then the blame game starts. And for some reason, I always get more of it." She smiled glumly.

"Why did you divorce?"

"Oh, I couldn't put it in a nutshell."

"So give me the long version," Sveta said, with a laugh.

"He knew too much about my previous boyfriends. He kept ruminating about my past. God only knows what he was imagining."

"How did he even find out?"

"He asked me, and so I told him."

"Boy, you're stupid."

"I know."

"You should never tell men anything."

"I can't be that way. They ask, I answer. My grandmother says I'd be worth my weight in gold in wartime, for my tongue." Lera giggled. "By the way, Artem is against abortions, like you. When he found out about mine, he said he pitied me, but... it was *the way* he said it! So high and mighty, like I was a cockroach and he was holding a shoe over me. The last thing I heard was 'Ech... I pity you.'"

"And he filed for divorce, strictly because of what he knew about your past?"

"I don't even really know why anymore. I probably just didn't measure up to his own refined standards, him being so very upstanding: 'oh, she didn't behave correctly'; 'she said the wrong thing.' When he found a video of me and my ex-boyfriend kissing, he packed up his things and went to his mother's while I was away. Before that, he'd read my diary, and even added some nasty comments in the margins."

"But all that was before he came into the picture, right?"

"Exactly, but it ate away at him. He said that since I'd kept the video, it was clearly dear to me, and he ordered me to destroy it."

"And what did you say?" Sveta sat on the edge of her seat, as though she were watching a soap opera.

"We can watch it now if you like. It's up there, on the top shelf." Lera pointed.

"So, you didn't listen to your husband, then," Sveta said, clearly amused.

Lera shook her head. "Nope. I said it was part of my life, and if I destroyed it, what would I look at in my old age, to remind me of how young and beautiful I once was. After all, he'd erased our wedding video."

"You rock!" Sveta extended her arm to shake Lera's hand. "I would've kept the video too. What a pity it would've been to get rid of it!"

"Of course it would! And it's not porn, just a completely innocent kiss! It's not just that. It's a walk through the Summer Garden and lots of other stuff."

"Why did he erase the wedding video?"

"He probably didn't want any physical evidence of the wedding he didn't like remembering."

"I guess. That's rough. So why do you keep seeing him?" Sveta asked, puzzled. "I like Oleg. He's so handsome, and calm, whereas this one... he seems so ill-defined. Why bother with the constant mind games?"

"I'm attracted to him. I don't know why, but it's so strong." Lera drank up her tea and set the empty cup on the stand. "It's mutual, by the way, from the second we see each other. But before long, we start grating on each other. Sometimes I think we should just have sex, preferably in silence, and then go home, respectively, because as soon as we start talking, the mutual rebukes start. He attacks, and I can't hold myself back from reacting. In the end, it all goes to hell."

"Oh, I don't know, Lera." Sveta finished her tea. "I've never been in your position, so I can't be the judge. To my mind, you're just wasting your time instead of finding yourself a normal guy and having a baby. You *do* want to have a baby, right?"

I froze.

"I do," Lera replied, confidently. "Oleg and I discussed it several times, and even considered renting an apartment, getting married, and having a baby. He wants a son, and he's even decided on a name. And then, as if to spite me, Artem comes back into my life. I didn't want to have to lie to anybody, and so I broke it off with Oleg."

"Too bad. Maybe you can still patch things up?"

At this point, I flew down off the curtain rod and sat on the stand alongside the tea cups, and shifted my eyes from one girl to the other, depending on who was talking.

"We didn't even really argue. It's just that I'm really embarrassed about the whole thing." Lera sighed. "He's a good guy, but I guess I'm just a glutton for punishment, a lovesick cockroach that keeps crawling back for more." She slapped herself on the forehead. "I mean, I love Oleg, too, just not in the same way. Not long ago, we celebrated our six-month anniversary, and then I pulled this stunt. I hate myself for it."

"Where do you know him from? How did you meet?"

"Oleg? We went to school together. We met by chance at a café in the downtown last summer, and then we went to the old neighborhood. We were next-door neighbors and classmates. We snuck into one of the high-rises through the back, and went up to the roof so we could enjoy a bird's eye view of the city. He was smoking and I suddenly saw *"I've been looking for you"* written on the wall, which is the name of one of my favorite Zemfira songs. He was standing beside me, and it seemed like it had been written about him. It suddenly occurred to me that this was a sign, and I thought, no way was all of this a coincidence. He was "The One."

"What does he do for a living?" the ever-curious Sveta asked with continued interest.

"Oleg's a psychologist, just starting out. Not long ago, he took a job as a consultant in a rehab center out in a suburb, working with alcoholics and drug addicts, but he hasn't been able to help me, probably because I'm not one of them." Lera laughed. "I'm not one of his patients, and so he just relates to me as a plain old person, not a psychologist. Too bad. He could psycho-analyze me, prescribe some 'anti-ex-husband' pills, and we'd live happily ever after!"

"Yeah." Sveta sighed. "Things are pretty screwed up for you!"

"You've got a pretty interesting conflict going on, too," Lera rebuked.

"And the one you could've had the baby with... what's he doing now?" Sveta just wouldn't let up, as if she'd been starving for 'information' while stuck between her four walls since she'd had her baby.

"I don't know anything about him, nor do I want to. I've already suffered through that pain. It screwed me up for a lo-o-o-ng time, too. I tried to pull myself out of it by the pigtails, like Munchausen, to distract myself, but nothing helped. So I got married, thinking I'd start a whole new life and stop feeling that pain, but I only made things worse. And not just for myself. It just went on and on, until I became godmother to a little boy, and... you know, it was so strange. That very day, it all just fell away! Before that, I was just sick about it all, as though my unborn baby was always with me."

I couldn't believe what I'd just heard. My presence had been making Lera sick! I wanted to hit myself. No wonder our department prohibited the souls of the unborn babies from visiting those who prevented their birth. Was it out of consideration for her, too? If that were true, would my reappearance make Lera sad again? I didn't want that.

"Well, maybe he really was there, beside you." Sveta said. "I mean, his soul. I believe in that kind of thing."

I looked at her with respect.

"Actually, I've got three kids!" Lera suddenly said, smiling. "Only they're all godchildren, two boys and a little girl: Peter, Roman, and Lyubov. They're the loves of my life right now."

"Well, that's a sign!" Sveta gave Lera an encouraging pat on the shoulder, and it reminded me of my last meeting with Elias, and the way he slapped me on the 'knee.' "And now you have to create a fourth, your own, out of your surplus love. My advice to you is to make up with Oleg. He's a pretty good guy."

"If he'll forgive me." Lera smiled sadly again.

"If he loves you, he'll forgive you!" Sveta assured her, and on hearing her baby whimper through the wall, she stood up. "I'll keep my fingers crossed for you."

"Please do," Lera said, clearly in better spirits. "I'll try. I don't want what we had to end this way. Just forget everything I've been blathering about. Consider it an early April Fool's joke," she added with a wink.

"What a long joke it turned out to be!" Sveta smiled.

"I guess brevity isn't always the soul of wit!"

Sveta went back to her own room, leaving the two of us alone. I snuggled up in Lera's red hair, which smelled so nicely of shampoo—the hair that was so dear to me. She scratched the back of her head, as though she'd felt something again, as she had when I first saw her. I felt like I was in a warm, orange ocean that was rocking me on its waves. I felt so good that I forgot about everything in the world, until I noticed the light from the computer monitor.

Chapter 42

Lera returned to her favorite online forum. On hearing a loud "Unbelievable!" I got down to reading what had amazed her so.

> *Orange, I know you log on regularly and will definitely see my message. I want to publicly confess that in these past few weeks, I've realized that I'm in love with you. It's hard for me to think that all our plans for a life together could be ruined by a person with whom, as you told me yourself, you had a 'three-week long relationship of an irresistible nature.' I've spent half of that time trying to find the strength to understand and accept it, as well as the strength to forgive you. And I seem to have succeeded! I'm a crummy psychologist, but I'm not a magician. I'm still learning, so please forgive me for that. It looks like you attract jealous men, but I'm working on myself, and I promise to invent some medication soon for 'resisting irresistible forces of nature.' I suggest we meet at our place at 8 p.m. on Sunday and discuss its components. P.S. In no sense should you consider this a joke. The timing just happens to coincide.*

The message was dated April 1, 2002, the contributor 'Flunky-Shrink.' The only comment under the post said "Respect!" from Potapiy, who'd written about the suit a long time ago.

Lera stood up and paced excitedly from one end of her narrow room to the other, alternating between outbursts of "Wow!" and "Unbelievable!"

I'd hardly ever seen her so agitated with happiness. Now I was in a hurry to see this Flunky-Shrink myself.

"Their place" turned out to be the Neva embankment by the Birzhevoy Bridge, on the Petrogradskaya side. I realized it was likely the cafe where the former classmates had met by chance. I could see the tall figure in black from a distance. This Oleg fellow sure liked black:

every single article of clothing he had on was black. The flunky psychologist turned out to be genuinely handsome and a real strapper. There was something monumental about him, his stony face expressing no emotions. He had the kind of piercing, gray eyes you'd expect of a psychologist. I can't say I liked him off the bat, but at least I didn't feel the kind of antipathy I had for Victor.

"Hi, Oleg," Lera said, walking up to him with a guilty expression on her face.

"Hello, Sunshine! I'm happy you read my message in time. Otherwise, I would've stood here freezing like an idiot until nighttime."

"Would you really have waited for me until nighttime?"

"Well, I didn't know exactly when you'd read it, but yes, I would've waited."

"Fate has sent me such a loyal fan, and here I am, messing around like a bonehead."

"We're going to close that topic, without even opening it, okay?"

Although he'd said it softly, I sensed a certain chill in his gaze.

Lera nodded. "Then how about discussing the ingredients in your pill for resisting the irresistible forces of nature?"

"I think I'll work on it myself." Stony smiled and pulled Lera close for a kiss. "When I'm all alone in complete silence, but right now, let's go somewhere. I got paid today, and I want to buy you dinner."

She beamed a smile. "Sounds good to me. As you know, I never object to going out for dinner."

They stood on the riverbank for another half-hour, talking and kissing, and I looked at an ancient boat resting in dry dock. What an amazing boat, I thought. Oh, to just get on it and drift far, far away, where nobody could control me, and it would be just Lera and me. Or maybe the three of us, I thought, peering suspiciously at Oleg's stony face. I wasn't sure about that. I'd have to examine him more closely. Stony was so odd, but he did seem to love Lera, truly, and she seemed to relate to him, heart to heart, but.... I definitely sensed a 'but' there, but couldn't quite put my finger on it.

They stopped into a little pub nearby, in a cellar, ordered two beers, some nuts, and something hot to eat. It turned out Stony was even wearing a black shirt under his jacket.

Hopeless. I sighed.

Meanwhile, Lera was dressed so colorfully, in her orange hat and scarf, a multi-colored jacket, and a striped top, in all the colors of the rainbow, and a pair of checkered pants—black, red, and white.

While they waited for their supper, she said, "You know, my friend Stasya and I are going to the Czech Republic for a week this summer, and next Saturday, Vlad and I are going skydiving! We've been planning to do it for at least two years."

"Oh boy!" Stony said, trying to crack open a pistachio nut with his teeth. "If you don't mind, I'll join you on the sky jump. I've always wanted to try that. Where in the Czech Republic are you going, and who's Stasya? How come I don't know her?"

"To Prague, Carlsbad, Kutná Hora, Český Krumlov, and somewhere else. I don't know the whole itinerary yet. Stasya really needs to go on a trip. All she does is sit at home, gathering dust. She won't even go out for a walk! I barely managed to convince her to go with me. Imagine: she's twenty-five years old and never been kissed!"

Stony let out a whistle and had a sip of beer. "Hard to believe, in this day and age."

I let out a whistle too. Just the kind of future mother I had in mind, not in any rush to conceive! I had to see this Stasya as soon as possible and let our 'spiritual' chancellery know that I'd decided on someone. Then, I could do whatever I wanted, at my own pace—there was no time limit on the rest! All they needed to know was that I was patiently waiting for my mom to meet and fall in love with a decent man, and that I would put all my energy into achieving that goal. I was so enthused and happy, I started flying circles around Lera's mug of beer.

"As you can see, it still happens," Lera replied, and continued the story of her old-fashioned friend. "She works in a library, is terribly indecisive but really nice, and she looks like a Barbie doll—all legs! Even with all that going for her, she constantly second-guesses herself, and she's afraid of everything, so I want to expand her world. Who knows, somebody might fall in love with her along the way." She laughed. "Then I'll help him pin her down for that first kiss. She'll like it there, and I'll loosen her up a little!" She burst out laughing. "The important thing is to get the ball rolling! Anyway, she and I are going to the travel agency tomorrow morning to pay for the package."

"You're forever fussing over your friends," Stony said, as if he were a little jealous. "Can't I go with you?"

"Would you get the time off? You just started working there, right?"

"Right, no vacation time." He sighed.

"The day I get back, you and I'll go to the Zemfira concert. Our newspaper is the media sponsor. There'll be free tickets." She caressed his hand. "Don't despair. I'll only be gone for a week. I hope you won't be jealous of me and Stasya."

"Not of Stasya, but what if somebody along the way falls for you instead?"

"Come on! My beauty pales to Stasya's! With those legs of hers, I don't stand a chance!"

"It's not the legs, it's the charm, and you're loaded with it." Stony seemed to know such things from experience.

"By the way," Lera suddenly said, "want to know a sure-fire way to get men to stop paying attention to me?"

Stony looked at her inquisitively.

"Knock me up!" She laughed. "Then the only thing on my mind will be motherhood, and whatever vibes I give off to men will diminish—dramatically!"

"Not a bad idea," the flunky psychologist said, grinning. "How 'bout tonight?"

"Oh, it won't happen tonight, for technical reasons, but you can definitely try it in about ten days," she said.

"Deal!"

The future parents held hands and laughed.

I was perplexed. Did that mean Stony would be my dad? Hmm... imagining him in that role made me uneasy. I looked into his eyes, but got nothing. Then I looked at his hands, his long, slender fingers, like a pianist's. Did I want these hands to hold me? I wasn't sure. Stony didn't arouse any warmth in me. Out of the two of them, I only loved Lera. Too bad things didn't work out for her with Artem. What mysterious force attracted them so irresistibly to each other, and what pushed them apart so quickly? I could only assume that, possibly, by some quirk of fate, they were meant to have a child together. But what had stood in the way? What if I was supposed to be that child, but wasn't because we were apart at the time? I couldn't ask about it, because I'd have to answer their questions about why I was so interested, given that Lera was out of bounds for me now.

I decided to resign myself to the will of the waves in the air, and go with the flow. I mean, did I really want Lera to be my mother? Yes! So, what difference did it make who would be responsible for my conception?

Que sera, sera, I decided. However, I had to meet Stasya, the only virtuous twenty-five-year-old maiden, as soon as possible and send that information upstairs. Then, I'd fly up to my own kind, tell them I found myself a new mom, and celebrate the event by dancing the traditional dance with everybody.

Yes! That will make it more convincing.

Stasya turned out to be a tall and pretty girl, with ash-colored hair pulled back in a tight ponytail. She really did resemble a Barbie doll, and even dressed like one — skinny jeans and a tight, pink sweater — but Barbie had Ken, and Stasya didn't. Then again, Barbie didn't have fashionable glasses like Stasya did.

"Hi Stas," Lera said, after finally meeting her girlfriend at the entrance to the Chernyshevskaya metro. "How come you're late? We have to hurry. I called the travel agency this morning and made all the arrangements. They're waiting for us."

"I don't know whether I should go or not. I've never even been on a plane!" Stasya said in the time it would've taken Lera to say twice as much.

"So this will be your debut!" Lera pulled Stasya by the hand.

"Well, I don't know... I've never even been out of the country. It's scary! I don't know any English, and I haven't got an international passport," Stasya went on, trying to find a reason not to go.

"So what? I speak English, and we'll always be together, I promise." Lera held Stasya's hand tightly. "By the way, they understand Russian there, and the agency will look after your passport. There's lots of time. What I can't believe is that, at twenty-five, you still don't have an external passport, not to mention everything else you still haven't done!"

"How easy everything is for you." Stasya sighed and followed Lera submissively.

Yes, this was an ideal candidate. With Stasya's approach to life, picking her as my mom would leave me plenty of time to take it easy. Flying to the Czech Republic with her and Lera would be cool. I'd never been to any other country, either.

I got her last name from the forms at the travel agency, and left them alone to figure out their holiday package while I flew up to the other souls. Knowing how well I'd thought things out, I felt light at heart. Now, they'd get off my back and I'd be completely free. I was so happy, I even felt like singing, but I controlled myself.

The first thing I did was inform the higher-ups of my decision, which earned me their praise for my efficiency. Then, in keeping with my plan, I flew over to my 'colleagues.' Knowing all about my sad story, the little souls surrounded me and demanded all the details. How stupid they seemed to me, especially the girls. They were constantly babbling, whispering and giggling about rumors. I gave them the minimum information, and as I prepared to fly off again, two future little girls caught up to me.

"Peace!" one of them shouted. "Hey, can't you hear me? Peace!"

I stopped and turned around. How did they know my angel's assistant name?

"You're Peace, right?" she said, catching up to me.

"I was, until recently," I replied cautiously.

"M-07091999 sent you a big hello!"

Masha's son?

It had been two years since he was supposed to have been born. I grew tense, expecting to hear the worst.

"He was born!"

Whew!

"I happened to be alongside him by coincidence, because my future mother is an obstetrician," she continued. "I met M-07091999 at the very second she delivered him. He begged me, if I saw a soul named Peace, to convey his greetings and a huge 'thank you' for his life."

"And do you know anything about what happened to the baby?"

"No, I only saw that he was born—a healthy little boy with dark hair."

"That's excellent news! Thanks for telling me."

"Good luck to you with your Stasya! May things work out this time!" she said.

"And do you know Lera, Stasya's friend?" the second little soul asked, jumping into our conversation. She had a clear voice. "I really like Oleg. Do you think I should choose her as my mom?"

I grew cold. "I know her as well as I do Stasya. I would say, don't choose her as a mom. I heard she has serious problems conceiving. She was just talking about it to my mom."

"What a pity. Oleg loves her so much! Maybe she'll start looking after herself and things will work out," she said hopefully. "Let's get introduced: I'm F-01152002."

I realized immediately by her number that she was a young and naive soul. I ended the conversation as quickly as possible, and flew away.

How positively annoying these future little girls are.

Chapter 43

I spent all my time with Lera now: I accompanied her to work and sat on her monitor in the office; I watched her eat lunch in the cafeteria in the company of her colleagues; and went with her to her godson Romka's birthday party—he had become an amusing three-year-old. Lera and I went to the movies together to see "What Dreams May Come," in which—and this is amazing—people had quite accurately conceived of a place where souls gathered together. They even said that these souls could imagine each other in whatever physical form they liked.

Lera took Sveta's advice and went to see the same doctor at the clinic; even I was happy to see the blue-eyed professor again. Neither he nor the surroundings had changed at all, and he greeted Lera with that same sympathetic smile as before.

"Hello, Sergey Aleksandrovich," she said. "Do you remember me?"

"Of course I do, my dear," he replied, glancing at her as he jotted something down about the previous patient. "Tanya, bring me the dossier, please," he said to the nurse, looking inquisitively at Lera.

"Vorobyeva," Lera said, loudly enough for the nurse to hear, smiling at her favorite doctor's slyness, "Valeria."

"Tell me what's troubling you, Valeria," he said.

"Well, I've finally found the right man, and we want to have a baby together, but there's something strange going on in my body. Sometimes, I don't have my period for six months. I don't want to have any problems conceiving, and so I decided to come and have you examine me, seeing as you're almost my family doctor," she concluded tenderly. "Even though, for the time being, my family only consists of one person, I've got great potential!" she joked.

"Good girl. You're doing the right thing. It's always better to visit your doctor before such an important step. Have a seat in that chair and I'll have a look at you."

I turned away toward the window and started looking out at the courtyard, where some kids ran around in the playground outside the building next door. I figured everything would be in order with Lera, and that they'd tell her she was worried for nothing, but that didn't happen.

The doctor took some swabs and sent her to get an ultrasound.

Here we were again, in the same office she and had visited two and a half years ago, but this time there was no sign of happiness on her face.

"Is there something wrong?" she asked the diagnostician, who slid the apparatus over her lower abdomen.

"Looks like polycystic ovary syndrome," the latter replied, continuing the process.

"What does that mean? Will I not be able to have kids?"

I touched her hand, which was ice-cold, and through it I felt the horror gripping her heart as she awaited her 'verdict.'

"Sure, you'll have kids," the diagnostician replied, neutrally, perhaps not wanting to upset the patient. "But not in the near future. The treatment you need will take about a year. First, we have to test your hormone levels, and then we'll do it again next year."

Lera was devastated by the time she left the office, clutching the specialist's report in her hand.

Her doctor had a look at the diagnosis and confirmed everything she'd already heard. Noticing the blank expression on her face, he tried to cheer her up. "Don't worry about it, Lera, it's treatable. Everything will be fine! You'll have a baby, maybe not as soon as you'd like, but you'll definitely have one! Anyway," he added unexpectedly, "it's not always up to medicine to decide these questions. Kids are sent from up there." He pointed at the ceiling with his index finger. "So...."

"I understand." She offered a glum smile and pointed up at the ceiling too. "I'll have to hope for a miracle."

"Oh, stop, will you! The lion is not so fierce as he is painted. Just rest up this summer, get your strength back, and in September you'll come and see me. We'll do all the tests, you'll have the treatment, and everything will be fine!"

"Thank you, Sergey Aleksandrovich, you're the best." Lera sighed and, after saying goodbye, left his office.

Well, how about that? It turns out that, without even knowing, I told F-01152002 the truth. I'll have to wait a year.

Well, I'd waited this long, so another year wouldn't make any difference. Besides, Stasya pretty much guaranteed the stability of my current state.

That evening, Lera and Sveta talked over tea again, and Sveta advised her not to mention anything about the diagnosis to Oleg for the time being. "He'll get upset, and that might be a mistake. Just try first, and maybe things will work out without the treatment."

Chapter 44

On Sunday, Lera had plans to skydive with Vladimir and Oleg. They'd all agreed to meet at 10 a.m. at the Moskovskaya metro station. When I finally got out of the dreaded metro, it occurred to me that this was where we'd set out for Romka's christening on the day they took me back up. This time we'd be setting out for Gatchina Park where, following two hours of instruction, whoever felt like it could jump from a height of eight hundred meters.

Lera and I arrived before the others; Vlad called to say he was waiting outside the station in the car, and the budding psychologist was late.

Stony showed up at 10:15 am with a companion: a big man with long jet-black hair. He looked ten years older than Stony, and wore a blank expression on his face as if he were lost.

The minute I saw him, I jumped: this person was Elias's double! The similarity was astonishing! I even flew around him twice just to see whether he had wings folded under his clothes.

"Lera," Stony said. "I'd like you to meet Elijah. We work together. He wants to jump with us too."

"Hello, Elijah." Lera extended her hand.

"Sorry we're late, Lera. It's my fault. I've been on a wild goose chase, looking for yesterday." Elijah said it gallantly and with a twinkle in his eye, like someone with an unusual sense of humor.

I still couldn't get over his remarkable resemblance to Elias—even his voice sounded similar—but it couldn't be Elias. So much time had passed! Anyway, people with amnesia were supposed to be in the hospital, not roaming the streets with the intention of sky diving.

"Let's go." Lera pulled Stony by the sleeve. "Vov must be tired of waiting for us by now."

They walked up to the Zhiguli so familiar to me, and Lera made introductions, and everyone shook hands.

Elijah suddenly behaved strangely, refusing to let go of Vlad's hand, and staring fixedly into his eyes. "Have we ever met before?" he asked, finally letting go of Vlad's hand.

Vlad glanced over at Lera in disbelief, as though he were waiting for her to answer for him, but she only shrugged her shoulders in surprise.

"I don't think so," Vlad finally said. "What a question! You're kidding, right, Elijah? I didn't get it at first." He laughed a little nervously.

"No, no, he's not kidding," Oleg butted into the conversation. "Elijah suffers from retrograde amnesia, complete memory loss. We met a month ago at the rehab facility where I'm a consultant, and he helps out as a volunteer."

"Please forgive me, for God's sake, if I frightened you, Vlad," Elijah said. "It's just that on seeing you, I suddenly had a vision of you and me, together, in a war or something."

"In a war?" Lera suddenly jumped in. "Wow! What exactly did you see?"

"I saw Vlad lying on the ground in a pool of blood, with some other wounded people beside him. Maybe it's a memory from a past life, when I was a nurse during The Great Patriotic War." He laughed and looked inquisitively at Stony. "I'm completely confused, guys. Forgive me, once again, Vlad." He turned to the psychologist. "Oleg, how can that be?"

"Vlad probably reminded you of somebody you knew before, but have forgotten. If he remembered you, we could untangle your history," Stony rationally explained. "But it seems he doesn't know you, right, Vlad?"

"Not that I remember," Vladimir affirmed, "although, two years ago, I did experience a situation much like the one you described, and ever since then I've had a limp. But it wasn't a war, just a battle, and only one participant was armed. You definitely weren't there. Forgive me, too, for not being able to help you out."

Vlad got behind the wheel and turned over the ignition, and I could see how difficult the sudden onslaught of those memories was for him.

While Vladimir and Elijah were talking, I was absolutely beside myself.

Dear, dear Elias, you've come back! No matter what they call you, you'll always be the guardian angel who turned my life around.

When everybody got into the car, I snuggled up to his chest and felt so happy. My favorite people were right here beside me.

Lera and Elijah sat in the back. She talked non-stop all the way there. It turned out that during a trip to the Black sea last year, she'd already flown in a parachute.

"There's this attraction there," she said "where they tie an open parachute to you with one rope and another to a boat. The boat takes off, the straps tighten, and off you go into the sky! The boat slows down and you fly lower—they almost dunked me in the water. What's most interesting is that I can't remember the moment between being on the ground and soaring through the air. Evidently, my brain erased that stressful moment from my memory. It's too bad we can't do that with everything we'd like to forget. I'd take advantage of it. Like in 'Men in Black'—*poof*, and it's gone, like it never even existed. Oh, Elijah, I'm sorry. For God's sake, I always talk before I think."

"Don't worry about it, Lera. It's fine!" He patted her on the knee, just as he'd done to me on the last day I saw him. "I'd like to have a device like that too, except preprogrammed to restore events—of any kind. I'd just really like to remember who I am and where I'm from."

I moved away from Lera and sat on his shoulder. "You're an angel!" I shouted in his ear, knowing full well he wouldn't hear me. I just wanted to try. "But they took away your wings and erased your memory!"

"My ears are plugged like on a plane," he suddenly said. "How fast are you driving anyway, Vladimir?"

"Not over the speed limit," my potential godfather replied laconically. "You sound like a traffic inspector, Elijah!" Vlad kidded, hitting the bullseye, but my ex-boss didn't recognize him, anyway.

"So, you just plain don't remember anything at all?" Lera asked.

"Unfortunately not. Three times I've bumped into people on the street, who seemed familiar to me, like I'd seen them before, but they all just backed away from me. Evidently, my appearance is too *out there*." He thrust his chest forward and pushed a lock of black hair off his forehead. "Maybe people think I'm a junkie when I ask such strange questions. I have dreams where I'm flying. They're very interesting."

"You're flying?" Lera perked up. "How exactly do you fly? I fly in my dreams sometimes, too."

"Promise you won't laugh though?" Instead of slapping her on the knee this time, he stroked it; luckily, Oleg didn't see anything from his position in the front seat.

"Okay." Lera shot a surprised sidelong glance at his hand. "I promise not to laugh."

"I'm often an angel in my dreams, with enormous white wings, and I'm swooping down from somewhere way up high. One time, I even dreamed the bronze angels on top of the Isaac Cathedral were my friends, and we were having a conversation."

"What amazing dreams!" Lera beamed. "I'm jealous. Mine are a lot more prosaic."

"Yes, but they're not helping me remember anything about myself. I couldn't possibly have been an angel!" Elijah laughed. "Even the doctors couldn't determine the reason for my memory loss. Nobody whacked me on the head. It feels like my memory was simply deleted, like an unnecessary file. It's almost mystical."

"What if you skydive and you meet some angels up there, and they recognize you as one of them?" Stony said, as a joke, turning around in the front seat. "I wouldn't mind having a friend who's an angel!"

They talked all the way there, and I could see that Lera was beside herself with admiration for their new acquaintance.

"You have a remarkable sense of humor, Elijah," she said. "I'm sure you were a creative person before your memory loss. Mr. Psychologist," she said, suddenly addressing her boyfriend. "If the jump helps Elijah remember everything, we can patent it as a non-traditional method of curing amnesia!"

"That would be cool!" Elijah said.

"Why not?" Stony said.

"Did you bring your diapers?" Vlad suddenly asked.

Lera burst out laughing. "I not only brought one, I'm wearing it!"

"What's that for?" the former angel asked, in surprise.

"The people at work kept bugging me when I told them I was going to jump. 'You better buy some diapers, because anything can happen when you're scared,' I told Vov, and he said the same thing. So, I went and got some, just in case."

Elijah stared at her in amazement. "I get it." He smiled. "I could tell right away that you're an unusual girl."

I watched the two of them with great interest, as there was clearly a spark of mutual affection between them. Even Stony couldn't help but notice.

After the training course, they determined their jumping order according to their weight, starting with the heaviest. Elijah would go first. It was a real spectacle: the former angel, preparing to step into the abyss from the height of a bird in flight, but without his wings. The instructor opened the door, and my beloved boss disappeared in midair without a word. I could see he was completely calm; Elias was returning to his element.

Then it was Stony's turn, and he, too, stepped bravely into the abyss, followed by another man. Then it was Lera's turn.

Come on, Mom, go for it!

She went up to the open door of the plane, looked down, and immediately shrank back. "No, I'm not jumping, I'm not," she mumbled to herself.

"Come on!" the instructor shouted, his patience having run out.

"I can't!" she shouted back. Her eyes were so full of terror, I thought they'd pop right out of her head. I'd never seen Lera so frightened.

"Go back, toward the wall," the instructor said, syllable by syllable, and slammed the door shut. The draft in the plane stopped.

I could see that Lera was terribly embarrassed, but her intellect had no control over her body, which had stubbornly refused to take that step into the void. I remembered that fateful morning when she made the decision not to have me. Maybe she was overcome by the same kind of uncontrollable fear of uncertainty then, too, the fear of taking on the responsibility for such an important step. I felt sorry for her. You're *my* coward, I thought, tenderly, remembering how she stood before the mirror in the semi-darkness, begging for my forgiveness.

Vlad was supposed to jump next, but because of Lera, the plane circled again. He looked at her in mute reproach, his big blue eyes seeming to say, "*Ech, you....*"

Hers seemed to reply, "*Vov, dear, forgive me, I can't.*"

I saw that she was fighting with herself with all her might.

When the instructor opened the door again, Vlad stepped out fearlessly, and behind him, the very lightest girl in the group jumped.

Lera was left alone with the instructor and her fear. Suddenly, she took a step forward. "Help me, please! I really need to jump, but I'm so scared."

The instructor nodded. "Stand up," he commanded.

On the way home, Lera recounted how the last thing she remembered was the door opening. Then next thing she knew, the parachute chords pulled taut over her head. I flew beside her and saw the way she just 'tuned out,' and the parachute opened automatically after three seconds. Conquering her fear and slowly descending under the cupola of the parachute, she'd yelled, "Vo-o-o-v, I jumped! Can you hear me, Vov? I'm fly-y-y-ing!" But Vlad was too far away to hear.

Once she'd landed, the gang headed back. Not much had changed: Elias's memory didn't come back, and the just-in-case diaper stayed dry, but Lera had overcome her fear, and that was the main thing.

Vlad said goodbye, and invited all the daredevils over to Petya's birthday party, which would take place on the same day Lera and Stasya would return from the Czech Republic.

Chapter 45

Time passes much more quickly in the spring. Back on the ground, I noticed that 'spring people' are in much better spirits than the 'fall or winter people' I'd seen as Elias's helper. Maybe this happened because spring brought more sunshine, and summer lay just ahead, and everybody had vacation plans.

I liked flying around the city, listening to the laughter and looking for all the spring smiles. Sometimes, I would run into other souls like me, who were doing the same thing, but I did so out of curiosity, whereas they were looking for parents. We'd acknowledge each other with a sign whenever we met, then go our separate ways. At times, I thought I felt the invisible presence of another soul, even when Lera and I were alone together.

I visited Stasya a few times at the Lermontov library, which sat right next door to where Vladimir used to live. It was an amazing old building, full of books and a constant pleasant silence. Secure as I felt, knowing that nothing in Stasya's life had changed, I used to slide down the wide slippery banisters of the marble staircase from the second floor, pretending to be a rowdy little boy.

Gradually, the time to go on our trip drew near. It would be my first plane ride, and I found everything terribly interesting.

"I'm afraid, Lera," Stasya moaned at the airport. "What if it goes down? They show plane crashes so often on television!"

"Ours won't go down," Lera snapped.

"How can you be so sure?" Stasya was so visibly worried, I felt sorry for her. She was an extremely dear but terribly insecure girl, always doubting things, or afraid of something. She needed a good psychologist.

"Because I found out this morning that I'm more than likely pregnant," said the person for whose sake I was prepared to do anything. "And I'm absolutely having this baby," Lera added.

If I could have fainted, I would have. Pregnant? How could I have missed that? There wasn't a living soul around us, except for me. I did sometimes get the strange feeling that one of ours was watching me, but no matter how hard I tried, I couldn't see anybody! How could I have missed the moment of conception? Who was in my mom? Me? Or someone else, whom I couldn't see for some reason?

"Where are you? What are you skulking around for? Show yourself, and we'll talk!"

"Lera, are you kidding?" Stasya's face brimmed with tenderness. "Now that's really news! Are you sure you should be flying? Maybe we shouldn't go," she suggested, grasping at the final straw.

"Stasya! If there really is something there, it's so early on that I feel funny even talking about it. We're going because we've already taken the time off, paid for the trip, and packed our suitcases. And in case you haven't noticed, we're already at the airport!" Lera said, raising her voice.

"Who's the father? Oleg?"

"Who else could be the father, if I'm only seeing Oleg and we're planning to have a baby?"

"You never told me that." Stasya shrugged her shoulders in embarrassment.

"I don't even know, for sure. The second line on the strip is very light. Maybe there was something wrong with the test, but it was too late to run out and get another one. I'll try it again in about a week."

At this point, a winded Oleg came up to the girls, as always dressed all in black, even though it was a hot day in July. "Hi girls, sorry I'm late. I couldn't get away from work, and then I was stuck in traffic for half an hour."

"All right, all right," Lera said, reproachfully. "Actually, we were hoping you'd drive us here."

"Sorry, sweetheart, it didn't work out." Stony leaned down and kissed her on the lips. "I'll do better next time. Nice to meet you, Stasya," he said, and gallantly kissed the blushing girl's hand.

"If there ever is a next time," Lera replied. "If everything is confirmed, I'll be getting fatter and fatter until next spring. Then come the diapers, the swaddling cloths, the terry jumpsuits, pediatricians, bottles, the nursing bra... there's no time to travel! I hope you won't be late picking me up from the maternity ward!" Lera tapped him lightly on the forehead. "Otherwise, somebody else will take me away, with charisma, baby, and all."

"I won't let it come to that," Stony said, hugging her. "I'll pick you up personally, and tie the blue ribbon onto little Greg myself."

"Oh my. You've even picked out a name!" Stasya blurted out. "What if it's a girl? You'll need a pink ribbon then."

"It's going to be a boy," Stony announced, confidently.

From that moment, even I started to like him. But how could I have missed the moment of conception? I should definitely have remembered that! Could seeing the amnesiac Elias have affected me so strongly that I lost my memory too? What if it was contagious?

Lera and Oleg—there was no way I could call him my dad, not even mentally—kissed goodbye.

The girls waved to him and disappeared behind the departure gate, where all the passengers and their carry-on bags were screened and even searched. Female guards searched the women and male guards searched the men, which seemed illogical to me but, obviously, those were the rules.

On the runway, the plane accelerated and noisily took off. How cool; we were flying! My happiness reminded me of my flight with Elias. I watched through the window as we passed through a layer of clouds and ended up in clear sight of the sun, shining directly into poor Stasya's eyes.

She was flattened against the back of her seat from sheer fright.

"Calm down, now, Stasya. Everything will be fine!" Lera stroked Stasya's head.

"I'll try," Stasya answered bravely, though her eyes were shut tight.

"Maybe you should have a drink. The stewardesses will be coming around with tiny bottles of liquor. Have one... for courage."

"I don't drink."

"So what? Have one anyway! You'll thank me for it, I guarantee!"

"No, I'll get myself right somehow, without alcohol."

"Okay, it's up to you. I'm probably not allowed to." Lera closed her eyes too, and dozed off.

The girls slept for most of the flight, waking up only for breakfast. Later, a male voice announced that they'd landed in Prague, and the passengers moved slowly toward the exit.

Prague impressed me deeply. On seeing it, I realized that St. Petersburg wasn't the only beautiful city in the world. I especially liked flying around the dark figures standing on a remarkably beautiful ancient bridge, across a wide river. Tourists waited in line before some of these, placed the palms of their hands on certain areas of them, which were worn down to a shine, and made wishes.

Lera closed her eyes and did it too, intensely, and even tossed a coin over her shoulder and into the water.

I didn't know what she was thinking, and I started to worry. If she was pregnant, somebody must've beaten me to it. Otherwise, I should've been able to hear her thoughts.

I saw an angel among the sculptures on the bridge and thought of Elias. I wondered what he was doing right now in that 'rehabilitation' center. The clinic for 'confused' souls, where I'd spent two years, was essentially the same kind of center.

Almost every morning, Lera, Stasya and I took our seats on the tour bus and visited some little Czech town. The one I considered the most fun and unique was Karlovy Vary, where people could drink the mineral water that came from the springs, so hot sometimes that it steamed.

The tour guide, who had a long stick with a ragged artificial flower on the end of it, so her tourists could distinguish their group from a distance, stood before the group and said, "Legend has it that if a girl manages to keep her finger in the water for a minute, she'll get married before the year is up."

"Really?" Lera had suddenly become interested in what the tour guide was saying. "It's very curious! Stasya, what do you think?"

"How you can believe in such fairytales?" Stasya countered. There was no limit to her skepticism.

"Oh, but you have to believe in them, if you want a fairytale life! Come on, give me your finger," Lera ordered.

"You first," the careful Stasya said.

"I'm already getting married. You need it more than me."

The girls argued about it for a minute. In the end, Lera did have to stick her finger under the stream of water, but she only lasted a few seconds. "I can't. It's too hot!"

"So don't. What did I tell you?" Stasya said, somewhat didactically.

"No, hang on a minute!" Lera moved toward the stand where the drinking cups were being sold.

"Now what?" Stasya followed her.

Lera put her hand up. "Just a second, I'll be right back." She came back with a tiny pink cup, filled it with the water, waited a little, and stuck her finger in it. "Time me!" she ordered Stasya, pleased with her own cleverness.

Stasya burst out laughing. "That's cheating!"

"What do you mean? The tour guide said, 'if a girl can hold her finger in this water for a minute....' She didn't say anything about not pouring the water into a cup. Come on, let's fill another cup for you. It's probably better not to use the same one. I mean, we don't both want the same husband," she joked.

Stasya got to hold her finger in a cup too.

"I can see you're skeptical about this." Lera sighed at the expression on her girlfriend's face. "That's too bad. The main thing is believing, because then, you could stick your finger in a cup of beer and still get married this year or early in the next year!" She laughed. "And too bad I can't drink now. I could really go for a mug or two. Being in the Czech Republic and not drinking Czech beer is a waste. Maybe I could have just one."

"I don't know." Stasya shrugged. "I wouldn't."

"You wouldn't anyway." Lera grinned. "I don't think one beer's going to cause any serious damage. We should find a place to have lunch, but first, let's go to the pool!"

The girls spent a whole hour at the outdoor pool, swimming in the warm mineral water. I wanted to go in the water too, to see what it was like for a baby in its mother's womb. I jumped in and snuggled up to Lera's belly the whole time, trying to pick up on any signs of life in there, but I didn't sense anything at all.

That evening, Stony texted her:

There's a tiny Me inside you.

They constantly texted each other on that theme, seeing as it was such an emotional subject for the two of them. Lera would tell him where she and Stasya were, and about the highlights of the trip, and they'd make plans for the future. It turned out that my Stony father was already looking for an apartment for his future family.

The week flew by in an instant. Lera didn't accomplish what she'd set out to do by dragging her homebody girlfriend abroad. Nobody fell in love with Stasya on any of their excursions; she wouldn't even give her number to a Czech guy at the disco who'd asked her to slow-dance a few times.

"Why didn't you at least give him your email address?" Lera blasted her on the way back to the hotel.

"I started having doubts," Stasya said. "What was the point? There's the language barrier, I'm not planning on leaving Russia, I don't have internet at home, and I haven't even set up an email account at work yet. How would I read his emails?"

"My God, so many reasons for doing nothing!" Lera rolled her eyes. "What language barrier? First of all, Czech is very easy to understand. Second, you could've given him my email address. I check it every day. Third, get an internet connection and your own email address! And about not planning to leave Russia... Masha left, and she's so happy, she doesn't want to come back."

"You mean, the Masha who had a baby and then put him in state care?"

"Precisely."

"Where did she go? And did she take the boy along?"

"She met the most amazing Swede who speaks Russian, and she went to Sweden with him, and yes, with her son, when he turned one. Plus, how she ended up meeting the guy is amazing: when she was at her very lowest, she sent a text out to the universe that said, 'Please tell me how I'm supposed to carry on' and got an instant reply."

"What do you mean, 'out to the universe?'"

"To a random number," Lera said, as if she were talking about the most ordinary thing. "Like a stab in the dark, as they say, and suddenly she gets a reply: 'I'll tell you. Let's meet.' She says, 'When and where?' and the reply was, 'Right now. I'm completely free.' Can you imagine? They met half an hour later, because he happened to be in the area, and they liked each other immediately. That's what I call fate! How can you not believe in it, after something like that, right? You have to believe! And sticking your finger in a cup of water doesn't hurt, either. It won't fall off!"

"What an unusual story! How did the Swede react to the fact that she had a son?"

"Wonderfully! They picked Vanya up together. At first, they lived here, and when Martin's contract work was done, they got married and left for Stockholm. My ex-husband and I were their witnesses — no guests, just the four of us. Straightening out the baby's papers was a hassle because he'd been registered to Masha's ex. By law, if the child was born less than three hundred days after the divorce, they automatically list the ex-husband as the child's father, but the bio-dad signed off, willingly, and now everybody's happy, especially him. He's a great guy all around, that Kolya!" Lera concluded, sarcastically.

"Wow!" said Stasya, the whole story having left quite an impression on her. "To be so 'bang on' with a random phone number!"

"And you know, there's an interesting sequel to that story."

"I'm intrigued," Stasya replied, all ears.

"It turned out, later, that same random number was on a sticker on Masha's fridge. She has no idea where it came from, and it was a different color than all the other stickers on the fridge. Even the printing wasn't hers. It was childlike. Masha wouldn't even have noticed it in the first place, if Martin hadn't seen it the first time he went over for supper, and asked why she'd stuck his number on the fridge, if it was already in her phone! The whole thing remains a mystery to this day. I mean, it's not like some Swede decided to sneak into a random Russian girl's apartment, write his number on a sticker, put it on her fridge, and disappear, right? Talk about miracles...."

Stasya was speechless.

"So, don't be a wallflower," Lera said, slapping Stasya on the shoulder. "You need to take advantage of every possibility life has to offer! Maybe you could send a group text with Masha's winning message and double your chances!"

Our return flight was leaving the next morning. Lera used another test strip before breakfast; it turned out her pregnancy had been a case of wishful thinking. At the appearance of the single strip, I heard a sad sigh right beside me, which didn't come from Lera or Stasya. I searched the whole room, even under the bed and behind the curtains, but I didn't find anybody.

Admittedly, the news elicited a sigh from me, too, but of relief. Secretly, I still hoped Lera would take up with Artem again.

Chapter 46

"Oleg!" Upon seeing Stony at the airport, Lera hugged him around the neck.

"Hello, Sunshine! I missed you so much! How was your flight?" He kissed her on the lips.

"It was excellent, and the trip was beautiful! The Czech Republic is an amazing country, and the language is a lot of fun. It's like Russian, only really disjointed, like they're doing it for fun. Some of the same words we use in Russian mean the opposite: 'forget' means 'remember,' 'beautiful' is 'horrible,' and 'fruits' are 'vegetables.' In schools, the top mark is a one instead of five! It was like being on another planet, where everything's upside down and backwards!"

Lera chattered away enthusiastically, the trip abroad having left a deep impression on her. "The people are so polite. Every day is a good day for them. All you hear them saying is, 'Good day, good day!' And the beer is good, too."

Oleg frowned. "You drank beer there?"

"Only one mug, symbolically." She sighed, justifying herself. "And now I regret not drinking more."

"Why do you regret it?" Oleg asked in his confusion.

"The pregnancy was cancelled this morning. Looks like we failed, again. Anyway, I should go and get tested properly."

"Right," said Stony, deeply saddened by the news. "Well, maybe next time. By the way, I found an apartment not too far from where Vlad and Natasha live. We'll go see it tomorrow."

"Great! Maybe it's for the best, right?" Lera looked him steadily in the eyes. "We'll just take things as they come, one step at a time, like normal people. We'll move in together, get married, and have a baby after that. After all, we're not in Czech Republic where everything's backwards." She laughed.

I just loved her way of finding the bright side to every situation.

Stasya joined them at this point. The airline had lost her luggage, and she was extremely upset. "Why do these things always happen to me?"

"Because you're a magnet for bad luck," Lera replied. "You remind me of a sad donkey Eeyore, although I'm like Winnie-the-Pooh, sometimes." She laughed and put her arm through Stasya's. "We'll go bawl them out about your suitcase, and dare them not to find it!"

Ten minutes later, the luggage problem solved, they piled into Stony's car, a maroon Zhiguli with a gray interior. A strange and pungent odor permeated the car, and I sent Lera a thought to open the window. It seemed as though our ability to contact each other had been renewed, because she reacted almost immediately.

Stasya sat comfortably in the back seat, looking pensively out at the road. "All in all, Lera, I'm glad you and I went to Czech Republic," she suddenly said. "At least I saw a little of the world, instead of just going to work and back everyday."

"Well, thank God!" Lera smiled. "Here I was, feeling like a tyrant—dragging you around while you resist."

"No, no, thank you. Now that I have a passport, and planes seem safe enough, maybe I'll even go somewhere else."

"You should go to Turkey for a couple of weeks. Your shyness won't fly over there. The men will be all over you!" Lera laughed.

They dropped Stasya off at her door, and went to pick up a cake. It was Petya's birthday today, and she'd bought his gifts in Prague: a big, plush mole, the star of a famous Czechoslovakian animated film, and a battery-operated old witch that jerked her legs and cackled at the sound of any loud noise.

At seven that evening, she and Oleg were going to a Zemfira concert.

"Is Elijah coming to the birthday party?" Lera asked. "Vlad invited him, too."

"Yes. He bought Petya a remote-controlled helicopter."

"Cool gift!" She sighed and added, "He won't even notice my plush mole after that."

"I've got a deluxe Erector Set for him in the trunk, too, so don't worry. He'll be very happy," Oleg said soothingly.

"Oh, you're so considerate of me," Lera cooed, and she kissed him on the cheek.

They came to a district of the city called Krasnoye Selo, which reminded me of where Olga and Klim used to live, not far from Lera and her parents but very far from the city center. It was quiet and green, and even grassy, not at all like the downtown area where Lera lived now, in her communal apartment.

"There's an apartment for rent on the next street over," Oleg said. "But we'll have to come back and see it tomorrow. The agent can't show it today."

"And if we take it, we'll have to come here every day." Lera looked puzzled.

"Don't you like it? At least you'll have plenty of green space to stroll around with the baby," Oleg argued. "Just look at it! And all the fresh air!"

"That's an irrefutable plus, but let's get going. We're already late, and we can't stay past six because there's no way I'm missing Zemfira's show. We're on the guest list, so we'll use the service entrance. Oh, will Elijah find his way here on his own?" she suddenly asked, anxiously.

"Don't worry about him. He's already here. He spent the day helping Vlad work on the car."

"Are they friends?"

"I guess so."

"Well, that's great. That's just what Elijah needs right now."

The young woman I'd seen on the street, the day I was 'liberated,' opened the door at Vlad's place. I didn't get a good look at her back then, but now I noticed how much she resembled Olga. At that very second, I remembered where I'd seen her for the first time: she was the nurse who'd brought Vlad his newborn Lyubochka at the hospital! So, one thing led to another, and Olga's children ended up with a new mom. As it turned out, Vlad wasn't left without a guardian angel after all.

"Hi, Natasha," Lera said, and the girls hugged.

"Hello, hello, come in!" Natasha responded. "Grandma and Grandpa came an hour ago. We've been waiting for you!"

"Happy Birthday! Gimme five!" Oleg said, as Petya came running to the door, and he shook the boy's hand.

The kid had grown taller and much thinner since that terrifying day. He smiled, but I could see the stamp of deep and eternal sadness in his eyes.

From behind me, I heard, "Greetings to the future first-grader, from his fairy godmother!"

I turned around and burst out laughing.

Lera stood there with a sparkling magic wand in her hand, and a pair of wings she'd made out of wire and purple chiffon. She looked terribly funny.

"Hello, little boy named Peter! I'm your fairy godmother, and I've flown in all the way from the distant planet 'Czechuri' to grant you three wishes!" she said in a sing-song voice. "If there's anything I'm not able to fulfill today on your birthday, you may write it down on a piece of paper for me, and I will definitely make it come true in the near future!" She gently tapped Petya on the head with her wand. "I will also see to it that Santa gets your letter to him," she whispered, as though this were a secret. "But in the meantime, your birthday presents!"

Petya was ceremoniously presented with the cake, the mole, the erector set, and old witch Baba Yaga, whose cackle frightened him at first. Having said, "Thank you," Lera's godson took her by the hand and pulled her into the living room.

"Godmother, look! Look what Elijah gave me! A helicopter with a remote! It flies just like a real one!"

My former boss was already seated and eating something at the table. Olga's parents sat beside him, Grandpa fiddling with the helicopter and trying to figure out how to get it going, while Grandma read fairytales to little Lyubov.

In honor of her brother's birthday, the little girl wore a fancy pink dress and two little pink ribbons in her blonde, curly hair, which looked just like the roses on the cake. F-12161998 looked so sweet in her earthly manifestation!

Natasha was busy in the kitchen, replenishing the empty dishes of assorted goodies for the celebratory dining table.

I'd missed so much, during my 'spiritual rehabilitation.' I didn't know anything about how things had developed in this family after their horrific tragedy, but I could see that, in spite of everything, they'd all stuck it out together, and that made me very happy. It was a pity Elias didn't remember anything. After all, if he hadn't shown up precisely when he did on that day....

"I'm having another déjà-vu," Elijah said, turning to Oleg. "I feel as though Natasha reminds me of somebody, too, and that I've even seen the kids before. I've decided to ignore these things now. It's as though my amnesia is mocking me. I mean, if I were among people I knew, they'd recognize me, and not the other way around!"

"If you want things to be the other way around, you should go and live in the Czech Republic!" Lera said, taking over the conversation, eager to talk about her trip. "Over there, the word 'forget' means 'remember!' What do you think of that?" she exclaimed, looking at everybody in the room and waiting for their reaction.

For some reason, Lera had gotten drunk very quickly, maybe because she hadn't had enough time to eat, telling everybody about everything. Also, she'd unexpectedly switched from wine to vodka. Maybe she was upset, subconsciously, about not being pregnant. Maybe it was all of the above. Anyway, she was on a roll and went on to list a few more odd Czech words, hoping to amuse the guests—and herself, while she was at it.

To make more room at the table, they'd put it in front of the sofa where they'd seated Oleg, Lera, and my favorite angel, whom Lera suddenly started bombarding with questions.

"And what exactly do you do at the rehabilitation center?" she asked, downing another shot of vodka, after the most recent toast of many more to come. "Oleg told me about all the drug addicts and alcoholics there. Is there any common ground between you and them?"

"I help around the kitchen," Elijah replied. "Actually, I do whatever they ask me to. I don't know what my profession was before this 'thing' happened to me, but it turns out I'm not a bad cook. So, they put me in the kitchen. And as far as common ground goes, I fell in with the addicts quickly. I ended up at the center, thanks to one of them. I'd approached him on the street, because I thought he looked familiar, and asked him if he'd ever seen me before. I'd asked a lot of people the same question, and Daniel was the only one who treated me like a human being! We started talking, and he took me to the center. He'd gone through the program not long before, and stayed on as a volunteer. That's how I found my new home. The important thing is that I really enjoy helping people. It comes so naturally, as if I've always done it."

"It's like a second life." Lera marveled.

I could see she liked Elijah more and more with every shot she downed. And I could see from the way Elijah looked at her that the feeling was mutual.

"And seeing as you don't remember anything, where did your name come from?" she asked.

"I was 'christened' on the Feast day of Elijah the Prophet. Before that, I was nameless for a few months. I kept hoping to find some relatives who could tell me who I was."

"And what was the first day of your new life like?"

"You'll laugh." Elijah smiled. "I'm not sure it's even worth telling you about."

"Come on, please tell me!" she whined, now quite drunk.

"I was found early in the morning, at the Palace Square, lying at the foot of the Alexandrian Column, unconscious and completely naked. There were no signs I'd been beaten, but they did find two big symmetrically situated red marks on my back. Nobody could figure out what they were, and a week later they were gone."

"I can just imagine. My God! Naked, on the Palace Square...." Lera shook her head in amazement. "Oleg, can you imagine what Elijah must've gone through?" She turned to Oleg, who sat there dark as a storm cloud, like his old Stony self, but Lera didn't seem to notice.

I was beginning to worry about her. Olga's parents were speaking amongst themselves, the birthday boy was watching an animated film, and Natasha had gone into the other room to put the little daughter down for a nap. Vlad was the only one observing the goings on with great interest, as though he were watching a movie.

"Hey, Lera," he said. "Maybe you should slow down a little. You two have a concert to go to. It's almost half past six."

Lera nodded, acknowledging the 'heads up,' bit off half a pickle, and continued with what she was saying to Stony.

"Listen, Oleg, I feel so sorry for Elijah, imagining everything he's told me! First, he wakes up naked on the square, then he wanders around aimlessly." She turned back to Elijah. "Did they put your picture on TV at least? Or online?"

"Of course, but nobody came forward. Anyway, don't worry about me. Everything will be fine." As was his custom in his angel days, he slapped her gently on the knee, but because of the short summer dress she had on, the gesture came across as more than just friendly.

Stony noticed, and grew even gloomier. A cloud of dark energy hung over his head, like the one I'd seen over Klim.

Lera remained oblivious. "Oleg, what if we were to take him?" she blurted out.

"Who?" he asked, dumbfounded.

"What do you mean, 'who'? Elijah!"

"But 'take him' in what sense?" Stony asked. He was confused, and so was I.

"Tomorrow, we'll rent the apartment you were talking about. You said there were two rooms. He can live with us! Why should he have to hang around that center with all those sketchy types? He needs a regular job and, well, just in general." Lera slurred her words.

"Yes, I get it now. I'm going out for a smoke," Stony said, calmly, and got up from the table.

"Oleg, where are you going?" Olga's mother asked.

"Out for a smoke," he repeated, even more calmly and succinctly. He went into the hallway, put on his shoes, and noiselessly shut the door behind him.

I watched Lera, expecting her to run out after him, but she kept blathering to Elijah as though nothing was happening.

"Lera, it's after six," Vlad said. "Are you going to the concert? I'm not trying to get rid of you, it's just that you've wanted to go to it for a long time."

"Of course I'm going," she said, suddenly remembering. She started to get up from the table, and spilled somebody's glass of red wine all over the tablecloth. "Oh, I'm sorry! Where did Oleg go?" She noticed for the first time that he wasn't beside her. "Okay, I'll get going. He must be outside, smoking."

She got her things together, kissed her friends on the cheek, one by one, said goodbye to Olga's parents, kissed Petya loudly on the head, put on her shoes, and left, slamming the door behind her, which made old witch cackle.

I hurried out after Lera. I'd had a nasty premonition about Stony, and I was right. There was no sign of either Oleg or his maroon car on the street. Lera called him, and a recorded message said the client was either unavailable or out of zone.

The huge Zemfira fan, already late for her concert, grew angry. There wasn't a single bus or shuttle in sight. "How am I supposed to get out of here? It's the middle of nowhere. Imagine living in this hellhole?"

The shuttle finally showed up at 6:25 p.m., and she had to get to Avtovo metro station, then take the train from there, and then transfer to another line.

I knew from experience that being late always made her nervous.

She ended up texting Oleg, hoping he'd turn his phone back on soon.

What happened? Where did you go? Going to concert. Meet me!

He replied an hour later, when she was almost at the rear entrance to the concert hall.

I left. Obviously, things aren't working out between us.

Lera couldn't believe her eyes.

Just then, the security guard, guest list in hand, asked for her name.

"Vorobyeva," she said.

Right behind her, a familiar voice said, "And while you're at it, check off Golubkov too!"

Lera jerked her head around to face Artem.

He looked as if he'd just come back from a tropical vacation, wearing a white suit that showed off his deep suntan. The only thing missing from his new, macho image was a cigarette in the corner of his mouth.

"So, we meet again," he said, smiling. "Did you finish your dumplings?"

"And did you find somewhere else to eat?" Lera quipped, trying hard to get a grip on herself.

"I always do."

"Well, looks like you found a meal ticket, anyway. Nice tan."

"Come on, let's go, my dear ex-wife." He pushed her gently forward. "The show's been on for a long time."

I flew in behind them, overjoyed, and unable to believe this sudden turn of events. I realized that, even stripped of his former duties and without even trying, Elias was still helping me to fulfill my destiny! Surely, this was no coincidence. Would everything finally work out the way I dreamed?

Chapter 47

Things had come full circle. The two of them attended a concert again, just as they had at the very beginning, when they first met. As they looked for a couple of seats in the press gallery, Zemfira sang a song I'd often heard at Lera's house.

> *He's your boy,*
> *You're his girl.*
> *He's a deceiver,*
> *And you're not exactly a song.*
> *You left a trail, but he didn't understand*
> *What it was, who else it could be...*
> *And out came the knives*
> *And hordes of recriminations.*
> *And you got lost in lies*
> *And personal feelings.*
> *He will kill you,*
> *But not until the end.*
> *And in the meantime, inhale the evil in spring, with*
> *whomever you like.*

The song could've been about them. Zemfira's lyrics always had a strong effect on Lera, and right now it was compounded by inebriation and raw emotion over Oleg's actions. She was rehashing everything she'd talked about at the birthday party, and she just couldn't understand why he'd decided to leave. She was too drunk to assess the situation properly.

I could see she wanted Artem to embrace and pat her like a little girl. She couldn't feel my embraces and, forgetting all their discord, she trustingly put her head on his shoulder. He looked at her attentively and stroked her hair. Lera moved in closer, and the irresistible attraction clicked in again. Yet even though Artem was tender and not against continuing the evening, I sensed he was cold inside.

The heartrending songs got the better of Lera, and the onslaught of emotion made her cry. With tears running down her cheeks, she lost all self-control and whispered in his ear, "Tema, tell me honestly, did you come to this concert purposely? I mean, you've never really like Zemfira, and you must've known I wouldn't miss it for anything."

"It's not a big deal!" he replied. "It's only because at the magazine I work for now, nobody else wanted to go. So, I figured, it's Sunday, it's summer, and rather than sit at home, I might as well go."

"You're always the same. You'd never just tell the truth and say you came because you wanted to see me."

"Because it wasn't like that!" he said, even more indignantly. "I really don't need this right now." He stared at the stage.

"Okay, okay." Lera trained her eyes on the monitor, where her favorite singer's face appeared in close-up.

> It's too late to think about anything,
> I can tell you need some air,
> We're lying in such a huge puddle.
> Forgive me, my love...

That was the last song of the night, and the crowd from the concert hall made its way to the metro. Afraid the former spouses would go their separate ways, I put all my energy into not wanting that. Squeezing my eyes shut, as hard as I could, I thought, *"Please, please don't part ways so soon!"*

When they got to the intersection, Artem said, "How about a gin and tonic?"

"Let's do it," Lera said. "I had a lot to drink at Petya's birthday party, but it feels like the concert cleared my head a little, and so I can drink some more."

"What a godmother — getting drunk at the kid's birthday party!"

"I am what I am, but I did it from the heart," she said, returning his jab.

"Do you remember when we first saw each other at the office, and you agreed to go to the Shevchuk concert, but said you'd rather go see Zemfira?"

"Vaguely."

"Well, you see? It happened. And do you remember when I asked you not to destroy my life?"

"I do, but I succeeded anyway, right?"

Artem glanced away for a second. "It's not so much that. You helped me become a different person."

"And what kind of person did you become?"

"Cynical and indifferent." He looked at her cheerfully, but I could see from his eyes that he wasn't kidding.

"And it's all because of me?"

"Well, there were other women after you," he admitted, pausing as though he were remembering each of them. "A lot has happened since then, but my first emotional upheaval was directly linked to you."

"Hearing you say that is kind of nice, but sad too. I'm a real swine, right?" She took another gulp of her gin and tonic.

"A captivating swine."

"When the victim finally becomes the perpetrator," Lera mused. "I've created a monster out of myself."

"It's alive, it's moving. *It's alive!*" Artem joked, quoting *Frankenstein*.

Having waited until after the first rush for the metro had ended, they finished up their gin and tonics, and went down to the station.

They got off at the Chernyshevskaya, near Lera's place.

"What's the deal?" Lera said. "Are you walking me home or coming over?"

"How about sitting in the park?"

"No objections here!"

They bought another couple of gin and tonics from a nearby store, and sat down on a bench in the Tavrichesky Garden. Before long, the alcohol hit Lera the wrong way — again — and she started to cry, bitterly.

"What's wrong?" Artem asked, frightened.

"Tema," she said between sobs. "If only you knew how badly I'm doing! I wish I could close my eyes, then open them again and — *presto!* — it would be two years later!"

"Why two?"

"I just think everything would be fine, two years from now, but I don't want to wait that long!" She bawled like a little girl.

I could tell by the look of amazement on Artem's face that he'd never seen his ex-wife this way. He sat closer to her, hugged her hard, and whispered in her ear, "Sh-sh-sh."

Lera couldn't help but start laughing through her tears. "You remember that?"

"Of course." He smiled. "Okay, stop bawling. Should we have one more each?"

I'd never seen Lera drink so much in one day. Her mood kept swinging from high to low—she'd get sad, then start laughing like crazy.

When it had gotten dark, Artem's phone rang.

"Hi, Julia," he said, getting up off the bench. His tone of voice had changed completely. "Yes, of course I can talk. I'm at the office, catching up on a little work."

Sitting on the bench, Lera choked on her drink.

"The security guard just coughed," he said in response to the female voice on the other end. "He choked on a sip of beer. He's always drinking on the job. I'm sure they'll fire him soon."

"Yup, that's how it is," Lera mumbled.

Then, she turned her head and looked exactly at the spot where I was sitting, as though she could actually see me.

"Can you imagine such a thing?" she said, looking right at me.

It was completely dark by then. I froze.

Can she see me?

"I can't," I answered.

"Me neither! But it's happening anyway." Then she turned to look at Artem again.

It was like being at the movies, when the people beside you are commenting on a scene in the film. 'Mr. Macho' was ending his conversation.

"Yes, I'll call you tomorrow. We'll go somewhere in the evening. Bye. Kisses."

"Wow, what a good liar," Lera said. "A real pro!"

"If you want to live, learn to lie."

"Yes, yes... and who's this Julia? Not that friend of mine you were necking with, when I had a crush on you?"

"When did you have a crush on me?"

"That summer, when you were necking with Julia," she said, pursing her lips in imitation of their kiss.

"Oh, I'd completely forgotten about that! No, she's another Julia, a sexy blonde with a big bust," he bragged.

"And big hips?"

"Normal hips," he replied, as though insulted by the comment. "I like them."

It was the first time I'd seen Lera jealous. Foggy from the alcohol, it took her a few seconds to assess Artem's response and draw the necessary conclusions, but her emotions compensated for the lag.

She got up off the bench, grabbed him by the lapels, and shouted, "Oh, so *that's* how it is! You like them bigger than mine? And a big bust, too!" She sounded as though half-kidding and half-threatening him.

"Lera, Lera, keep it down. You're drunk!" He giggled like a girl.

She kissed him first, and he didn't resist, despite the lingering presence of big-busted Julia on the phone. The kiss was long and passionate. They finally tore away from each other after no less than a minute, both breathing heavily.

Artem looked at Lera with mixed emotions, including love, bitterness, and anger with himself. "Christ, why... why am I so drawn to you?!" he said despondently.

"Are we going to my place?" said the irresistible force in Lera.

But the human organism is weak, and the lover of Julia's hips suddenly decided he needed to run behind the Suvorov Museum, directly across from their bench, and relieve himself. His first thought was to jump the fence, but he couldn't manage it, and he had to take an alternate route.

I decided to accompany him across the street, because he was drunk, too, and I was afraid for his life... and my own. He could get hit by a car, the idiot, and not be able to manage the one thing I'd striven so hard for! Luckily, not a single car appeared on the road at that time of night.

Having guided Artem across the street, against the background of the ancient mosaic decorating the museum of Russian General Suvorov crossing the Alps, I hurried back to Lera. It was so unbelievably funny to watch two drunk people trying to walk. Having gone around the museum from the left, and discovering her ex-husband, peeing, Lera was truly enthused.

"My God, what a sight!" she said. "Look at your profile in the moonlight!" She paraphrased Bulgakov's *Behemoth the Cat*.

"Get away," he snapped. "Let me pee in peace."

"I can't! You're making my heart beat so hard, it hurts!" She headed straight for him.

Once again, I was forced to turn away. The happiness that washed over me at seeing the two people I'd dreamed of being my parents together again really did make me feel 'all warm and fuzzy' inside. I looked at a building, where everybody was asleep and where only one window was lit up by a soft violet light. I imagined that maybe the people in there were busy doing the same thing, and that the soul of their baby was preparing to acquire its future body.

Stop!

What the heck was I waiting for? The required stream of energy was flowing, right now! There was absolutely no doubt in my mind that Lera genuinely loved Artem and wanted a baby by him. Even before they'd locked me up in the hospital, she'd admitted it to him. But Artem... well, ultimately, why should I care if he didn't stick around until I came into the world? The important thing was that my mom would be there, and I would always remind her of the one she loved... and of that unusual day, when she came back from Czech Republic, met up with the former angel and her ex-husband, and a future life was conceived in her.

While I worked myself up, the time came to act. I turned sharply toward my parents and swooped down the very second I heard the sounds that indicated they were almost done.

I made it!

The deed was done. I'd broken the rules, and nobody had any authority over me anymore.

Chapter 48

"Morning is never kind," Artem mumbled after he was awake. The first thing he saw was the orange window.

Lera looked at him. "Do you have a headache?"

He nodded and twisted his face in pain. "Do you have anything I can take?"

"Paracetamol. Is that okay?"

"Anything you have is fine. I won't be able to work with this headache. Why did we drink so much last night?"

"It was your idea. 'Let's have another. Let's have another!'"

"And you didn't refuse."

"Well, my head doesn't hurt, even though I drank a lot of vodka before that, at Vov and Natasha's."

"That's because you're not human," he moaned, taking the pill she handed him.

"Oh yeah? Gimme back the pill then, so you can feel human even longer!" She tried to take it back from him.

"And then we had sex all night long," Artem said, as his memory came back to him. "Unprotected, too. What if you get pregnant?" He sounded worried.

"I won't. I was at the doctor's recently. I have some serious problems, and need an in-depth examination, and then undergo treatment for a long time before I can conceive. I read a lot of things online about my diagnosis. There's nothing to worry about for a while."

"Well, at least you've calmed me down." Then he twisted his face again. "Ow! How can I work today? I have two important meetings, too. The first one's at ten."

"You better hurry, then, it's already nine. I don't have to go in until eleven, so I'm in no rush."

"I'll make it. The meeting's near here. You're in a good location."

"So come and sleep over, when you have an early meeting," she suggested. "It's too long a drive from your Kolpino. I had to come all the way from Krasnoye Selo last night. That's why I was late for the concert."

"I won't take advantage of your kind invitation, but thanks for your concern."

"As you wish. It was just a suggestion."

I sensed from her voice that she was hurt by his indifference, after everything that had happened between them the night before, but she pretended not to care one way or the other.

In keeping with their old family tradition, they had scrambled eggs for breakfast. Then Artem had to get going.

Lera took her keys and opened the door for him. "Say hi to Julia for me."

"Yeah, right." He sighed and scowled. "I don't know how I'll be able to look her in the eyes now."

"Don't sweat it. It doesn't count with an ex-wife," she said, giving him a friendly peck on the cheek and closing the door behind him.

I could again feel everything she felt, and hear everything she thought, and she wasn't herself for the whole day. When she got home from work that evening, she logged onto the forum on family relations and started a thread she called, 'Ex-Husband = True Love?'

> *This September, we will have been divorced for two years. I won't go into the reasons — it would take too long, and honestly, I still haven't exactly figured out why it happened. It had to do with his morbid jealousy about my past, my lack of restraint, etc. Basically, he suggested we divorce, and just live together. Funny, right? Our marriage lasted exactly nine months, such a sweet period, but we didn't manage to give birth to anybody.*
>
> *For a while after the divorce, we kept hooking up and splitting up. Our 'peculiar get-togethers' went on for about three weeks, and always ended with some stupid argument.*
>
> *Later, someone else came into my life, and we planned to stay together, have a baby... But then I met my ex again for exactly three weeks. The other guy understood and forgave me. At the time, I didn't realize I was in love with my ex. Yesterday, when we accidentally met again, I suddenly realized it, clearly. But it's too late. His feelings for me are gone, and he has another girl.*
>
> *Now, right when it seems like it's over, I understand that I just want to be by his side. I don't care that he doesn't have a place*

of his own and that he has a lot of problems. Together we can conquer them all! The problem is, there's no 'together' anymore. When I asked if he loved me, he replied that his feelings for me are warm and friendly.

I know you can't force someone to love you, and I don't even know what I want to hear from you. I can even predict some of your answers, like 'be patient if you want to be with him,' or, 'forget him and live your life,' but maybe there's still hope of winning back his heart. I realized, after meeting him yesterday, that I don't need anybody but him. When we're together, I don't even notice other men. They don't interest me, emotionally or physically. The physical part was always very important to me, and it's never been as good as it was with him. I've realized that even if I were to find someone else, I'd still be in love with my ex.

What to do? Bang my head against a closed door? There might be more experienced women out there, who've suffered something similar, or just some wise people. Give me some suggestions, please. Sorry this turned out to be so long. I guess it couldn't be any shorter.

She didn't want to use her handle, so she called herself, 'Confused.' The replies started coming in quickly.
I'm Anonymous Today wrote:

I was in the same situation. True, I was very young, only eighteen, but now that I'm ten years older, I realize that things were actually serious back then.

We were together for two years. Then I left, and he suffered terribly. He really loved me (he's a lot older than me), but when I decided to come back, he said the flame had gone out.

I used to visit him on weekends. He'd always greet me with a sigh – come if you want, but it's not like we'll get back together. Then he'd take my clothes off, and the whole time, I'd be crying a river. I wrote in my diary: 'Tears are the orgasm of the soul.' Pathetic. This went on for a long time, and then I got tired of it. He didn't love me. Okay, I'd live. I met someone else, and even though it was nothing serious, I decided to end it with him for good. How he wailed – my ex whose flame had gone out! 'I realize now you're my one and only. How could I have rejected you!'

Well, it made me so nauseous that I retched at the very sight of him. I realized I can't stand men who love you out of rejection. To this day, it nauseates me to think of him. He's been calling me over the past ten years, and even though he remarried, he says I'm still his one and only. I saw him recently. He makes me sick.

Someone named Max wrote:

Try looking at your situation impartially, without any elevated, all-justifying conceptions, if you really want to find a way out of your situation. We like to call everything we can't control with reason "love." In fact, this is so far from the truth (I'd even say it's 100% false, but you wouldn't believe me).

I can't say anything about your particular situation, because there's too little information for an outsider to give you any concrete advice. Try having a cup of tea and asking yourself what is going on in your life, and why. The answers will come.

Elf said:

Tell him everything, and he'll decide for himself.

Mother-To-Be wrote:

You've realized you're prepared to go back to how things were, which is why you get together with your ex, even if it's only for a while. But what's his goal in getting together like that? I'd hate to think he's doing it out of boredom. Serious feelings never die; there's always something left. He may be saying he doesn't love you because you hurt him.

A lot of people could tell you a broken vase can't be glued together, and that people don't step in the same river twice. But you know, I would try banging my head against the closed door, as you put it. You'll be fighting for your happiness. You know now that this is the person dearest to you and the one you need, no matter what. I think things will work out for you. The main thing is not to repeat your past mistakes, and to be more tolerant with each other.

Lera read the replies with her elbows propped up on the table and her chin in her hands.

I could feel how bad she felt. There seemed to be an invisible thread stretching out of her chest, looking for something to latch onto, like a tiny vine that winds itself around a tree and then feels safe. But there was no such tree for Lera's thread.

I felt so very sorry for her. I suddenly understood what I'd doomed Lera to, with my crazy desire to be born as Artem's son. I realized how hard things would be for her, if he didn't want to be with us. I started being afraid not only for her future, but for mine too. She was the only authority over me. There was no guarantee that Lera wouldn't be too afraid to have me without the support of my dad... again.

Chapter 49

A week later, Lera and I went to Kolpino and sat down near the building where Artem lived. According to her calculations, he'd be coming home from work soon. Now that I could hear her thoughts clearly, I understood her plan: *"If he comes home alone, I'll make overtures to him. If he's with his girl, I'll never call him again."*

We sat there for over an hour, watching from the children's sandbox in the courtyard next door. Artem showed up holding a tiny brunette with a super-short haircut around the waist. They were drinking gin and tonics and laughing.

Lera followed them with her gaze until they went into the building.

After having spent the night with Artem, she didn't try patching things up with Oleg—she was too ashamed. She chalked up her missed period to her medical problems, and now that she wasn't with anybody, she put off going to the doctor.

"Why bother with the treatments?" she told Sveta, when she was asked how the tests had turned out. "So that I can run into another jerk or two at the same time, like you did, and end up a single mother?"

"But you're going to want to have a baby anyway, so you shouldn't let such a serious problem slide."

"Okay, you're right. I'll do the treatment—later though, maybe in October when it starts raining. It's such a beautiful autumn right now! I don't want to ruin it with blood tests and all the medicines. Besides, they'll prescribe injections, and I'll end up being late for work every day."

"I could give you the injections," Sveta said, "I know how."

"What a remarkable neighbor you are. I really lucked out!"

"Have you had a pregnancy test?"

"When I was seeing Oleg, I did. It was negative, except at first it was a false-positive, and I even thought I was pregnant. As it turns out, tests lie."

"And you haven't been with anybody since?"

"With Artem, but only once."

"So maybe...."

"Stop it!" Lera waived her hand dismissively.

"Listen. Do a test!"

"You're such a pest!" She laughed nervously. "Fine, I'll do one – tomorrow, or the day after, or soon. Why do I always do what you say?"

As the week went by, she kept forgetting to stop into the pharmacy. The whole time, I watched my future little body growing inside her, developing more and more human features.

When she came home one evening, she met Sveta's inquiring gaze. "Okay, okay. Right now. I'm going to the twenty-four-hour one, even though it's so late, but only to satisfy your curiosity!"

As required, Lera did the test the following morning, put it on the table, and had a shower without even looking at the strip. When she came back, she froze: it was positive.

I got nervous and started flying around the room. I was really worried about what her first reaction would be. She picked up the strip, as though in a stupor, and walked out into the hallway. Just then, Sveta opened her door with nine-month-old Sonya in her arms, and Lera silently showed her the fateful stripes.

Sveta smiled and almost bounced. "But that's great!"

"What are you so happy about?" my mother replied, in a tone of voice that made me curl up into a tiny ball on her shoulder.

"Well, it's not so much me as you who should be happy! Meanwhile, you're black as a thunder cloud."

"I don't know how to react, Sveta. I don't understand what I'm feeling right now. Maybe I'll get my thoughts together in an hour, but for now I can't say anything."

"Give me a second to wash the baby up and I'll come over to your place."

"I'll put the kettle on." Like a zombie, Lera went back into her room for the teapot.

In the kitchen, the neighbors were talking, blinis were cooking on the stove, and the water was running in the sink. Things were really buzzing in the six-room communal apartment this Saturday morning.

Usually, Lera joined the conversations with great interest, but right now, having said "Hi," she filled her kettle, put it on the burner in silence, and left the kitchen.

The neighbors exchanged surprised glances, then continued discussing the pressing problems of the day.

Sveta came over, and she looked Lera right in the eyes. "If you have an abortion—again—just know that I'll stop talking to you."

This strong young woman, suffering all the trials of life as a single mom with a smile and good cheer, continued to inspire wonder in me.

"I haven't even said anything yet, so don't scare me." Lera, as always, armed herself with her sense of humor.

"Right now you need to just calm down, go out for a walk, and stop into the church. By the way, tomorrow's the name-day for Vera, Nadezhda, and Lyubov—Faith, Hope, and Love. Maybe it's no coincidence you found out about the baby on the eve?" Sveta took Lera by the hand, clearly trying to convince her.

"Hang on a sec. Tomorrow's Vera, Nadezhda, and Lyubov name day?" Lera acted as though she'd just remembered something.

"Yup."

"Wow!"

"Wow *what?*"

"You can't imagine what an amazing coincidence this is! If you hadn't said anything, I might not even have remembered."

"What's the coincidence?"

"Exactly three years ago, on this very day, I aborted the baby I told you about. Three years ago today...." Lera framed her face with her hands, like wings.

I watched wide-eyed, waiting for what would happen next, and for a second I thought they really did turn into wings, just like the ones they'd taken from Elias. I felt as though his wings had something to do with this coincidence, but how could that be possible?

"Yes, an amazing coincidence! Like a sign from above," Sveta said, as though mystified.

"It seems like that baby has come back to me, after three years to the day! I parted with it on September 29, and now I've been given a second chance," Lera seemed almost to be speaking to herself, not looking at her girlfriend anymore. "And in exactly the same situation."

Seeing what was happening, Sveta said, "Well, okay then, I'll get going. Just knock if you need me."

I heard Lera thinking: *"Could it be that my baby's soul has come back to me? It really is a sign, and the fact that his father doesn't want to be around is a sign too. The same situation on the very same day is a sign, telling me not to do what I did then. It means this is the road I must go down. Back then, I said 'no,' and now I have to say 'yes.' This baby is supposed to be born, no matter what. I'll manage! I do have to tell Artem, however, seeing as he's the father, and let him make up his own mind. Oh, why didn't the baby come earlier, when he still had feelings for me? Where were you before, kid?"*

"Where? They locked me up in a hospital!" I replied, mentally. "And you can't break out of that place. It's partly your fault because of what you did. I wasn't allowed to even try to become a person for two whole years!" It suddenly struck me, how similar my thoughts were to Artem's reprimands. Was I already starting to resemble him? "Mom, you must tell him about me! Maybe he'll decide to stick around after all, even if it's not every day."

"*I'll tell him,*" she thought. "*I'll call him today, arrange to meet him, and I'll tell him — come what may. No matter what he says, kid, you're going to born.*"

I hugged her and snuggled up to her red hair, which was already growing out a little. The longer it got, the closer she got to looking like that happy girl on that sunny day — the one I fell in love with at first sight.

Chapter 50

"Well, what did you summon me for?" Artem asked. He was wearing another stylish suit. "Everything's so secret, like in the movies. Why do you need to talk to me so urgently?"

They were sitting in a café on Nevskiy Avenue. Lera had brought with her the pregnancy test, which confirmed my material being, so she could show it to my dad.

"I wanted to see what you've become, Reindeer," Lera said, quoting *The Snow Queen*.

"Are you mocking me?" he asked, sipping a beer.

"Not in the least."

"Well, do I please you?"

"Very much. Such a man, such a man. It's really something!"

"You're malicious."

"You'll get over it."

"Ah, yes. I see your sense of humor is in fine form, as always," he said. "What about your personal life. Is that in fine form too?"

"It's striped."

"What color is it right now?"

"Black."

"Mine's the opposite—white. I've never had so many women who like me."

"Congratulations. Does Julia know about them all?"

"Julia's in the past."

"How come?"

"She found herself some married guy, and she's expecting twins," Artem scowled. It was clearly unpleasant for him to talk about it.

"You sure they're not your twins?"

"Absolutely. It's impossible. I must be infertile."

"How do you figure that?"

"I went to the doctor. I'm treating an infection from way back, and the side effect is infertility. I didn't catch it from you, did I?"

"I seem healthy enough. But thanks, I'll have myself tested. Did they really say you were infertile?"

"They told you, too. By the way, why aren't you getting a beer? Did you get an implant?" he asked snidely.

"Which brings us to the reason for today's meeting." She smiled and reached into her purse.

"What do you have in there?" He pretended to be worried. "A grenade?"

"Pretty much," she said, placing the test strip in front of him.

"What is it?" he asked, giving her an inquisitive look.

"It's a pregnancy test, with two stripes on it."

"I can see that, but whose is it?"

"My grandmother's! For crying out loud, Artem!" Lera was running out of patience.

"Congratulations to your grandmother, then. I guess you'll be having an aunt or an uncle soon!" he said, still playing the fool.

"Can we be serious?"

"About what?"

"What are we going to do about it?"

"You mean this has something to do with me?"

"In the most direct sense."

"Prove it," he said. He crossed his arms against his chest and leaned back in his chair, with a serious but questioning expression.

"Alas, I can only prove it after the baby's born," Lera said calmly, expecting a similar reaction in response.

"You've made up your mind to keep it?"

"I couldn't be more sure."

"But what about your diagnosis? Did you trick me?"

"No. I didn't trick you, but they could have made a mistake during the ultrasound. I don't get it, either."

"In that case, you should go back to that female doctor and demand compensation, moral and material."

"And will you be able to help out materially? Or at least morally?"

"Listen, the timing of all this is so bad. I've just moved out of my mother's place and rented an apartment. I'm spending a lot of money on chicks. Hang on, how can you be so sure the baby's mine? I mean, it could be anybody's!"

"For it to be just anybody's, I'd have to be hooking up with just anybody."

"So, you're trying to tell me you haven't been?" Artem finished his beer and ordered another.

"You won't believe me, of course, but I'll tell you anyway. I haven't."

"Well, yes, that is hard to believe." He drummed his fingers on the table.

I sat on the edge of the table, shifting my gaze back and forth from him to her, thinking, *"So, you people are my parents. What have your feelings for one another turned into? Is there anything left of them? The truth is, misunderstandings between people grow, if they don't realize they love each other, and this is exactly what's happened to you."*

I feared this meeting of my parents would more than likely be their last.

I could hear what my mom was thinking about my dad, and vice versa. It was sad but funny too, watching these two children discuss an adult problem. They failed to come to a single conclusion. At the end of their conversation, Lera got a nosebleed. I supposed it was either her blood pressure, or a bad case of nerves.

"Artem, do you happen to have a hanky?" she asked, her head tilted slightly back and her hand up to her nose.

"Hang on." He took one out of his pocket and handed it to her. "Keep it," he added, condescendingly. "What kind of mother will you be, if you don't even have a handkerchief?"

Lera didn't respond but I heard what she was thinking: *"How strange that I'm indifferent to whatever he says to me. It's kind of stupid, but I feel as though I'll be happy to have a baby that looks like him, even if he isn't around for it. Maybe, it's even better if he isn't, given the way he's turned out. What's with me? Is that what love is?"*

"Yes, Mom," I replied mentally. "That's what it is."

The ex-spouses left the café to go their separate ways. The sun shone brightly, and my mom looked up at the sky and squinted from the bright light. Flocks of birds flew around, again and again. It was the name day of Faith, Hope, and Love.

I snuggled up to her belly and saw that the person I would be in seven and a half months was sleeping peacefully, and my heart grew still and happy.

Chapter 51

Lera returned home from her mother's with a piece of celebratory cake, and logged on to her forum. She wondered whether to start a new thread, or add to her last post, and decided to read the beginning of what she'd posted a couple of months before. A new comment had appeared since then that made her jump.

The reply said:

> *Fight for your love, Lera! Don't listen to anybody. He's 'grown up' now and could fall head over heels in love with you a second time. A lot depends on your words and actions.*

What shocked her even more was his tag: 'Orange-2.'

She'd signed off as 'Confused'.

The first thing she thought was, *"What the...? How does he know my real name? I didn't even use it."* That was followed immediately by her second thought: *"Oleg! But how did he find it?"*

She replied to 'Orange-2,' still trying to veil her identity.

> *He hasn't grown up at all. And why 'Lera?'*

The next day, a reply came from her 'namesake,' which read:

> *So shake him up, live with him, and then — leave him. He may not get that he needs you. Dragging around somebody who's indifferent to you for two whole years is complicated and could prove thankless.*

At this point, Lera couldn't hold back any longer:

> *How did you come across this thread? I didn't even use my name! We shouldn't have split up last summer. I think we're*

compatible, and I love you too, only not the same way. We could've had a baby, and I would've been fine with that. But what's the point of that now, whereas my ex... It's easy to say, 'live with him.' Against his will? I don't know how to do that. I do have some self-respect left — not much, but some.

She signed off, 'Now you know.'

Every day for the next week, Lera came home from work and logged on to check for a reply, and it finally came:

I happened to log on for some reason — my sixth sense must've been in charge! I don't regret anything, even though I do love you. Well, I did, just to make it easier on you. And on me.

She replied immediately, without thinking:

Everything turned out so stupidly. You know, it looks like I'm going to be a single mom. How sad. But I'm really happy about the baby. Obviously, I got my body so ready for it with you, it just couldn't control itself afterwards. You say you love me? I'm not at all indifferent to you, either.

'Orange-2' answered a day later:

I'm happy about the baby. He'll have a good mom. Only don't call him Greg, okay? That's all. Sorry, I promised myself not to write anything else, so that's all. I'm going fishing, for striped and goggle-eyed lake elephants.

She wrote:

Screw the elephants, don't go! [Smiley Face Emoji] Oleg, do you really think I'll make a good mother? That's nice, if you mean it.

She signed off as 'Orange.' And so, they became a virtual couple.

True to his word, Oleg didn't write anything else.

Another week went by and Lera understood: it was over.

"It's a new beginning," she decided, "which means it's time to get rid of all my old junk, to finally clean my room, and to get rid of everything I don't need. Tomorrow. Today, I'll start with all the spam in my inbox."

Halfway down the third page, she came across a week old email from Oleg, which she'd almost deleted.

> Lera, I stopped posting on the forum because this is our private business. I've thought things through and I have a proposition: I'd like you to consider me in the role of your baby's dad. I don't have any experience in fathering, of course, but I'll try my best. We'll have a girl, and then later, a boy, like we always wanted.

Lera just sat there, hands on her head, digging her nails into her scalp. I tried reading her thoughts, but I couldn't hear a thing. She'd fallen into a stupor.

I reread Oleg's message and snorted.

So, you want to be my dad, eh? Well, well. Mom and I will have to re-assess the way you've behaved! And I'm not going to be a girl!

People who are so sure about their baby's gender in advance are often surprised when we souls do just the opposite. It's a good lesson for the overly confident. I'd fly up to my own kind and make a deal with a little female soul, to be my sister in a year or two—that is, if I found one willing to do that.

There you go, Stony!

I surprised myself. What was I doing? This guy had done me no wrong. In fact, he was offering to support my mom. Ultimately, what difference did it make to me if I had a sister or a brother? The main thing was for my mom to be happy!

Chapter 52

A week later, Oleg moved all his stuff from his parents' apartment into Lera's room. He turned out to be the ideal husband, taking care of my mom as though she were sick and not just pregnant. He bought juice and fresh fruit every day, saying she needed more vitamins in her condition.

Evenings, my mom read children's books to her belly, telling Oleg that the baby could hear everything, and that it would help in its development.

I thought it was funny, and felt like shouting, "I heard everything before, too!"

When she read, Oleg would sit beside her with his hand on her belly. He was always very tender to me, as though I were his own.

"Hi, Daughter!" he'd say, certain that I was a girl.

I even felt bad for having to disappoint him.

Every two weeks, my mom would go to the Mariinsky theater of opera and ballet. She'd buy the cheapest tickets and sit patiently in the upper gallery. She could barely see the stage from there, but she always did it with the same blessed goal: so that the fetus could listen to the music, and develop.

Why are you torturing yourself when you could just buy the CD?

She did, and now she played me lullabies every night.

At the end of November, my mom started keeping a journal in which the first entry was:

> *Hi, this diary is for you. I'm going to fill it with everything you might be interested in reading when you grow up.*

She glued her pregnancy test strip, thanks to which she found out about me, to the inside of the back cover. On December 8, she wrote:

> *I just saw my little bump for the first time. Even if I suck it in, the lower part stays rounded and sticks out anyway. You're already visible, kid.*

At the prenatal clinic, they weighed her regularly, measured the circumference of her waist, which was getting rounder all the time, and tested her blood.

The blood tests always reminded me of the day Masha sat in the lab mesmerized, staring at that picture of the sunflowers.

The friends only talked on the phone now, but because I loved listening in on Mom's conversations, I found out that Masha's son, Ivan, was a bright and creative little boy, and that he loved finger-painting.

"Lera," Masha said, "he's always painting! And yesterday, he suddenly painted a whole field of sunflowers with blue centers! It turned out so beautifully, Martin and I nicknamed him 'Ivan Gogh.'" Masha was so pleased with her son's accomplishments. "Pretty soon, we're having an exhibition of his 'works' here at home, and we're expecting you and Oleg to be our guests. By the way, Lera, the little toy you bought him that day is still his very favorite. He even sleeps with it."

Lera's pregnancy completely changed her life. She had a steady routine now. After work, she went straight home, stopping only at the grocery store along the way. She always had green onions and chocolate chip cookies on hand, not being able to go a day without them. Luckily, she had none of the nausea that had tormented Masha throughout her pregnancy.

Lera and Oleg were preparing to get married, and the only cloud over them was the apartment issue. Sometimes, they'd sit on the sofa figuring expenses with a calculator, and writing them down on a piece of paper. Judging by their gloomy faces, things weren't adding up.

The baby I would become was growing as fast as a beanstalk: in two months, he'd developed lips, a nose, and fingers, and at three, he could push out his hand if something was bothering him, or make a little fist. When he got a little older, I'd catch him sucking his thumb. It was so funny to see, and it made want to feed him. Most of the time, the baby slept. At four months, the amazing thing happened: he smiled at me, as though he were trying to say, "Hi there, my soul!"

At that stage, it was obvious for all to see that I would be a boy.

The bigger the baby grew, the more often I started staying home. I wanted to sleep constantly, and after accompanying Lera to the door, I slept on her pillow all day long. It could've been because it was winter again. That time of year always made me melancholy.

On one very cold evening, my mom flew into our little room, all rosy and happy. "Oleg," she exclaimed. "I have two pieces of news, and both are good!"

"Tell me both at the same time," he said, helping her take off her boots.

"The baby moved today for the first time—at least, it was the first time I felt it! They say it moves from the very beginning."

"What does it feel like?" Oleg asked, keenly interested.

I didn't think of him as Stony anymore.

"Like little waves of air bubbles," she said, "rolling around inside, very gently."

"Of course, it's gentle. She's still so little." He still thought he'd have a daughter. "Will you tell me when she moves? I want to feel it too."

"You're so sweet." Lera, moved by his attitude, kissed him. "Of course, I'll tell you, but I think I'm the only one who can feel it for now."

"And what's the second piece of news?"

"It's staggering!" She almost burst with enthusiasm. "They told me today that kids, who are born on the day of St. Petersburg's three-hundredth anniversary, will be given apartments! Not all of them, only the first, the twenty-seventh, and the three-hundredth. I mean, they can't give apartments to all of them. There'd be whole buildings full of anniversary kids!"

"I'm just imagining the sandbox for a building like that," he said, trying to follow her train of thought. "But what exactly are you trying to say?"

"That the baby is supposed to born precisely then. They told me after the ultrasound that I was due on the 27th or 28th of May, and the city's anniversary is on the 27th."

"Do you think it's possible to predict so accurately?" He shook his head skeptically.

She winked at her belly and said, "We'll work it out."

"Well, you can try." My future stepdad seemed to doubt the success of Lera's future undertaking.

"If it's an obedient baby, it ought to obey!" She laughed. "Take a picture of me today."

Lera had decided to photograph herself every two weeks from the side, so she could print all the photos after she gave birth and keep track of how fast her belly grew.

Oleg got the camera. "Smile! Look at the birdie!"

But he'd lied; there was no birdie. I felt as though I was distancing myself from him more and more with every passing day. His constant 'little daughter' obsession had gotten on my nerves.

What daughter?

If he could see the body part I'd already grown, he wouldn't talk like that. And one day he did....

During the next ultrasound of Lera's five-month belly, my male 'features' showed up on the screen, and the doctor froze the image so my parents could have a better look.

Lera looked anxiously at her future husband.

Oleg responded with absolute silence, saying he had to think about it.

He remained silent for an entire week.

"Vov, I don't know what to do," Lera said, complaining to my future godfather over the phone. "He's so hung up on having a son of his own that when he found out Artem's baby was a boy, he got depressed. I can't believe it myself. He's been coming home late every day for a week, stinking of beer. I can't even get him to talk to me, no matter how I try. What should I do? I feel like we're going to split up."

"Do you think he should talk to a psychologist?"

"You mean to himself?" She laughed. "I think that's what he's been doing all week."

"Then just wait it out. Don't jump to any conclusions, or do anything rash. He's probably working things out."

"He's his own psychologist." Lera laughed again, sadly this time. "At least we don't have to pay for it!"

"We'll make christenings of your son as soon as he's born, right?" Vlad asked.

"Hang on! Let me have him, first, preferably on May 27th, so we can get a free apartment."

"You believe in miracles?" Vlad laughed out loud.

"Go ahead and laugh, but I do. And seeing as it's impossible to predict when the twenty-seventh or three-hundredth baby will be born, the only option is for mine to be born first. At midnight, on the dot. Just to be sure."

"You're an eternal optimist," he said, which he called her all the time. "That's why I love you. Well, and because of everything else, too."

"Okay, hi to Natasha and the kids, and in the meantime, I'll come to an arrangement with my son. Artem hasn't called once since the day I showed him the test results, not even to find out if I kept the baby. If Oleg decides to leave now too, at least we won't all be crammed into my one room. When I look at poor Sveta, my neighbor, in that ten-square meter room with her daughter, she deserves a monument during her lifetime for that kind of heroism. Mine is only bigger by three meters. It's a good thing you and Natasha have a place to live. Can you imagine what it would be like for you in your little room on the Liteiniy, with two kids?"

"Only with great difficulty, especially since Natasha is aiming for a third."

"Oh boy! Good for you! Between the three of us, we'll have a whole kindergarten. We'll need a lot of space so we can visit each other."

"All right, so good luck with everything!"

Lera sat down on the sofa, put her hands on her belly, and started explaining her situation to me.

My beloved Mom, I heard everything.

Even though I was no magician, I would try to grant her wish, especially if our happiness depended on it. As her friend Anya had said, men come and go, but children stay with the mother forever. And I, as her only constant man, would do my best.

I'll try, Mom. You hear me? I'll try!

"You can hear me, right?" She leaned closer to her belly.

"I can," said I, sitting on her head.

"I feel like you can hear me."

"It's not just a feeling."

Soon enough, Oleg reconciled himself with the fact that I'd be a boy, and although he still dreamed of having a son of his own, he helped to come up with a name for me. He decided to put Greg aside, for his biological baby.

Lera was literally torn between the possibilities for my future name, even dreaming up comical plays on words, until my stepdad halted the flights of fantasy and suggested she decide on something 'peaceable.'

At that very moment, I pressed up against him warmly. He'd almost guessed my secret name!

Chapter 53

The less time there remained before my birth, the faster it rushed by. Lera and Oleg rushed into the district Civil Registry Office and became husband and wife.

My mom grew bigger every day, and some mornings she was so bloated, she couldn't even bend her fingers. She'd gained ten kilos and looked very funny. These days, she spent her time on a different forum, about pregnancy and giving birth, where women in her condition discussed what was happening to them. Once, after reading all the advice, she lay on her back and held her pelvis and legs vertically for half an hour, so the baby would turn upside down, instead of just asking him to get into the position.

Whenever she did that, the baby would scratch behind his ear and stick his tongue out at me.

When only two weeks remained until the due date, my mom got toxemia, and the poor thing would have to get up and run to the toilet, like Masha had. She was lucky, though, because the toilet was almost always available—a challenge in a communal apartment.

I remembered her plea, and as the due date approached, I started talking to the baby more often about when he was supposed to be born.

"Listen, buddy," I said while he sucked his thumb. "The day's coming when you'll have to make your way out of there. You're facing the demanding challenge of doing it at the right time. When I give you the signal, you break the water. Understand?"

The baby nodded, and I had no reason not to trust him. After all, together, he and I made a whole.

On May 26th, at 4 p.m., Lera came home from the grocery store and called my godfather.

"Looks like it's not going to happen, Vov. There haven't been any indications, although the doctor told me yesterday that I should be giving birth in the next couple of days. I don't think it's in the cards. I guess the baby didn't hear me."

"Forget about it. It was a utopian idea. Kids are born when it's their time. Up there, in the heavens, there are strict rules of conduct, you know."

"Rules everywhere." Lera sighed. "Too bad I've got such a stickler!" she joked.

"There aren't any rules, Mom!" I shouted. "I'm right here with you!"

And I gave the signal.

"Oh," Lera said. "I think my water just broke. Jeez, there's so much of it!"

"Holy smokes! You might make it after all!" Vlad laughed. "I'm taking the kids to their grandparents right now, so I can't come over for at least an hour and a half. Where's Oleg?"

"At work. He's not in the same field, anymore. He said he realized psychology wasn't his bag. Don't worry about me. The maternity clinic's not far, and I've made all the arrangements. My bag is packed. I'll take it slow and make my way over there. Midnight's a long way away."

"Good luck! Let me know when it's over. I have my fingers crossed for you!"

"Thanks, friend!" Lera hung up the phone. "Oh, my little boy, everything will be fine," she said to the baby. "You heard me, right? This is a miracle. To hell with the apartment and counting minutes! The important thing is that you're born healthy!"

"Mom," I said, "you're the miracle."

She wiped up from the floor the water, which the future me had been floating around in for nine months, like a fish in an aquarium. Then she called Oleg, telling him to come to the clinic right away.

"I'm on my way," he said in agitation. He insisted on being present at the birth. My "stony dad" wanted to see the 'groundbreaker'—he'd started calling me that when he found out I was a boy—make his appearance!

———— ⚬⟩⟩⟩⟨⟨⟨⚬ ————

I was so happy just before my birth that I felt like dancing, even though I was always skeptical of that type of spiritual self-expression. Still, my situation demanded it. After all, I was finally coming into the world! Waltzing like Karlsson, I flew around the lamp in the delivery room.

"Hey!" I yelled. "Can you hear me? I broke your stupid rules, and I got what I dreamed about!"

I was having fun, until I saw my mom in pain. She wasn't complaining or yelling, but only grimacing at every contraction. They got stronger, and so did the pain.

The doctors watched as the cervix, through which my big, smart head would soon appear, got wider. From their conversation, I understood that ten centimeters ought to be enough, but for some reason it was stuck at two.

I wasn't definitively connected to my body yet. That only happened at birth, but I could feel everything it felt. It was going through a rough patch. It had been without the amniotic fluid for a long time, and was feeling like a fish out of water.

"Let's do an epidural anesthesia," the obstetrician suggested. "It helps with the dilation and you won't feel the pain. It does cost extra, but if you agree...."

After getting Oleg's approval, my mom agreed. She quickly signed some papers, lay down on the cot, and turned onto her side. I didn't watch what they were doing to her spine, but from the peaceful expression on her face soon after, I knew her pain had eased.

Oleg walked around her with his video camera, immortalizing the process and asking her what she felt.

"I don't feel anything," she said with a tired smile. "May God grant everyone a birth like this one."

I was glad she wasn't suffering anymore, but this didn't make it any easier on the baby.

A kind-looking doctor walked up to Lera and said, "The anesthetic should last through the contractions. Do you know how to push and how to breathe?"

"I read about it but didn't practice much," she replied.

The doctor demonstrated.

She filled her lungs with air, held it in, and screwed up her face until she looked like she would burst. It was so comical, I burst out laughing.

"Got it?" the female doctor asked, maternally.

Lera nodded.

The doctor checked the opening again. "That's it — ten. Let's get into the chair!"

I turned away again. Couldn't help it. I would probably be a modest little boy, one who would close his eyes at every awkward scene at the movies.

Only a few minutes remained until I would anchor myself to my body, and only a few more days remained during which I would remember what had happened to me. As I thought about saying goodbye to my dear recollections, I suddenly realized, to my terror, that I forgot to do one very important thing. The clock showed 11:37 p.m. I had no more than ten minutes to go there and back, and I decided to put my birth 'on hold.'

"Please hang on for a bit, buddy," I begged the brawny little boy who was ready to start. "I'll be right back!"

As I flew out the air vent, I heard, "You're not pushing very hard."

"For some reason, I can't feel anything," Lera moaned.

Chapter 54

I'd never flown with such determination before—so much depended on my speed now.

The dancing of the future babies was in full swing.

With all the strength I had, I shouted, "My dear little souls! If any of you can't find a mother, identify yourselves!"

Through the dozens of replies, I heard the voice of a little boy-soul who sounded especially sad. "I can't find one anywhere."

In the space of a second, I was by his side, and blurted out as fast as I could, "There's a girl by the name of Stasya. You'll find her on the Liteiniy Avenue, at the Lermontov library. I was going to pick her as my mom, but I fell in love with somebody else. But Stasya is amazing! The only complication is that you'll have to match her up with a dad who'll make sure she stops second-guessing everything. Can you do that?"

The modest-looking little guy with gray eyes—that's how I saw him at that moment—who even resembled Stasya, nodded cheerfully.

"Do it now. I believe in you!" I said, slapping him on the shoulder, exactly like Elias used to do with me.

"Goodbye, everybody! I'm being born!" I informed them all, loudly, and left them for good.

Those who heard me waved as I left, wishing me luck. My return had only taken a couple of minutes.

As I flew back, I got the feeling that I wasn't alone. Someone was chasing me. Turning around, I saw F-01152002, the same future little girl who'd been checking out Oleg and asking me what I thought of Lera. I nodded at her and picked up speed, trying to get away from her unwanted company.

In the delivery room, the doctors prepared for a caesarian birth.

In my absence, the baby seemed to have fallen asleep. I could see from Lera's face, covered in burst blood vessels from all the unsuccessful pushing, that she was exhausted.

"Hey, kid, wake up. It's time!" I said, trying unsuccessfully to wake him.

"Please," Lera begged, "don't give me a caesarian. Maybe he'll still come on his own!"

"Unfortunately," the doctor said, "we're running out of time. The baby isn't getting enough oxygen. There's no alternative."

I had to do something, fast, but all I could do was gather all my energy and start pushing down on the motionless slouch, from the surface. The future me turned out to be very heavy, and despite my titanic efforts, he only moved a tiny bit closer to that precious light at the end of the tunnel.

"Prepare the anesthetic," I heard someone say.

Lera started to cry, barely audibly. She always said she was terribly afraid of having a caesarian.

I pressed down with all my strength on the feet I would be walking on, a year later. "Come on, buddy!" I shouted. "Don't let our mom down!"

Suddenly, I felt as though someone was helping me, adding their strength to mine. And thanks to my invisible helper, the unbelievably stubborn little baby finally decided he was ready. He pushed himself away and stuck his head out.

It remained so dark inside, I couldn't see whom to thank for helping.

"Who are you?" I asked. "And why are you helping me?"

"You sly one, you beat me to it," replied the familiar, clear voice of a little girl. "But so be it. You go first. I'll wait."

THE END

Acknowledgements

I'd like to send my regards to my son, Miroslav, for his existence, help and support.

About the Author

Hope Silver is a Russian author, born in Siberia. Her pen name is the translation of her lengthy given name, Nadezhda Serebrennikova.

Hope began her writing career as a journalist for several newspapers in St. Petersburg, before moving to Karlovy Vari in the Czech Republic, where she completed *Born – Against All Odds*, her first novel. After winning the green card lottery in 2013, she and her family emigrated to the United States.

In 2015, the Russian original of *Born – Against All Odds* won the 'Best Book of the Year' award in the fantasy genre at the International Russian Writers Competition in Germany. The following year, Krystyna Steiger's English translation was awarded second prize at the 2016 Open Eurasia 5th International Writers Competition in London. Hope now resides in Berkeley, California, with her husband, son and daughter, who inspired her to write this magical narrative, in which fantasy and reality seamlessly overlap.

Hope recently authored and published *Curious Things*, a collection of flash fiction, in which she endows inanimate objects with human emotions. She is an avid writer of children's stories and an active blogger, who writes about her travels and other adventures.

For more, please visit Hope Silver online at:
Website: www.HopeSilver.ru
Facebook: @HopeSilver (Nadezhda Serebrennikova)
Instagram: @HopeSilver77
Twitter: @HopeSilver77

More from Evolved Publishing

We offer great books across multiple genres, featuring high-quality editing (which we believe is second-to-none) and fantastic covers.

As a hybrid small press, your support as loyal readers is so important to us, and we have strived, with tireless dedication and sheer determination, to deliver on the promise of our motto: **QUALITY IS PRIORITY #1!**

Please check out all of our great books, which you can find at this link:

www.EvolvedPub.com/Catalog/

Thank you!